Praise for
Abby Finds Her Calling

"What distinguishes this from many other Amish romances is how it shows that forbearance and forgiveness take a good deal of work, and the Amish, like everybody else, gossip, bicker, and sometimes have less-than-ideal family lives. . . . King has created enough open-ended characters to entice the reader back to Cedar Creek for more."
—*Publishers Weekly*

"A new contemporary series, Home at Cedar Creek, from a talented author who writes from her heart. The story line's been around for decades, but King freshens it up and brings new life to it."
—*Romantic Times*

"*Abby Finds Her Calling* is a heartwarming story, beautifully told, of forgiveness, redemption, and the healing power of love in its many forms: love between individuals, family love, love within a community, and God's love. This story touched my heart."
—JoAnn Grote, author of "Image of Love"
from *A Prairie Christmas Collection*

"Naomi King writes with a heartwarming honesty that will stay with the reader long after the last page."
—Emma Miller, author of *Leah's Choice*

"A fresh new voice enters the world of Amish fiction with Naomi King's *Abby Finds Her Calling*. King's lyrical style shines in a tender tale of how love and forgiveness heal broken hearts and restore a family and a community. With its Missouri setting, King offers us a knowing look into a different Amish settlement. Readers will look forward to more Cedar Creek stories."
—Marta Perry, author of the Pleasant Valley series

OTHER BOOKS IN THE HOME AT CEDAR CREEK SERIES

Abby Finds Her Calling

Rosemary Opens Her Heart

HOME AT CEDAR CREEK

| BOOK TWO |

Naomi King

 NEW AMERICAN LIBRARY

New American Library
Published by New American Library,
a division of Penguin Group (USA) Inc.,
375 Hudson Street, New York, New York 10014, USA
Penguin Group (Canada), 90 Eglinton Avenue East, Suite 700, Toronto,
Ontario M4P 2Y3, Canada (a division of Pearson Penguin Canada Inc.)
Penguin Books Ltd., 80 Strand, London WC2R 0RL, England
Penguin Ireland, 25 St. Stephen's Green, Dublin 2,
Ireland (a division of Penguin Books Ltd.)
Penguin Group (Australia), 250 Camberwell Road, Camberwell,
Victoria 3124, Australia (a division of Pearson Australia Group Pty. Ltd.)
Penguin Books India Pvt. Ltd., 11 Community Centre,
Panchsheel Park, New Delhi - 110 017, India
Penguin Group (NZ), 67 Apollo Drive, Rosedale, Auckland 0632,
New Zealand (a division of Pearson New Zealand Ltd.)
Penguin Books (South Africa) (Pty.) Ltd., 24 Sturdee Avenue,
Rosebank, Johannesburg 2196, South Africa

Penguin Books Ltd., Registered Offices:
80 Strand, London WC2R 0RL, England

First published by New American Library,
a division of Penguin Group (USA) Inc.

First Printing, October 2012
1 3 5 7 9 10 8 6 4 2

NAL REGISTERED TRADEMARK—MARCA REGISTRADA

LIBRARY OF CONGRESS CATALOGING-IN-PUBLICATION DATA:
King, Naomi, 1953–
Rosemary opens her heart/Naomi King.
p. cm.—(Home at Cedar Creek; bk. 2)
ISBN 978-0-451-23797-2
I. Title.
PS3613.A277R67 2012
813'.54—dc23
2012013851

Set in Adobe Caslon Pro
Designed by Elke Sigal

Printed in the United States of America

In memory of my mom, who taught me how to work—
and how to work around

Acknowledgments

Once again, all praise and gratitude goes to You, Lord: without Your help and inspiration through some unforeseen events and distractions, I simply wouldn't have finished this book.

Thanks again and again to my editor, Ellen Edwards, for your patience as I completed this story. Many thanks, as well, to my agent, Evan Marshall, whose enthusiasm has brought me such a long way in my career. It's a joy and a privilege to work with both of you.

Special thanks to Jim Smith of Step Back in Time Tours in Jamesport, Missouri—the largest Old Order Amish settlement west of the Mississippi—for your indispensable insights and assistance as I write this series. Blessings on you, Jim! It's a real pleasure to work with you. Any mistakes in these stories are my own oversight, not yours.

Much love to you, Neal, for your unwavering faith in my abilities and for insisting we celebrate every success of every size.

He shall feed his flock like a shepherd: He shall gather the lambs with His arm and carry them in His bosom, and shall gently lead those that are with young.

—ISAIAH 40:11

I am the good shepherd, and know my sheep and am known of mine. As the Father knoweth me, even so know I the Father: and I lay down my life for the sheep. And other sheep I have which are not of this fold: them also I must bring and they shall hear my voice, and there shall be one fold, and one shepherd.   —JOHN 10:14–16

But he that is greatest among you shall be your servant.

—MATTHEW 23:11

Serve the Lord with gladness.   —PSALM 100:2

Rosemary Opens Her Heart

Chapter 1

Matt Lambright slipped out of the stream of nearly two hundred wedding guests who were filing out of the house and into the front yard after his aunt Zanna's marriage to Jonny Ropp. When he reached the pasture fence, he loosened his stiff white shirt collar. After more than three hours of sitting in front of the crowd as a newehocker, he was ready for some fresh air.

The April sun warmed his face and the breeze riffled his hair. Matt breathed deeply. He smelled the "roast" made with chicken and stuffing and the creamed celery, which were about to be served for the noon feast . . . heard the bleating of his sheep grazing in the pasture . . . saw his grandmother, Treva Lambright, walking toward her glass greenhouse, where long tables had been set up for the traditional Old Amish wedding meal. He saw so many smiles on the faces of family and friends who had come here to Cedar Creek, Missouri, from such far-flung places as Pennsylvania, Ohio, and Indiana.

His parents, Sam and Barbara Lambright, mingled among their many guests, looking happier than he'd seen them in a long while. Aunt Zanna was his dat's youngest sister, and she had given them all quite a shock last fall when she'd walked away from marrying James

Graber, their lifelong friend from across the road, because she was carrying Jonny Ropp's baby. Now that little Harley had arrived and Jonny had joined the church and reconciled with his parents, all was well. Family ties among the Ropps had been restored, and that was what mattered most.

Matt chuckled as he noticed James breaking away from the crowd, loosening the collar of his white shirt as though he, too, couldn't wait to get back into everyday clothes. Aunt Abby had made their new black trousers, vests, and white shirts, but—as perfectly as they fit—most fellows weren't keen on wearing their collars fastened for any longer than they had to. It was good to see James smiling, apparently enjoying the wedding festivities, considering how Aunt Zanna had forsaken him.

"Well, Matt, you look all dressed and ready to get married yourself," James teased as he came to stand beside the pasture gate.

Truth be told, Matt had been studying the single girls from his bench up front during the wedding service. Lately he'd been thinking about living somewhere other than his lifelong home, with someone other than his parents, his grandmother, and his three sisters. At twenty-two, with an established flock of sheep and some money in the bank, he was eager to move beyond rumspringa—his "running around" years—into a more satisfying life with a special someone . . . if only he could find her.

"Emma was gawking at you all during the wedding," James continued in a low voice. "My sister doesn't talk about marriage much, as busy as she is with our parents, but she's sweet on you, Matt. Or at least when she bakes brownies, most of them seem to end up at your place."

"Emma?" Matt shrugged, searching for a polite way to state his case. "What with living across the road from you Grabers and Emma's being at our house so much while she and Aunt Abby were growing up, she seems more like one of my sisters than somebody I might court, you know?"

"Jah, that happens," James murmured with a wry smile. "Sometimes we overlook someone who's been standing right in front of us for years even though the connection is obvious to other folks."

And what did James mean by that? Matt was in too fine a mood to pursue such a deep topic, so he searched for something else to talk about. "Would you look at that?" he said, gesturing toward the crowd beneath the trees. "Aunt Zanna's holding Harley to her shoulder, swaying from side to side as though she's rocked him all her life. Who ever thought she would take to raising a baby and making braided rugs? I didn't see this coming at all."

"Zanna's a gut mother." James nodded his approval, even if he looked a little wistful. "I wish her and Jonny all the best. It was God's doing, the way they worked everything out, and I hope God will reveal His plan for *me* sometime, too."

Matt sighed, wishing he had picked a better topic. "I'm sorry I brought that up. This can't be an easy day for you."

"It's all right, Matt. Everything has happened the way it was supposed to. Now that she and Jonny have tied the knot, I can move on, too, you see." James gestured toward the clusters of fluffy white ewes and lambs that dotted the rolling green hills behind the farmhouse. "Looks like you've done right well for yourself," he continued. "Something tells me you're better at shepherding a flock than you'd be at storekeeping. Or maybe your dat didn't want you going in with him to run the mercantile."

Matt acknowledged James's candor with a smile: the Cedar Creek Mercantile had been in the Lambright family for generations, so most folks would have expected Sam Lambright to pass the business down to him as the only son. "Never thought much about running the store," he replied. "Abby has her Stitch in Time shop up in the loft, so she helps Dat quite a lot—knows as much about the inventory and ordering as he does. And my sisters Phoebe and Gail have always been better at keeping the shelves straightened and making out the orders than I would ever be."

He drank in the satisfying sight of his sheep on the lush hillsides. "You know how it is," he continued in a thoughtful tone. "One business rarely brings in enough to pay for a large family. Just as there's not enough income from your dat's farm for you to support a wife and children, we Lambrights can't all be storekeepers. My dat has no time to farm his land while he's running the mercantile, so it's a gut thing for all of us that I can raise sheep and grow enough hay and grain to feed them and our horses, too."

"Jah, you've got that right. I apprenticed to make carriages right out of school because I was a lot more interested in running the roads than I was in raising crops," James said with a chuckle. "There's always a need for buggies and wagons amongst Plain people."

Matt raised a hand to signal for his two border collies. "Lois Yutzy was telling me her husband Ezra's brother, Titus, raises sheep over past Queen City and he might be looking to trade some breeding stock. He's supposed to be here today, but I haven't had a chance to look for him."

"You've drawn a big crowd today." James leaned down to rumple the ears of the two black-and-white dogs that had raced up from the pasture. "And you two pups are dressed up just like the rest of us, ain't so? Always in your Sunday black and white."

Folks often complimented Matt's border collies, which were not only well-disciplined flock dogs, but also eager to be friends with anyone who would scratch behind their ears. "Pearl will sit there all day if you keep rubbing her neck that way," he said as he watched the white-faced dog close her eyes in contentment.

When Panda stood at attention, Matt followed the dog's intense gaze and spotted a toddler coming toward them. She wore no kapp, and was still young enough for her pale blond pigtails to be braided and pulled back. Her airy white pinafore drifted above her blue dress with every determined step she took. "Puppy! Puppy!" she said as she approached them.

"Panda is the puppy with the black rings around his eyes," Matt said, smiling to encourage her, "and the one with the white head is Pearl."

The little girl stopped. She studied Matt and James for a moment, her expression serious until Panda let out a little *woof.*

When she laughed, Matt crouched beside her. "If you stand real still," he murmured, "Pearl and Panda will let you pat them. They want to be your friends."

When the toddler put a finger in her mouth, Matt thought she was the most adorable child he'd ever seen. James stopped stroking Pearl so the dog could focus on their little visitor, and then both border collies stepped cautiously toward her, as though they understood that such a young child could be easily knocked over. The girl extended a hand and then cried out in delight when Pearl licked her fingers. Not wanting to be left out, Panda nuzzled her other hand.

"Where's your mamm?" Matt asked, glancing toward the crowd now making its way toward his grandmother's greenhouse for the wedding feast.

"Can't say as I saw this little one during the church service," James remarked as he, too, scanned the group of guests. "Maybe she and her parents are Ropp cousins who came from out East."

The girl seemed unconcerned about her mamm's and dat's whereabouts. She was running her fingers along the dogs' silky ears, her expression rapt as Panda and Pearl patiently allowed her to touch them.

Then a woman cried, "Katie!" as she stepped out of the crowd. She was dressed all in black, from her kapp to her shoes, yet her melodic laughter and her wide-eyed, playful expression made Matt's heart pound. "Katie!" she exclaimed again as she broke into a run. "I've been looking everywhere and— Oh, punkin, be careful around those strange dogs!"

"Panda and Pearl love kids," Matt assured her as he placed his hands on the dogs' heads: he didn't want them barking and scaring the little girl as a reaction to her mother's noisy approach. An impish grin lit Katie's face, and she tottered away as though running from her mamm would be another fun game to play.

James scooped the escaping child into his arms. "She's been in gut company here. We wouldn't have let her go into the pasture or down the lane, you see."

The young woman opened her arms to take her child. "I can't turn my back for two seconds, or she runs off," she explained breathlessly. "I was just talking to Aunt Lois and suddenly realized Katie was gone and—"

"Lois Yutzy?" Matt inquired. Now that she had come this close, the woman looked younger than her black clothing had led him to believe. She had smooth, flawless cheeks and eyes as green as the trees that grew along Cedar Creek. Her sleek brown hair was pulled neatly away from a center part and tucked beneath a black kapp that seemed far too harsh for such a fresh complexion. She was awfully young to be a widow. "I'm Matt Lambright, by the way. Zanna's nephew."

"And I'm James Graber."

"Thank you for catching my little runaway. Katie's a handful." The young woman hugged her daughter around the waist, planting loud, exaggerated kisses on her cheek. Katie wrapped her chubby arms around her mamm's neck, happy to be where she belonged.

The sight of mother and child clutched at Matt's heart and he suddenly had a hard time making conversation. This woman must have been seated in the rear pews, back among the younger women, because he hadn't noticed her during the wedding. Lois and Ezra Yutzy had kin scattered all over northern Missouri, but Matt was sure he'd never seen this pretty widow. He would have remembered her face, no doubt about that.

"I—I didn't catch your name," he said.

She smiled shyly, her face half-hidden by Katie's dress and pinafore. "Doesn't matter," she murmured. "I'm not from around here." She turned and strode quickly back toward the throng of guests.

"But it does matter," Matt murmured as he gazed after her. Why hadn't she told him who she was? After the playful way she'd chased after Katie, he couldn't believe she was standoffish or unfriendly. Was she shy about being around folks she didn't know? Or modest because she was a widow?

"That was odd," James remarked. "We'll have to look around during dinner to see who she's sitting with."

Matt nodded as they headed toward the greenhouse. Through its big glass windows he could see the long tables draped in white where guests were taking their seats. He glimpsed the tall white wedding cake, too. But all he could think about was the young woman who had come to fetch her child. "Jah," he murmured. "Lois Yutzy's her aunt, so I'm going to find old Ezra straightaway . . . to ask him where he's been hiding his niece all these years."

Chapter 2

Rosemary Yutzy lingered at the table after she ate her baked chicken and stuffing, cradling a sleeping Katie on her lap. Was it her imagination, or was that fellow she'd met at the gate—Matt, the one with the wavy brown hair and dark, sparkling eyes—staring at her? Every time she looked up he seemed to be grinning at her from his seat at the eck, the raised table in the room's corner where the wedding party was seated.

Shifting in her chair, Rosemary followed Aunt Lois's conversation with the woman beside her, yet still she felt Matt's gaze. He was probably a nice fellow, but she saw no reason to encourage him: her husband, Joe, had died in a hunting accident last fall, and she still missed him terribly. She preferred to blend into the crowd until it was time to go home to Queen City with her father-in-law, Titus Yutzy, because today's festivities brought back memories of how she'd met Joe at her cousin Dora's wedding.

She had hoped to stay home today, but Titus was having none of that. "It'll do you gut to get out amongst folks again," he'd insisted. "It's not natural for a girl your age to spend all her time going between the stove, the washing machine, and the garden. It was Joe who passed away, not you."

That wasn't entirely true, however: a large part of Rosemary had died the moment she'd learned her husband wouldn't be coming home from the woods behind Titus's pastureland. Joe had apparently tripped over a tree root and landed on his rifle, which had then fired. They had gone looking for him when he hadn't come home by dusk . . . had found no evidence suggesting he could have been accidentally shot by another hunter. Their bishop had counseled them to take comfort in the fact that Joe had gone home to the Lord as a part of God's will for all of their lives, yet Rosemary still had trouble understanding that. Why would God take her husband, the father of her child? What had she done to deserve such a cruel, abrupt end to her marriage?

Cards and cash had poured in from readers who saw Joe's death notice in the *Budget*, the national Plain newspaper. For several weeks Rosemary had lived in a blur, grateful she had Katie to hold on to and thankful for each task that kept her hands occupied so her heart wouldn't cave in to a sadness such as she'd never known.

With the coming of the new year, however, her grief had begun to lift. Moving into Titus's home had given her a new sense of purpose, and she had finally reached the point where she didn't cry at the least little memory or mention of Joe. What a blessing it was, to believe God would take care of her when her husband could not.

These days Rosemary was happy to keep house for Joe's dat and to look after twelve-year-old Beth Ann, Titus's youngest daughter. His wife, Alma, had lost her battle to cancer just a few weeks before Joe had passed. Titus, Beth Ann, and Katie depended upon Rosemary to keep the household running. She was only half a mile down the road from her widowed mamm and her maidel sister, too. It was yet another blessing that all those who truly mattered to her lived within walking distance of the Yutzy homeplace.

Katie awoke from her nap. "Puppies?" she pleaded in her little-girl voice. "Play with the puppies now?"

"No, Katie," Rosemary replied firmly. "We're going to the kitchen to help clean up all these dishes."

"What kind of dogs do they have?" Beth Ann asked. She sat list-lessly at Rosemary's left, her head propped on her hand as she dragged her fork through her mashed potatoes.

"Black-and-white sheep dogs," Rosemary replied. "And you know the rule, Beth Ann. You'll get no pie or wedding cake if you don't finish your meal."

"But I'm full," the slender girl complained. "Aunt Lois put enough food on my plate for three people." Beth Ann was having a bad day because she didn't know any of the girls at the wedding—and she still missed her mother.

A movement at the eck caught Rosemary's eye. The groom had slipped his arm around his bride, and they held their son between them. Little Harley napped with an angelic smile on his rosy face.

Rosemary's heart constricted painfully. Jonny was smiling at Zanna as though he were the happiest man in the world . . . the way Joe had gazed at *her* when they'd held an infant Katie. Such intense love and devotion passed between the couple that Rosemary had to look away, blinded by hot tears.

Why was Joe taken from me? What were You thinking, God, when You left me to raise Katie alone?

A burst of laughter made her glance up. As Zanna and Jonny shared a joke with their newehockers, Matt Lambright was looking at Rosemary with a flirtatious grin—again. She lowered her head, hugging Katie closer. Matt was totally different from her Joe, whose dark hair, eyebrows, and beard had set off blue eyes that would for-ever beckon her in her dreams. She wanted no part of the playful invitation she saw on Matt's clean-shaven face. Her heart belonged to Joe forever, just as she'd promised at their wedding.

"Aunt Lois, I'm going over to the kitchen. Surely there are dishes to wash or pies to cut." Rosemary stood up and headed for the door without waiting for a reply. Occupying her hands and her mind seemed the best way to keep from weeping in front of all these happy wedding guests.

Walking toward the tall, white Lambright house, Rosemary inhaled the fresh air to regain control of her emotions. Across the lane, the pastures and trees glimmered with the bright green of springtime. The deep pink branches of the redbud trees swayed in the breeze down by the creek, which was lined with ancient cedars and dogwoods. The sheep bleated every now and then, a familiar sound that soothed her. Off in the distance two border collies were lying in the shade, keeping watch over a flock that looked somewhat larger than Titus's.

The peaceful scene reminded her of the Twenty-third Psalm, and some of the verses ran through her mind. *The Lord is my shepherd; I shall not want . . . He leadeth me beside the still waters, He restoreth my soul . . .*

Rosemary wondered wistfully if the Lord would restore her soul someday. She'd felt calm and accepting when they'd come here today, yet a glimpse of love shared between a man and his wife had upset her. "But we'll make it, Katie," she whispered staunchly. "We *will.*"

Her daughter snuggled against her shoulder. "I love you, Mama," she whispered.

Rosemary hugged her child—Joe's child—and hurried toward the house. For Katie's sake, she had to be strong. She hoped Titus wouldn't want to visit for hours with his brother, Ezra, and their friends here in Cedar Creek. The Yutzy brothers had grown up in this community, so his roots here ran deep. But she was itching to head home early.

"Rosemary! Wait for me!"

Rosemary turned to see Beth Ann hurrying from the greenhouse, her expression anxious. She chided herself: Titus's youngest child, the only one left at home, looked as lost and lonely as any motherless twelve-year-old could. What had she been thinking, to leave the poor girl in that crowded room full of laughing, talking strangers?

"I'm right here. I just had to get busy doing something." Rosemary saw no need to tell Beth Ann how Matt Lambright had been eyeing her during the meal, because nothing would come of that, anyway. "For sure and for certain there'll be a towel to fit our hands in the kitchen. With this dinner nearly finished and another meal to serve later, we'll find plenty of work to help with. There must be a couple hundred people here."

"And I don't know any of them, except for you and Katie and Dat—and Aunt Lois's bunch," Beth Ann replied, slowing her pace to match Rosemary's. "I could introduce myself to some of the other girls, but I haven't been in the mood, you know?"

Rosemary smiled ruefully. "I do know. Sometimes I have to make myself act cheerful and interested in what other folks are saying."

"Jah, nothing's been the same since Mamm got sick."

As they paused in front of the Dutch door to the Lambright kitchen, Rosemary lifted Beth Ann's chin and looked into her wide, gentle eyes. "Let's remember our deal," she said in the happiest voice she could muster. "While we're working on the dishes—or waiting on your dat to go back home—every now and again I'll look at you and send you a big, silly grin." Rosemary closed her teeth, opened her mouth in an exaggerated smile, and then rapidly batted her lashes.

Beth Ann giggled. "Okay, and I'll do the same for you. We can act happy even if we'd rather be home." She flashed her teeth, raising her brows and batting her eyelashes.

Laughing out loud made Rosemary feel better. This game was something she had devised for Beth Ann a few months ago, like a secret code to raise the girl's spirits. "Let's show these ladies how helpful we can be," she said as she turned the doorknob. "They've been cooking since before the sun rose, while we've been riding the roads and sitting for the wedding service—and eating their gut food."

"If I make myself really useful, may I have a piece of wedding cake? Even if it won't be as gut as if Aunt Lois had baked it?" Beth Ann asked with a demure smile.

Rosemary chuckled. Titus's daughter was by no means spoiled, but she had a way of coaxing what she wanted from the adults around her. "Jah, I suppose so. It's not often we get to eat goodies we didn't bake ourselves. I'm sure a cake from Mrs. Nissley's Kitchen will taste just fine or the Lambrights wouldn't have asked her to make it. But only one piece!"

Inside the kitchen a dozen conversations were going on at once. Several women stood by the sink, chatting as they dried dishes with flour-sack towels, while others worked around a long kitchen table, transferring leftover food from serving platters to plastic containers with tight lids. At still another table, younger women were counting out clean plates for the light meal they would serve later in the day.

At the sight of a blond girl about her age, Beth Ann brightened. "Here I go, Rosemary. Now *you* find a new friend." She made her way over to where the girl was wrapping silverware in paper napkins.

Rosemary sometimes envied Beth Ann's knack for striking up friendships. For a moment she stood in the midst of the kitchen activity, looking for a group to join. A woman in her late twenties glanced up from the sandwiches she was making. Her sparkling brown eyes and curved eyebrows suggested she was related to Matt Lambright. She wiped her hands on a towel and came over to where Rosemary was standing.

"Welcome to our kitchen!" she said as she tweaked Katie's nose. "I'm Abby Lambright, Zanna's older sister. And who might this little punkin be?"

Katie kicked, trying to get loose. "This is my daughter, Katie, and I'm Rosemary Yutzy," she replied. "We came in with Titus, from Queen City—"

"Oh, Ezra's brother!"

"Jah, and my sister-in-law Beth Ann just went over to wrap silverware," Rosemary said as she nodded in that direction.

"That's my niece Ruthie. She'll be glad for Beth Ann's help—and I could use another set of hands, too, Rosemary," Abby added as she went back to her spot. "We've made egg salad and sliced some ham, so it's just a matter of putting the sandwiches together for tonight's supper."

Rosemary followed Abby to the table and settled Katie in a high chair that had probably held a lot of little Lambrights over the years. "Denki, Abby. I can't help but notice how you look a lot like Matt—"

She stopped before she finished the sentence. Would Abby think she was interested in Matt? Rosemary began spreading butter on slices of fresh homemade bread.

Abby laughed as she spooned up egg salad. "Jah, folks notice that every now and again. Matt's my nephew, and he looks a lot like his dat, Sam, who runs the mercantile. Sam's my brother, you see." She pointed around the kitchen with her spoon. "The blond gal washing dishes is Barbara, Sam's wife, and those girls counting out plates are their daughters, Phoebe and Gail—and Ruthie, of course. My mamm, Treva, runs the greenhouse where we had the dinner. She's been out there refilling water glasses and visiting with folks."

Rosemary nodded, recalling the friendly woman who had poured their water and chatted with Aunt Lois. "It's a big day for your family, Abby. Zanna and Jonny look, um . . . real happy together."

Quickly she turned away. Would she be upset for the rest of the day after witnessing the look of love Zanna and Jonny had shared?

"Jah, we're mighty excited about Jonny joining the church so he could marry her, too," Abby remarked. "And their son Harley's the frosting on the cake, even if he came along before the wedding. It's a real blessing to see the three of them getting off to a gut start, considering some of the problems the Ropps went through—not to mention the way my sister broke her engagement to James Graber to marry Jonny instead," she said in an amiable rush. "But everything works out for the best if we trust that God's taking care of us, ain't so?"

"Jah. Gut things come to those who wait on the Lord." Rosemary considered what Abby had just told her. Despite a series of situations that had challenged the Old Order way, the Lambrights and the Ropps had apparently come through a time of trial and made it to the greener pastures described in the Psalm she'd just been recalling . . . so maybe the Yutzy family would someday emerge from the valley of the shadow, too. "We're waiting for Him to heal our hearts after my husband, Joe, died while he was hunting last fall," she murmured. "A few weeks before that, Beth Ann's mamm—Titus's Alma—passed after a nasty bout with cancer."

As Abby's brown eyes softened with sympathy, Rosemary's cheeks prickled with heat. Why on earth had she interrupted Abby's cheerful conversation with her gloomy story? "I—I'm sorry. I didn't mean to carry on about my own problems, when— I thought I was finally past feeling upset about Joe."

"Oh, Rosemary, I'm sorry you're going through such a tough time." Abby squeezed Rosemary's wrist. "We heard from Lois about a sister-in-law succumbing to her cancer, but I didn't connect that tragedy to you," she said in a concerned voice. "My word, losing your husband and your mother-in-law means you've suffered two huge losses. And then you stepped in for double duty, keeping your family going in Alma's absence. Titus is mighty lucky to have you."

Rosemary blinked. She sensed Abby had a talent for finding the silver lining in every cloud. "Denki, Abby. I—I appreciate the way you asked me to help with these sandwiches. This is my first wedding since Joe died, and I . . . Well, my tears took me by surprise at dinner," she admitted with a sigh. "I didn't realize how difficult today might be."

"I can't imagine." Abby smiled sweetly and went back to spreading egg salad on bread. "I have my moments during weddings, too, because while my friends and nieces and nephews are pairing up, I've decided to remain a maidel," she said. "Why pretend to love a man just so I can get hitched, if I won't be happy?"

Rosemary studied Abby more closely, admiring her glossy hair and kind smile. Why would Abby Lambright choose to live alone when she seemed so outgoing and friendly? Had she not yet met the right man, or did none of the local fellows measure up to her expectations? She wouldn't ask Abby such questions, of course, but they gave her something to think about.

Abby's face brightened as she sliced another loaf of bread. "You must be the niece Lois has often mentioned—the one who makes such fine pies," she said in a speculative tone. "She could really use your help in her restaurant. Mother Yutzy's Oven does quite a business, and with the summer tourist season coming up she'll be looking for extra help. Phoebe and Gail work for her a couple days a week."

"Aunt Lois has asked me time and again to bake for her." Rosemary tore a slice of the soft bread into pieces and laid them on the high chair tray. Katie immediately jammed one into her mouth, kicking gleefully. "But Cedar Creek's too far from Queen City to make deliveries practical. And right now, well . . . it's best I stick around home. Beth Ann's gut help, but she's in school all day, while Titus keeps busy with his sheep and the farming. He's not much of a fellow for putting together meals or washing the clothes."

"I can believe that!" Abby quartered the egg salad sandwiches by cutting them in an X pattern. At the sound of laughter from across the kitchen, she looked over to where Beth Ann and Ruthie were piling their silverware bundles into a large basket, racing to see who would finish first. "And how's Beth Ann handling her mamm's passing? She's at an age when a mother would be teaching her how to manage a household and—well, here again," Abby confirmed, "she and Titus are mighty blessed to have you helping them. Think how lost they'd be without you, Rosemary."

Why were Abby's kind words, spoken with the best intentions, upsetting her again? Rosemary turned, pressing a hand to her mouth. "Sorry," she mumbled. "I've been handling Joe's absence pretty well—until now. My emotions seem to run high and then low, like I'm riding a roller coaster at the county fair."

Abby squeezed Rosemary's shoulder. "You're doing the best you can. It takes time to get past losing someone you love."

Was that a catch she heard in Abby's voice? Rosemary went back to making sandwiches, determined to come out of this low mood. It surprised her that Abby was blinking back tears, too.

"Sam and Zanna and I lost our dat more than a year ago," Abby explained. "We miss having him here for today's wedding, but this big event and Zanna's baby boy have given Mamm and the rest of us reasons to rejoice again. You'll get to that point, too, Rosemary. In your own gut time—and in God's plan for your life—you'll open your heart to a whole new world of possibilities."

Rosemary smiled gratefully. Abby's story made her feel better, more confident about her future. "Denki," she murmured. "I'll do my best to remember that. I'll tell Beth Ann what you've said, too."

Again Abby glanced over to where Ruthie and Beth Ann were placing the last of the silverware into a very full basket. "You're gut at making pies, but what does Beth Ann enjoy doing?"

Maybe Abby was changing to a more pleasant subject so they'd both quit sniffling, yet Rosemary had a feeling that Abby rarely made idle chitchat. "Oh, she's a fine seamstress. She sews the family's clothes now, and always has a quilt in the works. Alma wasn't much for getting seams to lie flat or for adjusting patterns to fit different sizes, but Beth Ann naturally took to that sort of thing."

A smile lit Abby's face, as though she knew a secret she couldn't wait to tell. "Well, then, I know the perfect place to take her. We should have time to go before supper, while the others are visiting and singing."

What could Abby be hinting at? Wherever that perfect place was, Rosemary wanted to go, too—except Beth Ann deserved her own chance to feel special doing whatever this new friend had in mind. Abby seemed awfully good at making people feel better about themselves, and as she thought about it, Rosemary smiled brightly.

She *did* feel better. And as she and Abby made ham sandwiches to add to the supper platters, Rosemary promised herself that for the rest of the day she would keep her spirits light.

She looked across the busy kitchen and caught Beth Ann's eye. As Rosemary flashed her sister-in-law a silly grin and batted her lashes, the same ridiculous expression overtook Beth Ann's face. When they both burst out giggling, Abby's laughter joined theirs.

"Happiness is contagious, you know," Abby said as she covered the platter of sandwiches with a linen towel. "I predict that by the time supper's over, you'll be mighty glad you came to Zanna and Jonny's wedding."

Rosemary wanted to believe that. And maybe, if she gave this tiny seed of happiness a chance, it would take root and grow into a whole new outlook on her life.

Chapter 3

As Matt swung open the pasture gate and allowed Titus Yutzy to step through it ahead of him, he couldn't help but notice the old fellow's deep sigh, stooped shoulders, and black suit that hung loosely on his long-limbed body. While he resembled his brother, Ezra, Titus looked about a hundred years old as he took in the panorama of rolling green hills; the curving line of cedars, dogwoods, and redbud trees along the creek; and the scattered groups of ewes and their lambs.

"Pretty place you've got," Titus murmured. "Always liked it here as a kid, but when Alma's folks needed help running their farm, we moved there. Hadn't been married but a year or so."

"We do what we have to," Matt replied. "I'm real sorry to hear you lost your son and your wife, Titus."

"I'm sorry, too. Every single day I'm sorry." Titus let out a forlorn sigh.

Matt sensed that Titus's burden might weigh down their conversation unless he kept it centered on other subjects. How in the world did his daughter-in-law make it from one day to the next, shrouded in such oppressive sorrow? When Matt had talked to Ezra Yutzy earlier, he'd learned that Katie's mamm was named Rosemary and that she was the widow of Titus's son, Joe. No wonder she had acted so oddly when she'd come running after her adventurous toddler . . . But this wasn't the time to speculate about how to put a smile on Rosemary's pretty face.

"Ezra mentioned that you might want to trade some breeding stock to diversify your flock's bloodlines," Matt began in a more hopeful tone. "It could be as simple as trading rams—and I've got a couple of gut yearlings that'll be ready for breeding in the fall. Just a matter of hauling them to your place and bringing a couple of your rams back here, if that sounds reasonable."

"High time I paid more attention to my sheep," Titus agreed absently. "If I don't take care of my flock, it won't take care of me for much longer. My grass looks mighty thin this spring, on account of how Joe used to do the reseeding." He studied the cluster of lambs closest to them. "What breeds've you got here, Matt? Rambouillet and Montadale, judging from their wool."

"Jah, I've got a ram and some ewes of each of those breeds," Matt replied, "along with several crossbred ewes. I've had real gut luck with their lambing and with selling their meat and wool. They're devoted mothers, too."

"Mine are Montadales and Corriedales. The traits of the three breeds would cross well, most likely." A tiny spark lit Titus's eyes. "This is the best idea I've heard in a gut long while. I lost track of a lot of things this past winter, and it's time to come out of hibernation, if you know what I mean."

"A fella always feels better when the snow's gone and he can get out of the house, into his fields." Matt signaled for his dogs to come across the pasture. "You might like to meet my assistants, Panda and Pearl," he said. "Between the two of them, it's like having a hired hand when it comes to moving the sheep. They made friends with your granddaughter Katie before dinner."

As the two black-and-white collies loped toward them, a slow smile spread across Titus's face. "Katie's at an age when she thinks everything with four legs could be her pet. Hope she didn't make a nuisance of herself."

"She just wanted to meet them. Not one bit afraid of them, either." Now that Titus was talking about his granddaughter, he seemed brighter, so maybe it was a good time to wander onto another subject Matt was eager to know more about. "It must've been hard on Rosemary, losing her man when she's got such a young child."

"She's tougher than she looks. Has to be, to put up with an old coot like me." Titus let out a short laugh and stooped to rumple the dogs' ears. "Truth be told, Rosemary's the only thing that got me through this past winter. Don't know what I'd do without her."

Matt bit back his next question. Clearly, this lonely old man wasn't in the right frame of mind to suggest what a fellow might do to attract Rosemary's attention. "Jah, there's a lot to be said for having a cook in your kitchen—and a little one in your lap," he added. "We Lambrights are already wrapped up in Harley, and he's only three weeks old."

Titus continued stroking the dogs. "Ezra filled me in on some of the tribulations you folks have been through," he said softly. "But it all worked out, ain't so? Treva and even Sam—not a man to tolerate any nonsense—looked mighty excited today."

Titus glanced up at Matt then. "Rudy Ropp's come a long way, too," he remarked, mentioning Jonny's father. "Always was as prickly as a porcupine, but he and Adah have pulled their family together again . . . got their boys back into the fold after that house fire and Rudy's heart attack last Christmas. Hearing their story makes me dare to think I might make something of my life again, if I put my mind to it."

"No doubt you will, Titus." Matt was glad he'd called his dogs over, for Titus couldn't seem to stop running his hands over their soft coats. "It took my grandmother a while to get past losing our granddad Leroy, but now she's thinking to expand her greenhouse business—maybe add another glass building soon. She says she's gotten her energy back and feels like taking on new projects now."

Titus's smile made the lines around his eyes crinkle. He glanced behind them, gazing at the building made of glass squares, which sat alongside the two-story mercantile. "Leroy and Treva made a fine pair. They got married the same November Alma and I did," he reminisced. "Your granddad turned the Cedar Creek Mercantile into the best general store in this part of the state. He treated folks fair—Plain and English alike. He listened to what they wanted and made sure he carried it for them."

"My dat's mighty busy these days," Matt agreed. "Folks from all the towns hereabouts say they'd rather do business with him than go to a big discount store. That's a fine compliment, when you consider how those places can price a lot of their merchandise lower because they handle so much more volume."

Titus straightened to his full height, a thoughtful expression on his face. "I know your dat has closed his store today on account of the wedding, but I bet Rosemary would be tickled to stock up on baking supplies. She makes pies for the cafés in Bloomingdale and Queen City, you see."

"I'm sure Dat would be happy to sell her what she needs," Matt replied. "Or Aunt Abby could help. It wouldn't surprise me if she goes over there anyway, to fetch whatever else they might need for tonight's supper."

Was it Matt's imagination, or did Titus have more color in his cheeks now? Once again the old farmer was looking out over the pastures, letting his gaze wander across the road to the Graber place, as though he had some ideas he wasn't ready to talk about yet. "Merle Graber's not looking too steady," he remarked quietly. "I suppose James supports that family with his carriage making nowadays."

"Jah. They raise enough hay to feed their horses, but Carl Byler does their farming for them—same as he works Paul Bontrager's place next to it." Matt waited to see where this thread of conversation might lead.

"Jah, but by golly, Paul's still making cabinets and he preached a gut wedding sermon this morning. Must be nearly ninety, don't you think?"

"Getting close," Matt agreed. "His boy Perry works at James Graber's carriage shop. He and Salome live in the main house now, so Paul's got somebody looking after him."

"All the more reason I need to give myself a gut swift kick when I think my troubles are worse than anybody else's." Titus hooked his thumbs around his suspender buckles. "My older kids are married, and Beth Ann helps Rosemary when she gets home from school. And Rosemary—now, there's a gal who can put a meal on the table even after she's been helping me with the sheep all day, or tending the laundry and the garden. I've got no call to complain when I see how the fellas I used to run around with are slipping a notch or two."

"That's a gut way to look at it." Matt smiled at Titus as they turned toward the gate again. "And for the rest of today, why—you can catch up with your old friends and stay for supper and still make the drive home before it gets dark."

"Jah, I think I will. Rosemary wanted to head back right after the wedding, but I'm real glad we stayed." He extended his hand. "I'll get back with you in a day or so about exchanging rams, all right? If we do this soon, they'll be accustomed to their new homes come time to turn them in with the ewes in the fall."

Matt grasped Titus's sturdy hand, pleased with the turn the conversation had taken. After all, a trip to Queen City with a couple of rams would give him another chance to see Rosemary. "Both of us can upgrade our flocks and it won't cost us anything but some travel time. Can't beat a deal like that."

Matt latched the gate behind them, signaling for the dogs to return to the pasture. He scanned the clusters of folks who stood chatting in the yard between the greenhouse and his home, but he didn't find a particular young woman dressed in black. "I'll see that Rosemary gets to shop in the mercantile, if she wants to. There's Dat, right over there, so I'll go ask him."

Titus focused in the direction Matt was pointing. "I'll go with you and congratulate the brother of the bride. Haven't talked to Sam in a long while."

As they strolled across the yard toward where Matt's father was chatting with James and Merle Graber, who were seated in lawn chairs, Matt felt a hopeful thrum all over his body. He knew almost nothing about Rosemary Yutzy. Yet even in her stark black clothing, the way she'd laughed and played with Katie had made him *want* to know her. The sooner he could talk with Rosemary alone, the better.

As Matt was planning how to arrange a chat, the kitchen door opened and Aunt Abby stepped out with a young girl close behind her. Rosemary followed them, holding Katie against her hip—and wearing a wide smile that made her face glow like a springtime day. Abby's expression told him she was on a mission, and when she waved at him, Matt couldn't help grinning. Was she helping his cause without even knowing it?

"Matt, have you met these girls from Queen City?" Abby called to him. "We're on our way over to the store, to see the spring fabrics and baking utensils Sam just got in." As the four of them stopped in the lane, Abby placed her hand on the girl's shoulder. "Titus, I've had the nicest time getting to know your family. They've been such gut help to us. Matt, this is Titus's daughter, Beth Ann—"

"Nice to meet you, Beth Ann," Matt said. She looked to be all legs and arms, like a young foal, yet anyone could see she was excited about going to the mercantile.

"—and this is Rosemary Yutzy and her daughter, Katie," Abby finished.

Matt's heart was pounding, and he reminded himself not to say anything stupid. "Katie came over to play with Panda and Pearl earlier," he said, tweaking the toe of her tiny shoe. "We're glad you came today, Rosemary. Titus was saying you'd probably like to see the mercantile, and it's just like Aunt Abby to make all the right things happen."

Matt held Rosemary's gaze until she lowered her eyes. Was that a blush on her cheeks, or was that wishful thinking on his part?

"Abby's been mighty nice to us," Rosemary murmured. "Beth Ann loves to sew, and she wants to see the nook where Abby runs her Stitch in Time business."

Titus, who had been following this conversation with great interest, fished his money clip from his pocket. "You girls get yourselves something you'll enjoy," he said as he handed Rosemary some folded bills. "And if you see things you might want later—for making us some clothes or stocking the kitchen—we'll have Matt bring them. He'll be hauling a couple of rams to our place as soon as I pick out two of my yearlings for him."

Matt's pulse surged. "If you need help loading your packages into the carriage, Rosemary, let me know," he said. All of a sudden, it seemed that everyone around him was making his fondest wish come true. Who could have known Zanna and Jonny's wedding day would turn out so well for him, too?

Chapter 4

Abby opened the back door to the Cedar Creek Mercantile. "The sign out front says we're closed for the wedding, so if we come in this way, folks on the road won't expect us to let them in," she explained as they stepped inside. "This is our workroom, where we fill resealable plastic bags with spices and cookie sprinkles and whatnot. We store our bulk nonperishables in the warehouse to our left. That door leads to the main store."

Beth Ann walked ahead of her and stopped in the doorway with a delighted gasp. "Oh, Rosemary, look!" she said. "Two levels of shopping! And it's so much homier than the big discount store in Kirksville, ain't so?"

Abby chuckled. She had known in an instant that Beth Ann would buzz like a honeybee when she saw the new spring fabrics and all the craft supplies Sam kept in stock. "Take your time," she encouraged the girl. "The fabrics are to your right."

"Jah! And look at those colors—like spring flowers!" Beth Ann exclaimed as she hurried into the main room. "Oh, Rosemary, you would look so pretty in that shade of lavender over there. It reminds me of wild thistles."

Rosemary glanced apologetically at Abby. "You're probably right, Beth Ann," she called after the girl, who was rushing down the aisle. "But that's hardly a proper color for me to wear. Pick out fabric for your own new dress, and we'll get a length of Triblend to make your dat some new work pants, too. Every pair he has is worn thin."

Abby smiled to herself. It was just like an Old Order woman to put the rest of her family's needs before her own. But Beth Ann was right: the new poly-cotton crepe in the color of a thistle would lift Rosemary's spirits while it complemented her rosy complexion. "What can I show you?" she asked. "We just got a shipment of glass pie plates and paring knives, as well as fifty-pound bags of flour and buckets of lard. And we carry scented soaps my friend Marian Byler makes and other things every woman needs around her home."

Balancing Katie on her hip, Rosemary discreetly counted the money in her hand. "Truth be told, the metal pie pans in Alma's kitchen are stained and beat-up, and I threw away three rubber spatulas last week because the tops came off."

"We've got what you need right here in aisle five." While Abby wasn't surprised by Rosemary's thrift, it touched her that this young woman still referred to the kitchen as Alma's. "Did you move to Titus's place from the house you and Joe lived in, then?"

Rosemary smiled ruefully. "Joe and Katie and I were living with my mamm and my sister—which worked out fine because my dat's been gone for several years. Joe was farming his land," she explained. "We'd bought the acreage between my folks' farm and the Yutzy place. Had it all paid off. A local carpenter was drawing up plans for a house, but . . ."

Abby squeezed Rosemary's shoulder. "It has to be hard, having all your hopes and dreams go by the wayside. And it's not the same, moving into another woman's home."

"Jah, and Titus refuses to change anything. He wants the place left the way it was when Alma was alive." Rosemary shifted her toddler on her hip, as though deciding how much to reveal. "Alma was about four inches taller than I am, so I needed a stepstool to reach the ingredients for my pies and even the dishes we eat from every day."

"That sounds inconvenient," Abby remarked as she led Rosemary to the display of kitchenware.

"Dangerous, too. One day I nearly brought a stack of glass bowls down on my head," she continued in a low voice. "I ducked in time, but I wasn't happy about those bowls shattering on the floor. I changed things around in that kitchen right then and there—and thank goodness Titus is none the wiser."

Rosemary's expression lightened as she reached for a stack of disposable foil pie plates. "These are perfect for the pies I take over to the cafés in Bloomingdale and Queen City," she said as she took two bundles. "And Alma's old egg beater hardly cranks anymore," she added as she reached for a new one. She turned to look at Abby in wide-eyed exasperation. "You must think I sound ungrateful for the home Titus has provided me, or that I want everything to be my own way, or—"

"Not at all." A real liking for Rosemary welled up inside Abby. "It's only natural for a woman who bakes so much to want her kitchen gadgets to work and to rearrange the cabinets for everyone's safety. Let me get you a shopping cart."

As Abby walked up the aisle toward the checkout counter, she glanced over to where Beth Ann was fingering the fabrics. The girl looked totally enthralled, as though she could imagine herself wearing a new cape dress in each of the fresh colors, even though she had to limit herself to one or two. "When you've picked out all your yard goods, let me know," Abby called across the tops of the shelves. "And whenever you're ready to see my Stitch in Time corner, we can head upstairs."

Beth Ann's head bobbed up. "Oh, I'd love to look around in your shop and see what all you've made, Abby!"

What a compliment, coming before the girl had seen any of the quilted jackets, placemats, or pleated white kapps displayed on Sam's shelves. Abby grabbed the handle of the nearest cart. "On the pegboard to your right, Beth Ann, you'll see one of the rag rugs Zanna has crocheted, as a sample for folks to order from," she said. "My sister's doing a real gut business at that. We never figured her for a rug maker, but it's perfect for her while she starts a family."

"Oh, Rosemary, this rug would look wonderful-gut in the kitchen!" Beth Ann exclaimed. "That poor old thing we have now has been on the floor since before I was born."

Dismay flickered over Rosemary's face. She handed her supplies to Abby and went to see what Beth Ann was looking at.

Abby placed the items in the cart. How could she convince Titus Yutzy to allow for a few new things in the kitchen? Men had no idea how minor changes could make a woman's work easier . . . and how much better a homemaker felt surrounded with fresh colors. Surely a new rug wouldn't be a betrayal of his wife's memory . . .

"Jah, this rug's a gut size for in front of the sink, Beth Ann. Such cheerful colors in it, too," Rosemary agreed, but then she hesitated. "We'll ask your dat before we buy one, though. He likes to keep the house the way your mamm had it—"

"But Mamm was ready to make a new rug!" Beth Ann protested. "She had the strips torn and the ends sewn together, but she got to feeling so puny from her chemo that she didn't have the patience for it."

Again Abby's heart went out to Rosemary and Beth Ann. If she could think of a way for a new rug to appear at the Yutzys' house . . . or if she could convince Beth Ann to send those fabric strips to Zanna for crocheting into the rug Alma Yutzy had intended to make . . .

"Which two colors of this crepe do you like best, Beth Ann?" Rosemary asked, steering the conversation along a different route. "As fast as you sew, you could make yourself a couple of new dresses before this Sunday's church service. Your dresses from last summer might be too short by now. You've gotten taller these last couple of months."

Beth Ann immediately pointed to a bolt of cornflower blue and to another one the color of butterscotch. "I could make you a dress, too, Rosemary," she insisted again, pointing to the bolt of lavender. "That way you'd have a pretty dress ready for whenever you feel like wearing it."

"Plenty of time for that—but denki for thinking of me. We could make a dress for Katie from that lavender, though . . . and another one from that dark gold you've picked out for yourself." Rosemary's expression said they would discuss her wardrobe no further, so Beth Ann pulled out the three bolts of fabric they had chosen.

Abby picked up the sharp shears from the table where she measured customers' cloth. "This poly crepe is sixty inches wide," she said as she unrolled a length of the cornflower blue. "How much would you like, Beth Ann? Probably takes about two and a half yards for a new cape dress in your size."

"Jah, that'll do for me. And it won't take but a yard for each of Katie's." The young girl looked frustrated, but apparently she knew not to argue with Rosemary. "And cut eight yards of the black Triblend for Dat's pants, please. That should be enough for three pairs, plus some patches for the old ones he wears to muck out the barn."

Abby fetched a thick, heavy bolt of the Triblend denim most women made their men's work pants and jackets from—a blend of denim, nylon, and polyester that didn't fade or fray like cotton denim, so the garments lasted a lot longer. As Abby measured, Beth Ann marveled over the ginghams and calico prints Sam kept on hand for quilting. The Cedar Creek Mercantile supplied many of the area's English and Plain women with fabrics for their clothing and crafts, so it wasn't unusual for their customers to spend a long time in the fabric section.

"Oh, Abby, did you make this?" Beth Ann asked in an excited voice. "What a nice jacket for spring."

Abby glanced over to where Beth Ann was holding up a light-weight collarless coat pieced from pink and green prints. "Jah, I make a lot of those. The English tourists seem to like the mixed-print jackets best, but I sew them in solids for Plain gals—and we sell the pattern for it, too."

Rosemary was already walking toward the tall file cabinets where the sewing patterns were stored. "Now there's a gut idea for you, young lady," she said to Beth Ann. "Perfect to wear to school so your Sunday coat will last another season, don't you think? And you've got a lot of solid colors to choose from in this twill, too."

"Can I have the royal blue?" Beth Ann asked eagerly.

"Jah, you *may* have that color," Rosemary corrected in a teasing voice. "And I'll buy that for you myself if you'll make me a jacket from the gray."

"I can do that!" Beth Ann was hurrying down another aisle, toward the yarn in the store's far corner. "And could you teach me to crochet, Rosemary? I could make a new afghan for the back of the couch. Or I could make a rag rug from the strips Mamm was sewing together."

"Maybe someday," Rosemary answered with a laugh. "We've lined up several projects for you already."

Abby smoothed the blue crepe over the small channel in the table that kept her shears cutting in a straight line. "It's gut to see her so excited about sewing," she remarked. "These colors will make everybody feel like a new season's come along—and Katie," she added, tweaking the toddler's cheek, "*you* will make everyone smile when you wear these pretty new dresses."

"Smile—and chase after her. This little imp moves faster than any of us think her legs can carry her," Rosemary remarked with a shake of her head. "It's a gut thing Beth Ann sews our clothes. I no sooner get settled at the machine than I have a daughter on the loose. I don't know how mamms with more than one child get their work done."

"Before you know it, she'll be wearing kapps and going to school," Abby replied. "Next she'll be Beth Ann's age and then entering her rumspringa in the blink of an eye."

"I can't think about time moving that fast right now. But thank you, Abby, for bringing us into the store," she went on. "Beth Ann asks for so little. This is a real treat for her."

"I was that way, too—ever so long ago when I was twelve." Abby laughed as she folded the fabric she had cut. "Take your time looking around while I show Beth Ann my Stitch in Time nook."

"Oh, she'll love that. She's always said she'd like to earn money sewing at home, once she's finished school."

Abby laid the armful of fabric in the shopping cart while Rosemary secured her baby in the seat. As she strode to the steps, her heart swelled. While most Plain girls learned to sew as a matter of course, not many of them got as excited about it as Beth Ann did. She apparently had a God-given gift for it, too.

"I see you've found my little corner," Abby remarked as she turned at the top of the stairs. "When I sit at my sewing machine, there beside the railing, I can see almost everyone in the store. If Sam's busy with a customer or unloading the supply truck, I can go downstairs and help other folks with what they need."

Beth Ann nodded, wide-eyed, as she sat in the chair that faced the old treadle sewing machine. Her gaze flitted from the shelves of sewing notions and projects Abby had in the works to the curtained closet that served as a fitting room. "So what all do you make?" she asked. "Do you mostly sew for folks who order stuff? Or do you keep busy making those placemats and jackets to sell in the store?"

"That's a very gut question. It means you're really thinking." Abby noticed that Beth Ann's legs and arms seemed long in proportion to her body, as though she would grow tall like her mamm one of these days, while her adolescent face gave only a hint of how her features would finish out. "I started out sewing placemats, napkins, and jackets for our store when I got out of school. And a couple years ago, I made the curtains for your aunt Lois's restaurant—"

"Mother Yutzy's Oven? She makes the best sticky buns on the planet," Beth Ann said matter-of-factly.

"Jah, she does. I made matching tablecloths for her place, too." Abby picked up a scrap of periwinkle fabric, smiling fondly. "I sewed Zanna's wedding dress from this fabric, and I made Matt and Jonny's pants, vests, and white shirts. I also sew for a lot of older fellows who have lost their wives."

Beth Ann was nodding. "I could do that, maybe even before I finish school," she said in a faraway voice. "When I'm at the machine, with my feet going in a gut, steady rhythm on the treadle and my mind focused on what I'm stitching, I lose all track of everything else, you know?"

"Jah, I do that, too," Abby whispered, feeling a tug at her heartstrings. This child, lonely for her mamm, had discovered the perfect remedy for times when her soul sagged. "I get lost in my sewing and when I look up, I think Sam has surely moved the hands of the clock forward to fool me."

When Abby glanced at the regulator clock above the stockroom, her eyes widened. "I should ring up your bill and get back to helping with the supper now," she remarked. "See there? Getting to know you and Rosemary has made the afternoon fly by!"

The smile on Beth Ann's face gratified Abby immensely, and as the two of them descended to the mercantile's main floor, she had a prayer in her heart. *Lord, You've blessed me with so many fine moments during Zanna's wedding, and now with two new friends. I hope You'll bless Rosemary, Beth Ann, and Titus, too, and bring them peace as they move into the future.*

A few minutes later, the three of them were walking toward Titus's carriage with a paper shopping sack of fabric and another full of kitchen supplies. From the greenhouse, where a few windows had been opened, came the sound of dozens of young voices singing a favorite hymn. While the married women finished preparing the evening meal in Barbara's kitchen, most of their men were scattered around the lawn visiting and enjoying the warm afternoon.

"Can you believe it's almost time for supper?" Beth Ann remarked. "Seems like we just finished our dinner."

Abby held the carriage door open while Beth Ann arranged their bags in the back. "And I thank you both for helping us with the sandwiches and the silverware—"

"Beth Ann!" a familiar voice called from the house, and then Ruthie hurried down the gravel lane toward them. Because she was still in school—too young to attend singings—she was in high gear, helping the adults keep the festivities on track. "When they finish singing this hymn, it'll be time to put out that silverware we bundled, and the plates. If you'd help me, it would go lots quicker."

Beth Ann's face brightened. "I can set a table faster than you can!"

"Puh! We'll see about that, won't we?"

As the two girls hurried off, Abby closed the carriage door. "Ruthie is certainly glad you two came today. And if your Katie needs a nap, I'll be happy to take you to my place," she added, pointing toward the smaller house beyond Sam and Barbara's two-story home. "She can snooze on my guest bed."

Rosemary's green eyes glimmered with gratitude. "Denki for all you've done for us, Abby. We left home before dawn, so Katie might not be the only one who curls up for a few winks, depending on when Titus plans to leave. I'll go ask him."

Abby walked alongside her until they got to Sam and Barbara's house, where several women were carrying food from the kitchen to the greenhouse. "See you later," she said, patting Katie's dimpled knee.

As Abby left the kitchen a few minutes later, balancing platters of sandwiches, the young people surged out into the fresh air so the greenhouse could be readied for the evening meal. Already in the yard, Matt wore an expression that made Abby chuckle: her nephew had apparently been watching for the Yutzys to leave the mercantile. He beelined toward Rosemary, but remained several steps behind her when he saw that she was approaching Titus. Meanwhile, he was making funny faces at Katie, coaxing the toddler to laugh at him over Rosemary's shoulder.

And wasn't *that* interesting?

Abby entered the greenhouse and placed her trays on two of the tables. She watched Beth Ann and Ruthie setting out the silverware while Beulah Mae Nissley, Adah Ropp, and Bessie Mast swept beneath the tables. What a blessing that they could serve today's meals in this glass building. Cut flowers and bridal bouquets had no place at a Plain wedding, but the potted hyacinths, tulips, and daffodils her grandmother had grown to sell in Treva's Greenhouse made such a beautiful addition to the white-draped tables. The late-afternoon sun brightened the entire room so much it would almost be like they were eating outdoors.

As she glanced outside at the gathering crowd, Abby caught sight of James Graber. He was facing in her direction as he laughed with Gideon and Jonny Ropp . . . Such a wonderful smile he had, and such a forgiving heart. Not many men would have accepted Zanna's rejection as gracefully as he had. And not many fellows would befriend the man who had stolen his bride, either. James had designed and constructed Jonny's new horse-drawn van and had completed the special vehicle ahead of other buggy orders so that Jonny could start his mechanical repair business sooner.

And weren't James's gentle smile and his forgiving nature just two of the reasons Abby wished he would see her as more than a friend? She headed back to the house for another tray of food, returning James's wave when he caught sight of her. Maybe—if she was lucky—a little of the romance in the spring air would bring them closer today. It couldn't hurt to hope so.

Chapter 5

Rosemary stood alongside a cluster of gray-bearded men, hugging her daughter while waiting to get Titus's attention. Katie was in one of her giggly moods, so Rosemary swung her from side to side, reveling in her smile and the golden highlights the sun brought out in her braids.

Titus was having a fine time catching up with fellows he'd known as a boy in Cedar Creek. It was good to see him enjoying conversation that didn't concern Alma or Joe or what he'd been missing since their deaths. Maybe coming to the wedding would improve all of their moods, if only because Joe's dat had forgotten his sorrow for these hours he'd spent among friends.

When Uncle Ezra finished his story about an old fishing hole they had frequented as boys, Rosemary spoke up. "Will we be staying for the supper, Titus?" she asked quietly. "We've loaded our shopping bags into the carriage—"

"And I'm assuming you had enough money?" he interrupted with a purposeful gaze.

Rosemary reached into her skirt pocket for his change. "Denki for letting us choose a few things. Beth Ann will be busy sewing up dresses for herself and Katie and new work pants for you, too."

"And did you find anything for yourself, Rosemary?" Sam Lambright asked with a kind smile. Weddings were one of the rare occasions when Amish men assisted their wives with meal preparation so the young girls could socialize: he was pulling a high-sided wagon loaded with clean dinner plates, and he had stopped to chat with these friends on his way to the greenhouse. Sam was more outgoing than most of the other men, probably because he did business with so many folks in his store. He chucked Katie under the chin, which made her wiggle her feet and giggle again.

"I found several things, jah," Rosemary replied. "It was awfully nice of Abby to take us inside, considering how busy you've all been with the wedding today."

"If you think of other supplies you want later, I hear our Matt will soon be coming your way with some rams," Sam remarked. "He'll be glad to bring along whatever you need."

Rosemary smiled politely. Why was everyone so set on telling her that Matt Lambright would be driving to the Yutzy farm? Sam's son seemed like a nice enough fellow, but she had absolutely no interest in getting better acquainted with him. What would be the point?

"We'll eat our supper here," Titus said. "It'll save you from having to cook after the long drive home, when it'll be time to put Katie down for the night."

Rosemary nodded, hoping she appeared more grateful than she felt. It was indeed a treat to eat a meal someone else had prepared, but she sensed that a certain pair of playful brown eyes would be seeking her out again. Soon it would be time for the tradition of "going to the table," when Zanna and Jonny would pair up the unmarried wedding guests for supper, so Rosemary decided to disappear to the kitchen, where she could wash dishes. She certainly had no place among the unmarried folks, though, at twenty-three, she was younger than some of them.

She hadn't gone ten steps toward the house, however, when she noticed Matt Lambright leaning against a tree. Katie laughed at the silly face he was making, clapping her hands over her eyes to imitate him. Had Matt been the reason her daughter was so wiggly while she was talking to Titus? Had Matt been waiting to see *her*?

He stepped toward her, smiling. The breeze sifted through his wavy brown hair and, as he closed the distance between them, Rosemary noticed how his black vest accentuated his broad shoulders . . . how fit and strong he was compared to the older men she'd been spending her time with lately. "I was hoping we'd have a chance to visit before they call us to supper," he said.

"Puppies?" Katie piped up. She pointed toward the pasture gate.

Before Rosemary could nip that idea in the bud, Matt put his fingers to his lips. With a loud, piercing whistle he summoned his border collies, and even as Katie covered her ears with her hands, she was squirming to get down.

"I'm not so sure this is a gut idea," Rosemary protested, struggling to keep hold of her child. "I was going to help your mamm and Abby set out the supper."

"With all the neighbor ladies and the Lambright women—Dat and I are the only two fellas in the family, you know—I'm thinking our helpers will be tripping over one another." Matt turned toward her again, a smile lighting his entire face. "How about if you be our guest for the day, Rosemary? It's your turn to be the served rather than the server."

Her heart fluttered, yet she frowned. Matt's words were very thoughtful, but she had no intention of spending the rest of the day with him. Had he told Zanna he wanted to be matched up with Rosemary for supper? "I'm about to put Katie down for a nap—"

"No nap!" Her daughter squealed and clapped her hands together. Matt's two black-and-white dogs were loping toward them, their tongues lolling and their gazes alert. "Puppies! Play with the puppies now!"

Matt held out his arms, entreating Rosemary with his chocolate-colored eyes. "Maybe if I hold her, down here where she can pat the dogs—"

"Pleeease?" Katie pleaded as she reached for Matt. "Wanna play with the puppies, Mama."

Utterly frustrated, Rosemary turned her daughter over to Matt . . . and was dismayed by how rapidly Joe's child grabbed this stranger around the neck. Katie danced in the air as Matt lowered her to the ground. Thank goodness the two dogs sat with their ears pricked up, remaining absolutely still while Katie fussed over them.

"Stand right here with me, Katie, and I'll show you some tricks my dogs know," Matt instructed quietly. "It's always best to get their attention first, calling them by name. Can you say 'Panda'?"

Katie gazed into Matt's face as he crouched beside her. "Pan-dah!"

"Jah, you've got it. Can you say 'Pearl'?"

The toddler frowned, as R's were still difficult for her to pronounce. She studied the way Matt's mouth moved as he said the dog's name again, more slowly. "Puhh-el?" she mimicked.

"Jah, that's the girl dog's name," Matt confirmed, "the one with the white face. Now say, 'Panda, speak!'"

"Pan-dah—speak!"

The male dog *woof*ed and wagged his fluffy tail. Beside him, Pearl quivered with the same excitement, waiting for her turn to perform. While Rosemary enjoyed watching well-trained dogs—and she realized how important Matt's two helpers were in his sheep business—it was another thing altogether that Katie had become so enthralled with this man and his border collies.

"Now let's give Pearl a turn," he suggested as he kept an arm crooked around Katie's waist. "Say, 'Pearl, shake hands.'"

Katie focused intently on the white-faced dog. "Puhh-el," she said as clearly as she could, "shake hands!"

The female dog immediately lifted her paw.

"Nice and easy now," Matt murmured, "you can shake Pearl's paw."

Rosemary held her breath. Katie loved every animal she met. She had to be reminded that horses were easily spooked when they were approached from behind by little girls they couldn't see and that birds and squirrels weren't as tame as the kitties that lived in the barn. As her daughter reached for the dog's paw, it was a wonderful thing to behold Katie's enthralled grin even as Rosemary realized this was a game her daughter would want to play every time she saw a dog.

But isn't it nice when something so simple can make someone so happy?

Rosemary blinked. Where had such a thought come from? And while she knew Katie should be around men besides her grandfather, her mother's heart—her widow's heart—was reluctant to let go . . . to allow her toddler to delight Matt Lambright the way he was so effortlessly enchanting Katie. It was too soon after Joe's death to even consider the attentions of another man. Rosemary simply didn't have time for a new relationship. Keeping house for Titus, raising Katie, acting as a stand-in mother for Beth Ann, and baking pies for two cafés required every ounce of energy she could muster.

How could she tell Matt she wasn't interested in him without ruining the joy he'd created for Katie? As Rosemary considered her words, a loud voice rose from the crowd of young people who'd gathered near the greenhouse.

"It's time for our unhitched friends to partner up," announced Jonny Ropp, standing behind them. "As we read your names, you fellows are to take your girl by the hand and go inside. We did our best at matching up all you cousins and friends from out of town."

Rosemary's heart pounded painfully. She turned to look at Jonny Ropp, the handsome young groom, as he stood beside his new wife. Their faces glowed with happiness—and a hint of mischief.

"Oh my," she gasped as she reached for Katie. She wanted no part of this matchmaking. Such a wedding game was for folks who were still searching for their life partner, and that didn't include her. "Come on, punkin, it's time for your nap."

"Nooo!" Katie howled, struggling against the hands around her waist. "No nap! Play with the puppies!"

Rosemary's face felt like it was on fire. No doubt her daughter's outburst had brought Jonny's announcement to a halt, and the whole crowd was gawking at her, thinking she had no control over her child. But this was a minor, momentary humiliation compared to sitting beside some poor fellow she didn't want to talk to as they endured the evening meal.

"Rosemary, it's all right." Matt leaned closer to make himself heard above Katie's wailing. "I'd be honored to sit by you—"

"You don't understand." Rosemary held Matt's gaze as best she could, considering she had a toddler kicking and screaming in her arms. "I still miss my husband too much to— Surely Zanna's picked a nice girl from Cedar Creek for you to sit with." Holding fast to her crying child, Rosemary hurried toward Abby's tiny white house. Like Katie, she needed a place to settle down so she wouldn't spoil the matchmaking game for the other guests.

But Matt didn't take the hint. He raced ahead to open Abby's front door, and then he gazed earnestly at her. "Can I call you tomorrow, Rosemary?"

Her mouth fell open. "I—I bake pies on Friday mornings, to deliver in the afternoon," she insisted as she stepped inside. Katie's wails echoed in the simple, clean front room, yet Matt didn't seem to notice.

"What about Saturday?" he insisted. "Or if Sunday after the preaching service would be better—"

Rosemary muffled Katie's cries against her shoulder. Her temples were starting to pound, and all she wanted was a quiet place to be alone. "All right then, Saturday afternoon," she rasped. "But please understand, Matt. I'm not ready for another man in my life. And maybe I never will be."

"And maybe I can change your mind about that." He placed his hand lightly on Katie's shuddering shoulders. "After what Titus has told me, I hope you and I can be gut friends, Rosemary. Close friends, in time."

What could she say to that? It seemed much too soon to consider a relationship, yet he was already counting on one. And how was it that Matt's touch seemed to be calming her daughter's crying fit?

"I'll call you around two then—after dinner and before you'd be starting supper. Will that work?"

She blinked. Men seldom had any notion about timing their activities around hers. "I—I suppose I could talk for a bit then."

"Wonderful-gut!" Matt gazed at her, still rubbing her daughter's shoulders. "Katie seems more ready for a nap, so I'll slip out now. Talk to you on Saturday."

As he departed with a shine in his brown eyes, Rosemary could only stare after him. What had she just gotten herself into by agreeing to take his call?

At a serving table inside the greenhouse, Abby cut a peach pie into eighths and slid the pan over so her friend Emma could place the slices on plates. A pleasant breeze came through the open windows and the places were set at the long tables draped with white cloths. The sandwiches and salads had been put out, awaiting the young couples who would enter as Jonny called out their names. The white wedding cake graced the eck, the raised corner table where the wedding party would eat. Once the plates of pie were arranged on this serving table, she and Emma could relax.

Emma lifted a wedge of pie with her metal spatula. "Do you suppose Zanna and Jonny matched us up with anyone?" she asked as she glanced at the crowd outside.

Abby was wondering the same thing. She had declared herself a maidel when she'd had her home built, after starting her Stitch in Time business, and yet . . . it would be a nice surprise if she got to sit beside James, wouldn't it? But if her sister had matched her up with another fellow because there wasn't a more suitable young woman to pair him with, well, she was beyond feeling the evening would be ruined because of that. Emma, however, was a few years younger than she, still eager to court and marry.

Abby raised her eyebrows at her best friend. "Anybody who's between sixteen and thirty is usually included in the bride's pairing up," she pointed out. "That includes us—and you'd be mighty happy to be matched up with Matt. Am I right?"

Emma's expression wavered between hope and despair. "Seems he's mighty interested in that gal with the little girl, showing off his dogs and—"

A loud wail made Abby glance outside, but with such a crowd around Jonny it was impossible to see whose child had begun to fuss. "Rosemary Yutzy came with her father-in-law, Titus, today, not so much because she wanted to but because he refused to let her stay home."

"And they drove all the way from Queen City?"

"Jah. Seems Titus wanted to talk to Matt about his sheep." Abby heard envy and frustration in her friend's voice, and she understood Emma's predicament perfectly. She, too, loved a man who seemed to have no notion of her feelings for him. The fact that she and Emma were sweet on each other's kin and lived right across the road from them added an ironic twist to their situations.

"Maybe Matt'll lose interest in her," Emma replied tartly. "James has driven us to Queen City for the last few holiday dinners, and it's a long couple of hours. Or maybe the trip seems endless because Mamm fusses at Dat, and he doesn't want to hear her."

Outside, Jonny's voice carried over the crowd around him. "Owen Coblentz and Phoebe Lambright," he called out. He waited for a few teasing whistles to die down before announcing the next couple. "Gideon Ropp and Gail Lambright."

"Oh, that'll make Gail happy," Abby murmured. The wailing of that fussy child got louder, and she caught sight of Rosemary Yutzy heading down the lane toward her house with a squirming, screaming Katie on her hip—and Matt jogging ahead to open the door.

Abby glanced at Emma, relieved that she was too busy cutting pies to notice the way he was talking to Rosemary in the doorway. "I'll take these empty pie pans to the house," she said, carefully starting toward the rear exit of the greenhouse with a stack of them in her arms. "I'll be back in a few."

"Save me a spot in the kitchen," Emma called after her. "I'll probably be eating there with all the parents, you know."

"Matt Lambright and Emma Graber," Jonny announced in a loud voice.

Abby turned in the doorway to grin at Emma. "You'd better head outside so Matt can find you. Have a gut time tonight!"

"Jah, well—" Emma looked flustered yet indescribably happy. "I'll need to thank Zanna for her gut taste in pairing us up, ain't so?"

Abby wondered how Matt would react to this match. However, she was more concerned about the harried young mother she saw stepping inside her house, trying to control a wailing, frustrated child. Rosemary and Katie were probably both exhausted. And it was obvious that as long as Rosemary missed her husband so desperately, she wasn't ready to find another one.

"Noah Coblentz and Maggie Ropp," Jonny continued, reading from his list. Abby was nearly to Barbara's kitchen door, walking as fast as her wobbly load would allow, when she heard, "James Graber and Abby Lambright."

Abby's heart stopped. She nearly dropped the stack of pie plates. Luckily, Beth Ann was standing inside, where she could see how full Abby's arms were through the glass. She swung open the door. "It's a gut thing we saved back a few pies here in the kitchen," she remarked as she removed several pans from Abby's stack. "My favorite has always been coconut custard. What's yours?"

Abby carried the rest of her load over to the sink. Sam, Rudy Ropp, and Amos Coblentz were setting up tables in the front room for the married adults so the younger folks could have their fun with the bride and groom in the greenhouse. "If it's a cream pie, I want lemon with lots of meringue. But cherry's my favorite fruit pie, hands down." Ever so carefully, she set the pie plates in the warm dishwater. She needed to check on Rosemary and Katie, yet she didn't want James to think she had run off. Glancing around the kitchen, which bustled with women and school-age girls, Abby spotted Ruthie taking a platter of sandwiches from the fridge.

"Ruthie, can you do me a favor?" she asked. "I'd like to see if Rosemary needs my help, but the bride and groom have matched me up with James for supper—"

"I wonder who told them to do that?" Ruthie teased. "Come on, Beth Ann! Let's make up a wild story about Aunt Abby while we go find James. Nobody ever said that courting couples are the only ones who can have fun this evening."

Out the two girls rushed, slamming the door in their excitement. Abby's mamm and her sister-in-law, Barbara, were taking the lids from bowls of applesauce and slaw. "You've been helping with meals all day, Abby, so go on now! Eat with James," her mother insisted.

"Jah, this would be a gut time for me to get better acquainted with Rosemary and that little girl who seems to think Matt hung the moon," Barbara joined in. "We saw him out the window, showing off his dogs. And now he's chatting with her at your place."

Abby smoothed her apron, pleased that she didn't have to keep James waiting any longer. "Meanwhile, Zanna has paired Matt up with Emma for supper—and Emma also thinks he hung the moon," she replied. "That's fine with Rosemary, who's missing her husband today. But Matt's smiling at young Mrs. Yutzy like I've never seen him look at a girl."

Mamm and Barbara walked with her to the door and peered outside. "Well," her mother said, "the thing about young love is, it either works out—"

"Or not," Barbara finished. "We all have to learn how to handle that. So you go have a gut time, Abby. Leave things between Matt and Emma—or Matt and Rosemary—to work themselves out."

"Could be he won't court either one of them," Mamm added as they stepped outside. "Folks hereabouts all thought Leroy Lambright would hitch up with Alma Bender—"

"The same Alma that Titus Yutzy married?" Barbara cut in.

"Jah, she was just one of the gals who was sweet on Leroy, back in the day." Abby's mother raised her eyebrows. "But catching a man's a lot like fishing, you see. You've got to toss out the right bait."

"Mamm!" Abby gasped. "Maybe we'd better save this story for another time—if it's not too embarrassing to tell."

"There's nothing to be embarrassed about, young lady," her mother declared. "When you're ready for some advice about landing a gut man, I'll tell you all my secrets. We want to see you happy at whatever life you choose, Abigail."

And what was this talk about bait and secrets, coming from her mother? Abby hurried down the lane toward the greenhouse. Her dat, Leroy, had been gone for more than a year now, but this was the first time since his passing that her mamm had seemed so . . . playful. Happy and ready for whatever life brought her next.

And wasn't that the best way to spend each day? Happy and ready for whatever God offered? Abby looked toward the young folks who awaited Jonny's next announcement. When she saw James, who was talking to Beth Ann and Ruthie, her heart fluttered. She might well have a home and a business of her own, but wasn't there room in her heart for more love?

Chapter 6

James laughed with the two young girls who had concocted an outrageous reason for Abby being late to join him for the supper. Hadn't this been a day of surprises? By the looks of it, Ruthie had taken the Yutzy girl under her wing and they had become fast friends. Titus Yutzy seemed like a man come back from the edge of the grave, chatting about his new partnership with Matt. And meanwhile, Matt had taken a very obvious shine to Rosemary.

And what had come over *him* today? After the wedding ceremony, Abby had told James he was a fine man for accepting the way Zanna—originally *his* intended bride—had married Jonny Ropp instead. She had been holding Zanna's baby to her shoulder, and he had blurted out that Abby surely must be made of love and sunshine, like little Harley.

What had possessed him to say such a thing? He had seen Abby holding each of Sam's four kids when they were babies, so what was different about the way she cradled Zanna's infant son?

Didn't you, just for a moment, imagine Abby was holding her own firstborn? And didn't you, just for a moment, put yourself in the role of that child's father . . . Abby's husband?

Now, hours later, such thoughts seemed risky. While it was the right thing to move beyond Zanna's rejection, that didn't mean he was ready to court another woman. He had loved Zanna with all his heart. He had believed she was the woman God had chosen for him. A man didn't recover from such a deep personal wound in days or even weeks. Lately, James had even been wondering if God intended for him to remain single—to assist Emma with the care of their parents so perhaps *she* would have the chance to marry.

And yet, as James watched Abby coming down Lambright Lane, it wasn't hard to imagine the possibility of spending more time with her. After all, hadn't Jonny Ropp informed him last fall that Abby had been sweet on him ever since they'd been scholars coming up through the grades in school? He had been surprised that other folks had noticed her feelings for him, too . . . and how could it be a bad thing, if she felt attracted to him? Abby was the picture of solid, honorable Amish womanhood, yet as she approached him her lips twitched with the same playful grin he recalled from when they were in their teens.

"I didn't mean to head the other way when Jonny called our names," Abby said in her lilting voice. "I had an armload of dirty pie plates and a young mother wanting to put her fussy child down for a nap in my guest room." She stopped a few feet in front of him, clasping her hands at her waist, looking at him in that direct way she had.

Could Abby read his thoughts? Did she have any inkling of how vulnerable and confused he felt right now where women were concerned?

On such a happy occasion, it seemed better to go with Abby's lightheartedness than to dwell on his misgivings. "The way these girls tell it," James teased, "you kept back the best cherry pie to eat all by yourself, rather than come to the table with me."

Abby's eyes widened as she laughed along with Ruthie and Beth Ann, and then her expression softened. "If a woman chooses to eat dessert all by herself rather than join a fellow for supper, well . . .

she's missing out on one of the sweetest parts of a meal—or of a wedding celebration."

Abby looked again at the girls, who were following this conversation closely for signs of—what? Romance? Wasn't that on most young ladies' minds at a wedding? "I did save back the most wonderful-gut cherry pie," she continued with a straight face, "but while you two girls have been carrying tales to James, your dats have probably gobbled it all down. Too bad for you!"

Ruthie's face fell, but then she chuckled. "Come on, Beth Ann. I think Aunt Abby's fibbing about setting a pie back, but it couldn't hurt to find out before Dat does."

"Jah, my dat gets Rosemary's pies all the time, but he's always ready for a piece of somebody else's," Beth Ann replied. "Let's go!"

As the two girls hurried toward the house, James nodded toward the guests who were entering the greenhouse. "Shall we show the rest of them how this is done?" he asked. "I almost joined my parents for a bite in the kitchen—figured I was too old to be in on the matchmaking. As I looked around at the crowd of Jonny's and Zanna's friends, it struck me that I remember when most of them were born."

"Jah, and I changed the diapers of more than a few of them." Abby smiled up at him as they walked. "But I was tickled to hear my name called with yours, James, instead of being matched up with some poor out-of-town Ropp cousin that Zanna didn't know who else to pair with. That's what happens when an unattached woman reaches a certain age, you know."

James had often wondered why Abby hadn't settled down with one of the local fellows. Perry Bontrager and Mose Hartzler had both been eager to court her at one time, yet nothing had come of it. Then, when Abby's dat had helped her build her little home up the lane, the men had stopped asking her out. Yet Abby was by no means old or mean-spirited or difficult to get along with. She knew how to cook and sew and organize her time, and she had a fine head for business, too.

But he had no room to talk about still being single, did he? "Jah, and when a man reaches that age—"

"You'll be thirty next month, if I recall."

"—folks think he's either too set in his ways for a woman to tolerate him, or that he can't find one who'll look after him like his mamm did," James continued in a low voice. "Or the younger girls consider him a gut catch because they assume he's built up a big bank account."

"Unlike the boys their own age, who want to run around with their friends, sampling all the worldly temptations they'll put aside when they join the church." As they entered the greenhouse, Abby stopped to gaze around the large, airy room. "What a beautiful place this is," she murmured. "Look at how the light sparkles on the glass panes . . . the way the hyacinths and daffodils glow when the sun hits them. It feels holy here, like God surely must be present."

Mesmerized by Abby's rapt expression, James held his breath. How like her it was to find something extraordinary about everyday places like her mother's greenhouse. It was probably Abby's doing that Beth Ann Yutzy had come out of her shell, too. And although Rosemary had gotten upset about being here today, James was certain Abby had done her best to comfort and reassure the young widow.

Love and sunshine. Maybe those words hadn't been so outlandish after all. Maybe his heart was trying to tell him something and he should listen more closely. After all, if he had truly forgiven Zanna— he had spent the past six months getting over her rejection—wasn't it time to open himself to seeing someone new?

As James stood with Abby, he was aware of other couples coming in around them, yet he saw only this woman who smiled so steadfastly at him, wearing a dress the shade of lilacs. "Abby, you have a way of making me look beyond the surface of the situations I'm in. You seem to see inside me—and everyone you meet—to know exactly what we all need," he murmured. "I realize now that as much as I loved your sister, Zanna and I would have had some major differences and disagreements once the rosy glow of being newlyweds wore off."

Abby cocked her head, thinking. "Every husband and wife disagree now and again. Part of becoming a gut, solid couple is learning how to deal with life's ups and downs."

James steered her to a chair at the end of a table, where they would have a few more moments to talk before the other seats filled. "And how do you know these things?" he whispered. "Now that I see Zanna standing beside Jonny, holding their child, I believe God worked it out just right. Your sister would never have found that sort of happiness with me, no matter how much I wanted to give it to her."

"James." Abby rested her hand on his arm with a serene smile. "You gave her the very best you had to offer. Zanna's a lucky girl to still have you for a friend, truly forgiving her for the way she behaved last fall. Any woman would be blessed to call you her husband, James. Don't be so hard on yourself."

James blinked, caught up in the depth of their conversation. He sensed that a lot of couples he knew couldn't speak this openly about matters of the heart. "And I'm blessed to call you my gut friend, Abby," he murmured.

Jonny Ropp clanged his knife against his glass until everyone in the greenhouse got quiet. "Let's return thanks before our meal," he said, and all heads bowed. After a few moments of silence the groom spoke again. "We're happy to have you all here. Let's enjoy the rest of our big day!"

The open room filled with the chatter of couples, who passed platters of sandwiches and bowls of salads. "We should get more in the spirit of this wedding supper, instead of being so all-fired serious," James said. "I didn't mean to spoil your fun, Abby."

She nodded toward a table across from them. "Looks like you and I are having a party compared to your sister and Matt. Goodness, what a frown Emma's wearing."

After he accepted a bowl of slaw from Owen Coblentz, James glanced at them. Emma sat with her chin in her hand, looking away from Matt as though she were ready to burst into tears.

"I'm sorry to see that," he said. "My sister is responsible for our parents while I work in the shop—she does all the housework and cooking—and she deserves a nice fellow to have some fun with. At twenty-two, she's wondering if time and the chance to marry are passing her by."

"I'd go talk to her," Abby said as she chose two triangle-shaped sandwiches, "but this isn't the place. Emma's well aware that Matt's had his eye on Rosemary all day. It's one thing to be paired with a fellow you've got your heart set on, and another thing altogether when he doesn't return your feelings."

James spooned applesauce onto his plate. It struck him again how Jonny Ropp had told him—months ago—that he'd been acting just as unaware of Abby's feelings as Matt seemed to be of Emma's.

Something inside James shifted. What if he was missing out on the opportunity God had in mind for him? What if Abby had been the right woman for him all along? Maybe he should ask her out sometime—

Ask her now. When will you have a more perfect opportunity?

She turned toward him, a sandwich at her lips, as though she anticipated something wonderful. He saw himself reflected in her large, doelike eyes and all rational thought left him. And wasn't that a silly reaction? It wasn't like he was a young, tongue-tied adolescent without any experience around women. He'd known Abby all his life. And being here at Zanna's wedding certainly proved that he'd learned how to handle rejection, should Abby decline his invitation.

James took a deep breath. "You know, I'm building a buggy for a company that gives horse-drawn tours of New Orleans," he began before he lost his nerve. "Would you want to join me for a test drive after I finish it next week?"

The words hovered between them while Abby chewed and swallowed, her eyes wide. She looked delighted. "Does that include a tour of the countryside around Cedar Creek?"

"It does if that's what you'd like, Abby." And didn't it feel good, to know he had just made her so happy?

"I'd like to bring a picnic," she replied pertly. "With the dogwoods and the redbuds in bloom, it's the perfect time to enjoy the spring weather, don't you think?"

James was beyond thinking. As Abby squeezed his hand, he could only nod happily. Wasn't this yet one more surprise Zanna's wedding day had brought about?

Chapter 7

On Friday morning, Rosemary sat forward on the seat of the buggy, willing old Gertie to trot faster. The restaurant in Bloomingdale wanted ten pies for the weekend, but she was too agitated to bake. Titus and Beth Ann had chatted all during breakfast about the fine time they'd had at the wedding yesterday. After that, when she'd checked the messages in the phone shanty by the road to hear how many pies the café wanted, Rosemary had also discovered a message from Matt Lambright.

"I'm calling for Titus Yutzy and for Rosemary," he'd said in his energetic voice. "Titus, I've got you two fine yearling rams picked out—a Montadale and a Rambouillet—and I'll bring them over whenever you're ready. And while I'm there," he added, "I'm hoping to visit with you, too, Rosemary. I really enjoyed meeting you and Katie yesterday. I'll call you tomorrow afternoon, like we agreed."

Rosemary's heart had pounded so hard she could barely take down the phone number. She'd been tempted not to tell Titus that Matt had called, but that would have been the wrong way to handle this situation. Instead, she'd erased the message and left the phone number on the table for her father-in-law before hitching Gertie to the buggy. The best remedy for her racing thoughts was to visit with her mamm and Malinda, her sister. Surely there, at the home where she had grown up—and where she and Joe had been living—she would find the support she needed.

Was she the only one who felt it was too soon to embrace all this excitement about sewing and sheep and Cedar Creek? Beth Ann had rhapsodized all the way home about Abby Lambright and her Stitch in Time business, as well as about the incredible assortment of fabrics at the mercantile. Titus had gotten new ideas for improving his flock, and he couldn't say enough positive words about Matt. And just the mention of Matt's name made Katie ask repeatedly about his border collies. Thank goodness her little girl was riding quietly now, anticipating a visit with her grandmother and aunt.

Rosemary drove past the parcel of land she and Joe had bought, sadly imagining the orchard and the beehives they had planned to put behind their new house. It would have made such a pretty place to call their own, but now . . . She sighed. The weedy, unplanted fields and the clumpy grass along the fencerows resembled the way she felt this morning: needy and ignored and in total disarray.

She clapped the reins on Gertie's broad back. Five minutes later she pulled onto the familiar lane, where her maiden name, KEIM, painted on the mailbox had faded over the years. Rosemary waved at Malinda, who was hoeing the freshly tilled vegetable garden, and hitched the mare at the post beside the front porch. "All right, Katie, we're at Mammi's," she said as she helped her daughter down. "You're to stay in the house with your grandmother and me, understand? No slipping out the back door while we're visiting."

Katie nodded, her fingers in her mouth, but the twinkle in her eye told Rosemary she would have to watch her daughter every moment. Up the porch stairs they went, with Katie clutching her hand as she took each tall step. "Hullo, Mamm!" Rosemary called out as she entered the kitchen.

Her mother answered from upstairs, so Rosemary steered her

toddler toward the staircase in the front room. As they walked past the two recliners, she noted how the scuffmarks on the walls showed up more in the morning light. Joe would have painted these rooms by now, if he were still alive. He had been doing so well with his new remodeling business. Because of the downturn in the economy, he'd lined up a lot of jobs with English folks who were updating their homes rather than buying new ones.

As she helped Katie up each step, Rosemary forced her thoughts away from all the unrealized dreams Joe had left behind. She put a determined smile on her face. "And how are you this morning, Mamm?" she asked as she entered the bedroom her parents had shared for more than fifty years.

"Wasn't expecting you girls to drop by, what with you being gone yesterday." Her mother looked up from the clean sheets she was tucking around the mattress. "So how was the wedding?"

Rosemary stepped to the other side of the bed to help. "Nice enough. But I'm mighty tired of Titus saying how much greener the grass is on the Cedar Creek side of the fence and Beth Ann declaring how *wonderful* it would be to live closer to Sam Lambright's mercantile, and—"

Rosemary bit her lip. She should speak more carefully. Her daughter had picked up the faceless Amish doll from the hand-carved cradle in the corner, which her mother kept there for her to play with. Katie was only three, but she had a knack for repeating what she'd heard—usually at the most inopportune times.

"Sorry, Mamm," she murmured. "I didn't intend to dump all my complaints on you. Yesterday was . . . more difficult than I had anticipated."

Her mother smoothed the Dresden plate quilt with her hand. Bertha Keim was quiet by nature, so she didn't respond except to raise her eyebrows.

"I felt like a fish out of water," Rosemary explained. "Everyone else was having such a gut time. Beth Ann made a new friend and

Titus gave us money for fabric and kitchen supplies, so now she's all excited about the new clothes she'll make for herself and Titus and Katie—"

"You didn't pick out fabric for yourself?" her mother asked. "You ought to oblige Titus when he offers to buy you things, Rosemary. You've done him quite a favor, moving into his home and taking care of him and Beth Ann."

Rosemary bit back a remark. While her mother's reply was true enough, she had hoped for more . . . support. "It's just not time for colored dresses yet, Mamm. And while Titus arranged an exchange of rams with the Lambrights' son, our girl here"—Rosemary tilted her head toward Katie, who sat on the floor, rocking the doll— "couldn't stop playing with the D-O-Gs. To make it worse, the owner of those D-O-Gs kept gawking at me, even though I told him I wanted no part of his attention. Then he called this morning, saying he had Titus's rams picked out and that he was . . . looking forward to bringing them to Queen City. I don't know why I agreed to talk to him on the phone tomorrow."

Her mother stuffed a fat feather pillow into a fresh pillowcase. "And does Treva Lambright still run her greenhouse there on the county road, alongside the mercantile?"

"Jah, that's where they served the two meals." Rosemary grabbed the other pillow and jammed it into the remaining pillowcase.

"I've been wanting some hostas to plant under the tree out front," Mamm mused aloud. "And maybe Malinda will want to go to Cedar Creek this week for some tomato and cabbage plants. A tree branch fell on her cold frame—broke it open—and the deer ate her seedlings."

Rosemary squeezed her eyes shut. Why didn't anyone understand that she had no interest in Treva's Greenhouse or in the Cedar Creek Mercantile—or in Matt Lambright? "You could find starter plants closer to home than— Oh, forget it," she said with a sigh. "Just forget it."

Her mother glanced at Katie, who was now spinning in a circle, swinging the doll by its arm. "Sounds like a gut time was had by all except for you, daughter," she remarked. "Time marches on. The world won't stand still because you lost your Joe. You've got a little girl to raise, and you need to find a new life for yourself—something besides being Titus Yutzy's housekeeper and Beth Ann's stand-in mother. What don't you like about the Lambright boy? He comes from a gut family."

And what did that mean? Surely her widowed mother understood the heartbreak and loneliness she was going through . . . It wasn't like Mamm had been looking for another husband, even though that's what she was telling Rosemary to do.

"I . . . I'm still in love with Joe, Mamm. I miss him every day."

"I didn't say those feelings for him would go away. But they'll get easier to bear, with time—unless you keep dwelling on the past," she added matter-of-factly. "You'll shrivel up like a grape that rolled behind the fridge if you don't mix with other folks . . . and other fellas."

Her mother angled the pillow against the walnut headboard. "You're too young to be alone, Rosemary. Malinda and I worry about you, shutting yourself away at the Yutzy farm, cooking and cleaning and making pies. It keeps you busy, but there's no future in it."

Was her mother jealous because she'd moved in with Titus instead of staying here with her and Malinda? Or did Mamm mean what she'd said about finding another husband so soon?

"Sorry I bothered you," Rosemary said. "I wanted some time here to settle my nerves. If you'll look after Katie, I'll be downstairs in a few."

Mamm sighed. Then she smiled at her granddaughter and opened her arms. "Mammi baked snickerdoodles yesterday, Katie. Shall we go down and have us some?"

Katie dropped the doll and rushed into her grandmother's embrace. As they went down the steps, her mother's voice echoed in the stairwell, leading Katie's as they sang "In der Stillen Einsamkeit" to the tune of "Twinkle, Twinkle, Little Star." Mamm loved to sing in church, and she was tickled that her granddaughter had some musical ability and a clear voice.

Rosemary picked up the muslin doll, which was dressed in a blue cape dress with a white apron and kapp, and crossed the hall to the pale yellow bedroom she and Joe had shared. Here, she often found comfort remembering the plans she'd discussed with her husband while they had gazed out the back window, where they could see part of the land they had bought.

Rosemary sat in the old rocking chair where she had rocked Katie to sleep on many a night. She closed her eyes and took a deep breath. Since her husband's death, she had come here to pray and to call up the special feeling she considered Joe's presence. Being in this room calmed her when she'd had a trying week dealing with Titus's refusal to change anything in his home, or his remarks about how Alma had fried her chicken more to his liking.

Clutching Katie's doll, Rosemary waited for that indescribable peace that had always surrounded her in this room . . . and then she waited a little longer. After several moments she opened her eyes, which stung with unshed tears. Why wasn't it working? Why weren't memories of Joe comforting her after she'd had such a hard time at the Lambright wedding? Hadn't she remained true to him, as she'd promised when they exchanged their vows four years ago?

Be true to yourself now. Follow your dreams and live your life to the fullest.

Rosemary blinked. That hadn't sounded like Joe at all, talking of dreams. Was her husband, in spirit, leading her toward the changes she needed to make to feel whole again—or were her own thoughts struggling to be heard in the chorus of advice everyone else was giving her?

Rosemary had often wondered if Joe should have pursued his own ambitions sooner, rather than dutifully helping his father with a flock and a farm he'd had no real interest in. Her husband had delayed starting his remodeling business when Alma had been diagnosed with cancer, so it had taken them a year longer to pay for their property . . . a home he hadn't lived to enjoy.

The idea of following her dream disturbed Rosemary, though. The *Ordnung* taught that faith in God came first, followed by respect and love for one's family. Paying attention to her own desires seemed selfish, especially when Titus, Beth Ann, and Katie needed her like a pie required a crust to hold it together. This sense of duty had been ingrained in her since she was Katie's age. Yet hadn't her mother been telling her to make a new life for herself, just as that voice in her head had?

Rosemary stood up suddenly, leaving the chair to rock crazily behind her as she went to the window. Her property, with its overgrown grass and the underbrush along the fencerows, seemed foreign to her now. She no longer felt connected to the untamed acres that had become hers when Joe passed away. And worth a pretty penny, they were, because the parcel had enough flat, tillable land to become profitable someday. She felt Joe's memory slipping away from her, too.

For a moment, Rosemary couldn't remember what he looked like. She tried to call up Joe's voice in her mind, but couldn't hear it. And that frightened her.

She realized then that she was clutching Katie's doll as though she were holding on to the last thread of her sanity. And when she looked at its round, featureless face, which reflected the Plain belief that nothing should imitate the image of God or his human creation, Rosemary swallowed hard. Just as the doll had no eyes or nose or mouth—no signs of a soul or a self—she felt that she, too, might have lost these basic elements of her identity.

If I'm no longer Joe Yutzy's wife, who am I? And if I can no longer follow the dreams I shared with my husband . . . how am I to spend the rest of my life?

These were startling questions for a young mother of twenty-three. Rosemary's heart began to throb painfully. She tossed the doll onto the bed, which was covered with the Grandmother's Flower Garden quilt Mamm had made for her hope chest before she had met Joe. She couldn't leave the room fast enough.

Down the stairs she rushed, her footsteps clattering with the same loud discord she felt inside herself. "We're heading home, Katie. Bring your cookies," she snapped as she lifted her startled daughter from the old high chair. "I've got pies to bake. I'll see you soon, Mamm."

"Jah, well, Katie and I, we were just— Are you all right, Rosemary?" her mother called after her. "You're as pale as milk."

"I'm fine," Rosemary fibbed as she let the screen door bang behind her. Malinda, barefoot, with garden soil clinging to her ankles, was coming toward the house, but Rosemary hurried on over to the buggy. She urged Gertie down the lane at a trot, waving to her befuddled sister.

And why *wouldn't* Malinda look confused and hurt? Rosemary knew exactly how that felt because she hadn't been so upset—so afraid and overwhelmed—since the day Joe had died. What did she hope to accomplish by leaving her mother and sister so abruptly?

Rosemary didn't have any answers. Her heart pounded to the rhythm of Gertie's hoofbeats—*clip-clop! clip-clop!*—as fear pulsed through her body.

Then she caught the expression on Katie's face: her daughter sat beside her, clutching a snickerdoodle in each hand and looking terrified. Her eyes were wide. Her chin quivered as though she wanted to cry but was afraid to.

Rosemary pulled over to the shoulder, set the brake, and drew her toddler into her lap. Katie was her only living, breathing memento of Joe, for she saw him in the angle of their daughter's brows and her long, lush lashes. "I'm sorry, baby girl," she murmured against Katie's silky hair. "Mama didn't mean to scare you. Sometimes I miss your dat so much I don't know what to do with myself."

"Dat?" Katie repeated in her high, childlike voice. She looked at Rosemary with a hopeful expression. "Play with Dat's puppies now?"

Rosemary gaped. What on earth was her daughter talking about? Joe had never owned a dog—

Is she talking about Matt's puppies? Is she confusing the words "Dat" and "Matt" because they rhyme?

Or did Katie think Matt *was* her dat? Their daughter had barely been two and half when Joe had died, so she didn't recall anything about her father. Maybe she had drawn that conclusion because Matt was a man, and he had crouched down to talk with her, just as Joe often had.

Oh please, Lord . . . Will Katie want to spend time with Matt Lambright now? I'm not sure I can handle one more person believing I should like him.

When Rosemary got back to the Yutzy farm, the sheep stood blathering near the barn, waiting for their day's ration of grain. She carried Katie into the kitchen and sat her in the high chair with a handful of animal crackers and a few cubes of cheese. Down from the shelf came the can of lard and the bin of flour. Without a second thought, Rosemary measured enough of each ingredient for ten double-crust pies and began to cut the lard into the flour. She sprinkled water over the dough, mixing until its texture felt right. Then she divided it into twenty balls, which she set aside beneath a damp towel so they wouldn't dry out.

As Rosemary opened jars of ruby-red cherry filling from Alma's cellar shelves, she silently thanked her mother-in-law for putting up so much of it before she'd gotten sick. She also opened a few quarts of sliced peaches and thickened their syrup with tapioca, on the stove. Only a few quarts of gooseberries remained in the cellar, so she kept those back because Titus was especially fond of them.

And what's your favorite kind of pie?

She heard the words in her mind just as Beth Ann had asked Abby Lambright the same question . . . and Rosemary realized she didn't have an answer. She made so many kinds of pies for other people—mostly for folks she didn't know—yet she'd never considered her own preference. At other folks' homes, she ate what was put in front of her without thinking about what she would *rather* have.

Rosemary stopped rolling out her crusts, stunned by this revelation. She snatched the pan of peach syrup from the gas flame before she scorched it, lost in thought. Katie was playing with her animal crackers, singing the same tune she'd shared with her Mammi, but Rosemary really needed an answer, so she interrupted her.

"Katie, what's your favorite kind of pie?"

Her toddler kicked her legs happily. "Peach! Katie wants peach pie!"

Rosemary sighed. Even her three-year-old knew, without a doubt, what she liked in the way of pie.

What was going so wrong? Why did her world seem to tilt in a different direction today? First she'd gotten upset at Matt's message, then she'd fussed at her mother, and then she'd lost her connection to Joe. And now she had no answer for the simplest question. She had been so busy pleasing everyone else that she hadn't considered what she truly wanted for her future—or even for tonight's supper.

What's wrong with me, Lord? I think I might be losing my mind.

But crying wouldn't get her work done, would it? Rosemary rolled bottom crusts and fitted them into ten aluminum pie pans. She filled some of them with the ruby-colored cherry filling and arranged sliced peaches in the rest before pouring the thickened glaze over them. Finally, as she positioned the top crusts and crimped the edges, it came to her: she was afraid of losing everything she had ever known. If Titus and Beth Ann were so excited about Cedar Creek, if her mother insisted she should find another husband, and if she no longer felt Joe's presence in the room they had shared—where did that leave her?

The bang of the porch door brought her out of her woolgathering. Titus was washing up in the mudroom, and she'd been so preoccupied that she hadn't even thought about what to cook for their noon meal. She was tucking the last of her pies into the second oven when he entered the kitchen and noticed the unset table.

"I'm running late," she explained as she hurried to the fridge. "I drove over to see Mamm and Malinda and lost of track of time. Sorry."

Titus hung his straw hat by the door. He sat down in his chair at the end of the long kitchen table. "Guess I'll wait," he remarked with a shrug. "Maybe Katie'll share one of her animal crackers with me."

Rosemary had braced herself for a much sterner response to a late meal. She was amazed to see Titus trotting a cookie giraffe around the high chair tray to entertain Katie. She unwrapped a ham slice she'd taken from the deep freeze early that morning and dropped it into a cast-iron skillet. "How are the ewes and lambs looking today?"

"Gut. I got a section fenced off behind the barn for those rams Matt's bringing." Titus bounced the giraffe in the other direction, dodging Katie's attempts to grab it.

Rosemary relaxed. In another skillet, she simmered diced onion in butter before she added slices of leftover baked potatoes. If Titus had built a pen for those rams, to get them accustomed to their new home before he turned them in with the ewes, he surely had every intention of staying here in Queen City.

"So how's your mother?" he asked.

"Fine," she replied over the sizzle of the ham and onions. "She was changing the bedsheets and my sister was planting the garden."

Titus scratched under his beard, as he often did when he was considering a new idea. "Seems to me we'd all be better off if your mamm and sister came to live here. It's silly for them to keep up that big old house while the four of us are rattling around like dried peas in a shoebox at this place."

Rosemary stared at him. Where had this notion come from? "Mamm's no more ready to leave her home than you are. It's the house Dat built her when they got married."

"Jah, but maybe she'd like some company, same as I would. Maybe I should mosey over there to see what she'd say to hitching up," he mused aloud. Then he laughed until his shoulders shook. "At our age, it's not like we need all that newlywed romantic stuff."

Rosemary didn't know whether to laugh with him—or *at* him. Bertha Keim was every bit as set in her ways as Titus Yutzy was, and she seemed quite content to live with Malinda even if they didn't use some of the rooms in their farmhouse anymore.

But Titus sounded settled and no more likely to leave his home than Mamm was to leave hers—which meant that once he traded rams with Matt, there wouldn't be any more contact with folks in Cedar Creek. Everything would continue just the way it had been since Alma and Joe passed.

Rosemary turned the ham slice, inhaling its salty-sweet aroma. It occurred to her then that no one else had forced her to feel so agitated today: she had worried all morning that everything in her world was changing, fearing Titus would pull up stakes and move back to Cedar Creek. That obviously wasn't going to happen if her father-in-law was thinking he'd propose to her mother. And that wedding wasn't going to happen, either, if she knew her mamm.

Smiling, Rosemary flipped the simmering, nicely browned potatoes. What a relief to realize that it was only her imagination that had run off. Titus didn't know it, but he had brought her wandering thoughts right back where they belonged.

Nothing serious would change, after all. She could go on about her day now.

As she transferred the crisp potatoes onto a serving platter, Titus's chair scraped against the floor. "You know," he said quietly, "you're probably right about your mamm not wanting to come here. And now that I think about it, I'm not so sure I could tolerate a woman who ran the house her way, different from how Alma did. And when you add in your sister, that would make three grown women and two girls under my roof."

"Jah, that's the way I see it, too." Rosemary carried their food to the table, relieved that Joe's dat had come to his senses. She went to the cabinet to fetch their dinner plates.

"I'm going to call Matt Lambright . . . tell him to hang on to those rams," Titus continued in a faraway voice. "I'll ask him to keep an eye out for any property going up for sale in Cedar Creek, too. What with Joe gone, I'd be better off moving closer to Ezra—taking my flock there, where Matt and I could help each other with the lambing and the shearing and such. Now, there's a fella who knows the sheep business!"

The old Melmac dishes slipped from Rosemary's hands and clattered noisily on the plank floor. As she leaned against the stove to pull herself together, her heart raced. Did Titus really mean what he had just said?

Chapter 8

Matt polished off his plateful of meat loaf, mashed potatoes, and glazed carrots and then accepted the warm pan of raspberry cobbler from his dat. He and the rest of his family had spent Friday morning cleaning up after Zanna and Jonny's wedding, and now the newlyweds were on their way to see some cousins near Bowling Green, Missouri. It was the first of their weekends collecting wedding gifts from kin, and they planned to visit in three different households before they returned late on Sunday.

"Gut to get the greenhouse all put back to rights and the pew benches on their way to Ezra's place for preaching this Sunday," Matt remarked as he spooned out a huge helping of the cobbler. "Two hundred guests can make quite a mess!"

"Jah, but it was a gut sort of mess," his mother remarked from across the table. "I'm pleased so many folks were willing to come."

"Zanna's happier than I've ever seen her, and she's got a gut start on her family and her life with Jonny," his father remarked. Sam wasn't a man who carried on about other people's happiness, so he was in a fine mood today even with all the physical work of taking down tables and hefting benches into the pew wagon. "I think I'll keep the mercantile closed this afternoon to catch up on some book-keeping and inventory work. How about you girls? What are your plans today?"

Gail and Phoebe were scraping the dirty dinner plates while the cobbler made its way around the table. "Lois Yutzy wants us to bake rolls and sheet cakes for an English reception she's catering tomorrow," Phoebe replied. She looked at their grandmother, sitting next to Abby near the other end from their father. "Or do you need help at your greenhouse? I saw a lot of our guests taking home potted hyacinths and tulips when they saw how pretty they looked."

"Jah, Treva's Greenhouse did right well selling flowers yesterday, considering the shop was closed." Their grandmother chuckled. "If I wanted to branch out, I could rent out that big space for other folks' weddings, too—not that I'd want to face cleaning up that sort of mess every time, let alone doing all those dishes."

Phoebe smiled as though she were keeping a secret. "Maybe we can call Zanna's wedding gut practice and remember what all worked well and what we'd do differently next time," she hinted. "And it's probably a gut idea to plant a big section of celery in the garden this spring . . . if you know what I'm saying."

"You and Owen are getting hitched?" Gail blurted, and then she grabbed her sister's hands. "So he asked you yesterday? Like you thought he might?"

Matt watched this little drama unfold while pouring milk over his cobbler. He wasn't one for listening to girlish notions and wedding plans . . . but then, he'd certainly had Rosemary Yutzy on his mind all morning while he'd been cleaning up. He had called Titus's place earlier today, hoping she would answer the phone—but maybe their shanty was too far from the house for her to hear it ring. He'd called a second time, just in case she had been on her way down the lane or out planting in the garden.

Phoebe was blushing, nodding at them all. "Jah, Owen finally popped the question during the supper. We were keepin' quiet until we decided on a date."

"Well, congratulations!" Aunt Abby exclaimed. "You two have been looking cozy for quite some time now."

"You and James looked mighty cozy at supper, too, Aunt Abby," Gail piped up. "Do tell!"

Abby's face turned pink as she helped herself to the cobbler. "Puh! James and I were saying how we remembered when most of you young folks were born," she protested. "And we were grateful that Zanna didn't pair us up with guests from out of town."

Matt watched a smile bloom on his mother's face as the news of Phoebe's engagement sank in. "So this means you and Owen will be taking your instruction to join the church soon," she said, nodding at her eldest daughter in approval. "Unless I miss my guess, we might see several young people in Cedar Creek get hitched in the next year or so. That can only make us a stronger community, especially if we can keep our families close."

Still focused on his dessert, Matt was taking in all this talk . . . especially his mother's views on joining the church and staying around town to raise a family. Everyone hereabouts considered it a miracle that Jonny and Gideon Ropp had returned to Cedar Creek after the way they'd left their dat's dairy farm a few years ago to start other businesses outside the Amish community. It was mostly Zanna's doing, Jonny had confessed, that he realized he needed to live closer to his parents again and that he should give up his cars, his motorcycle, and his driving business to support his young family in a way that honored the *Ordnung*.

And what does this mean for you, if Rosemary lives clear over past Queen City?

Matt wasn't sure why that question had popped into his mind. After all, he'd met Rosemary only yesterday—and he had gotten better acquainted with Titus and Katie than he had with the young widow who clung to memories of her husband.

But maybe it was the way Rosemary had devoted herself to her man and was now taking care of Joe's father and Beth Ann that appealed to Matt. Sure, he had noticed Rosemary's pretty skin and he had already imagined how long and soft her glossy brown hair would be when she unpinned it, but he wanted to spend time just talking with her, getting to know her, too. She seemed to be just the right height and size, and more than once yesterday he had wanted to put his arms around her and comfort her. He imagined himself as the man who could coax a smile back to her face.

And when had he ever considered such notions before?

When laughter erupted at the table, Matt blinked and looked around him. His dat and mamm, his two sisters, Aunt Abby, and his grandmother were all looking at him as though they'd said something funny and he'd been so lost in his thoughts of Rosemary that he'd missed it.

"Matt's mind is miiiles away," Phoebe teased.

"Jah, about as far from here as it is to Queen City." Gail giggled over her first bite of cobbler. "Katie was pretty excited about meeting your dogs, Matt."

"Too bad Rosemary didn't feel the same way," Phoebe joined in. "And poor Emma's probably wondering if you even knew she was sitting beside you, the way you kept gawking out the window."

Matt's face went hot. He hadn't intended to ignore Emma. She'd brought him a lot of brownies lately, as though she liked him a lot, but why should he pretend he had special feelings for her? "I didn't mean to make her feel bad," he mumbled, "but it wasn't my doing that she got paired up with me. Why do I suspect you girls and Ruthie had a hand in making out Zanna's list of matches?"

"We men don't stand a chance, outnumbered by women the way we are," his dat remarked with a shake of his head. "I haven't seen a wedding supper yet where girls didn't get their hopes up and their feelings hurt. We all have to learn how to handle disappointment."

For a few moments everyone ate in silence. Matt had the urge to excuse himself to see to his sheep chores, as he didn't care much for having his romantic notions discussed by all the women in his family. But if he left now, his sisters would only tease him more.

"Rosemary's a very nice young woman," Aunt Abby finally said. "I really enjoyed getting to know her and Beth Ann. It's not an easy row to hoe, living with Titus after his wife and son have died," she pointed out. "I suspect Rosemary's having a tougher time of it than she lets on."

"And from what I could tell while she was putting Katie down for a nap," Barbara joined in, "Rosemary needs time to figure out what comes next. She and Joe had bought a piece of land between her mamm's place and Titus's, and they were having plans drawn up for their new home when Joe died. She has a lot on her mind right now."

Rosemary owned a piece of land? Matt considered this as he scraped the last of the sweet raspberry filling from his bowl. What if she planned to go ahead and build that house? Did that mean she intended to live out her life as a widow, raising Katie in Queen City?

It was awfully soon to be wondering about such details, since he'd only exchanged a few words with her yesterday, hardly the basis for making any long-range plans. And her response to him had been anything but encouraging. Maybe he should take the hint and forget about her . . .

But Matt couldn't get her pretty face out of his mind. Despite the way she had laughed and played with Katie, he had sensed a deep loneliness in her . . . a need for the same warmth and caring she was so good at giving to others but didn't know how to accept for herself.

The sound of dishes being stacked brought him out of his thoughts. "Guess I'd better see to my bottle babies," he said, referring to twin lambs whose mother had died. "And I need to figure out which wagon to use for hauling those two yearlings over to Titus."

As Matt stepped into the afternoon sunlight, he smiled at the perfect springtime day. Robins were hopping in the yard, gathering dried grass for nests, while overhead he heard wrens warbling. A thick border of bright red and yellow tulips swayed in the breeze in front of the house, and as he walked toward the sheep barn, his horse, Cecil, nickered at him from the corral. It would soon be time to sharpen the blades on the rotary mower and clip the lawn—just as it was almost time to wean this crop of spring lambs from their mothers.

Even as his flock's needs were foremost on his mind, Matt glanced at the phone shanty by the road and headed in that direction first. Maybe Titus had left him a message. He had a feeling the fellow from Queen City wouldn't let much time get by before he prepared a place for his two new rams . . . and just maybe he would phone the Yutzy place again. It was silly, hoping to hear Rosemary's voice, yet Matt grinned. He was twenty-two and he'd lived happily at home all his life, but maybe it was time to change that situation.

His heart skittered when he saw the red message light blinking on the phone. He slipped into the small white building and sat in the old wooden chair at the table supplied with a notepad and pens. He reminded himself that customers might have left orders for the Cedar Creek Mercantile, Treva's Greenhouse, Graber Custom Carriages— or someone might have called any of the Lambrights or the Grabers. Yet in his heart, he hoped . . .

Matt pushed the Play button. Sure enough, the first two messages were for James Graber from companies in Kansas City and Orlando, inquiring about his prices for special touring carriages. A lady had called from Clearwater to see if his dat had any bulk pectin in the mercantile for making jelly from the grape juice she'd kept in her deep freeze over the winter.

Then a familiar voice came on with a chuckle. "This is for Matt Lambright, and this is Titus Yutzy calling from Queen City," he said as Matt listened eagerly. "I'm gonna ask you to keep those two young rams for now, son—"

Matt's hopes plummeted. What had made Titus change his mind when he had sounded so excited about the exchange yesterday?

"—on account of how I'm thinking to move to Cedar Creek. With my kids scattered around, it'll put me closer to my brother, Ezra, you see," the old farmer continued. "Will you ask around town and find out if any land's up for sale? The sooner I know about this, the sooner I can make my plans."

Matt stared at the phone, his thoughts spinning wildly. If Titus moved to Cedar Creek—if, indeed, there was a place for him to move to—would Rosemary come along? Or would she build that house she and Joe had been planning and stay behind?

He replayed the message, hanging on every word, and then he stepped out of the phone shanty. The CLOSED FOR WEDDING sign still hung inside the front door of the mercantile, so Matt went around to the back door. Through the workroom he hurried, fighting a grin as he looked around the store's huge main room. His father sat at the checkout counter, bent intently over the order he was filling out.

"Dat!" Matt called out as he strode past the shelves lined with bags of bulk flour and yellow cornmeal. "Do you know of any farms for sale hereabouts? Is anything posted on the bulletin board?"

His father looked up, raising his thick eyebrows. "Does this mean you're looking for a place of your own?" he asked, only half teasing.

"Not anytime soon." Matt stopped at the counter, careful not to scatter his dat's inventory lists. He laughed, still in disbelief at what he'd heard over the phone. "Titus just called me, asking about property so he can move back to Cedar Creek. Says he wants to be closer to his brother," he explained. "Since all the news gets talked about here at the store, I figured you might've heard if anybody was looking to sell out."

His father considered this for a moment. "There was a time last December, while we were rebuilding the Ropp house, when some of us wondered whether Rudy's family would decide not to move back there because they'd lost their savings in the fire," he replied. "But right now I don't know of anybody turning loose of land. Most of it gets passed down rather than going up for sale."

Matt nodded, thinking. If Titus moved his flock here, they might be able to share some of the chores, like shearing, or lower some of their expenses by buying larger quantities of veterinary supplies or feed supplements. Titus would certainly bring Beth Ann with him, so maybe . . . maybe Rosemary would come along, too. That possibility inspired Matt to pursue even the remotest chance that somebody might sell off a parcel of land.

As he glanced through the front windows, where he could see the Grabers' front porch, Matt got an idea. "What with Carl Byler farming a gut bit of the Graber place, now that Merle can't handle that sort of work, do you suppose Merle might sell some of his property?"

His dat pushed up his rimless reading glasses. "Carl farms a lot of Paul Bontrager's acreage right next to the Grabers, too," he replied as he thought about it. "But be careful, son. Talk to James real quietlike, when Merle and Eunice aren't around, or you'll get them all upset. And we wouldn't want Preacher Paul hearing rumors that somebody wanted to buy him out," Sam remarked. "We can't forget that those families depend on the income from the crops Carl raises for them, either."

Matt nodded, already envisioning what a perfect arrangement it would be if Titus could pasture his flock right across the road. He was fighting a smile, imagining he was already courting Rosemary . . .

"Another consideration," his father said, "is that Titus'll need a house. I can't see him as the sort to build a new place at his age."

Matt sighed. "Jah, there's that. I'll think about it before I say anything."

He returned to the sheep lot. As he refilled the wooden creep feeder at the pasture gate with finely ground grain for the new lambs, to get them accustomed to solid food before he weaned them from their mothers, Matt tried to remain objective about Titus's request . . . reminding himself that Rosemary might have different ideas altogether from Titus when it came to moving away from her home. Even so, as he gazed across the county blacktop toward the Graber acreage, separated from Preacher Paul's cornfields by only a wire fence, he could envision sheep grazing there. Such a conversion would mean feeding Titus's sheep more processed rations—or pasturing them here, with his own flock—until those cropland acres across the road could be plowed and replanted with pasture grasses. It would require some sturdy new livestock fencing, too, which wasn't cheap.

But it could be done.

His dat was right, though: while Titus would willingly invest in the changes required to keep his sheep, building a house was a far-fetched proposition for a fellow of that age who didn't have a wife. Even with a daughter to raise and Rosemary looking after him, Titus wasn't the sort to spend any more than he had to on a place to live . . . Matt had heard of displaced Amish families living in trailers or manufactured homes, but that idea went against the grain here in Cedar Creek. His dat and other folks had donated lumber and supplies, and local carpenters had built Rudy and Adah Ropp's new house in less than a month—in freezing December weather—because they believed in helping each other live in real homes, which fostered permanent roots.

Matt filled the bucket feeder, equipped with two big nipples, and watched his orphaned twin lambs suck their milk. He rubbed his dogs' ears, smiling at them. "All this thinking isn't doing one bit of gut—for me, or for Titus, either," he murmured as Pearl and Panda leaned into the strokes he was giving them. "You pups take care of the flock while I go across the road. I won't have any answers unless I ask some questions, will I?"

As soon as he'd finished his chores, Matt headed for the Graber Custom Carriage shop, which sat closer to the road than the rambling white house where James, his sister Emma, and their parents lived. It was a relief to see that Emma wasn't out working in the garden. He wasn't eager to talk to her while he was on this mission for Titus. He entered the shop's front door and then paused to look around.

The large, open work area was filled with a couple of farm wagons and an enclosed carriage in various stages of completion, while along the walls shelves and workbenches held the tools of James's carriage-making trade. Noah Coblentz, who was now an apprentice here, waved at him from the bed of the wagon he was painting, while Perry Bontrager, the preacher's son, stood at the rear of the other wagon, welding a wheel. The whine of a pneumatic saw filled the big room until Leon Mast spotted Matt and shut it off.

"Hey there, Matt," he said with a grin that split his thick, dark beard. "Let me guess—you've come to order a courting buggy. After the way you were watching that gal from over Queen City way—"

"Nope, you guessed wrong, Leon." Matt hoped the sudden heat in his face wouldn't give away his embarrassment. Had every guest at Zanna's wedding noticed the shine he'd taken to Rosemary? "I was hoping to have a word with James."

"Other room," Noah replied, pointing with his paintbrush. "He's finishing another of those fancy-dancy carriages like a princess would ride in for a parade."

"Jah. Denki." Matt walked carefully around Perry's sparks and smoke. He knocked playfully on the welder's helmet and then made his way past the new carriage's fiberglass body.

He hadn't given it much thought, but Leon was on target with his remark about a courting buggy: most young Amish fellows looked forward to the day when they received a fine new rig, usually when they had a special young lady in mind to drive home from singings or for long rides on warm summer nights. Up to this point, Matt had been content to drive the buggy his dat had bought a few years back. If he ordered a courting buggy now, maybe—if he offered a bonus—James would complete it in time to escort Rosemary around Cedar Creek and the surrounding Missouri countryside this summer. And if she refused to see him, well . . . he would have a nice vehicle ready for when the right woman came along.

Matt stepped into the back room, which was almost as large as the one he'd come from, to see James stretching a piece of deep red leather over a curved seat section. Lately the carriage maker had received several orders for specialty vehicles from places all over the map—tourist attractions and theme parks, mostly—and James insisted on doing the intricate finishing work on these buggies himself while his employees built the wagons and carriages Plain folks had ordered. Matt stood quietly, watching, until James straightened to his full height.

"Gut afternoon to ya, James. I've got to say that's the most *colorful* carriage I've ever seen," Matt said with a chuckle.

"Jah, 'colorful' is a gut word for the Mardi Gras in New Orleans, the way I understand it." James brushed his hair back from his damp face. "But you haven't seen the half of it. Along with this devil-red leather upholstery and the ebony trim, there'll be a giant mask on the front and another on the back, all covered with faceted light bulbs in purple, green, and gold. They flash in patterns while another electrical current follows the lights around the outline of the mask. Chaser lights, they call them."

Matt's eyes widened. "And you know how to do all that electrical work?"

James chuckled and stepped down to the floor. "I tell the folks who order these carriages that I can produce whatever they want—and then I get a lot of on-the-job training," he replied. "For what they pay me, it's fun to tinker on new systems and make a rig look and handle better than they expect. The only thing I won't build them is a horse to pull it."

"So this one's almost finished?" Matt walked around the gleaming vehicle, admiring the fine craftsmanship. A globe-shaped network of wiring formed a nearly invisible canopy that arched above the two passenger seats, which faced each other behind the open carriage's driver's seat.

"They tell me a Mardi Gras mask wouldn't be complete without feathers, and they sent some big ones for me to use. I have to figure out how to attach them, though, along with some fake jewels." James looked delighted with this project even if no Amish fellow would be seen driving it. "I'll ask Abby to help with the trimming, as she's handier with that than I am. She's agreed to go for a test ride, too. Won't that be something, rolling through Cedar Creek with all those flashing lights?"

"Better put blinders on your horse and hope you don't spook any-body's bulls. I'd like to watch it roll by just to get the full effect." Matt was nodding, still trying to figure out how to ask his question while he was alone with James.

"So what's on your mind today?" James asked after a short si-lence. "A courting buggy, maybe?"

"All right, so I made it pretty obvious I was interested in Rose-mary Yutzy," Matt protested. When he heard how his voice echoed in the high-ceilinged workroom, he stepped closer to James. "Truth be told, I'm here on account of how Titus called—because he wants to move to Cedar Creek!" he explained in a lower tone.

"Jah? I sure didn't see that coming."

"Well, here's the real question for you." Matt glanced behind him to be sure none of James's employees were in the doorway. "Far as I know, nobody has any land for sale hereabouts. Since Carl's farming most of your acreage, I'm taking a long shot, asking if you'd consider selling those lower fields that join on with Paul's."

James's eyes widened. "Well, now, I wasn't expecting you to ask *that*."

"And if you need time to think about it or to ask your dat—"

"Oh, I can already tell you Dat's not ready to part with any land—and not so much because he depends on the income," James clarified. "This place belonged to his dat and his grandpa Graber before that. Mamm would have a fit, too. She'd figure we must be getting low on money, and that wouldn't sit too gut. The carriage shop makes us plenty to get by on, but Dat considers the farming income his contribution to supporting the family, you see."

"I figured you'd say that," Matt said with a sigh. "But Titus asked me to check around. I thought about asking Perry Bontrager the same question, but since Paul gets no pay for preaching, I'm guessing he needs the income Carl's crops bring in."

"Jah, and Paul has aged to the point where he doesn't do much cabinetry work, either. Just smaller pieces and some repairs on days when his hands are steady." James crossed his arms, thinking. "You know, I can't recall the last time a place came up for sale here in Cedar Creek. Lots of families have had kids move elsewhere, but there's always been a son to carry on and keep the homeplace."

"Jah, and what with the improvements it would take to convert that land for Titus's sheep, I can't see him building a new house, either." Matt sighed. "Just thought I'd ask."

James nodded and focused again on the seat he'd been covering. "If I hear of anything, I'll let you know. We'd rather have Plain families buy land around Cedar Creek before English folks get wind of it being for sale."

Matt headed for the side door. "Have a gut afternoon, James. See you around."

The carriage maker's face lit up. "Jah, you just might," he replied. "If you're watching out your window tomorrow night, could be you'll see a Mardi Gras carriage going by. Imagine how your Aunt Abby will look riding in that!"

Chapter 9

Around one thirty on Saturday afternoon, Rosemary was trying not to let on that she was expecting Matt to call. While she had tried to dissuade him at the wedding, she intended to state her case firmly today—which was easier when he wasn't gawking at her with his playful eyes. Or maybe she should ignore his call altogether . . . except if the phone kept ringing, Titus might pick up his extension in the barn. There was no reason to let Matt think she would ever change her mind, and no way to know what he and her father-in-law might have discussed when she was out of earshot. That left her at a distinct disadvantage.

While Titus hadn't said anything more about moving to Cedar Creek, he had worn a smug smile all during dinner. What did that mean? Beth Ann had helped with the dishes and then returned to her sewing. Already she had finished three pairs of work pants for her dat, and she had nearly completed a new dress for the preaching service tomorrow, as well. As the young girl sat at the old treadle machine, which had belonged to her mother and to Alma's mother before that, Rosemary envied Beth Ann's ability to immerse herself in a task she enjoyed.

"You're sure you don't mind watching Katie while I work outside?" Rosemary asked. She had gardening to do—onions to thin out and peas to pick—which would keep her close to the phone shanty out by the road.

"She'll be no trouble at all," Beth Ann replied. "Katie plays with my spools and scraps. I can already tell she's going to like her new dresses by the way she picks up leftover pieces of the lavender and gold we bought for her."

"Jah, well . . . I'll be back in a while. Denki for your help, Beth Ann."

Katie looked up from the corner where she sat arranging fabric scraps. "I love you, Mamm!" she chirped.

Rosemary still got goose bumps every time her toddler said that. In a lot of Amish families, affection wasn't openly expressed, but she believed it was important for Katie to know she was loved, and to express her feelings, too. "Jah, and I love you, too, punkin," she replied. "Be a gut girl for Aunt Beth Ann while I'm in the garden."

She fetched her baskets from the shelf in the mudroom. Out the door and across the yard she went, noticing how the grass already needed cutting—and goodness, what a crop of dandelions they had! She was just crouching at the outermost row of green onions when the phone rang.

Should she answer it? It might not be Matt—and if it was, what would she say to him? She had been riding such an emotional seesaw that she had no idea what words might come out of her mouth. If she let it ring, he would eventually figure out that she didn't want to talk to him.

But if Titus answered, he would encourage Matt's attentions.

Rosemary made it into the shanty just in time to keep the message machine from kicking on. "Jah, hullo?" she said breathlessly.

"It's gut to hear your voice again, Rosemary. This is Matt." He sounded so close he could have been calling from the other side of the wall while looking in the window at her. "I thought you might not answer. I didn't mean to come on like a fire truck at the wedding."

Rosemary closed her eyes. If she didn't set him straight right off, there would be no convincing him that she meant what she said . . . and no way she'd be able to say what she meant. She hadn't talked to a man this way since Joe had courted her, and she felt as nervous as a girl at her first singing. "You need to understand that Joe and I were so happy that, well— You're a nice fella, Matt. But don't get your hopes up."

"You're talking to me, though. That's all I want for right now."

Rosemary gripped the receiver. Why couldn't she spell out her feelings—or just hang up?

"Ezra says you bake a better apple pie than your aunt Lois," Matt continued, sounding comfortable and confident. "What's your secret?"

"Brown sugar instead of white," she replied without a second thought—and then she realized that he had cleverly kept her talking by changing to a safe, everyday topic. And what else had Uncle Ezra told him? Had Titus contacted him about moving to Cedar Creek? Her mind was spinning with so many possibilities that her tongue couldn't seem to cooperate.

"What do you like to do in your spare time?" Matt asked. "Say, on Sunday afternoons?"

Was he going to ask her for a date? Planning to come to Queen City rather than attending tomorrow's singing in Cedar Creek? On alternate Sundays when they didn't have church, Amish families often went on longer visits, so maybe he was planning a week ahead. "Well . . . I don't have an answer for that because—because I don't have any spare time," she blurted out.

"You know, I haven't had much fun lately, either," he replied. "I keep busy with my sheep and my dogs, mostly. Maybe if I had company other than Panda and Pearl, my life would take on more sparkle."

Sparkle? Why would a Plain fellow care about that?

Rosemary recalled Matt's shining brown eyes and wished they hadn't looked so happy all those times he'd held her gaze on Thursday. His voice, low and smooth, was affecting her, too. But she couldn't fall into any more conversational traps. "I saw plenty of single girls at the wedding who'd enjoy being with you," she stated.

"I've known them all my life." His reply was so clear, she could imagine him shrugging . . . tilting his head the way he had at the wedding, when he'd been listening carefully. "I'm twenty-two and I haven't found the right woman, Rosemary. I have a wonderful-gut family—lots of girls as friends—but it's time to start a home of my own."

"Matt, I can't just up and leave Titus!" she protested.

"Why not?"

Rosemary swallowed hard. It had been *her* idea to move in with Joe's dat. The household chores had been overwhelming Beth Ann, and she'd believed that sharing their grief might help them all heal sooner. But she couldn't explain such notions to Matt, could she? Her Joe had been five years older than she was, more reserved and settled than this fellow who was challenging her with his new ideas . . . his life-altering questions. Rosemary fidgeted with the pencil and scratch pad.

"Titus lived a gut long life with Alma," Matt continued in a persuasive tone, "and no matter how hard you try, you can't replace her. Not that Titus wouldn't miss you, understand. And—"

"I never intended to replace Alma!" she blurted out. "It's just that—"

"—I can see why you wouldn't want to leave the area where you've lived for most of your life. So if Titus finds a place here in Cedar Creek—"

So Titus *had* talked to Matt about moving there. Rosemary's lungs were running out of air, just as she was running out of ways to counter Matt's ideas.

"—maybe I could move to Queen City!" he suggested gleefully. "Ezra says you've got a piece of land where you and Joe had planned to build a house. I can't imagine you living in a new place or in Titus's house after he leaves and trying to raise Katie alone."

"Matt, you haven't heard a thing I've said!" Rosemary blurted out. This conversation was getting way out of hand. "I'll not be moving to Cedar Creek, and you'll not be moving here, either. I—I have to go now!"

"Tell Katie that Panda and Pearl say hi!"

She banged the receiver down so hard the clatter echoed inside the tiny building. What a lot of nerve for Matt Lambright—whom she'd met only two days ago—to suggest that he could take Joe's place even as he told her not to fill in for Alma! Rosemary stepped outside, but the fresh air did nothing to settle her emotions. In all her years with Joe, she had never felt so frenzied, so pushed into doing something before she was ready.

Joe was the slow-but-steady type. He did what needed to be done on the farm, ran his remodeling business, and relied on you to run the house. No challenges. No surprises.

Rosemary drew in a deep breath, glancing around the yard. No one else was in sight, so she could use this time in the garden to clarify thoughts that had boiled over like an unwatched pot. Truth be told, her husband's reticence had irritated her at times. More than once Joe had planned a joint trip to town or had assumed she would help him with sheep chores when she had figured on canning vegetables with Mamm or had promised pies to the Clearwater Café.

But didn't every wife figure on being inconvenienced now and again? Wasn't it part and parcel of marriage that the man of the family made the decisions and the woman went along with them? Yet Matt didn't seem to fit such a predictable mold . . .

Rosemary walked toward the garden again and was struck by the bright yellow-green of the leaf lettuce and the way the bean plants had popped out of the ground practically overnight. New growth . . .

a fresh season, and all of it happening from the planting of seeds and the gentle rains God had provided at just the right time.

Maybe she was overreacting to Matt's enthusiasm. By nature she was as bubbly and vibrant as her Katie, yet these past months she'd worn black clothing and stayed dutifully busy to keep her loneliness at bay. Her husband had provided her a good, steady life, but his own mother had remarked about how Joe and Titus seldom laughed out loud. *As somber as a couple of crows perched on a hearse,* Alma had said on more than one occasion.

Rosemary had met Matt only a couple of days ago, but she couldn't imagine anyone comparing him to a blackbird at a funeral. As she knelt to cut lettuce for their supper, her thoughts returned to what Matt had said during his call. *You bake a better apple pie than your aunt Lois . . . What do you like to do in your spare time? . . . I haven't had much fun lately . . .*

For sure and for certain, *fun* wasn't one of Titus's priorities. And hadn't Mamm told her there was no future in staying with him? Matt was stating the same idea but with different words . . . more convincing reasons, even if he had tried to rush her into a relationship.

Still, she felt obliged to look after Joe's dat. It was important for Katie to grow up near Joe's family. Wasn't it?

As she clipped some spinach, Rosemary had a flash of memory from the wedding, when Katie stood fascinated by the two black-and-white dogs . . . with Matt's arm around her waist as he encouraged her. Her daughter had been so enthralled by those dogs and so enamored of Matt—so trusting. But what did a three-year-old know about love and life and what it took to get from one day to the next?

Maybe more than you realize. What if Katie has the right idea, reaching out to a man whose future shines as brightly as his eyes?

Rosemary blinked. How had her thoughts taken such a turnaround? Thank goodness there were so many onions to pull and peas to pick and radishes to gather and—

Chapter 10

Abby stepped back from the Mardi Gras carriage to study the arrangement of fake jewels she'd just glued to one of its doors. "Is that what you had in mind, James?" she asked, holding the cordless glue gun so it wouldn't drip. "Seems to me, if we add one more row of the green beads as a border, it would finish off the design and cover the edges of the inset, too."

"I knew you'd have the right eye for my trim work," he replied, "even if you think a wicked witch ought to be riding in this carriage."

Abby grinned. When had she ever spent a Saturday afternoon working in James's shop on such a flamboyant project? "After sewing dark work pants for Matt and Sam all morning, this is a lot more fun—and certainly more colorful!"

When James smiled at Abby, her heart danced with anticipation. He fitted his epoxy gun with a very small tip and came to stand beside her. "I'll secure the jewels you've set so far, so they'll stay rock solid in place before you add the border." He raised his eyebrows playfully. "You never know how fast this carriage might travel in New Orleans, considering how speedy it looks just sitting here in the shop."

As their laughter rang out in the big, open workroom, Abby chose the same number of purple, gold, and green faceted stones for the design on the opposite door. While she had known James Graber all her life, today felt special. Since two days ago, the light in his eyes at the wedding supper, when he'd invited her for a ride, had lit up her imagination—her whole sense of who she was and what she might hope for.

"I've sliced some ham and made coleslaw for our picnic," she said as she positioned three gold octagonal beads in the center of the inset. "And when Sam saw I was making fried pies, he threatened to come with us if I didn't make him some, too."

"The more, the merrier, right?" James's eyes teased her over the tops of the carriage doors. "So what kind did you make him?"

What a fine face James had: the lines at the corners of his eyes crinkled and a dimple came out to play in each of his cheeks. Abby returned his gaze and then focused on keeping hot glue from dripping all over the carriage door. "Sam likes pineapple-lemon filling, so I made a batch of those, as well as a dozen or so with cherry, and another batch with apples and lots of cinnamon." She squeezed the glue gun's trigger to affix more beads. "That'll give them enough for tonight's dessert as well as some for tomorrow's lunch after the preaching service. Barbara has a couple of midwifing visits over toward Clearwater today and Mamm's planting flats of bedding plants in her greenhouse, so I'm the designated baker."

"I can't lose, whichever flavors you bring along, Abby," James assured her. "It's been a long time since I went on a picnic." He was intent on squeezing out the clear epoxy in just the right amount, so he stopped chatting until he'd finished going around the beads she had affixed. "Emma and the folks seemed mighty surprised when I told them why I wouldn't be at supper tonight. Surprised but pleased."

Abby reminded herself that James's social life was his business, yet she suspected he hadn't taken anyone out since Zanna had abandoned him last October. "And your parents are doing all right? Your mamm is usually weeding her flower beds once it gets this warm."

"Jah, she and Dat are usually glad to get out of the house, just to sit a spell on the porch of an afternoon. But they're saying it's still too chilly. They don't have the energy they did last fall."

Abby thought about this as she positioned lozenge-shaped purple beads between the gold ones she'd already glued. "Do you suppose that's because of all the ruckus Zanna caused when she didn't marry you?" she asked quietly. "I know it would've been a big change for them, having her in the house, but—"

"I suspect you're right about that, Abby." He looked up from his work. "Mamm was one for fussing at Zanna and pointing out her faults, yet she and Dat were excited about having some grandchildren right here at home, too. They don't get to see Iva and Sharon's kids much, what with them living on the other side of Queen City."

Once again Abby was reminded of the repercussions of Zanna's walking away from her marriage into the Graber family. She also told herself not to get her hopes up after years of wishing this fine man would notice her, but that didn't stop her from enjoying every moment she spent with him.

"Looks like the mailman just pulled away," James said as he glanced out the window. "I'll be right back. It's Saturday, and Dat likes to look at the *Budget* as soon as it arrives. He reads your piece first, you know."

As Cedar Creek's scribe for the national Plain newspaper, Abby wrote a weekly report of the local goings-on, usually with a few reflections on them. "Take your time, James. Tell your folks hello for me."

"I'll do that. Kind of you to think of them." James put on his straw hat and strode out toward the road.

As Abby went around to the other side of the carriage to work, she glanced outside. James stood at the mailbox, thumbing through the mail: his broad shoulders were accentuated by the suspenders that crisscrossed the back of his shirt . . . a shirt she had sewn because Emma kept so busy with housework and looking after their parents that James had chosen to pay Abby to make his family's clothes. He opened a large white envelope. As he was reading, his expression suggested news of a totally unexpected nature. He looked toward the shop as though he were gazing right at her and flashed a dazzling smile.

"Here's your mail, Dat," he called as he jogged toward his family's front porch. "I'll be in after Abby and I finish this carriage. Won't be but a few minutes."

Merle leaned out over the porch railing to take the paper from his son. "If it were me and I had a perty young woman in my shop, I'd not be in any hurry to come home," he teased. "Go out and have a gut time, son. You know how it goes on a Saturday night—your mamm'll be readin' me reports and recipes from the *Budget* whether I wanna hear them or not."

Abby arranged a few more beads on the carriage door, thinking most folks around town would also be reading the *Budget* tonight . . . although she could imagine Eunice's reedy voice getting louder and more piercing as the evening wore on, to keep Merle from nodding off in his recliner.

When James hurried back into the shop, his eyes were wide. "What do you make of *this*?" he asked in an excited voice. "You remember that white princess carriage I made last fall?"

"The one where I sewed the beads on the seat cushion? Jah, that was a mighty pretty coach—and there it is!" She pointed to the magazine page he was waving, and he held it still enough for her to read. "'In Praise of Plain Craftsmanship.' Now, isn't that a fine title? And it looks like you had quite a princess riding in your coach, too."

"Jah, I'm not sure what all being Miss America means," he said in a rush, "but when she heard that an Amish fellow had made the carriage she rode in a Disney World parade, she really talked it up. So here it is—my carriage—in a magazine, no less! Although," he added, "I'm sounding mighty proud of my work now. And that's not so gut."

Abby gazed at the photograph, which featured the open white carriage in semidarkness, with its canopy grid of sparkly white lights. A young woman stood alongside the impressive Clydesdale it was hitched to. Her hair was swept up and she was wearing a sequined dress of morning-glory blue. The banner draped from her shoulder read MISS AMERICA.

"There's nothing wrong with a job well done, James," she reminded him. "And the article doesn't single you out so much as it draws attention to the craftsmanship we Amish believe in. When you consider all the cars and computers and other fancy items manufactured in English factories," she went on in a thoughtful tone, "isn't it nice that those same folks recognize the careful work Plain people do with their hands, in shops that sit right alongside their homes?"

James blinked. "Jah, it is. And denki for the way you pointed that out, Abby. You have such a talent for making folks feel gut about what they do and who they are."

Her face went hot. Abby focused on placing the last green beads around the edge of the bright design. "You say the nicest things, James."

It didn't take her long to finish the insets. Meanwhile, James was inserting huge green and purple feathers into short pipes he'd welded along the sides of the Mardi Gras masks that decorated both ends of the carriage. Abby studied the front mask when he finished it. "I can't figure out what all of this means, or why folks would want such a gaudy carriage, but . . . well, I guess it takes all kinds."

James looked up from inserting the last feather. "You're not backing out of our ride, I hope?"

"No, no. We have to maintain that quality craftsmanship the magazine article talked about, don't we?" she teased. As Abby dropped the leftover beads back into their box, she felt giddy yet almost shy. "I'll go pack our picnic now. See you whenever you're ready."

"Give me about half an hour to check on the folks and clean up."

Was it her imagination, or did James look every bit as excited as she was? Did he consider this a first date, or was that wishful thinking on her part? Abby decided to stop analyzing so she could enjoy the evening's ride, no matter what they called it. After all, a dream she'd clung to for the past several years was about to come true.

As James hitched Mitch, his bay gelding, to the finished Mardi Gras carriage, his hands trembled. That hadn't happened since early in his courtship with Zanna, yet this date with her older sister gave him an entirely different feeling. While Abby's personal life wasn't an open book, James had no doubt about the woman he was riding with this evening. He knew of no one he respected more. While Bishop Vernon Gingerich and the preachers Paul Bontrager and Abe Nissley were esteemed leaders of the Plain community hereabouts, Abby had a kindness and a decency that he also admired greatly. He had always liked Abby a lot—had always appreciated her bright mind and her sunny disposition.

So why didn't Abby's finer traits seem relevant while you were courting her sister? Too carried away by Zanna's pretty face and blond hair? Her carefree giggle . . . and her kisses?

Would he kiss Abby tonight? James gazed across the road toward the small white house that sat a ways up Lambright Lane. What if he did kiss her and she wasn't ready for that? Or what if she didn't like the way he kissed? Or what if he didn't kiss her and then felt her disappointment stabbing him in the back as he started for home?

He'd forgotten how jittery first dates could be—and who would've thought an evening with Abby Lambright would make him nervous? James laughed at himself and vaulted into the seat of the colorful carriage. It wasn't dark yet. He wanted to save the best surprises for later, so he didn't flip any of the switches on the dashboard panel.

"Geddap, Mitch," he said. "Let's get this show on the road."

Down Lambright Lane his horse trotted, and as he passed Sam's farmhouse he waved at the folks who were peering out the kitchen door. Abby stepped off her narrow front porch, holding a picnic hamper, gazing at the carriage and then at him. He hopped down, placed the basket on the floor behind the seat, and then gave Abby his hand as she ascended the wrought-iron steps. She had changed into a magenta dress and her freshly pressed kapp set off a face he'd known all his life and yet . . . she looked like someone he'd never met but certainly wanted to.

"Ready?" he whispered.

"Jah." She looked at the open carriage's unlit canopy made of tiny light bulbs, running her hand over the rich red leather seat. "Who would ever have thought I'd be riding in such a flashy vehicle—and seated beside a man whose work was featured in a magazine, no less?"

James clapped the reins against the bay's back. "We haven't yet begun to flash," he teased. "The carriage has headlights and taillights to be legal, but there'll be no danger of anyone running into us tonight. We'll be lit up like a carnival ride."

As he again passed the Lambright house, James felt like a teenager on his first date: Sam, Barbara, their four kids, and Treva had all come out onto the front porch and were gawking at them. "That's my sister with you, Graber," Sam called as he waved at them. "Behave yourselves, hear me?"

"When do the lights come on?" Ruthie asked.

"Owen and I will be out later, watching for a carriage lit up like a circus," Phoebe called out. "We'll be able to see every single thing you're doing, you know!"

Abby's face turned pink. "You'd think I was sixteen, just entering my rumspringa," she murmured.

James checked for traffic at the end of the lane and then said, "Gee!" The horse turned right and trotted smartly past the phone shanty, the Cedar Creek Mercantile, and Treva's Greenhouse. He relaxed then, looking over at her. "Truth be told, I'm happy you're not sixteen. We've both made something of ourselves, but we've also become involved in our community and committed to our faith—and to our families—in ways kids just out of school have no idea about."

"Jah, we have. But I'd like to think you and I can be comfortable talking about what we need . . . what matters most to us," Abby replied. "And I hope we'll still be gut friends if it turns out we've got different priorities."

"I'm with you there, but this seems like awfully serious talk for a first date. How about if we just cut loose and have some fun?"

"I thought you'd never get to that part!" Her brown eyes sparkled. "Do you remember that sleigh ride years ago, when we raced the Ropp brothers across Sam's pasture? I want to go that fast again—except this time, no one will turn over, all right?"

James clapped the reins lightly on his horse's back. "It wasn't my fault Jonny dumped himself and Gideon on that snowy hillside," he reminded her. "But it was *you* telling me to go faster and faster. When we reach the next straightaway, I'll give Mitch his head. I have to see how the carriage handles under all kinds of conditions, after all. At the very least it has to keep up with a spirited horse."

Abby's mischievous grin made his insides flutter, and—as had happened on that wintry day when Jonny Ropp had dared him to race—James delighted in her challenge for more speed. When he saw there were no cars on the road, he urged Mitch into a faster trot . . . a canter . . . a gallop. With one hand Abby held the strings of her kapp to keep it from flying off as she gripped the seat with the other. She was leaning into the wind, her face alight with a giddy happiness that James hoped he could put there again and again. He dropped his hat to the floor, relishing the sense of freedom he always felt when his favorite horse and his latest carriage went flying down the highway as one.

For about half a mile they clattered down the blacktop, until the distinctive stone silo on Vernon Gingerich's corner marked the intersection where he wanted to turn. He eased Mitch back to normal road speed. "Still got stomach enough to enjoy our picnic?" he teased as they headed west onto the gravel road. "I've got a spot in mind alongside Cedar Creek, where the redbuds are at their peak."

"Puh! You think *that* little run scared me?" Abby elbowed him playfully. "I loved riding the Tilt-a-Whirl and the roller coaster at the county fair when we were kids, you know."

James recalled those carnival rides and suddenly felt the same swooping surge of speed and force, as though his stomach had leaped off a cliff. It had been years since those rare summer nights when their parents had bought them cotton candy and tokens for the rides, before their dats had watched the livestock judging and their mamms had fingered the quilts and looked at the vegetables entered for prizes. But indeed, he recalled Abby Lambright's face all aglow— the way she'd laughed hysterically, carried away by the exhilaration of the fastest rides and the scariest roller coasters on the midway.

"Maybe I should ask if you can endure a peaceful meal beside the creek," he said. "I don't want to bore you, after all."

As he pulled the carriage into a clearing, Abby smiled. "I can't recall a single moment when I felt bored while I was with you, James."

Wasn't it just like her to say that? As James helped her down from the carriage, he realized yet again that while she loved a fast ride, Abby was the embodiment of Plain womanhood—simple and kind and caring . . . not to mention a fine cook. After they bowed for a silent grace, they feasted on ham and coleslaw, with fresh bread and glazed carrots kept warm in a crockery bowl. As they sat on the old quilt she'd spread on the creek bank, with the sunset peeking between the cedars and the redbud trees, James couldn't recall enjoying a meal so much. It was a far cry from hearing his mamm fuss at Dat for dribbling gravy on his shirt while watching Emma grow weary after another day of caring for them. Little pink petals from the redbuds drifted on the wind, landing on Abby's kapp and her cape dress like confetti from heaven.

James bit into his first fried pie. As the creamy sweetness of lemon filling and crushed pineapple spread across his tongue, James moaned with the sheer pleasure of it.

"Are you all right?" she asked

James grabbed her hand. "Abby, this fried pie is wonderful-gut. I'd thank Sam for demanding his favorite filling, except I'm glad he's not here."

Her cheeks flushed. "We make fried pies a lot, you know. They're nothing special."

"They're special because I'm eating them with *you*, Abby."

Her awestruck expression made him pause. Had he said too much? Led her to expect more than he was ready to give? *What wouldn't you share with Abby? Where will you ever find another woman like her?*

James took another bite of the tart-sweet pie. He realized then what was making him antsy: such romantic thoughts brought back his dates with Zanna. He'd been so eager to say how much she appealed to him . . . so quick to admit how crazy in love he was with her. He had believed Zanna was the woman God meant for him to spend his life with, and he had been so wrong—and then so disappointed.

Abby squeezed his hand. "This picnic and our ride in your new carriage is the most fun I've had in a gut long while. Let's enjoy them for what they are without complicating everything with words."

James paused, his final bite of pie poised at his mouth. "Denki for saying that. You somehow anticipate when I'm about to make a mess of things."

Her smile released the tension that had tightened his stomach.

Then she shrugged. "I'm pretty gut at telling fellows to put on the brakes. Which explains why I'm a maidel, ain't so?"

"*No*," he insisted. "It means you know what your heart needs, and you won't settle for less." James held her gaze, wishing relationships weren't so complicated. "I'm glad you told those other fellows how you felt, Abby. If you hadn't, I wouldn't be here with you now . . . having more fun than *I've* had in a long time."

Abby took a big bite out of a fried pie, cupping her hand to catch the cherry filling that gushed out. "See? You're not the only one making a mess. It's gut we understand that about each other—and gut we can laugh about it, too. Most folks don't laugh nearly enough, in my opinion."

Wasn't that an astute observation? As they packed away their plates and the leftovers, James again realized how lucky—how blessed—he was to have Abby as a friend. Twilight was falling, and as James placed the picnic basket back in the carriage, Abby wrapped a pale gray shawl around her shoulders.

"Stand right here in front, where you'll get a gut look at all the lights," he said as he sprang up into the seat. "If any of the bulbs don't work, or the lights don't flash in patterns like they're supposed to, I'll need you to point out what should be fixed when we get back. Ready?"

Abby nodded.

One by one, James flipped the switches, which were powered by a car battery tucked beneath the seat. The Mardi Gras mask on the front of the carriage flashed on and its different sections began to flicker. Then the lights that formed the border started racing clockwise for a few moments before reversing direction.

"Oh, James! Oh, my stars!" Abby stood with her hands framing her face and her mouth open, while her eyes tried to follow the swirling patterns of the green, purple, and gold lights. "As far as I can tell, all the bulbs are working. They're flashing so fast—"

James turned a dial backward to adjust the speed, reveling in

Abby's reaction. He'd tested these lights in his shop last night, but it was a lot more fun to show them off for an appreciative audience.

"Jah, that's better." She leaned forward for a closer look. "The patterns are repeating now. It's a wonder Mitch isn't stomping, ready to race off. He's not used to so much flickering and flashing."

"He's a retired racehorse, remember. He had to handle all sorts of noises and flashing signs at the track." James moved his hand to a different control button. "Now let's check the lights in back."

Abby hurried to the rear of the open carriage and grinned like a kid when those bright lights came on, as well. "Looks like they all work back here, too. I'll get up into the seat— Oh, my stars!" she gasped when he flipped the final switch. "Would you look at that? So many twinkly lights, like a fairy cage made of green and gold stars above where the passengers will ride!"

"And would you like to ride there, Abby? Like a Mardi Gras queen?" James swiveled in the driver's seat to catch her reaction.

Abby didn't have to be asked twice: she was already springing up the wrought-iron steps and into a red leather seat behind him. She perched on its edge, gazing at the shimmering grid of lights above her, as rapt as a child. "Who needs a fancy parade, James? I have you to drive me, and we couldn't ask for a nicer night. But don't leave me back here too long," she added playfully. "The whole point of a date is to spend time *together*, after all."

As Mitch's hooves clip-clopped down the highway, James smiled in the darkness. The carriage was performing beautifully, the air was sweet with spring, and Abby Lambright was sharing her happiness with him. Nothing could be better.

Chapter 11

As she waited in the line of women who were filing into Ezra and Lois Yutzy's large home for the Sunday-morning preaching, Abby couldn't keep a grin from her face. This was the time for folks to prepare their hearts and minds for worship, yet her evening with James flashed through her mind. What a time they had enjoyed, rolling along the roads in that bright, sparkling carriage.

After James had turned off all those green, gold, and purple lights, she'd sat beside him again as they toured the countryside around Cedar Creek. They had both noticed fluttering curtains and faces at an upstairs window while the horse trotted past Sam's place, a sure sign that Gail and Ruthie were watching as James set the brake in front of Abby's small house and then came up on the porch with her. She'd felt like a teenage girl wondering if he would kiss her . . . A kiss would have been a sure sign that he finally saw her as a woman he might like to court seriously.

Instead, James had honored her wishes to keep things between them uncomplicated: he had grasped her hands between his big, strong ones and gazed deeply into her eyes. "It was a wonderful-gut evening, Abby," he had whispered. "And I want our first kiss to be something only you and I share—without an audience, jah?" So Abby had nodded and squeezed his hands, content to wait.

This morning, as the women filed slowly into the kitchen side of Ezra and Lois's home while the men entered from the front door, folks seemed to be taking extra time greeting Bishop Gingerich and the preachers. Then a rapid-fire *clip-clop! clip-clop!* came down the road and a carriage rumbled along the Yutzys' lane. Salome Bontrager, Perry's wife, climbed down into the driveway rather than parking alongside the other carriages.

"What's going on?" Eva Detweiler whispered in front of Abby. "Salome's face is all puffy and red from crying."

"Did I hear somebody in the kitchen asking where Paul was?" Hannah Hartzler wondered aloud. "He's usually the first of the preachers to arrive, no matter where the service is held."

Abby stepped out of the line to meet Salome in the yard. Salome had moved to Cedar Creek from a district on the other side of Clearwater when she married Perry, and now she was pregnant with their third child. She and Perry had been living with her father-in-law, Paul, these past few years to help him keep up with his farm after his wife died.

"Salome, what's going on?" Abby whispered as they clasped hands.

"It's Perry's dat," she replied in a shaking voice. "We thought he'd gone ahead to church, like he always does—gets himself mentally ready and prays real early, in case he gets picked to preach, you know. But he was still in bed. He—he passed on in his sleep, he did, and I've got to let Vernon know."

"Oh, Salome, I'm so sorry." Paul Bontrager had lived across the road from Abby's family since long before she was born. "Would you like me to tell the bishop what's happened?"

"Jah, denki so much, Abby. Perry's more upset than he'll let on. His dat had seemed to be doing so gut lately, rolling along toward his ninetieth birthday, and—" Salome sniffled loudly and swiped at her wet face. "Well, I guess we never know when the Lord's going to call us home. It's a comfort that he went in his sleep, with a smile on his face like he was already seeing the glory that awaited him."

"How could it be any other way?" Abby assured her. "He was a gut man and a faithful servant. You give Perry our best. After the common meal, Mamm and I will be over to help. If you'd like me to sew Paul's white burial clothes, I'd be happy to."

"Oh, Abby, what would we do without our gut friends? Jah, that would be a gift to me and a fine send-off for Perry's dat."

As Salome hurried back to the carriage, everyone in the lines was watching Abby for word of what had happened. First, however, Bishop Gingerich needed to be informed so he and Preacher Abe Nissley and their deacon, Pete Beachey, would know how to proceed with the service. "Excuse me," she whispered to the curious women in the doorway. "I've heard some news I need to share with Vernon."

Abby passed through the kitchen, which was crowded with women waiting to be seated. The table and the counter space were covered with loaves of bread and pies for the meal they would eat after the church service. Vernon and Abe stood at the doorway to greet folks as they filed into the front room, which had been expanded by removing wall partitions. Rows of wooden pews faced a center area where the preachers sat and spoke.

"If I could have a word, Vernon," Abby murmured. Because he was stooped, he didn't stand quite as tall as she did, but his piercing blue eyes told of an alert mind despite his age. When he stepped away from the crowd, Abby drew a deep breath. "Salome Bontrager just told me that Preacher Paul has passed on in his sleep," she said near his ear. "Perry's taking it pretty hard, so Salome went back home. I told her we'd be there right after the meal to divvy up the chores and help with the funeral details."

"Oh my." Vernon's eyes misted over. He grasped Abby's hand,

pausing to deal with an emotional moment. "Denki, Abby. Abe and Pete and I will talk this over upstairs, during the first hymn. But we'll let folks know before the service so they can pray on it."

Abby walked past the older women in line to resume her spot between Eva Detweiler and Emma Graber, who took her elbow.

"Preacher Paul has died?" her best friend whispered.

"Went peacefully in his sleep. And that's about the best any of us can hope for," she murmured. "To meet Jesus in our dreams and leave our body behind, without hospital beds or lingering sickness or being an extra worry to our families."

Emma nodded sadly. "Dat's not going to take this well. He and Paul were such gut friends, and even closer after his wife, Edna, passed. They went fishing at that pond in back of Paul's pasture. Now I doubt Mamm'll let him go there anymore, what with Paul not around to watch after him."

As they got to the doorway, they heard Vernon announcing Paul's passing to those who were already seated. Abby wasn't surprised to see Sam, James, and Adah Ropp—neighbors who lived closest to the Bontrager place—immediately clustering around the bishop to confer with him.

The news spread quickly down the line of women waiting outside, too. As Abby entered the kitchen and then the front room with her friends, the familiar faces around them were shadowed by the news about Paul. After everyone was seated, they shared a moment of silence. One of the men sang the first note of the first hymn, and as the rest of them joined in, the preachers entered the crowded room and removed their hats in one sweeping motion. At the beginning of the third line of the song, the three leaders retired to an upstairs bedroom to confer about the service and decide who would preach the first sermon and the main sermon that morning.

Although a cloud hovered over them all during the service—Vernon's sermon, Pete Beachey's reading of the day's Scripture, and then Abe Nissley's longer main sermon—their worship proceeded at its usual unhurried pace. After the closing hymn, Bishop Gingerich announced a short Members' Meeting.

"Paul Bontrager has left our earthly congregation to join the heavenly bands who praise God in eternity," Vernon began in his mellow voice. "The Lambrights, the Grabers, and the Ropps have assured me they will see to the immediate needs of the Bontrager family by preparing meals and caring for the livestock there. Sam and his mother have offered to host the funeral and the lunch in their barn and greenhouse, while Matt and James Graber will take charge of the parking," the bishop continued, turning to address both sides of the room. "Adah and Rudy Ropp will see that distant kin of the Bontragers are notified, and Beulah Mae Nissley will coordinate the meal after the funeral."

Standing beside him, Preacher Abe Nissley nodded solemnly. "At such times as these, we're truly grateful to be a close-knit community bound by God's love and compassion. We'll hold the service on Thursday morning, to allow time for the burial preparations. I'm sure we'll all visit about this during today's common meal and see that Paul's family is well cared for."

"Such a loss necessitates the selecting of a new preacher, too," Vernon added, gazing purposefully at the rows of men seated nearest him. "I ask you to prayerfully consider the married men among us and have your suggestions ready for the preaching service four weeks from today, on May twenty-first."

The meeting ended, and as Abby entered the kitchen to help carry food, the women were abuzz. Vernon Gingerich, Paul Bontrager, and Abe Nissley had all served the Cedar Creek district for more than twenty-five years, so the younger folks among them couldn't recall when anyone else had been a minister, and they had never witnessed the drawing of the lot. While serving the Lord and the Plain community was an honorable role, it involved giving many selfless hours without pay, for the remainder of a preacher's life.

"I sure hope my Mervin's not called to serve," Bessie Mast fretted as she cut a chocolate cake. "He's getting so he can barely keep up with the farm."

"Jah, preaching doesn't come easy to some fellows, either," Nell Coblentz remarked. "I can't see my Amos standing in front of everybody like he knows what he's talking about. He was born to be a carpenter, for sure and for certain."

"Could be the lot'll fall to a younger fellow," Lois Yutzy speculated as she took platters of sandwiches from her refrigerator. "We have a promising crop of men married only a few years. But we've watched them grow up here, and we've trusted them all along."

"Jah, like Mose Hartzler or Carl Byler, neither of them thirty yet," Adah Ropp said in a thoughtful tone. "My Jonny's married now, but I don't expect anybody considers him ready to take on the ministry, considering how he drove cars and lived amongst English before he hitched up with Zanna."

Laughter rippled among the women—except for Hannah Hartzler and Marian Byler. Neither woman relished the thought of her husband being called away from his businesses or his young family. Mose Hartzler was a chimney sweep and owned a thriving orchard, while Carl Byler did a lot of custom farming for elderly men who couldn't handle the heavy labor and equipment any longer.

"There's Zeke Detweiler, too," Eunice Graber remarked as she repositioned her thick eyeglasses. "And we can't none of us forget how Sam Lambright handled all the trials and tribulations of Zanna running off and leaving my boy, James—and how he stopped us all from squabbling at each other, too. Fine man, Sam is."

Abby smiled to herself. It was easy for women like Adah and Eunice to recommend fellows from other families when it was unlikely their husbands or sons would be up for consideration. She glanced across the kitchen at Barbara, who raised her eyebrows in concern. Everyone in the Lambright family—indeed, everyone in town—knew about the long hours Sam devoted to running the Cedar Creek Mercantile.

"While we believe preachers are nominated for service by the people and chosen by God himself," Sam's wife said quietly, "I wouldn't want to think about my husband spending his time and energy on being a minister while he's keeping up with the store. He'll collapse, because he'll not take time for any sleep."

The women scattered then, carrying bowls of slaw and cut pies to the tables, which the men had set up in the front room. As they moved in and out of the kitchen, however, their talk continued. "Too bad James Graber's not married," Lois Yutzy remarked. "Now, there's a fellow who knows how to deal with disappointment and how to forgive. Fine man, James is."

"And there's your Ezra, too, Lois," Eunice Graber piped up again. "He's built up his pallet-making business enough that he's hired a lot of local fellows to keep it running. A gut, steady man who starts a job and sees it through, Ezra is."

Abby carried a platter of her fried pies to the front room. In the coming weeks, folks would spend a lot of time speculating about the new preacher—as well they should. Preacher Paul had been one of their spiritual leaders for nearly half his life, and suggesting a handful of men worthy of replacing him, even though God made the final choice, was one of the most serious responsibilities their district had faced in many years.

As the older members sat down to eat for the first shift, their conversations were mostly about Paul and recollections of times each of them had spent with him, or his more memorable sermons. Many of these folks had kitchen cabinets, built-in bookcases, and other carpentry projects that Paul had built for them over the years, and he was mentioned with a lot of fondness and laughter.

And wasn't it a fine thing, the way plans had fallen into place before all of Abby's fried pies had disappeared during the second shift? Beulah Mae Nissley arranged for several of the women to provide side dishes for the funeral lunch. Barbara and her three daughters planned to meet Adah Ropp and her two girls at the Bontrager place to help Salome clean in preparation for the visitation, which would be held at Paul's house all day on Wednesday. Sam had men coming to set up tables in Treva's Greenhouse, as they had done for Zanna's wedding, and to clear out the largest room of the barn and bring in the pew benches for the large crowd they expected.

Abby glanced around the noisy front room in Lois's home, grateful she lived among such faithful friends. Everyone would take part in bidding Paul Bontrager farewell, including the young folks. Phoebe, Gail, and Ruthie were nodding earnestly as they talked with Emma and the Ropp girls, and Matt—

Abby stopped eating to watch her nephew. Matt had a curious smile on his face. He was seated near Owen and Noah Coblentz and the Ropp brothers, as he usually was for these meals, yet he appeared to be lost in thought while the other young men visited around him. And wasn't *that* interesting?

Chapter 12

Matt filled the bucket feeder and watched his orphaned lambs suck milk from the oversized nipples, but his mind was on another subject altogether. All during the common meal he had itched to get home and call Titus Yutzy. Wouldn't it be something if now that his father had died, Perry Bontrager didn't want to keep all of their pastureland? It wasn't his place—or the proper time—to ask Perry such a question, of course. But all sorts of possibilities had crossed Matt's mind while his friends had been discussing which girls they wanted to drive home after tonight's singing.

As he left the barn, Matt corralled his thoughts. While he intended to call and leave a message for Titus, wasn't it possible that Rosemary might answer the phone? He was still disappointed that he wouldn't be delivering rams to the Yutzy place, because he had no idea how their property was laid out. How far was the phone shanty from the house? Had Titus installed an extension in the barn? Some Amish farmers did that, especially if they lived too far from neighbors to make sharing a phone practical.

He slipped inside the small white shanty located at the roadside in front of the Cedar Creek Mercantile, directly across from James's carriage shop. His eyes widened: the red ten lit up on the phone meant that either his family or the Grabers had received a lot of calls this weekend. Amish folks all over the Midwest were just getting home from preaching services and the common meals that followed, so it was unlikely that Plain callers had left so many messages in the last few hours.

He itched to play the recordings, but instead he called Titus. With Rosemary's smile in mind, Matt dialed the number and waited for the *beep* after the recorded announcement. "Jah, Titus, it's Matt Lambright from over in Cedar Creek," he said. "I thought you'd want to know that Preacher Paul Bontrager passed on in his sleep last night. The funeral's to be on Thursday," he began earnestly. "I mostly thought—since his place sits across the road from ours—that you might want to see how Perry feels about letting you have some pastureland. What with him being the only son and working full-time for James Graber, he might consider a rental agreement if he doesn't want to sell."

Matt paused, hoping he hadn't overstepped by passing along this news. Upsetting Perry was not his intention. After all, if someone were to ask him about selling off a parcel of Lambright property, he would refuse immediately. "You wanted to know about property availability hereabouts, so there you have it," he continued. "I hope you and your family have had a gut Sunday. Bye now."

His pulse thrummed. It seemed that opportunity might be knocking, and pretty loudly, too. As much as Titus's mood had lifted after the wedding, when they'd talked of sharing some labor and business expenses, Matt felt as if he might be offering Ezra's brother a chance to return to his boyhood home . . . maybe giving him a whole new lease on life.

Curiosity won out then, and Matt pressed the Play button on the answering machine. While he doubted folks had left so many messages for his dat with orders for the store, it was possible that some of their out-of-town kin had been trying to reach them with important news. The first man's accent sounded anything but Amish, however.

"I'm calling for James of Graber's Custom Carriages," he said in a businesslike drawl, "in regards to an article about a carriage you built for Disney World. If you'd call me back as soon as possible, Mr. Graber, I'd like to order some similar vehicles for my horse-drawn tour business here in Memphis."

Matt's eyebrows rose. He played two more similar messages, and then the fourth recording filled the shanty with a woman's sophisticated voice. "Mr. Graber, I'm assuming you've read the magazine article I sent you, which featured the carriage Miss America recently rode," she began. "It would be my privilege to interview you for an upcoming issue of our publication. So many readers have called wanting to know more about you and your carriage business. I can't wait to speak with you!"

Matt scribbled the woman's phone number below the previous three he'd taken down. Aunt Abby had mentioned the magazine article with a photograph of the white princess carriage, but who could have predicted this sort of response to it? He tore off the scratch pad page and stepped outside to gaze across the road. The Grabers had returned home from Lois and Ezra's shortly after his family had, so he jogged across the blacktop to speak with James. It wasn't often he had such exciting news to share, and phone messages like these certainly lightened a day otherwise filled with talk of Paul Bontrager's death.

He took the porch steps two at a time and pounded loudly on the Grabers' front door. If Eunice and Emma were in the kitchen and James wasn't nearby, there was a chance Merle would be napping in his recliner and wouldn't hear him. Matt waited a moment and knocked again, louder this time.

As footsteps came through the front room, a big grin overtook his face. Who wouldn't be happy for a friend whose hard work had resulted in so many calls to order specialty carriages—plus a request for an interview? It wasn't the Plain way to boast about such accomplishments, but didn't it glorify God when folks outside of Cedar Creek acknowledged good work produced by Amish hands?

The door swung open and Matt's breath left him. "Emma! I—" He crushed the piece of paper in his hand. Why hadn't he figured Emma might answer the door? "If James is around, I've got some news for him."

When the hopeful smile fell from her face, Matt felt lower than an earthworm's belly. He hadn't come here to make Emma feel bad, after all, and he hadn't planned to discuss how he'd ignored her at the wedding supper, either. But here she was, standing in the doorway.

"Matt." Her tone told him she'd be going after some answers. "I'm sorry if I did or said something at Zanna's wedding to upset you, or to make you think—"

After all the years he'd known her, such a difficult moment probably called for holding her hands, but he didn't have the heart to let these mismatched feelings continue between them. "Emma, it wasn't your fault," he insisted. "I know how everybody's saying you and I would be a gut match, but—but that isn't going to happen. I'm sorry."

Emma's face crumpled. Her breath escaped her like air leaking from a balloon. "Oh."

Oh? How did he respond to that? Wouldn't it only complicate matters further if he elaborated on his situation? "I can't pretend to have feelings for you just because folks think I should, Emma. That would be more cruel than telling you the truth, ain't so?"

"So, what *I* think doesn't matter?" She turned away, crossing her arms. "It's because of that Rosemary from Queen City, isn't it?"

Matt closed his eyes. The excitement he'd felt for James's phone messages drained out like water from a punctured trough. Why did relationships with women—both Rosemary and now Emma—have to be so difficult? "No," he murmured, "it's because I can't let you keep bringing brownies and—and looking at me with all those wishes in your eyes. I'm sorry, Emma. Let James know I came by, all right?"

As he stepped out of the doorway, Matt felt her closing the space between them. She shut the door, probably so her folks couldn't hear. "Fine and dandy, then!" she said in a rising voice. "If it doesn't work out with Mrs. Yutzy, at least you'll have your dogs for company. Which is pretty much what you deserve!"

Matt strode across the Grabers' front yard, knowing that whatever response he gave would only anger Emma further. He hadn't heard the last about this issue.

Later that evening, as James sat in the phone shanty playing more than a dozen messages left for him on the phone, he shook his head in disbelief. Who would have believed one magazine article—one photograph of the white carriage he'd crafted last fall—would inspire such an avalanche of calls? All in all, he had three requests for interviews and potential orders for at least ten more customized carriages. Never had his work received so much attention. And for an Amish fellow, that became a problem.

It wasn't only the fact that he, by himself, couldn't possibly fulfill so many special orders. Who could he hire to help with the technical details these English customers expected on their vehicles? Pete Beachey, who had taught him his trade long ago, was beyond the age when he wanted to work full-time. And while Perry Bontrager and Leon Mast were good, steady employees, he needed them to keep up with orders for ordinary farm wagons, courting buggies, and other vehicles his Amish customers depended upon. His apprentice, Noah, would probably be a fine carriage maker in time, but he'd worked in the shop less than six months.

And then there was the issue of reporters from national magazines wanting to talk with him. Apparently the outside world was fascinated by all things Amish these days, but it went against the most basic tenets of Plain belief to accept the adulation of anyone—most especially curious English reporters.

James raked back his hair and put on his straw hat again. It was another warm spring evening, and since Sundays were intended for visiting, he hitched Mitch to his buggy and drove down Lambright Lane to seek some advice. True enough, this was the courting buggy he'd driven Zanna in . . . but it was too fine a vehicle to leave in the stable just because he wasn't courting anyone. *Yet.*

He knocked on Abby's door. While she might be at Sam's, discussing plans for Paul's funeral with Treva, Barbara, and the girls, he was hoping to catch her without an audience. Right now, with so many phone voices in his head, he could use a quiet chat with a woman who would see through to the heart of his dilemma.

She opened the door at last, and the sight of Abby's face settled his churning thoughts. "Could we go for a ride?" he began. "You won't believe how many phone messages I just listened to, all on account of that magazine article I showed you! Some for orders—mostly for more of those fancy parade carriages—and three requests from magazine reporters for interviews, and I—"

"Vernon will know just what to do, James," Abby said. "And no doubt the bishop will be pleased to hear some gut news after dealing with Paul's passing all day long. Let me fetch my shawl."

Wasn't it just like Abby to suggest that he go to a higher power? James relaxed all over. "Denki, Abby. I'll wait right here."

The voices, the demands, the requests . . . they all stopped spinning in his head. He sat down in Abby's porch swing, aware of the mild spring evening, of the glow of the sun in the western sky, and the whisper of the leaves in the maple trees that shaded Abby's home. While moments ago he had felt caught up in a whirlwind, he could now put his trust in Abby, and in Vernon Gingerich—and in God—as he decided how to handle this unexpected rush of publicity.

Moments later, he and Abby were rolling down the county

blacktop. The *clip-clop! clip-clop!* of Mitch's hooves created a happy rhythm to accompany the sparkle in Abby's eyes. "It was gut to see you at my door, James, and even better to hear of so many folks wanting your work."

"Jah, it was nice to hear so many customers telling me they want my carriages," he agreed. "But it'll be impossible to produce those specialty rigs as fast as these English folks will expect them. They have no idea that my shop employs just two full-time fellas and an apprentice, besides me, and that we already have a backlog of orders."

"English apparently have no concept of limiting their businesses, the way we do." Abby looked over at him, her face alight with the setting sun. "From listening to them when they visit Sam's store, I gather it's a constant scramble to grow their companies bigger and to make more and more money."

"Which doesn't always improve their lives," James remarked. "Vernon has always stood by the Old Ways of working close to home and spending time with family. I have a pretty gut idea about what he'll recommend, and I'll let his wisdom guide me."

As they approached the corner where the old stone silo marked the Gingerich property, James grinned like a mischievous boy. "Maybe we could skip our visit with the bishop and go down that road toward Cedar Creek instead," he suggested, half serious. "Our picnic yesterday was one of the nicest times I've had lately, Abby. And it was such a private spot, too . . . maybe for that kiss I didn't get last night."

The gleam in her eyes told him she had been thinking about a kiss, as well, but when he pretended he might drive past the Gingerich lane, Abby elbowed him playfully. "Better stick to business first, or all your gut intentions might go astray, ain't so?"

James gave her a quick peck on the cheek, mostly to watch her blush, and then steered Mitch into the gravel driveway that led to the bishop's home. The main house, two stories high and built of stone and brick, dated back to when early settlers had come to this part of Missouri, while the one-story wing Vernon had added when his two aunts moved in was made of clapboard painted white. Vernon was a retired master carpenter who now devoted his time to leading the Cedar Creek church district—and to finishing out Angus cattle, which his nephew Abner then butchered to sell to regional markets and restaurants.

"It's always a grand sight, looking out over Vernon's pastures where those black cows graze," James remarked as he parked the buggy alongside the house.

"I'm sure Abner thinks so, too." Abby grabbed his hand as James helped her down. "It's been a gut arrangement for Vernon, having his aunts and a nephew here. Remember how, when Dorothea died, we all thought he'd wither up and blow away without a wife?"

"Jah, especially since they couldn't have kids," James agreed. "But with Nettie and Florence keeping house for him, and Abner to tend to his barns and pastureland, it's the perfect setup for a fellow who stays too busy to do such work himself."

"And would you look at how the ivy and the rose of Sharon bushes have grown!" Abby exclaimed as they approached the front door. "I'll have to tell Mamm how well her cuttings have done."

As they waited on the front porch for an answer to his knock, James became more aware of the woman who stood beside him. Was she hoping this trip would end on the same romantic note as their previous ride? He'd been so focused on his carriage-making quandary, he hadn't considered Abby's expectations. "Denki for suggesting I talk with the bishop," he said softly, "and for coming along with me, too."

Abby lowered her eyes, flushing modestly. What a beauty she possessed, radiating from the inside out . . . And wasn't *that* a thought he'd do well to ponder? When the door opened, however, James focused on the stout, silver-haired woman who stood before them. "Gut afternoon, Nettie," he said. "And how are you?"

"Come in, you two! How nice to see the both of you." The bishop's aunt waved them into the front room. "If it's Vernon you're looking for, I'll fetch him from the barn. He and Abner are tending a couple of contrary calves who tangled with a barbed-wire fence—and the fence won."

"Tell him we're in no hurry, if he's not at a gut stopping point," James replied.

"You can wait for him in the study." Nettie beckoned for them to follow her. "I'll bring you in some tea and sweets."

James and Abby passed through the large front room, furnished with sturdy sofas and chairs in soothing shades of blue and green. Beside a large picture window, Nettie's older sister, Florence, sat at a quilting frame where the sun shone over her work. When she straightened in her wheelchair, her oxygen hose became visible. "Gut afternoon to you. You'll have to pardon me if your names have slipped my mind."

"Gut to see you, Florence," Abby replied as she stepped over to the quilt frame. "This is James Graber and I'm Abby Lambright, and we live a little way down the county blacktop. My word, but this is an intricate pattern you're quilting."

"Jah, keeps me outta trouble. This one's for a niece who's getting married, and another three quilt tops are waiting for me—from gut friends who don't have the eyesight for this close work anymore," she added. "Mighty lucky, I am, at eighty-five."

"We're every one of us blessed," James agreed. "And Vernon is one of the blessings that keeps the Cedar Creek district going so strong, too."

"Jah, he takes gut care of us all," Florence replied. "Who else would've built on to his house so my sister, my son, and I would have a home after our places washed away in the flood of ninety-three?"

"And he hasn't known a quiet moment since!" Nettie preceded them down a hallway to the study where Vernon often worked on the records he kept as a bishop. A beautiful carved library table and four matching chairs occupied the room's center, while a modest desk filled one corner. "I'll be back in a few. Make yourselves at home."

James pulled out a chair for Abby at the library table and then sat down. "I'm guessing Vernon built these pieces himself," he said as he ran his hand over the smooth surface of the oak table.

"Jah, I did, James—many moons ago, as a gift for Dorothea." Vernon Gingerich entered, wearing work pants and a patched blue shirt. He'd brought some barn aroma inside with him, yet his ethereal blue eyes left no doubt that he was a man who followed God. "It was a sad morning, learning of Paul's passing, but we rejoice for him because the Lord keeps His promises and grants us His grace. I sense, however, that another matter has brought you here."

The bishop's gaze embraced the two of them as though he wondered if they had come calling as a couple. Once again James wondered how other folks had apparently noticed how compatible he and Abby were while he had remained oblivious for so many years. "Something unexpected has come up, Vernon," he said, unfolding the magazine page that featured his white princess carriage. "I need advice and objective opinions, so Abby steered me here to visit with you."

Vernon's bushy eyebrows rose as he looked at the photograph. "One of your custom creations, jah? Not a vehicle we'd drive through the barnyard," he added with a laugh, "but a lot of folks would enjoy parading along in this pretty coach. So what's on your mind?"

James relaxed, grateful for the bishop's manner. Vernon was as fatherly as he was friendly, and that made for a nice combination of traits in a community leader. Other districts didn't have such an understanding man with whom to discuss perplexing issues. "They say success breeds success," James began, "and as of this afternoon, I've gotten a dozen calls from English folks wanting carriages for their horse-drawn tour businesses. Three others were from reporters wanting to interview me for magazines."

"Ah." Vernon nodded. "So you've come up against a production crunch. Not enough fellows in your shop to do all this work and not enough hours in the day. Unless you expand in a hurry."

"That hits the nail on the head. Not that I could find qualified employees or increase my shop space anytime soon."

"And then there's the magazines wanting to shine their worldly light on your work—and on you as the man who does it so well." The bishop looked up when Nettie knocked. She held a tray with a ceramic teapot, cups, and a plate of sliced breads. "It's gut we have tea to lubricate our thoughts and some of Nettie's fresh banana bread to fortify our intentions, jah? Denki, Nettie."

After her footsteps faded down the hallway, he refocused on the issues before them. "Your situation brings to mind the story of the Israelites enslaved in Egypt, where the Pharaoh had them making bricks. When they demanded time off to worship, Pharaoh stopped supplying their straw, yet he insisted they produce just as many bricks while having to go out and find the raw materials."

James nodded at this familiar story, as did Abby. "Jah, Pharaoh was calling out 'more bricks, more bricks!' while giving his slaves less material to work with and less time to make those bricks," James replied. "I'm starting to feel that way."

"And if you take on all the orders you're receiving, while telling these new customers you can meet their time frames," Vernon continued, "you'll feel as if Pharaoh's sitting on your shoulder, making you a slave to your carriage business and to the ways of the world, as well."

"This, while you're helping Emma take care of your parents," Abby added.

"Jah, there's that." James looked at the photograph of his white coach with Miss America beside it. "And while my sister would never expect to live in the style this young woman has become accustomed to, she can't take on all of Mamm and Dat's day-to-day care and have any time for herself—either to find a husband or to honor Sunday as a day of rest. We're seeing that already."

"So what's your response?" The bishop handed James the plate of banana bread as Abby poured three cups of fragrant orange-spice tea for them.

"I'll answer the calls in the order I got them, with a calendar at hand," James replied firmly. "I'll figure out how much time to allow for the special detailing of each rig—and if a customer can't wait that long, I'll decline the order." He shrugged. "It's all I can do. I can't rush Noah's apprenticeship, and I have to figure Perry and Leon—and Emma and my parents—might need my time along the way."

"There are only so many bricks a man can make," Vernon agreed. "And you probably realize that those who interview you might want photographs and that such attention in worldly publications will distract you from doing your best work with your God-given skills. Not to mention inviting pride into your life."

James sank his teeth into the moist, sweet banana bread, glad he'd come to confer with Vernon. "For craftsmen, pride is a tightrope we walk when we become gut at what we do. I'll call those reporters and tell them it goes against our Plain principles to talk to them."

"Or," Abby chimed in, "if there's a way to serve God by lifting up our Amish values—maybe to talk about the other craftsmen in Cedar Creek and the other home-based businesses our families run."

"That would take the spotlight off James and benefit other members." The bishop nodded, his curly gray beard brushing the front of his shirt. "Seems to me if you chose *one* of those reporters and requested the interview questions ahead of time—with the understanding that you and I would choose which ones to answer—we could work this out to the common gut."

"And I, for one, would enjoy listening to the interview!" Abby's eyes shone over the top of her teacup. "James is a fine man to speak to our beliefs and practices. If he sat in the doorway and spoke out toward us, anybody who wanted to gather around the phone shanty could follow along."

"That would be a first for Cedar Creek," James replied. Abby's idea impressed and inspired him: limiting himself to a single interview solved a lot of problems that might arise from appearing in a magazine.

"We've settled it, then." Vernon polished off his banana bread and drank deeply of his tea. "Wherever two or more are gathered, we draw upon the Lord's power to accomplish His will here on earth. And that's always better than going it alone, thinking we humans can set the proper limits and avoid worldly temptations."

After the three of them chatted briefly about Preacher Paul's funeral service, James stepped outside with Abby, into the twilight. A pink glow hovered at the horizon where the sun had just set, and while the temperature had dropped, the evening was still pleasant. As Mitch trotted down the bishop's lane, they waved to Vernon, who watched them from the doorway of his rustic stone home. Once they were clip-clopping along the blacktop, James gazed at the woman beside him.

"Don't let this go to your head," he said lightly, "but you were absolutely right about taking this matter to the bishop. It all worked out so much better than if I'd tried to manage these orders and interviews by myself."

"You would have figured it out, James," Abby replied. "But other folks from Cedar Creek will want to share your success and listen to the interview. If there's anything else you need help with, you know whom to ask."

Abby's laughter rang around them. Her eyes told him she was hoping for the kiss he'd promised her last night. He was ready to hug her close and—

For a fleeting moment, it was Zanna flirting with him, teasing him with her carefree mirth and her flawless face until he couldn't help but love her. His stomach clenched as he recalled how that love had ended.

James faltered. His imagination had played a cruel trick on him

just now, and he could *not* tell Abby her sister's image had come between them. The two Lambright girls barely resembled each other—
Abby had Sam's darker hair and brows while Zanna was a blonde
like Phoebe, Gail, and Ruthie—yet they shared mannerisms. A certain arch of their brows . . . a pattern to their laughter. Just enough
to pinch him with the memory of his intended bride's betrayal, even
though he thought he'd gotten past it.

So James let the romantic moment pass. He focused on the road
again, recalling how he and Abby had sped along this straightaway
in the Mardi Gras carriage last night, laughing and having fun together. He could feel Abby's bewilderment as surely as the evening
seemed chillier now as the sun went down. He had just disappointed
both of them.

"It's gut you have the patience of a saint, Abby," he murmured.
"You might need it while I work my way through these next several
weeks, figuring out my schedule."

Abby's face fell. She tugged her shawl around her shoulders,
looking away. "Jah. I just might."

Chapter 13

Later that evening, Abby brushed out her hair and then sat on her bed with her writing tablet. It was time to send in her weekly letter for the *Budget*, the national newspaper for Plain folks. But how could she write, considering her excruciating disappointment? She had seen a kiss written all over James's face, but he'd stopped short. All through school she'd loved him . . . had discouraged other fellows' attention, knowing they would never measure up. For *years* she'd waited for him to return her affection, and after the fine time they'd shared the previous evening in his Mardi Gras carriage, she'd believed her chance had come at last.

How much longer could she be as patient as James claimed she was? It wasn't as if she or James had never kissed anyone. Why had he changed his mind? Was he wary of taking up with her after her sister had betrayed him, even though he'd claimed he was ready to move on? Or had she seemed too eager to tell James how he should live his life and set his business priorities?

Abby wiped away her tears. She reminded herself that she was secure in her little home, with her Stitch in Time business to support herself . . . But still her heart ached. It was sure to be a long, dark night of soul-searching, and she needed her rest for a full day of making a comforter and curtains for a customer tomorrow. Stewing over her crushed feelings wouldn't get her column written, either. Abby picked up her pencil and began with the community's most obvious news.

It was a sad day for Cedar Creek. Paul Bontrager, not quite ninety and our preacher for more than half his life, went to his reward this morning. For many of us, he was a leader we respected and looked to for guidance our entire lives. We ask your prayers for his family, and—

Someone pounded on her front door. Abby set aside her tablet and slipped into the robe that hung on the back of her bedroom door. Surely James wouldn't be knocking this late, coming to make amends. And if he was, well, her hair was down and no proper unmarried Amish woman kept company with a fellow in her nightgown. But when Abby peered out the window beside her door, she saw a familiar figure in a white kapp and a gray shawl. "Emma! What brings you over at this hour?" she asked as she swung open the door.

Her best friend stepped inside, pressing a small covered container into Abby's hands. "Finally got the folks off to bed, and when James came in, scowling and refusing to say what had happened with you this evening, I was just too peeved to stay home," she replied. "Between my brother and Matt—the way they've both acted today—I'm ready to give up on men altogether! Aren't you?"

Abby lifted the container's lid. While she and Emma had shared secrets since they were girls, she wasn't ready to elaborate on what had—or had not—gone on between her and James. "Lemon bars? When did you have time to bake these?"

"I made an extra batch when I was getting ready for today's common meal. And after Matt told me not to bother making him any more brownies, why—" Emma's breath came out in a huff. "Lemon bars are a treat I can share with *you*, Abby. I know you'll be my friend, no matter what."

"Come sit down. Treats like these deserve a gut cup of tea while you tell me what's happened." Abby led the way into the kitchen and lit the lamp on the wall. She put on the teakettle, noting how Emma's eyes were as puffy as her own and how she seemed too agitated to sit at the small table by the back window. They made quite a pair. Misery loved company.

"Matt told me he didn't want to be *cruel*," Emma said with an edge in her voice. "Didn't come out and admit it, but he's head over heels for that widow, Rosemary. *Isn't* he?"

Abby reached for the tea bags, hoping to console her friend. But there was no way around it: the truth wasn't going to make Emma feel any better. "It was one of those unexplainable things," she murmured. "Matt laid eyes on Rosemary and he's thought of little else since then. I'm sorry it happened this way, Emma. I don't know what else to tell you." She carried two steaming cups of water to the table and then dropped in the tea bags.

"But, Abby, what'll I do now? He . . . well, Matt's the only fella I've ever been seriously interested in."

As Emma slumped in a chair, Abby squeezed her shaking shoulders. What with getting her parents ready for church and spending the day at the Yutzy home, Emma may not have had a chance earlier to deal with her hurt feelings. "Maybe it's best to have a gut cry about it and then leave it be, Emma," Abby suggested. "Time to get Matt off your mind and move on to somebody else."

Easy for you to say. Could you take your own advice if James told you he didn't want to see you anymore? Abby sat down next to Emma and dunked her tea bag again and again, not wanting to think about that.

The tear streaks on Emma's face, shining in the lamplight, accentuated her dejection. "It's not like fellas'll line up to court me, knowing how snappish Mamm gets and how Dat is losing track of his thoughts from one minute to the next. And I—I really don't want to end up alone, Abby. I've always wanted a family . . . a husband to love."

Ah, but Abby knew the heartache of a maidel's singular life—except she'd been blessed with several options. Her Stitch in Time business and this cozy home had put her in a better position for a fulfilling future. Abby picked up a lemon bar. "Oh my," she whispered as the tart-sweet filling spread over her tongue. "It's been a long while since I had one of these, and yours are the best, Emma."

"And what gut does that do me? Who else besides you and the folks will ever know how they taste?" Emma pulled a tissue from her pocket and blew her nose. "They're James's favorite, too—and what's *his* problem now? He was whistling last night after your ride, yet he came home this evening looking like a whipped dog."

Abby crammed the rest of the lemon bar into her mouth and took a long sip of her tea. Emma's problem was far more serious than her own, yet there was no getting around the question. "He's gotten a lot of calls this weekend from folks wanting more of those specialty rigs than he can make—"

"Puh! The look on his face was not about carriages, Abby." Emma gazed at her in the dimness, expecting an answer.

"All right, then. He was ready to kiss me last night—told me so, even—but the girls were watching out their bedroom window, so . . ." Abby sighed. "Just when it seemed he was going to carry through on our way home from Vernon's this evening, he changed his mind. I have no idea why."

"Well, if that isn't the most ridiculous— You know, if it weren't such a waste of my time and ingredients, I'd put a pie in his face. And I'd smash one all over Matt's, too!" Emma grabbed a lemon bar and consumed half of it in one bite. "Why are fellas so *dense*, Abby? How could James possibly do better than hitching up with you? I tried to tell him that when he started seeing Zanna, but did he listen?"

Emma's bewilderment had turned to righteous indignation, and suddenly Abby felt better. Having a close friend share her frustration—realizing that Emma had a much harder row to hoe—put her disappointment into better perspective. After all, if James was acting as though he'd let her down, a chance remained that he'd make that missed kiss up to her, while for Emma, finding another beau seemed less likely.

"Denki, Emma," she murmured. "What would I do without a gut friend like you?"

Emma inhaled the aroma of her tea and then finished it. "I knew I could come here any hour of the day or night and you'd hear me out, Abby. This tea hits the spot, too. Chamomile, is it?"

"Jah, real nice before bedtime to settle you down." Abby drained her cup. "Just out of curiosity, what kind of pie would you pitch into James's face? Picturing that makes me giggle."

"Oh, gooseberry! He screws up his mouth and refuses to eat it. Says it's too puckery." The lines around Emma's eyes relaxed. "And for Matt . . . wouldn't blackberry make the biggest mess? Can't you see that dark goop running down his face, his eyes all wide and white in the middle of it? Neither of them would believe I could do that, but it's fun to think about, ain't so?"

"Jah, it is." Abby slung her arm around Emma's shoulders. "Another cup of tea?"

"I'd best get back. Lots of laundry to do tomorrow, and Dat gets up earlier and earlier these spring days," Emma remarked. "He cat-naps a lot during the day, so he doesn't rest real solid at night. Or maybe that's on account of Mamm's snoring."

They rose from the table and Abby walked her friend to the door. "Sure glad you brought those lemon bars, Emma. And I—I hope you get to feeling better about the situation with Matt. Hard as it is to accept, he's a gut young man. Not one to be mean or hateful."

Emma shrugged. "Maybe it's time to rethink my future. I'm not happy about that, but you've been a real help, Abby. See you soon."

"Jah, take care, Emma." Abby held the door open, watching as the moonlight made her friend's kapp glow. "Keep a pie handy. And you'll come get me if you put it in one of their faces, ain't so?"

Emma's laughter trailed behind her as she headed up Lambright Lane. And didn't that put a better ending on the evening for both of them? After Abby washed their cups and saucers, she returned to her bedroom and picked up her tablet. It amazed her, how ideas came from the most ordinary situations. She finished the paragraph about Paul Bontrager's passing and then pressed her pencil eraser against her cheek, thinking, before she completed her column.

Some of us have dealt with disappointment this past week, and it seems to me that instead of making lemonade from such lemons, maybe a pan of lemon bars—or a lemon meringue pie!—would be a better way of chasing off our negative moods. We have to take the sour with the sweet, and when you bake up a pie or a batch of bars, you spread happiness along with your treats. I wish you someone wonderful to share them with this week.

—Abigail Lambright

Abby glanced across the road, to where James's lamp still burned in his upstairs window. She prayed that Emma would find peace and that James would figure out how to handle all the business success that had come his way. And as for whether he would ask her out again? Well, God would have His own ideas about that, and she would wait for whatever the new week might bring.

Chapter 14

Titus sat down at the table for breakfast on Monday morning wearing an expression that told Rosemary he had something on his mind. Something he was downright tickled about. It was a rare day when Joe's dat cracked a smile before he'd had his coffee and a full meal, so while Beth Ann set out the maple syrup and honey, Rosemary stood at the stove turning their French toast in the cast-iron skillet, hoping it wasn't another life-changing announcement. She'd endured enough of those these past few days.

"Thought I'd wait until you didn't have any dishes in your hand to say this, Rosemary," he began with a chuckle.

She looked over at him, expecting a reprimand for dropping that stack of plates the other day, even though the Melmac hadn't broken. But he looked like a boy who was trying to keep a secret yet itched to tell someone about it. "I'm listening."

Titus chucked Katie under the chin as she sat in her high chair. "Got word from Matt Lambright that Preacher Paul Bontrager, over in Cedar Creek, passed away during the night on Saturday."

Rosemary swallowed, sensing another shoe was about to drop. "I'm sorry to hear that," she murmured. "I know he was one of your friends from a long time ago."

"Was he the really old fellow who gave the first sermon at the wedding?" Beth Ann asked.

"Say there! Watch your tongue, when somebody's got a lot of miles on him!" Titus laughed, apparently unconcerned about his own mileage—which was a huge improvement over the mood he'd been in for most of the winter. "Jah, that was Paul, who also owns the farm across the road from the Lambrights. His pasture adjoins the Graber place," he continued. "And when I go to Paul's funeral on Thursday, I'll be asking his son, Perry, if he'd be interested in selling that property—or at least a gut chunk of it. Perry works at Graber's Custom Carriages, you see. He doesn't work the land himself. Has Carl Byler raising the crops there."

Rosemary's heart stopped. Oh, but she knew where this conversation was going. She stabbed the first pieces of French toast with her fork to keep from making a remark she might regret.

"So why would you buy land clear over in Cedar Creek, Dat?" Beth Ann looked perplexed. Like her father, she'd enjoyed visiting for the wedding, but she hadn't realized how *much* Titus had liked it there.

Rosemary dipped another slice of bread into the egg and milk mixture, allowing it to absorb the liquid. It was best to let father and daughter have this conversation while she got her runaway pulse under control. It was easy to imagine how tickled Matt must be about this situation.

"After talking to Matt about our flocks, and after visiting with your uncle Ezra and other fellows from Cedar Creek—friends I've known since I was your age," Titus added emphatically, "I'm figuring out a way to move us back there, where we'll be close to family. With your older brothers and sisters married off and scattered all over, it seems like a gut thing to do."

As this news sank in, Beth Ann's face fell and she looked ready to cry. "But what about *this* farm? And this house? And where will I go to school? And—" She stopped abruptly when her dat's expression warned her that she was crossing a line.

Rosemary's heart thudded. She hadn't considered Beth Ann's position in all of this talk of a potential move: leaving her school, not to mention her homeplace, would mean a total upheaval for the twelve-year-old girl.

"I've got some ideas about this place, and there's no need for you to go worrying about it." Titus gazed steadily at his youngest child, not angry but not apologetic, either. "It's my job to see that we've got a roof over our heads and food on the table. We can do that just as well in Cedar Creek as we can here. Maybe better, if Matt and I share the work and expenses for our flocks."

Beth Ann shot Rosemary a worried look and then busied herself with setting silverware at their places. No matter how she felt about so much potential change, she knew better than to protest. Plain girls learned early on that while their fathers loved them, they wouldn't consult their wives or daughters about decisions or pander to their wishes.

Rosemary lifted three more pieces of crispy, fragrant French toast from the skillet and carried the platter to the table. She took the plate of bacon from the warming oven and, after they were all seated, they bowed their heads for a moment of silent thanks.

As they ate, Titus talked about the lay of the Bontrager land and how much easier it would be for him to manage his flock with Matt as a partner. He had obviously spent a lot of time considering all the benefits of a move. Beth Ann ate about half of her French toast and then began to drag a piece of it through the syrup left on her plate.

Rosemary glanced at the clock, sighing inwardly. Titus's plans would get his daughter's day off to a worrisome start, but this wasn't the time to discuss Beth Ann's emotions . . . the friends she would miss, and the way leaving this house would mean leaving behind reminders of her mother, as well. "Won't be long before the Schlabachs and the Millers are waiting out by the mailbox," she said gently. "Have a gut day at school."

Beth Ann rose from the table, plucked her lunch bucket from the countertop, and grabbed her shawl from a peg by the door. "Bye, Dat," she murmured. "See you when I get home, Rosemary."

"Jah, Katie and I'll be waiting for you." Beth Ann and the other children along this road walked about a mile to the one-room schoolhouse situated on a corner of Bishop Chupp's property, so they got an early start each weekday morning.

Rosemary glanced at Titus's plate. "More French toast? Or some eggs, maybe?" She broke more of the fried bread into pieces for Katie.

Katie grabbed the largest chunk and dunked it in the puddle of strawberry preserves Rosemary had spooned onto her plate.

"A couple of eggs would be gut," Titus replied, and then added, "Make it three. My appetite seems to be coming out of hibernation, maybe from thinking about all the effort it'll take to shift us from this farm to a different one."

Rosemary rose to fix the rest of his breakfast. "Well, you dropped enough weight while Alma was sick that your pants got baggy. So maybe this means you're coming around now, back to normal."

"Normal?" Titus let out a short laugh. "Whatever *normal* is, I feel like I've gone way beyond it. I'm excited, Rosemary—even though I'm in for a lot of work if I'm to make all these plans come to pass."

She cracked three eggs against the edge of the counter, dropping them one by one into the skillet in which she'd fried the bacon. Even before Alma and Joe had died, her father-in-law had never sounded so exuberant about *anything*. "So . . . what if Perry Bontrager doesn't want to sell?"

"Why wouldn't he?" Titus replied with a shrug. "With his dat gone, he's in the same situation I am—most of his kin scattered someplace else. His wife's family lives over around Clearwater, so what's to keep him in Cedar Creek? Especially if I make him a gut offer."

Rosemary's heart constricted. How was it that, less than a week after Zanna's wedding, so many major changes had taken place? Was it God's doing when circumstances seemed to mesh so quickly? As she stood by the stove, watching the eggs crackle beneath a shaking of salt and pepper, she fought a new surge of anxiety.

What's to happen with your *land? You can't leave Joe's investment behind or let Titus blend it in with his farm when he sells it. Or would you stay here in Queen City, near Mamm and Malinda? He can't make you move to Cedar Creek . . .*

Rosemary flipped the three eggs, not caring that some grease splattered the stovetop. Realizing that she had options—that she did not have to go along with every move Titus made—gave her a different perspective on this surprising development. After all, she had blueprints for a new home . . . plans that she and Joe had made before tragedy turned the Yutzy family upside down. It had been her choice to keep house here for Titus, so it could also be her decision to stay in Queen City.

"I'm thinking you should go to the funeral with me, Rosemary. Get yourself out amongst people in Cedar Creek."

That was *not* what she had in mind. Titus's statement hung in the kitchen as she lifted the fried eggs from the skillet onto his plate. Rosemary considered defying him, and yet . . . she might be able to use Thursday's trip to her advantage, as far as her own future was concerned. Maybe, since Titus had been making decisions that took her by surprise, she should use the same strategy on him. After all, hadn't he reminded her on the evening before Zanna's wedding that it was Joe who had died, not her?

Rosemary carried the rest of his breakfast to the table, her thoughts simmering. "Let me know what time you'll be leaving. I'll be ready."

"This is a surprise," Titus said as he stepped up into the carriage early on Thursday morning. "The way you've been reacting to Matt Lambright's calls, I figured you'd back out of going to the funeral today."

Rather than answer, Rosemary checked the pie carriers at her feet to be sure they would ride upright. Not often did Joe's dat admit he hadn't predicted what she would do. It *would* be difficult to endure the service for Preacher Paul, but it was time she started rising to challenges again.

"And you could've pushed me over with a feather when you took Katie to stay over at your mamm's yesterday," Titus added. As the horse trotted onto the wet blacktop, he looked sideways at her from beneath the brim of his black hat. "I thought you'd be using your little girl as a distraction, for when Matt got too friendly."

Oh, but she wanted to reply to that remark! Instead, Rosemary considered her answer. "You probably think one of those six apple pies I baked is for him, too, don't you? But they're a favor to Aunt Lois. When I called Tuesday, she said the Bontragers are expecting a lot of kin from Indiana and Ohio. Lots of mouths to feed."

Truth be told, Rosemary wasn't sure she was ready to sit though a funeral. Joe's service had been the last one she'd attended. But a trip to Cedar Creek seemed a better way to spend a dreary day than stewing over Titus's dealings with Perry Bontrager. If she was at the funeral, she could watch facial expressions while Titus and Perry—and probably Matt—discussed the possibilities of buying that land. It seemed inconsiderate to rush into such talk with a fellow who had just lost his father, but it wasn't her place to tell Titus that, was it?

As the miles rolled by and the rain pattered against the carriage roof, Rosemary enjoyed a newfound sense of freedom, having a day away from the housework. Abby would be at the funeral, of course, and the prospect of getting better acquainted with Barbara and Treva Lambright appealed to her because—well, she had kept herself so focused on her daily tasks at Titus's that she hadn't gone to any quilting frolics or other activities over the winter. She craved the company of other women right now. And she would enjoy talking to them a lot more without Beth Ann's long face or Katie's squirming to contend with.

"If we move to Cedar Creek, Lois would welcome your help at

her pie shop," Titus remarked. "She'll reach a point someday where running Mother Yutzy's Oven is too much of a strain."

"Jah, she's told me that several times," Rosemary replied in a faraway voice. "But I might not move to Cedar Creek. Joe and I had blueprints drawn up for a house, and if I gave the carpenters my go-ahead, I could be living in it by fall. I'd be right next door to Mamm that way."

Titus's eyebrows shot up. "Now, why would you want to go building a house? That's just silliness, thinking you should go through with the plans you and Joe made—locking yourself away in the past and living by yourself."

Ah, but what if Matt Lambright moved to Queen City to be with me? What would that do to your plans?

Rosemary looked away so her father-in-law wouldn't see her furtive grin. She had no intention of letting Matt share her house, of course, but wasn't it fun to watch Titus squirm? He apparently assumed that she had signed on with him until she found another husband. And maybe, no matter what he said out loud, he was hoping she wouldn't remarry. That way, his laundry would get done and his meals would appear on the table—and she could navigate Beth Ann through her teenage years and her rumspringa, so Titus wouldn't have to handle those matters as a single father.

And while Rosemary didn't regret stepping in to help Titus, Mamm's assessment might be correct. She had made life a lot more convenient for Joe's dat. If she slowed down some, and even got back into circulation, what might life be like? Even as gray clouds shrouded the sky, and though she still wore the black kapp and dress of a widow, Rosemary felt happier than she'd been in a long while. Just for today, it would be good to keep Titus guessing.

As they approached Cedar Creek, carriages were streaming in from both directions on the county blacktop, toward the mercantile and the carriage shop, where fellows in dark slickers were directing them where to park. From their place in the stalled line of folks who had come to pay their final respects to Paul Bontrager, Rosemary could see through the windows of Treva's Greenhouse, where long tables were again set up. Although this occasion wouldn't be nearly as cheerful as Zanna's wedding, it provided a way for far-flung members of Paul's family to gather, while folks from around town would see to the meal after the service and the livestock chores at the Bontrager place so Salome and Paul wouldn't have to worry about them.

Such thoughts brought to mind the day they had buried Joe. Rosemary recalled the November wind biting through her coat . . . the *thud* of the soil being shoveled onto his plain pine coffin. She sat straighter, determined not to cry. She yearned to rise above her own loss—to give help today rather than needing to receive it. When she caught sight of a slender young woman beneath an umbrella coming down Lambright Lane, she slid open her door.

"Abby!" she called out. "Where should I put these pies?"

It was good to see her new friend's face light up, and as Abby hurried toward them, Rosemary sensed her day had taken a turn for the better. "Since we've come to a stop in the line," she said to Titus, "I'll save us from carrying these pies all the way from wherever you have to park."

"Gut to see you, Rosemary! Gut morning to you, too, Titus," Abby said as she reached the side of their buggy. She grasped the first pie carrier—a tall covered basket designed to hold two stacked pies—as Rosemary handed it out to her. "Mighty nice of you to bake for us today, Rosemary. We've got a large crowd already, even though it's an hour before the service starts."

Rosemary handed the second carrier to Abby and then stepped down to the pavement. "Happy to help. It's the least I could do after your warm welcome last week. Aunt Lois was thinking you might need every pie you could round up."

Rosemary grabbed the last carrier, took one back from Abby, and followed her along the side of the carriage-congested road. It occurred to her that she had just walked away from Titus without even thinking about it, because she had someone to visit with. She had a mission and a new friend, so she didn't have to hunt up Aunt Lois to keep her company anymore.

And wasn't that a blessing? Another little freedom she had allowed herself.

Rosemary noticed the glowing green of the new leaves on the trees as the sun came out from behind the clouds and how rows of red and yellow tulips brightened the front of Sam and Barbara's white house. Had the rose of Sharon bushes been this full of blooms last week, or had she been too agitated to notice them? As she enjoyed these signposts of spring, she saw two familiar figures: James was motioning for carriages to proceed to the back of his carriage shop, while on the other side of the road Matt directed drivers coming from the other direction to park in the Lambrights' big front yard. He caught sight of Rosemary and held her gaze.

She stopped. She waved and then followed Abby into Treva's Greenhouse, where several women were setting the tables. No sense in letting these folks—especially Titus—witness any sort of connection between her and Matt. She hadn't come to this funeral to flirt, after all.

As Rosemary set her carriers on the table and began removing pies, Abby handed her a clean knife. "Denki," she murmured. "I hadn't expected to be back in Cedar Creek anytime soon, so it's gut to see you."

"And we're glad to have you here, too. So where's Katie today?" Abby deftly drew her knife through one of the apple pies.

"I thought she'd have a better day with Mamm and my sister." Her four quick cuts made eight evenly sized pieces. "Beth Ann's in school, of course—and I'll have you know she's already made Titus's work pants, those two dresses for Katie, and her own new dresses, as well."

"Sounds like she's a wonderful-gut seamstress." When she heard the door opening behind them, Abby turned. "And I'm guessing Matt saw you and figured he'd better see what kind of pie you brought."

"There's no figuring about it," Matt replied in a low voice. He came up to the table and lifted the pie Abby had just sliced. "Rosemary's specialty is apple pie, made with brown sugar and fresh lemon zest, and this one has my name all over it."

Rosemary's eyes widened as Matt snatched a fork from the nearest table. Was he really going to eat a piece right out of the pan?

"Matt, let me get you a plate." Abby hurried over to where the dessert dishes were stacked.

"No need. It's not like anyone else gets a taste—unless Rosemary wants some." Matt forked up the tip of one piece and held it in front of her with a wicked grin. His brown eyes sparkled with mischief, yet he was serving her the first bite as though he wouldn't take no for an answer.

"I—you don't really intend to eat this whole pie, do you?" Rosemary blurted out.

Matt's dimples teased her. "I'll save some of it for the funeral lunch and some for later today," he replied, still holding the fork in front of her. "I've never sampled one of your fine pies, Rosemary, and I want to enjoy every bite of it. If you'll share it with me, it'll taste even better."

Rosemary's breath caught. When had a man ever gazed at her this way, as he held out an offering of far more than filling and crust? Something indescribable passed between them—something sweeter than pie. She opened her mouth. When Matt slipped the fork between her lips, his gaze grew more intense. Then he turned the fork's handle toward Rosemary so she could feed him the next bite.

She could hardly swallow. This exchange came too close to the way a bride and groom shared the first bites of their wedding cake. If she went through with what Matt was silently suggesting, it seemed they would forge a profound connection even though they'd never been on a date. Even though they knew very little about each other.

But she saw no graceful way to refuse him. Rosemary closed her eyes over the bite of pie, savoring the rich sweetness of the brown sugar and butter, the texture of the sliced apples . . . the tang of lemon zest and the tenderness of the crust. It was like no other bite of pie she could recall—and wasn't that a silly idea? She'd been making and eating her own pies since she was Beth Ann's age.

Matt's expression, however, told her he didn't find this moment silly at all. His lips parted in anticipation. His eyes closed and his long lashes brushed his cheeks. Quickly, before she got any more caught up in how kissable he looked, she forked up a big bite and slipped it into his mouth.

His groan gratified her. As she removed the fork, Matt caught hold of her hand. He chewed slowly, holding her gaze, apparently delighted by the blend of flavors and textures. "Rosemary, that's the best apple pie I've ever tasted," he murmured matter-of-factly. "But then, I knew it would be. Denki for bringing it and for sharing it with me."

She had no idea what to say, so she nodded. When Matt took the fork back, she once again became aware that while Abby was still cutting pies, the other women bustled about the tables as they laid out plates and silverware.

Rosemary reminded herself to breathe. It seemed that while she had felt suspended in time and space, removed from reality, the world had not come to a standstill, nor had anyone apparently noticed the little ceremony that had just taken place. Yet Rosemary felt changed. Matt had initiated an unspoken agreement between them, and she had willingly entered into it. And what did that mean?

Matt offered her another bite, but she shook her head. As he polished off that piece of pie, Rosemary felt an inexplicable happiness. She had passed his first test.

Joe would never have done that. Not in public, anyway.

Rosemary looked away, removing herself from all thoughts of her deceased husband. Joe had been a fine man, if more private about his feelings than Matt was. But he didn't have a place here today. She had come to explore a whole new realm of possibilities without being bound to her past as a wife and a mother. Today she was Rosemary, a young woman seeking her future, even if it was too soon to believe Matt would play an important part in it.

Abby elbowed Matt as he lifted the crimped crust edge to eat it from his fingers. "I'll cover this and set it aside for you," she said, pointing to a closed cabinet along the wall. "You know, of course, that if your sisters or your mamm see you eating it straight from the pan, you'll catch a lot of teasing when they learn it's Rosemary's pie."

"Not the first time they've teased me," he said with a shrug. "And if a fellow can't tolerate some talk for pie like this—or for a woman like Rosemary—well, he's not much of a man."

Matt laid his fork in the pie pan and handed it to Abby. "I'd better get back to parking buggies, but I'll find you after the funeral, Rosemary—if you'll let me sit with you at dinner," he added as he waggled his eyebrows at her.

Again, she saw no easy way to refuse him. They'd be seated among hundreds of other people, after all. "All right. But if you need to talk with Titus about your flocks or—"

"Titus will have to wait his turn."

As Rosemary watched him walk out the door toward the road, which was still lined with carriages, her pulse pounded. Matt seemed so confident about his feelings for her. What if she was getting too caught up in the rush of his emotions and the attention he was paying her that she wasn't considering how *she* felt? She had a young child to consider, and a piece of ground, and Mamm and Malinda, and—

"I've never seen Matt so happy." Abby's brown eyes, so much like her nephew's, glimmered as she squeezed Rosemary's wrist. "I know he's taken you by surprise, Rosemary, but he's a gut man. Not a fellow to string girls along and then cast them aside. God has brought you together today, so don't be afraid," she added softly. "All the right reasons and details will fall into place, if we give ourselves over to His will."

Chapter 15

As Abe Nissley preached the first sermon of Paul Bontrager's funeral, Matt shifted so he could see between the men sitting in front of him. He peered across the crowded barn, studying the women who faced them in row upon row of black dresses . . . past his grandmother and his mamm and behind Aunt Abby, Marian Byler, and Eva Detweiler. Because the eldest sat in front while girls Ruthie's age were in the rear, he knew approximately where to find Rosemary. But with so many out-of-town folks swelling their number to nearly two hundred and every woman wearing her hair tucked under her kapp from a center part, it took longer to study the faces.

". . . and we are thankful to God for the many years of Preacher Paul's service," Abe was saying. "In all he said and did, Paul served the Lord with gladness of heart and generosity of spirit. The man God chooses to take his place will have big shoes to fill."

As Matt continued to search for Rosemary, Preacher Abe's phrases lingered with him: gladness of heart . . . generosity of spirit. Were these qualities Joe Yutzy had possessed? Would he have big shoes to fill if he convinced Rosemary to court and marry him? Could he be a good father for Katie?

Mighty soon to be concerned about those details. One slice of apple pie and a few smiles aren't enough reason to hitch up with any woman.

When he found Rosemary in the crowd, his heart stilled. She was wiping away a tear—not unusual at a funeral—yet the sight of her sorrow made Matt realize she had a lot more at stake than he did if she agreed that he could court her. While no one doubted that Rosemary could keep a home running and be a loving parent while she baked pies to earn money, he could offer little proof that he would make a good husband.

Had Rosemary been happy with Joe?

"We now commend our brother Paul Bontrager into the Lord's eternal care," Preacher Abe was saying, "with the assurance that he has gone to his reward in Glory, to serve God in the hereafter just as he served us here in Cedar Creek."

Matt shifted on the hard wooden bench. He glanced to his left at Jonny Ropp, who sat close enough that their shoulders touched. On his right, Mose Hartzler looked ready to nod off, maybe because he'd been up late with his wife, Hannah, who was due to deliver their third child any day. It struck him then that these fellows, along with a good many of his friends, had married and started families while he was still living at home and keeping his sheep.

Would Rosemary wonder why he was twenty-two and uncommitted? Would it concern her that he hadn't yet taken his instruction to join the church?

You'd better be speaking to Vernon about that, he thought as the bishop rose to read the words of a hymn. Funeral services, being more solemn, included no singing—and he wished they didn't have to sit through a second, longer sermon without the musical relief of raising their voices. All he could think about was Rosemary . . . where he might take her to enjoy another slice or two of that apple pie . . . what he might say to win a "yes" from her.

Matt closed his eyes, recalling her expression when he'd offered her that forkful of pie. He had definitely surprised her with that move, so how could he keep coming up with ways to impress her as no other fellow ever had? Rosemary's deep green eyes fascinated him, and as she had gazed up at him with the fork still in her mouth, accepting what he'd fed her, he had yearned to share more moments of such closeness today. Would it be wrong to kiss her? Would she think he was too bold and presumptuous if he held her close? Surely she was as hungry for affection as he was . . .

"Oh!" Matt gasped when Jonny elbowed him. On his right, Mose was trying not to snicker, and Carl Byler turned around to see what the commotion was. Even the bishop looked his way as he kept speaking about the true measure of a man.

You've gone and done it now. Got so caught up in your thoughts of Rosemary that you must've made a telltale noise.

Then he realized that Rosemary was looking right at him from across the crowded barn. Had he attracted everyone's attention? Made a fool of himself? Matt returned her gaze, and after a moment she lowered her eyes.

For the rest of the long, somber service, Matt sat up and paid attention even as he longed to be outside in the fresh air. His stomach rumbled. He tried not to think about those seven remaining pieces of apple pie . . .

At last Bishop Gingerich pronounced the benediction, and the men filed out one side of the barn while the women exited through the other door. Because the Cedar Creek cemetery was just down the hill, below the Bontrager place, Paul's wooden coffin would ride in the horse-drawn black hearse but everyone else would walk to the graveside service. Beulah Mae Nissley, Matt's mamm, and other neighbor ladies would stay behind to make the final meal preparations so the Bontrager family would be greeted with a hot dinner when they returned from laying Paul to rest.

As soon as he stepped out the door, Matt followed a hunch. Sure enough, he saw Rosemary enter the greenhouse with Abby and his grandmother. It didn't surprise him that she would help serve the meal rather than attend the burial of a fellow she hadn't known—especially so soon after her husband's death. Into the greenhouse he went, and despite curious glances from Eunice Graber and Adah Ropp, he walked directly over to Rosemary.

"May I have a word?" he whispered, gesturing toward the front room of the shop.

Rosemary looked startled, yet she followed him through the swinging door and into the area where his grandmother displayed her potted plants and the woven baskets some of the local ladies made to sell. "Jah? What's on your mind?"

Matt knew better than to elaborate on the thoughts he'd had during the service. Instead, he reached for Rosemary's hand. "With so many older folks here and Bontrager kin from out of town, it'll be a long while before it's our shift to eat," he murmured. "How about if we take my pie and slip into the house to fill a couple of plates after the burial? Then we could sit out back in the swing together."

Matt wasn't sure where that idea had come from on the spur of the moment, yet Rosemary's expression made his heart pound.

"I—I don't see why not. We'd be outside, in plain sight, and, well—truth be told, Abby said they have a gut many helpers for the meal and . . ." Rosemary's voice trailed off, and she glanced toward the door.

Matt held his breath. Was she having second thoughts?

"If I eat with you early on, I can be washing the dishes from the first shift," she said resolutely. "And while your mamm and sisters are eating, I can help at the tables, if need be. How's that sound?"

Matt squeezed her hands, keenly aware of how small yet sturdy they felt. "Perfect. It sounds just perfect, Rosemary."

The next forty-five minutes flew by in a flurry of preparations for the funeral meal. Rosemary got into the flow quickly, slicing hams and cutting up baked chickens that Beulah Mae Nissley had prepared at her café. As Rosemary put the meat back into its large metal catering pans to keep it warm, Abby and her mother were setting plates of pie at each place on the long tables, while Barbara and her girls poured water into glasses. Large covered pans of hash-brown casserole and mixed vegetables waited on the serving table, too, so folks could help themselves as they came in. Aunt Lois had baked dozens of loaves of bread, and as Bessie Mast sliced them, Eunice and Emma Graber filled baskets and set them on the tables beside the butter plates. Rosemary had discovered that no matter where she went among Plain folks, the church services were the same—and so were the basic tasks that went into serving food for a large crowd of hungry people.

"The first folks are coming down the road from the cemetery now," Treva announced as she glanced out the window.

Beulah Mae began removing the lids from the pans, while Barbara set out serving spoons. Rosemary was brushing crumbs from the table when a familiar face greeted her from the swinging door of the shop.

"I jogged ahead of the crowd," Matt said breathlessly. "Looks like if we fill our plates real quick-like and I grab my pie, we'll be on our way to a picnic, jah?"

How could she refuse? It might not be entirely proper to eat before the Bontrager family, but when Abby waved them on, Rosemary followed Matt down the length of the serving table, filling her plate. The two of them were walking across the yard toward the Lambright home as the others were entering the greenhouse to go through the line.

"Was this a gut plan, or what?" Matt held his pie in one hand and a piled plate in the other. "I thought Vernon would never finish the service. And it seemed Preacher Abe spent nearly as long giving Paul's send-off as it took Gideon Ropp and me to dig the grave yesterday."

Rosemary willed herself not to recall the gaping hole in the ground where they had laid Joe to rest. "We women stayed busy, believe me. Made it handy that Beulah Mae Nissley and Aunt Lois could cook most of the meal in their restaurants and keep it hot in their big catering pans."

Matt led her past the side of his white house, around to a double swing in the backyard. Made of white wooden slats and suspended by chains on a freestanding A-frame, it sat facing out over the pastures. He wiped the wet seat with napkins he'd grabbed in the serving line and nodded for her to be seated first. "What I was trying to say," he continued in a softer voice, "was that I couldn't wait for all the formalities to be finished so I could spend time with *you*, Rosemary. It was a fine surprise this morning to see that you'd come with Titus."

As he slid onto the wooden seat, careful not to jostle her, Rosemary felt her cheeks flush. Now that she was alone with Matt, she would have to respond to his pleasant chitchat. "Jah, well," she began, feeling suddenly tongue-tied, "when Titus said he planned to speak with Perry Bontrager about buying that land across the road, I . . . I wanted a chance to look things over firsthand."

Matt's dimples winked at her. "You can look me over all you want, Rosemary," he said before he took a big bite of ham.

The way he chewed made her watch his lips—until she caught herself. She focused on her forkful of cheesy hash-brown casserole. "If Paul's land does come up for sale, I won't necessarily move to Cedar Creek with Titus, you know. I have a lot of decisions, now that he wants to be your partner in the sheep business."

For a moment Matt looked like a puppy who'd been punished, but he recovered quickly. "Jah, you have a lot more to consider than I do," he replied. "But let me tell you this. I've never before met a woman who made me feel like I'd have a great big hole in my life if I didn't see her again. It was love at first sight, for sure and for certain," he continued earnestly, "and I'm not saying this to make you nervous, Rosemary, or to get you to say the same thing back to me."

Rosemary had a hard time swallowing her hash browns. Her heart was pounding so hard she couldn't think straight. Matt had cut right to the chase, hadn't he? And even if he didn't expect her to love him right now, he obviously wanted her feelings to catch up to his as soon as possible.

She focused on the rolling green pastures dotted with woolly white sheep . . . the bursts of pink redbud blossoms and white dogwood blooms set off against the dark green cedar trees growing along the creek. The Lambright land made a peaceful scene, and it was a view she could grow to love. Still . . .

"I don't know a thing about you, Matt," she blurted out, gripping her plate so it didn't slip off her lap. "We haven't spent any time together, or—"

"Which is why I invited you to eat with me," he pointed out. "Maybe you know more than you think, Rosemary. You've seen my flock, and you're already aware of what goes into keeping sheep. You've been inside my home and met my family. And you know how Katie already loves my dogs and isn't the least bit afraid of me. Those things are important, jah?"

Rosemary took a bite of ham, stalling, because Matt's answer made perfectly good sense. "So—what do you know about *me*?" she asked, mostly because she couldn't think of anything else to keep her side of the conversation going. Her pulse pounded with that reaction they had called "fight or flight" in school. She certainly wasn't a fighter and she didn't want to run from this conversation, but it made her uncomfortable to talk so seriously so soon.

"Well, besides the fact that the proof of your pie is in the eating, I admire the way you chose to look after Titus and Beth Ann. Titus has told me you could just as easily have stayed at your mamm's." Matt lifted a crispy chicken leg to his lips, chewed a bite, and then swallowed. "And you've taken on all the work his wife, Alma, once did, plus you're raising a child and baking pies—and you're seeing to Beth Ann's growing up at a tough time in her life. I've got a lot of respect for a woman who voluntarily cares for her husband's family, Rosemary."

Matt glanced at her over a forkful of broccoli and cauliflower. "So—even without getting into how your smile does crazy things to me and how pretty you are—I've touched on some important traits. You're a gut woman, and I hope I can win your trust and love. I've decided to take my instruction to join the church, so you'll know I'm a solid fellow with the best of intentions for taking care of you and Katie."

Rosemary gripped her fork. Matt sounded sincere and steadfast. And those were traits she had treasured about Joe. "I—I need time to think about—"

"You need a man to make you laugh and to hold you when you cry," Matt said softly. "And seeing how you love little Katie, I'm thinking you'll want more children someday. I want to be the husband who helps you raise them."

Rosemary's fork clattered to her plate. "I—I—"

Matt slipped a hand gently behind her head, leaned toward her, and kissed her on the lips. It was a soft, sweet kiss, and for a few moments Rosemary wanted it to last longer. She had forgotten the pleasure of sharing a man's affection . . .

Then she grabbed her plate and sprang from the swing. "This is happening way too fast!" she cried out. "If I say the least little thing to encourage you, or agree with everything you've just said, you'll think I'm all set to marry you! And that's not going to happen!"

Rosemary hurried around the frame of the swing, toward the back door that led into the Lambrights' kitchen. Her throat was so tight she could hardly breathe. Matt called her name, but she stepped into the house without a backward glance. Once inside, she fell against the door to close it, desperately trying to rein in her galloping doubts.

Thank goodness the kitchen was empty while the other women assisted with the meal in the greenhouse. It wouldn't do for them to see how agitated she was. Their questions would lead her to reveal what Matt had done to put her in such a state. She inhaled the aromas of chicken, ham, and hash-brown casserole left warming in the ovens for the next shift of guests.

He kissed you. Was that so wrong?

Rosemary set her half-full plate on the counter. She found the dish soap and began to run hot water in the sink—anything logical and purposeful. When her hands were busy, her thoughts were less likely to rush into places where they shouldn't go. As the steam rose, along with the lemon scent of the liquid soap, she closed her eyes.

Jah, he kissed me, Lord. And maybe I liked it a little too much. And maybe I'm afraid that with all the plans Matt seems to have, my own ideas might get swept aside . . . like they sometimes did with Joe.

Her eyes flew open. It wasn't proper to think ill of the dead, especially since Joe Yutzy had been a dependable husband and was the father of her child. And yet . . .

Forgive me, Jesus. While I didn't always like to submit to my husband's will, as a Plain wife is supposed to do, I believe I am to submit to Your will, first and foremost.

She placed several cooking utensils in the hot, soapy water and began to wash them. She had to admit it was a thrill to hear a nice fellow like Matt say such wonderful-gut things about her. Was she being prideful or immodest? Was she running scared from the secure future God was arranging for her? She must turn her doubts and fears over to God for now, but she wasn't giving Matt any answers just yet either.

As she set several glass pie pans in the hot water to soak, Rosemary inhaled the warm, citrus scent and felt her emotions settling. This always happened after she took a moment alone to talk to God. Through the window she saw Matt heading back to the greenhouse, probably to refill his plate. No doubt she had hurt his feelings, but she'd been afraid. And fear had no place in a serious relationship between a man and a woman.

But hadn't Matt also said he admired and respected her? It was rare to hear an Amish fellow express such sentiments—as well she knew, after living with her stern, stoic dat and then with Joe and Titus. From what she could tell, Matt was as dependable and sincere as Abby had said he was. Had he meant it when he'd hinted over the phone that he would move to Queen City to be with her? If she had that house built from the blueprints, Matt could bring his sheep to her land and they would have a home of their own, and Titus wouldn't feel compelled to move to Cedar Creek. She would still live just down the road from Mamm and Malinda. Life as she and Katie knew it would be so much simpler . . .

But I'm getting as much ahead of myself as Matt was, Lord. So for now I'll just wash these dishes and leave the future to You.

Chapter 16

Abby was standing at her mamm's greenhouse sink, scraping the crusty hash-brown casserole from the sides of an emptied glass pan, when James came to stand beside her. "I owe you a big apology for my behavior the other night," he murmured. "Can we talk about it somewhere?"

She recognized the same pain in his expression that she'd been feeling since Sunday evening, but what had taken him so long to come around? *Does that really matter? Hear him out, so you can put your doubts to rest.*

Abby glanced behind them. The big glass room was noisy, with so many folks chatting as they ate their meal, so the two of them would be able to converse quietly here. As was the Amish custom, the Bontrager family and the older members of the Cedar Creek community had been seated first, so she and James—the folks their age and younger—wouldn't fill their plates until this round of guests had finished their dinner. "I'm listening," she said as she ran water over the pan.

James gently grasped her wrist. "Abby."

She stopped scrubbing the baked-on cheese, drawn in by his earnest gaze.

"You're the last person in the world I want to hurt." He leaned closer to speak near her ear in a wistful voice. "I got cold feet because— Now don't take this wrong, Abby, but just when I was ready to kiss you the other night, your laughter sounded like Zanna's and I saw her in the way you raised your eyebrows—"

Abby blinked. This wasn't what she'd expected to hear, yet James's desperate expression told her he was completely sincere. He looked exasperated with himself and spooked by what had happened.

"—and I would *never* compare you to your sister, Abby," he continued earnestly. "I ruined a wonderful-gut ride, and it's bothered me all week, and . . . I didn't know how to tell you. Can you forgive me, Abby? Please?"

Oh, but his gaze delved into her lonely heart, enough that she could set aside her momentary disappointment that he'd thought about pretty, vivacious Zanna instead of delivering that kiss they'd both wanted. But hadn't it taken great courage to tell her the truth? Some fellows would never bother trying to explain.

And forgive us our debts, as we forgive our debtors.

It was the only line of the Lord's Prayer that placed responsibility on the one asking God for such things as daily bread and delivery from evil. And hadn't everyone in Cedar Creek witnessed the forgiveness James had granted Zanna?

Abby's heart fluttered. Her disappointment released its grip. "Jah, James, I'll forgive you. I'm glad you asked. Glad you told me what happened."

James exhaled. He rested his forehead against hers for only a moment, but his gesture soothed her soul. "Denki," he whispered. "I know I need to make up for the way I hurt you, but I still want that kiss, you know. Don't think for a minute that I've forgotten about it."

Abby felt a pleasant rush of warmth. She considered giving him a peck on the cheek, but with so many folks in the room this wasn't the time or the place. "Gut, because I haven't, either." She eased away from him, thinking of a safer topic, should anyone come up behind them. "So—tell me what's going on at Graber's Custom Carriages now that you've gotten all those calls."

James placed the catering pans Abby had just washed in a wagon with high sides and a handle so they could haul them to the house for refills. "It's going to be an exciting new venture, but I'll be mighty busy. I've taken orders for three more parade buggies. Another fellow wanted half a dozen hay wagons for the Agricultural Hall of Fame in Bonner Springs, Kansas, so Perry, Leon, and Noah will have extra vehicles to work on, as well."

"And every one of them will be wonderful. Sturdy and well crafted," Abby replied with a nod.

"I'm grateful to Vernon—and to you, Abby—for helping me keep this flurry of business in perspective." James smiled at her as though she were the only person in the huge, crowded room. "I turned away orders for five more special rigs because I can't guarantee their quality if I take on too much work. I see no practical way to expand my shop space or to hire any other experienced carriage makers right now."

"It's gut to set limits." Abby reached for another glass pan to scrape, feeling mischievous. "We don't want anyone to say that all work and no play has made James a dull boy, you know."

His laughter rang out, and then he leaned in closer so only she would hear him. "I don't want *you* to think I've become dull, Abby. There's more to life than welding and painting and wiring light panels, ain't so?"

Abby's pulse sped up, but as she was about to respond, the door from her mother's front shop swung open and Matt stepped through. He looked ready to cry—or to cuss, the way some young fellows did during their rumspringa. As her nephew gazed down the length of the serving table, his empty plate in his hand, she stepped away from James.

"We'll be bringing fresh pans of everything from the house in just a few, Matt," she said. Rather than ask why his mood had changed so drastically, she buttered a slice of Lois Yutzy's fresh rye bread, knowing it was one of his favorites. "So . . . after another slice or two of that apple pie, you're not full?"

"I've ruined it." He shook his head forlornly. "I've ruined everything, Aunt Abby."

"How's that?" James inquired as he joined them. "Last I saw, you and Rosemary were slipping into the swing for a nice chat and—"

"I kissed her," Matt confessed. "I couldn't help myself. And she jumped out of the swing like she couldn't run away fast enough."

Abby shared a glance with James. Wasn't it ironic that a kiss—or the absence of one—had caused so much commotion lately? What could she say to make her nephew feel better, preferably before his friends or his sisters quizzed him about his dejected expression? "I've heard more than one widow admit it was difficult to accept affection from a new fella. Maybe—"

"She was trying to tell me she needed more time, that I was moving too fast, and what did I do?" Matt chided himself. "I raced right along on my own excitement, not paying her one bit of attention."

"Because she's just what you've been searching for, and you couldn't wait for her feelings to catch up to yours," James said, clapping Matt on the back. "You're not the first fella who's ever done that, you know. Could be that after Rosemary settles down, she'll realize she *liked* that kiss. And truth be told, you can give some gals forever and a day and they still won't come around. Or they'll fall for some other man in the meanwhile."

Abby winced. "Let's hope it doesn't come to that. Rosemary's a very sweet woman and awfully young to be alone for the rest of her life. I'm thinking things will work out, Matt. Patience is a virtue."

"Jah, but it's obviously not a virtue of mine." He looked through the nearest window, toward the house. "Guess I'll stay out of the kitchen . . . eat another slice or two of that fabulous apple pie, and leave her be."

"Time and pie heal all wounds, Matt," James remarked with a nod.

Abby glanced around the noisy greenhouse. Her mother, Barbara, the girls, and the neighbors helping with this meal were all here, pouring water and refilling the bread baskets as they visited with those who'd come to remember Paul today. "Seems like a gut time to head to the kitchen for more food," she said as she grasped the handle of the cart. "Maybe I can smooth things over so Rosemary won't go home feeling bad about how your picnic ended."

"Jah, thanks, Aunt Abby. Rosemary likes you a lot, so whatever you say to her will go over better than anything I could come up with." Matt looked glumly at James. "I'd better fetch that pie from the swing before the dogs find it. Bring a fork and I'll share a piece."

"Best offer I've heard all day." James found a clean fork on the back counter and then slipped his hand around Abby's for a moment. "How about you let me pull this cart to the kitchen door, and when you've refilled the pans I'll bring them back. By then it should be safe to come into the kitchen."

"Denki, James. Bringing the hot food sounds like the best way to be first in line for the next shift, ain't so?"

He laughed and followed her through the back door. "I can't get a thing past you, can I?"

As the three of them crossed the yard, Abby wondered what she might say to calm Rosemary's jitters. Or should she let matters take their own course? She'd never lost a husband or taken on responsibilities for a family other than her own, so she had no idea about all the concerns the young widow might be facing. As Matt held open the back door to the kitchen, James rolled the loaded cart inside and Abby stepped in behind it.

Her mouth fell open. All the glass pie plates were washed and stacked on the counter. The utensils they had cooked with all morning were clean and neatly arranged on the table, and Rosemary was draping her damp dish towel over the drying rack. "My word, Rosemary! We didn't expect you to clean up all by yourself," she exclaimed. "Barbara and Mamm will be mighty glad you came today—but then, they'd be happy to have you here even if you hadn't lifted a finger."

"How could I not help? It's what I know how to do," Rosemary said with a shrug. "And without Katie to look after, well—I'm not used to having free time and empty hands, you see."

When Abby lifted the metal pans to the tabletop, Rosemary was beside her immediately to assist . . . not ready to talk about why she had escaped into the kitchen. And that was all right, wasn't it? Sometimes a little peace and quiet set a lot of things right in a woman's heart. "It's nearly time to serve the next shift, so let's fill these pans with ham and chicken. James will take them back for us."

Nodding, Rosemary opened the wall oven and carried pan after pan of meat to the table. "You and James make a gut team, Abby. He's a mighty nice fella—and you'd never know he went through such an ordeal with Zanna," she remarked. "Maybe he's finally seeing the way *your* light shines, ain't so?"

Abby looked up from the hot pieces of chicken she was transferring. Matt had been so concerned that he'd upset this young woman, yet she seemed collected and composed now—not to mention observant. "James and I had our first date last weekend. And isn't that a funny bit for a maidel like me to be admitting?"

"I think it's very sweet. Another way of understanding that love comes in its own gut time."

"That's gut advice no matter what your age or your situation." Abby placed the lid on the first big pan of chicken pieces and then lifted another of Beulah Mae's metal bins to the table. "Truth be told, James nearly kissed me, but he's saving it for when I don't have nieces peeking out their window. I've . . . almost forgotten what kissing felt like."

Rosemary chortled as she fetched a pan of sliced ham from the oven of the big metal stove. "You can quit beating around the bush,

Abby. I know gut and well that Matt's told you why I rushed into the kitchen."

"Ah. Well, then, I'm glad to see you've recovered." Abby shook her head. "Matt's been coming on like a runaway train, hasn't he? He's kicking himself for whatever he said to you."

Rosemary retreated into her own thoughts as she arranged hot ham slices in the catering pan. She then stacked the glass pans the meat had been warming in and carried them to the sink. Abby had no doubt that this young woman kept Titus Yutzy's house clean and well organized . . . and that she would be a good match for Matt, who tended to clutter things up. "I should stop being such a nervous Nellie, I suppose," she finally admitted. "Matt means well, and he'd be a gut fella to hitch up with, but—"

"If you're not ready for that, you should stand your ground," Abby said. "Nothing's to be gained by rushing into a new courtship only to find out you disagree on some important issues after you've invested yourselves emotionally."

Rosemary smiled ruefully. "Denki for understanding my side of it. Titus and Mamm and—well, just about everyone I know—have been saying it's time for me to let go of the past. I have all faith that I *will* move forward, Abby. But I want to do that on my own terms. Once I'm a wife again, I might not be making my own decisions, you see."

"Jah, that's happened to some of my friends who married in a flurry and now . . . well, they're seeing to their husbands and their young children, and they sometimes wonder if they'll ever have time to be themselves again. That's one of the reasons I've remained un-married." Abby set the heavy lids on the two catering pans. "Too hardheaded and set in my ways, you see."

"Something tells me James doesn't think so. I predict that by the time summer's in full bloom, you two will be setting a date," Rose-mary replied. "Better plant a big patch of celery soon."

Abby felt her cheeks go pink. "We're already doing that for

Phoebe, you know. She and Owen Coblentz got engaged during the supper at Zanna and Jonny's wedding."

"Well, then, there must be something in the air here in Cedar Creek." As Rosemary went to the oven for the final pan of ham, she glanced out the window. Her expression became more speculative. "And there's something else afoot, too, seeing's how Titus and Perry Bontrager are heading across the road together."

Abby was about to ask what Rosemary meant when the door opened and James stepped inside, followed by Matt, who held a pie pan with only three pieces left in it. The two fellows stood there taking in the metal pans on one end of the long kitchen table along with the clean dishes stacked on the other end.

"Time for me to cart these to the greenhouse," James remarked as he found a big pair of potholders. "The first shift of folks is moving outside. Beulah Mae and her helpers are headed this way."

Rosemary looked toward the greenhouse. "Jah, such a big crowd is a nice tribute to Preacher Paul." She turned then, clasping her hands in front of her. "Matt, I'm sorry I spoiled our picnic. I overreacted," she said. "Maybe someday we can take up where we left off. But not today."

Matt's face lit up even though Rosemary had made her boundary clear. "And I'm sorry I bungled things, Rosemary," he rasped. "It's gut of you to give me another chance."

Abby smiled at James as he carefully lifted the first hot, heavy pan into the wagon. Wasn't love a fine thing when the folks involved made an effort to truly understand each other's feelings?

As Rosemary sat beside Titus in the buggy, she kept her thoughts to herself, which wasn't difficult because her father-in-law couldn't stop talking. He had eaten in the first shift before speaking to Perry Bontrager, and then decided to drive back to Queen City ahead of the crowd, knowing how heavy the horse-drawn traffic would be once everyone else decided to head home. "Jah, there were quite a number of Paul's kin there I hadn't seen for nigh onto forty years," he remarked as he urged the horse into full road speed. "And the more I heard some of them speculate about what Perry might do with that farm, the more I figured I'd best have a word with him before somebody else did."

Even in his somber black vest and pants, with his black broad-brimmed hat riding low on his forehead, Titus seemed more cheerful and upbeat than he'd been since Alma had started feeling so poorly from her cancer treatments.

"So I asked Perry what his plans were, and we walked across the road," he continued. "What with his wife just a few months from having another youngster, he wasn't keen on uprooting his family, and yet—"

Titus shifted his hat back, chuckling. "I could tell the idea might take root if I planted the right seed. His outbuildings are in pretty fair shape, although the fences would need to be replaced on account of how he hasn't kept much livestock lately. And, of course, those fields would have to be plowed and planted in grass rather than crops," he continued matter-of-factly. "Meanwhile, I'd be out the expense of feeding the flock or renting pasture nearby until the new grass got established. It's a lot to think about, but it could be done. Having Matt right across the way will make the whole shift a lot easier."

Rosemary closed her eyes, letting the afternoon sun warm her face as the breeze played with the strings of her kapp. Titus was talking as if he had already bought the place. And there was no question in his mind that Matt would be staying in Cedar Creek rather than moving to Queen City.

And wasn't that wishful thinking, assuming you could keep things the way they've been for so long?

Yet as Titus kept talking in a voice that rose on a tide of rare excitement, Rosemary no longer felt the fear that had overwhelmed her earlier. Oh, it would be a horrendous job to clear out Titus's big old house. Forty years of his and Alma's living there meant that long-forgotten personal possessions would come out of cubbyholes and attic boxes and trunks that Titus had no idea about. Women took care of such matters—just as she had donated Joe's clothing to an Amish relief program months ago—but Titus had insisted that Beth Ann leave her mother's belongings where they had always been.

What if he says all of Alma's personal effects must go to Cedar Creek? How will you make everything fit into a house that doesn't appear to be as big as the Yutzy place?

Rosemary shifted on the seat. Plenty of time to deal with that situation, the way she saw it. As she recalled Matt's hopeful, contrite smile when he'd said good-bye . . . she realized she didn't feel edgy or upset anymore. She wasn't ready to rush ahead, yet she could consider relinquishing her roots in Queen City now that she'd had more time with Matt and had experienced his affection and exuberance. Truth be told, his anticipation of their happiness together was blowing through her soul like a breath of spring.

Matt wanted to be with her. He had established a fine flock and a steady income. All he lacked, as far as she could see, was a physical house where they could make a home. While she liked the Lambright family, living with his parents, his three sisters, and his grandmother in their busy home as a new bride—with Katie—seemed a bit . . . intimidating. And not at all private.

And who's rushing ahead now?

"And you know, as we walked around in the house," Titus was saying, "I realized that if you and Matt were to get hitched, you'd have plenty of room to raise a family while I'd have the dawdi haus, where Paul was living while Perry and Salome's family used the main rooms. A fresh coat of paint, and the place would be like new."

It was time to ask the same question that had sprung to her mind on the ride into Cedar Creek that morning. "You're talking like Perry's already said he'd sell out," Rosemary remarked. "He's worked at

James Graber's carriage shop for a lot of years, so why would he want to move? And what if his wife has no intention of leaving so close to her due date? They have to find someplace else to go, you know—and when you asked Matt about property available around Cedar Creek, there wasn't any. What with their little ones and all that clearing out and packing to do, why—"

She shook her head, boggled by the sheer effort it would require to shift Perry Bontrager's family out of their home. "*I* certainly wouldn't want to tackle that move, if I were Salome."

"Ah, but you're not." Titus gave her a sideways smile. "I could tell from the way Perry was talking that the decision to move would be his. As well it should be."

Rosemary pressed her lips together. Titus's attitude matched most men's, as far as expecting women to say "jah" and go along with whatever their husbands decided. Joe would've responded the same way.

And what about Matt? Would he consult you about such a major move, or would he announce his decision and expect you to get everything packed by the date he set?

She had a lot to ponder. Yet surely by the time Perry and Salome found another place to go, their new baby would be here . . . With this being the end of April, figuring on at least a couple of months to pack up and deal with Paul's carpentry equipment, she didn't see how they could possibly be out of the house before August or September.

Truth be told, she didn't see this sale taking place. Too many circumstances didn't support Titus's optimistic opinions about his future in Cedar Creek. He was caught up in his own form of wishful thinking, just as she had been, except that while he believed all these changes—all the pieces of this puzzle—would fall into place, she was still half hoping their lives would stay the same.

Maybe it wasn't so far-fetched to think about building that house on her property. If Matt moved to Queen City and they found a place for his sheep, wouldn't Titus be just as happy? And wouldn't life be a whole lot easier for all of them?

Rosemary sat back against the buggy seat, hiding a smile. Maybe the partnership Titus wanted depended more upon her ownership of adjoining land—which could be converted easily enough into pasture for Matt's sheep—and the construction of her new home than her father-in-law wanted to believe.

And wasn't *that* something to think about?

Chapter 17

James got to the phone shanty early on Friday afternoon to lift its window and prop the door open. It was a beautiful first day of May, so while he hoped several friends would stop by for his interview with Lacey Piranelli, the magazine writer, he also realized the mercantile would be busy, as would Treva's Greenhouse. English customers often ventured into Cedar Creek on Saturdays to shop and then eat at Mother Yutzy's Oven or Mrs. Nissley's Kitchen—a very good thing for everyone in town after a cold winter had limited the tourist traffic.

And here came Abby out the mercantile door, waving at him. "Are you ready for your interview, James?" she called over to him. "It's a big day for you!"

"Jah, I don't often tell Leon and Perry and Noah not to return after dinner," he replied. "I gave them the afternoon off with pay because, with all those specialty orders, we'll all be putting in some overtime."

As Abby stopped in front of him, James allowed her confidence to settle his nerves. "It'll be different, talking to a woman about the carriage business," he admitted as he checked his handwritten list of questions for the dozenth time. "I hope I won't bore her or stumble over my tongue while I talk to her."

"James." Abby reached for his hands. "I've never known anyone—especially women—to be bored with you. Your interview will fly by before you know it."

"And Sam can spare you this afternoon?" he inquired as he glanced at the buggies and cars parked in the mercantile's lot.

"Phoebe and Gail are working in my place. I wouldn't miss this for the world."

He wanted to hug her, but this was too public a place. "Jah, it would take two people to replace you, Abby. But I'm glad you're here. If I stumble over my tongue, I can look at you and I won't be so nervous."

Within the next few minutes, Vernon Gingerich was hitching his horse to the post beside the mercantile, and Mervin and Bessie Mast pulled in, as well. Emma was stepping out the front door with their parents, too, as Mamm and Dat had been buzzing like bees all morning. Everyone exchanged greetings as they placed their lawn chairs or blankets close to the shanty. James's heart swelled: where else on earth would folks be so excited for him?

"Here you go, Dat," he said as he took a lawn chair from Emma and set it next to the door. "We'll put you here with your better ear closer to the phone—"

"And don't you be yackin' with anybody or interruptin' James while he's talkin' with that reporter lady," his mother instructed with a shake of her finger. "If you start actin' up, I've told Emma she's to march you right back to the house, mister!"

James winced. His poor father found few enough activities to enjoy these days, now that his close friend Paul had passed, and it seemed his mother's tongue cut sharper with each passing week. He and Emma exchanged a knowing look, and as his sister settled between their parents on a folding stool, he was pleased that Abby stood behind her. Although she never complained, Emma didn't get nearly enough time to chat with Abby or her other friends these days.

The ringing of the phone made everyone sit up in anticipation. James slipped into the chair and closed his eyes. *Lord, let this be a chance to hold up our Plain ways so the outside world understands us better. And please don't let me say anything stupid.*

He picked up the phone and let out the breath he'd been holding. "Jah, hullo? This is James Graber speaking."

"James, it's such a pleasure to talk with you. This is Lacey Piranelli from *Town and Country*, and I can't tell you how excited everyone here is that you've agreed to an interview." She sounded young and energetic, but sincerely interested in whatever he might say.

"Everyone here in Cedar Creek's excited, too," he replied. "Several of them are gathered around to listen while I talk to you."

"And is your bishop there? That was a very good idea, requesting the questions in advance, as it gives me a way to learn more about Amish ways without unwittingly offending you."

"Vernon's here, jah."

"And who else is with you? I think it's fascinating that your friends and family are sharing this experience with you, James," she said with a lilt in her voice. "It speaks to a very special bond you Amish share."

"Jah, there's that," he said, pleased at the direction this conversation was taking. "My parents, Merle and Eunice Graber, and my sister Emma are here, and our friends Mervin and Bessie Mast, and Vernon Gingerich, our bishop—"

"Sounds like you've got quite a group."

"Jah, and here comes my gut friend Matt Lambright, who raises sheep across the road from our place, and his sister Abby is here, too," he added, enjoying the way her face lit up when he mentioned her name. "Abby has a seamstress business in the loft of her brother Sam's mercantile, and we've known each other all our lives. That's how it is here in Cedar Creek, you see. Our roots go deep, on land that belonged to our dats and their dats before that."

"So how did you get started building carriages, James?" Lacey went on. "You've told me you built that white princess carriage yourself, using very few factory-produced parts. You don't sound old enough to have mastered such a craft."

As James explained about his apprenticeship with Pete Beachey when he was fourteen, the words flowed like Cedar Creek, rippling along on their own easy current. His parents looked so tuned in and interested. Abby stood with her hands on Emma's shoulders, silently cheering him on—just as older folks like Vernon and the Masts were. Noah Coblentz moseyed over and sat cross-legged in the grass and then Leon Mast joined his parents. Perry Bontrager arrived with his young son Eli riding on his shoulders.

As Lacey asked him about building his carriages and about everyday Plain life in Cedar Creek, James sensed that this reporter from New York City wasn't really so different from the young women he'd grown up around. Sure, she had a job with a big-time magazine and she probably drove a fancy car. Yet she spoke of growing up with siblings and the importance of going to church with her fiancé—the same Christian faith and traditions his family and friends honored, but in a different setting.

"Well, it's been mighty nice talking to you," he said as she wrapped up her remarks.

"I've enjoyed it, too, James. Can you believe an hour and a half has passed?"

James hung up, gazing at the friends and family gathered at the phone shanty. "Well, I wouldn't want to give interviews every day, but it was gut to discuss our ways and the work of our hands with an English gal who respects them."

His father chortled. "Can't say as I ever talked to a woman for that long in my life," he remarked. "But sometimes your mother carries on for that long, and I don't get a word in edgewise. Does that count?"

"Merle Moses Graber!" his mamm retorted as she glared through her thick glasses. "We were goin' along just fine without you sayin' that!"

The Masts and the bishop said their good-byes, while Emma folded the lawn chairs. "I'll be in for supper in a few," James told his sister, and as most of the folks headed into the mercantile to shop, he gazed at Abby. "Did I do all right? I was too caught up in following her quick way of speaking to notice how folks were reacting."

"You sounded real gut, James," Matt replied. "Made me proud to be living in Cedar Creek, the way you talked about us."

Abby beamed at him. "I thought it was a wonderful-gut chat, James. Bless them, your parents were hanging on every word. I hope that reporter sends us a copy of the article she writes."

"She said she would, jah." James relaxed, satisfied by the way his unusual afternoon had gone. "Denki for taking a break from your work to listen in. You could've sewn up a couple of dresses in that time, no doubt."

Abby shrugged. "And who amongst us couldn't go a couple of hours without a new dress? I will get back to the store, though, as it looks like Sam and the girls might be awfully busy now."

James watched her walk toward the entry to the Cedar Creek Mercantile, gratified because Abby wouldn't give him anything but her honest opinion. This being Saturday, and with tomorrow being a non-preaching Sunday, he tried to think of someplace he and Abby might enjoy themselves this evening. It seemed like a chance to celebrate his recent orders and today's interview, because, after all, hadn't God provided such opportunities for him?

"James, might I have a word?" a familiar voice behind him asked.

He turned, smiling at Perry Bontrager. The lanky fellow with the bushy black beard had been in his class at school, had apprenticed in Pete Beachey's shop with him, and had then come to work in Graber's Custom Carriages when James had started up nearly ten years ago. "It was nice of you and Eli to spend your afternoon off listening to me rattle on about the rigs we build," he said. "I should've handed you the phone. You're every bit the carriage maker I am."

Perry's expression wavered. "I—well, that's partly what I wanted to talk about," he said in a tight voice. "After all the years of working for you, it's—it's not an easy thing for me to say, James, but I've gotten an offer on Dat's land. Salome's always had a hankering to live closer to her family over toward Clearwater, so now we've got our chance to go."

James's heart thudded like an anvil being whacked with a mallet. "You—you'd leave Cedar Creek?" he rasped, glancing at Matt for support. "But how will you make your living there, Perry?"

Matt's eyes lit up with surprised interest, while Perry's smile went sideways. "Well, you just said I'm a pretty gut carriage maker, ain't so? Always a call for that kind of work in Plain settlements, and the fella there's about ready to hang up his hammer," he explained in a low rush. "I can take over his shop, equipment and all, he says. And selling off Dat's land will pay for that place and leave enough money to build us a bigger house."

James blinked, reeling as this information sank in. "So—where'll you live in the meantime? What with Salome nearly ready to deliver—"

"Her mamm and dat are ready to shift into their dawdi haus, so it'll be a lot like living here with Dat. Except I'll have my own shop." Perry's smile wanted to break out like the sun from behind clouds, for what man didn't want to own his own business? Yet he glanced at the ground and shifted young Eli to his other hip. "I feel bad about leavin' when you've taken on all that new business, James. But it'd be best to get Salome settled in with her folks before this baby comes."

"Jah, I understand that, Perry."

"And what with these details comin' together so quick-like, with a few phone calls, I feel like it's the hand of God movin' us forward," Perry continued earnestly. "Before now, I wasn't even considerin' a move, but—well, it's too gut an opportunity, close to family, to pass it up."

James felt the blood was draining from his head. Yet what could he say? Perry sounded like he'd made all the right decisions . . . had a new life falling into place just days after he'd buried his dat. "Well, then, gut luck to you and may God bless."

"Denki, James. I'll stay on for another couple weeks, if that's all right."

"Jah, that would be gut." James gazed down the county blacktop toward the rolling hills of the Bontrager place. "So who's to be our new neighbors?"

Perry gave James another lopsided smile and then he gazed at Matt. "I'm guessin' neither of you have heard the latest. Titus Yutzy made me this offer after Dat's funeral, and I gave him my answer this morning. He'll be bringin' his flock here to Cedar Creek— partnering with you, Matt, the way I understand it."

"So we're gut to go?" Matt threw his straw hat up in the air, letting out a yell of pure joy. "This means that— Well, I hope Rosemary'll come with him, but either way I've got my work cut out for me, ain't so? Wait till the folks hear *this*!"

Off he ran, up Lambright Lane toward the house, as excited as James had ever seen him. And rightly so. It seemed that for Matt, a lot of hopes and dreams had just come true. Little Eli kicked and laughed in his dat's arms, as though he wanted to get down and race Matt up the driveway.

"Well, I'd best get along home to supper," Perry said as he held more tightly to his wiggly son. "Lots to talk about. Lots to do in a little bit of time."

"Jah, you've got that right." As James watched Perry hike home with his young son riding high on his shoulders, he felt like a deflated balloon. All the fine energy from the successful interview had fizzled out, and the excitement Matt and Perry felt was lost on him as he made his way across the road toward home.

At least Mamm and Dat weren't here to hear this news, but it'll get out soon enough. If I'd known about Perry's move a few days ago . . .

James gazed at the sign that said GRABER'S CUSTOM CARRIAGES across the top of his shop. What a joy it had been to declare himself his own boss at the age of twenty. As his parents' only son, he'd been pleased to support his family with the skills he'd learned and the abilities God had given him.

He prayed now for help in meeting the challenges ahead of him and for some insight into what special plan God had in mind for him.

Chapter 18

After a few moments of silent thanks before their evening meal on Friday, Titus reached eagerly for the platter of hamburger steaks. "Well, it's official! Perry Bontrager's sellin' me his dat's land. They'll be moved out by the first of June—well before Salome has her baby."

Rosemary's jaw dropped. Today was May 1, so did that mean Titus planned to be out of this house in just four weeks? So much for her second-guessing about why this sale would never go through.

Beth Ann's fork clattered to her plate and she burst into tears. "But, Dat, that means I have to leave all my friends and—and I won't know anybody in—"

"But you get to finish out the school year here, daughter. We'll not be moving until the new place is ready for the sheep, after all," Titus replied.

Wasn't it just like a man to put his livestock before his daughter's feelings? Rosemary took a thick onion-studded hamburger steak and then handed the platter across to Beth Ann. "Well, this way you'll have the summer to meet new friends around Cedar Creek before school starts in the fall," she said gently. "And Ruthie Lambright will be glad you're moving across the road from her, too. Didn't seem to be a lot of girls her age in that community."

"Seems to me your wish about living closer to the mercantile has just come true," Titus added as he piled mashed potatoes on his plate. "Busy as that store is, you might even get hired on someday."

Beth Ann's chin quivered, but she knew better than to do any more crying at the table. She cut a piece of meat in half, leaving the other half on the platter, and took only a small spoonful of potatoes. "So . . . what's to happen to this house, then? And to Rosemary's land?"

Rosemary silently thanked her young sister-in-law for asking that question. While it was good to see Joe's dat looking so pleased with the way his plans were coming together, she and Beth Ann would have to handle all the practical details, such as packing and redding up this big old house for the final time—and, of course, getting the Bontrager house ready to move into. Right now, those tasks seemed overwhelming. She spooned some mashed potatoes onto Katie's plate and put the little fork into her daughter's hand with a purposeful look.

"I've got some visiting to do tomorrow," Titus continued with a mysterious lift to his eyebrows. "At my age, I don't want to take on a mortgage, so I'm selling out. Starting fresh—but the new place will be paid for in full."

He looked pointedly at Rosemary as he handed her the bowl of peas and carrots. "Do what you want to with your property, but whoever buys this place might offer you a fair price for your land, as well. Or do you really figure on staying behind, building that house you and Joe got the blueprints for?"

Rosemary nearly dropped the vegetable bowl. Titus's abrupt tone told her he was more interested in knowing whether he'd have a housekeeper in Cedar Creek than he was concerned about her future. Or was that an unfair assumption? Was she hearing this whole conversation through her dismay at the prospect of moving so far from her own family and friends—and on such short notice?

"Maybe that depends on the offer I get for my land," she hedged. It wasn't fair that Titus had information he wasn't sharing, yet he expected her to give an answer that would determine her entire future. "Who do you have in mind to talk with? Joe paid a gut price for our ground, buying it from an English fella, but that doesn't mean I'll let it go cheap just because an Amish buyer thinks he'll be doing me a favor, taking it off my hands."

Titus's eyes widened. "You could show some gratitude for the home you'll have in Cedar Creek, Rosemary. You'll be closer to Lois's shop, where you can sell your pies. Not to mention living right across the road from a young fella who wants to get hitched."

Beth Ann's eyes got as wide as saucers. "You and Matt Lambright are gonna get married?"

"NO!" It was all Rosemary could do to stay at the table. How had this conversation strayed so far down this path, and so fast? "Your dat is jumping the gun, just like he seems to forget that I came here of my own accord to help out."

Beth Ann's wavering expression warned Rosemary to tread carefully. Her own feelings weren't the only ones she had to consider. "While it's true you both welcomed me into your home," she went on, cutting chunks of hamburger steak for Katie, "I have my mamm and sister to consider. Just like it will be hard for you to move away from folks you've known all your life, Beth Ann, going to Cedar Creek will mean I'll be leaving my family and friends behind, as well."

"But . . . but without you, Rosemary, we won't be a family."

The kitchen got very quiet. Beth Ann's wistful words hung over the table like a rain cloud. Titus looked ready to reprimand his daughter, but Rosemary held up her hand. Oh, but this was a prickly patch of nettles they had strayed into, and she had no idea how to get out of it gracefully . . . lovingly. She had seen this crossroads from a distance, as though she'd been driving a buggy, looking for the turn-off to a place she'd never been. Now that she'd reached the intersection of Move Forward and Stay Put, the decision loomed larger than she had anticipated. And her choice would affect Beth Ann and Titus as much as it would determine her own future.

"We will always be a family, Beth Ann," she said. "But just like you'll someday meet a fella and move out of the house to start another branch on the family tree, I have choices to make for Katie and me that might shoot us off in a different direction. Sometimes we lose branches in a storm and sometimes we grow new ones, but it's still the same sturdy tree."

Titus sat back. He looked grateful for the way she'd framed her answer. "I'm seeing this as a chance to get back to my roots—a fresh start, even at my age." He ladled gravy over his meat and potatoes. "I suppose it's only fair to Joe's memory—to the investment he made in that piece of ground—to see what offers you get before you make your decision, Rosemary. But as for me and my house," he quipped, rephrasing the verse from the book of Joshua, "we'll be moving to Cedar Creek when the Bontrager place is emptied out."

"As well you should. Seems like the whole situation has come about mighty fast," she replied. "I'm happy for you."

For the rest of the meal an uneasy peace prevailed. Titus seemed intent on eating twice his usual amount while Beth Ann drew her fork through her potatoes and gravy, lost in thought.

"Mama! More!" Katie crowed, pointing to the bread basket.

As she buttered another slice of the bread she'd baked that morning, it struck Rosemary that *more* was exactly what they all needed right now. Beth Ann craved more love and attention at a difficult time in her young life, while Titus wanted more companionship from old friends and his new partner, Matt.

And what do you want more of?

The question lingered in Rosemary's mind after Titus went out to do his sheep chores, as she and Beth Ann washed the dishes.

Would God think she was ungrateful for all He had given her, if she wanted a life of her own choosing? Did God, like Titus, figure that as a woman, she should be happy with whatever the men in her life provided for her?

"Guess I'll finish our new jackets," Beth Ann murmured as she draped the dish towels over the drying rack. "Sounds like I'll be packing up my room pretty quick, with no time to sit at the sewing machine for a while."

"Jah, we'll be plenty busy, you and I, getting ready for whatever comes next." Rosemary stood in front of Joe's little sister, squeezing her shoulders. "Your dat acts like it's all to be smooth sailing and moving forward, but he'll hit a few bumps come time to leave this house," she said softly. "No matter what happens, though—no matter whether I go to Cedar Creek or stay here—I love you, Beth Ann. And you can talk to me whenever you need to. I'd miss it a lot if we couldn't do things together."

So why would you leave me? Beth Ann's forlorn eyes seemed to ask.

It was a question that would torment Rosemary until she made her final decision to go or stay.

Beth Ann went upstairs, and within moments Rosemary heard the steady whirring of the treadle sewing machine in the spare bedroom above her. Meanwhile Katie had opened the lower cabinet door to haul out the pots and pans, but Rosemary wasn't in any mood to hear her banging on them. "Outside we go, punkin," she said as she scooped her daughter into her arms. "Let's cut the lettuce and spinach. And who knows? Maybe the bunnies will be playing in the garden."

"Bunnies?" Katie's face lit up, and Rosemary laughed. She plucked her baskets from the mudroom shelf, and as she stepped outside into the early-evening sunshine, she felt better. Planting loud, playful kisses all over her giggling daughter's face lifted her spirits, too, and when she set Katie down she marveled at how much steadier those little legs had become. Her toddler took off across the yard, squealing when a rabbit sprang from behind the leafy rhubarb plants at the garden's edge.

What a difference it made, getting out of the house, after baking and delivering her pies this morning and her terse conversation with Titus. It seemed the rows of carrots, beets, lettuce, and onions had grown taller since the last time she'd worked in the garden, and the recent rain had made the weeds pop up. As Rosemary cut the tallest leaf lettuce, she heard the phone ringing. Ordinarily, she might let the caller leave a voice mail, yet after receiving so many surprises over supper, something prodded her up off her knees. She sprinted to the shanty and grabbed the receiver. "Jah, hullo?" she said breathlessly.

"Rosemary, it's Abby Lambright. I'm glad I caught you close to the phone."

Who wouldn't feel better, hearing that happy voice? "Well, I'm glad, too, Abby. How are you?"

"We're all gut here, thanks—and we've got some plans brewing for a sewing frolic next Saturday." Abby paused for a moment. "You probably know by now that Salome Bontrager's got a baby due in August—and that she and Perry plan to move soon."

"Jah, I've heard about that, all right."

"Well, we're making it one big get-together for all the neighbor gals, sewing baby clothes and a new quilt here at the house. We'd love for you and Beth Ann to join us," Abby continued in an excited rush. "I thought it might be a gut way for you two to get better acquainted here in Cedar Creek. And truth be told . . ."

Abby apparently assumed Rosemary had decided to move to the Bontrager house with Titus. That aside, wouldn't a sewing frolic be a fine way to spend time with Beth Ann, doing what she loved best?

". . . Matt was already thinking of coming your way for a visit with Titus about his sheep," Abby went on. "So he'd be willing to leave here bright and early, pick you girls up, and then drive you back to Queen City after supper that evening."

That meant Matt would be in for a very long day, and spending nearly eight hours of it on the road. But that was his choice, wasn't it? "Is this your sly way of putting Matt and me together again?"

Laughter erupted from the receiver. "You saw right through me, then?" Abby teased. "But honestly, Mamm and I had been looking for a gut time to host a party for Salome, and with all that's happened for the Bontragers—and for you—these past couple of days, we thought we'd better have our frolic sooner rather than later."

"Mighty nice of you to think of us, Abby," Rosemary murmured.

"And why not have Beth Ann bring those strips for the rag rug her mamm was going to make?" Abby continued. "Zanna will be here, and there's nobody better for showing Beth Ann how to crochet those strips into a pretty piece she can remember her mother by."

Rosemary's heart welled up with so much gratitude, she gripped the phone to keep from crying. "Abby, that's the sweetest, most thoughtful idea. It was awfully nice of you to think of Beth Ann this way. What time should we be waiting for Matt?"

"He'll probably be there by eight, eager as he is to see you." Abby laughed softly. "I've told him to take it a little slower, to give you time to adjust to all these changes in your life, but—well, Matt will be Matt, ain't so?"

Yes, Matt *would* be Matt. But before Rosemary had to fend off his exuberance again, she would spend a week clearing out closets . . . pondering the big decisions about where she would live and what she wanted to do with her life now. And didn't a sewing frolic sound like a better way to spend next Saturday than packing?

"We'll be ready to go when he gets here," Rosemary replied. "And, Abby, denki so much for this invitation. You've just made my week a whole lot brighter."

Chapter 19

Matt wondered if he looked totally idiotic as he clapped the reins lightly on his horse's back, but he couldn't help himself. After a brief assessment of the flock that Titus would be moving, Matt was leaving the Yutzy place on a sunny Saturday morning with Rosemary seated beside him, and he'd never felt so grand. Sure, Beth Ann and Katie sat behind them in the buggy, but if their presence made Rosemary more comfortable, he was fine with that.

And wasn't this what it felt like to drive a family around? It could be *his* family someday. He guided the horse onto the county road, looking for a good start to a conversation.

"It was a nice surprise last week, to get Abby's invitation to the frolic," Rosemary said, sitting primly against the far side of the seat, hands clasped in the folds of her black dress and apron.

"Truth be told, I was happy to get out of the house and come for you," Matt confessed. "Dat and I will be making ourselves scarce while you hens—er, you *girls*—do your sewing and chitchatting."

"Gut thing, too. Gives us more of a chance to talk about you while you're not around. Not that we'd gossip, of course," she added.

She was keeping a straight face, but oh, Rosemary's green eyes had a special glimmer when she teased him this way! Matt shifted so his thigh nearly touched her skirt . . . wanting to sit closer, yet aware they had an audience. "Meanwhile, we fellas will be helping Perry get his equipment out of the sheds," he said. "That also involves making decisions about what to do with his dat's woodworking tools and lumber left from his cabinetmaking, in that shop behind the house."

"Jah, we'll have that on our end, too," Rosemary said more solemnly. "Won't be easy for the Bontragers or for us, moving away from homes full of memories and belongings of people who won't be going with us. But we'll figure that out. We'll handle it, come time."

Matt was sorry he'd introduced a topic that had made Rosemary's sunshine duck behind a cloud. They rode in silence for several moments.

"Matt? Matt!" Katie piped up behind them.

He turned to grin at her. She was perched on the seat beside Beth Ann, watching him intently.

"Matt, hi!" she said, waving her hand.

"Hi yourself, Miss Katie. It's gut to see you this morning," he replied. Who wouldn't be captivated by this little pixie in her dress the color of a butterscotch pie?

"Puppies?" she replied hopefully.

"Jah, Panda and Pearl are back home, watching the sheep," he said with a nod. "They'll be glad to see you."

"Me, too." She stuck a finger in her mouth, fixing him with her gaze.

Rosemary chuckled. "Katie went running out into the yard and scared up a bunny in the rhubarb patch yesterday. That was exciting."

"Jah, we've had to shoo the bunnies from Mamm's garden, too," Matt said. "The dogs love to chase after them in the pasture. Which do you like better, Katie? Bunnies or puppies? Or kitties? We have barn kitties, too, you know."

"I love bunnies," the little girl sang as she began to rock from side to side. "I love puppies . . . I love kitties. And I love *you*, Matt!"

His heart leaped up into his throat. How did he reply to that without making Rosemary or Beth Ann feel awkward?

And why are you worried about them? Hasn't this little girl just wrapped you around her finger—and her heart?

Matt let out the breath he'd been holding, giving the only reply that made sense. "And I love you, too, Katie. Wherever you go, you're a ray of sunshine."

She giggled. "Jah. I know."

Beth Ann grabbed her playfully in the crook of her elbow, and it struck him how close the two of them must be . . . Most likely, things were pretty quiet for a young lady of twelve, out there on Titus's place. As the girls tussled, he turned his attention to Rosemary again. She was looking into the distance, maybe because Katie's declaration of affection had startled her. "You've got yourself quite a little sugar pie there," he murmured. "One of these days you'll be beating off the boys with a stick."

"It's too soon to be thinking about that," Rosemary declared. "Just got her out of diapers not so long ago, and—but I don't suppose a fellow like you has reason to talk about such things."

"Puh! Zanna brings Harley over nearly every day, you know. I'm not saying I know how to pin a diaper on him, but I can sure tell when it's time to pass him off to his mamm again."

When Rosemary burst out laughing, Matt suddenly felt like fireworks were *pop-pop-popping* in his soul, in bright colors that climbed higher with each ecstatic beat of his heart. Rosemary's cheeks glowed, and it was easy to imagine her sitting beside him in a summer dress in a pretty color with an apron and kapp of white rather than black.

"So now you know what you'd be getting yourself into, if you took up with the likes of me," he remarked. "A little rough around the edges and maybe wet behind the ears, but sincere. And trainable—mostly."

Oh, how his insides quivered when Rosemary looked at him. "We'll see about that."

Matt got so lost in a romantic fog, he wasn't sure how they arrived in Cedar Creek and drove up Lambright Lane. But he knew the next ride with Rosemary couldn't come soon enough.

Rosemary listened to the many conversations going on in the Lambrights' large front room. Barbara had taken down some partitions, as they did for church, to allow space for large tables where some of the neighbor ladies were cutting pieces of bright-colored calicos. This had also opened up the room where the sewing machine was, and Treva sat there seaming cut pieces into a Friendship Star design for a quilt top that was already coming together beautifully.

Abby smiled at Rosemary. "We told Salome the frolic started this afternoon, and meanwhile these gals came over with their fabric scraps." With one swift, firm motion, she drew the rotary cutter over several layers of marked calico. "So by the time Salome gets here, figuring we're having a baby shower—which we are—we'll have a pretty quilt top for *her*, too, made by all of us here in Cedar Creek."

"What a wonderful-gut gift." Rosemary stacked the triangles Abby had just cut. "Something new, yet made from pieces that belonged to all her friends here. And why do I suppose *you* were behind this idea, Abby?"

Her friend shrugged as she arranged fabric pieces for another couple of cuts. "Perfect way to visit while we make a quilt that would've taken any one of us several weeks—for a gal we'll all miss," she added.

Rosemary glanced over toward the corner where Zanna sat between Beth Ann and Ruthie, patiently demonstrating the technique of crocheting braided rugs with a large plastic hook. Little Harley wiggled in his infant seat on the floor, laughing as Katie held a stuffed patchwork puzzle ball beyond his reach—and then quickly tickled his face with it.

Rosemary's heart swelled. "Now, there's a sight to see. Look at how fast Beth Ann's catching on to rug making."

Her young sister-in-law's face glowed as she nimbly crocheted the first length of braid, which would form the center of her rug. Her slender wrists and fingers found their rhythm quickly, stitch after stitch. Zanna nodded her encouragement while she crocheted another strip so Ruthie could see the movements again.

"I figured it would be that way," Abby said. "Ruthie was so glad Beth Ann would be here today—and it's gut for Zanna to share her skill, too. She and Jonny were to be visiting some Ropp cousins, collecting a few more wedding gifts today, but everyone there had a stomach bug. So they came home last night."

"No need for them, or Harley, to be catching whatever that was," Rosemary agreed, handing Abby another stack of fabric pieces marked with the template for the design's center square. "I'm glad Beth Ann could start this rug, too, now that she'll be leaving the home where her mamm lived. She's had some tough moments since Titus broke the news."

She focused again on the fabric pieces Abby had cut, matching up four triangles and a square of the same color, which Treva would join with ivory triangles to form a finished block. Just as all the various colors the local women had brought from their scrap baskets would look fresh and cheerful when the blocks of the Friendship Star quilt were sewn together and pressed, so it was with the community of women here in Cedar Creek. Their personalities and ages and situations differed from one household to the next, but when they came together in a common purpose, they formed a warm comforter big enough to cover everyone in town.

Rosemary's heart stilled. These women were no different from her friends in Queen City. They loved to sew, and they loved to help their neighbors—mostly while they talked. And they had already included her in their circle . . .

Considering how she spent most of her days in a quiet house with Katie, the noise level here was amazing. Rosemary recognized many of the faces she'd seen at Zanna's wedding and Preacher Paul's funeral. "Let me see if I'm remembering names and connections," she said. "Zanna's your younger sister, and the lady at the sewing machine is your mother, Treva, who owns the greenhouse out by the road."

"Jah," Abby confirmed. "So who're the gals at the table with your aunt Lois?" Abby asked, testing her.

Rosemary thought for a moment. "The one in the thick glasses lives across the blacktop—Eunice, isn't it?"

"Right again. She's James and Emma's mamm."

"And then there's Bessie Mast in the teal dress, and Beulah Mae Nissley—Preacher Abe's wife, who runs the other café—and Adah Ropp."

"And that's Emma, with the light brown hair, sitting beside Mary and Martha Coblentz," Abby continued, gesturing to the table beside the one where the older ladies sat. "The twins are easy to remember on account of their red hair. So, see? You're getting us all down pat, Rosemary."

Abby again drew the rotary cutter over her stack of fabric, forming more squares. "I hope that makes you feel gut about coming here. You'll be just as uprooted as Beth Ann when Titus moves—maybe more so, since you've lived in that area all your life," she added softly.

Something made Rosemary stop before insisting that she could stay behind in Queen City if she chose. While Abby, as a single woman with her own home, would understand that idea better than most, Rosemary decided to ride on this wave of contentment . . . this gathering of souls who served the Lord today by making a quilt for a friend who was leaving them. "We'll all have our difficult moments," she remarked, "because, for sure and for certain, we'll find unexpected reminders of Joe and Alma while we're packing up."

"Jah, that's why Matt and Sam and the other fellas are over at the Bontragers', helping Perry deal with his dat's equipment," Abby remarked. "Moving from one place to another gets overwhelming if you take it on by yourself. It's a gift to have the help of friends. And it's a lesson we all need to learn, about accepting that help."

Rosemary pulled a large piece of thistle-colored twill from the box on the floor. While Abby wasn't pointing any fingers, her comment felt like a shoe that had grown too tight. It had been a while since she'd allowed anyone to help her. She stayed too busy, proving she could handle life's major changes all by herself . . .

At the table next to theirs, three women about Abby's age had gathered to cut and hem flat diapers from bird's-eye cotton. "I don't know how we're gonna manage if the lot falls to Carl to be the new preacher," the woman with black hair remarked as her needle flew along a diaper's hem. "It's all he can do now, what with farming for the Grabers and Pete Beachey and raising his ducks for specialty restaurants." Her brow puckered as her voice rose. "And now that Perry's moving, Titus Yutzy has asked Carl to work up more of those fields and plant them in pasture grasses as soon as he can get to it. He's got no time to learn how to preach, believe me."

"That's Marian Byler," Abby murmured into Rosemary's ear. "She makes the scented soaps we sell in the mercantile, and her little baby's name is Bessie. And beside her is Hannah Hartzler, Mose's wife, and Eva Detweiler. They were all in my class in school."

Rosemary nodded, still listening to the three women with her other ear. "I can understand their concern," she murmured. "Preaching is a big job and it takes a lot of time."

"Jah, it's the same with my Mose," Hannah agreed as she laid out another length of the cotton to cut more diapers. "What with his chimney sweeping and doing tuck-pointing and masonry repair when he's not laying brick for Amos Coblentz, he's not home enough to study up for preaching—not that I could see him standing in front of folks to deliver the message of a Sunday morning," she added wryly. "He'd be so scared, he'd jump out of his skin!"

Hannah's two companions laughed loudly enough to attract the attention of the other women in the room.

"Same could be said for my Zeke," Eva Detweiler chimed in as she snipped a thread. "That man catches himself coming and going, installing dairy equipment in Clearwater and Bloomingdale—and everywhere in between. And now that Joel's too big for me to heft in and out of his wheelchair, well—" Eva's slender face furrowed with concern. "Seems the Lord has already given us plenty enough work, and we've got more expensive surgeries in the future for our son. I'm hoping nobody mentions Zeke's name to the bishop when he sets up for the drawing of the lot."

"You know who I think would make a gut preacher? Sam Lambright!" Hannah declared. "Takes a fella with some age and experience to lead a congregation."

Adah Ropp, who was carrying cut squares and triangles for Treva to sew, countered the idea. "Jah, but with Vernon and Abe getting up in years, we might do better having a younger fella—"

"But it's no different for Sam," Marian pointed out. "Who'll mind the mercantile while he's tending to folks who need confession? Or—"

"Zeke says the men are in a stew about picking a new preacher, too." Eva spoke shrilly above the other ladies. "True enough, when a man marries, he vows to accept the role of preacher or deacon if the lot falls to him. But when you're young, you've got no idea what you're agreeing to."

Rosemary noticed that Abby had stopped cutting quilt pieces as she followed this conversation. She wasn't surprised when her friend stood up, clasping her hands in front of her crisp white apron. "Ladies, we've got no reason to wear ourselves into a frazzle over picking a preacher."

Abby had by no means raised her voice, yet her tone quieted the entire room. All hands went still. Treva stopped pumping the treadle of her sewing machine. The three young women at the next table looked a little sheepish, but they turned in their chairs to hear what Abby would say next.

"It's a wonderful-gut thing, the way the *Ordnung* maps out our path when it comes to important matters of our faith," she continued. Her voice projected the same warmth and confidence that shone on her face as she spoke to the roomful of women. "And it's best for everyone—men and women alike—that God chooses our leaders, ain't so? Who among us could possibly pick the best replacement for Paul Bontrager? And who would serve, or let her husband serve, if we allowed our personal concerns and excuses to pile up?"

A lot of the women had lowered their eyes. Rosemary noticed, however, that no one looked ready to challenge Abby's opinion. Instead, each of them had been moved to consider what she'd just said.

"Jah, my excuse pile gets mighty high some days," Adah remarked.

"I'd be a lot better off if I let God do His job—every single day," Zanna said from her spot in the corner. "And it's a gut thing I don't have to pay His wages, too. My rug money wouldn't go far!"

Rosemary chuckled with the others. "It's like when we take on caring for folks in our extended families," she ventured. "We can't think about the cost—or the wages that go by the wayside—in the case of a fellow being picked as a preacher. We trust that God will see to everyone's needs when we can't and that He'll provide us the best opportunities to grow in our faith. Even when we don't much feel like growing, jah?"

Where had that sentiment come from? And why had she felt compelled to share it in this roomful of women she barely knew? Rosemary wasn't sure about those answers, and yet . . . most of the gals around her were nodding.

"You said a mouthful, Rosemary," Abby remarked. "A new friend's voice can refresh us like a breath of springtime."

"Jah." Beulah Mae Nissley spoke up. "Sometimes we don't realize how we gripe about the same worries day in and day out—not that it improves our lives any. With Titus taking over the Bontrager place, bringing you three girls along, why, we'll not be missing Preacher Paul's family nearly so much."

"Gettin' an old friend back amongst us, too," Bessie Mast joined in with an enthusiastic nod. "We'll not be concerned about the new folks in town being somebody we don't know, or English snapping up our land. It's a blessing all around, your coming to Cedar Creek, Rosemary."

"Matt could've told you that, Bessie!" Ruthie piped up from her corner.

Rosemary felt the heat rising into her face, yet it seemed everyone gazed at her with a whole new interest. How long had it been since she'd felt so welcome—even if these women seemed to know a lot more about her situation than she knew about theirs? True enough, they assumed she would be coming along with Titus and probably didn't realize she had the option to build her own house. Yet once again she didn't feel like bringing up that subject.

"Seems to me we've got another frolic or two in our futures," Barbara said from the kitchen doorway. "What with the Yutzys moving into a different home, wouldn't it be nice if they had fresh curtains and quilts and rugs?"

"What a gut idea! I'll hold a sewing frolic," Zanna offered. "It'll be a chance for all of you to come see our new house."

"I'm thinking a bunch of us could make quick work of painting over there, too, once Salome and Perry have moved out," Phoebe said, grinning in Rosemary's direction. "It'll be a snap with all the furniture gone. And Owen's got the ladders and tools we'd need, too."

"I love to paint," her sister Gail chimed in. "It'll be a painting party!"

"I'm in on that one," one of the redheaded Coblentz twins volunteered, and her sister beside her said, "Jah. I'd rather be rolling paint on a wall than trying to keep itty-bitty quilting stitches looking the way they're supposed to."

"And if we do these frolics after the lot falls to the new preacher, think about what all we'll have to talk about," Eunice Graber remarked in her reedy voice. "I can't climb a paintin' ladder no more, just like I can't see gut enough to quilt. But I can chat with the best of ya."

Friendly laughter filled the big room, and it seemed to Rosemary that within the last few moments her attitude, and maybe her whole future, had shifted in a wonderful way. How had that happened? While Abby had set up today's frolic out of the kindness of her heart, she couldn't possibly have planned the generous suggestions that would transform the house on the Bontrager place into the Yutzys' new home.

"Come fill your plates," Barbara suggested, waving them all toward the kitchen. "What with Salome feeding the men as thanks for helping Perry today, we've got ourselves an all-day hen party. Denki to all of you who brought dishes to share."

As they surged toward the door, where heavenly aromas of chicken and cheese and hot rolls welcomed them, Rosemary suddenly became the center of attention. Every woman present asked if she needed help packing and moving—or unpacking when their furniture got to Cedar Creek. Who would have dreamed that women she'd met only at a wedding and a funeral would offer to travel all the way to Queen City with boxes Sam had emptied in his store? As she took helpings from a variety of casseroles, salads, and goody trays, Rosemary couldn't recall the last time she'd felt so singled out for so many blessings.

Beth Ann, too, was having a fine time with Ruthie, Zanna, and Mary and Martha Coblentz—so caught up in their chitchat that she'd forgotten her qualms about leaving her school friends in Queen City. It was a sure sign she would do just fine in her new hometown when she scooped Katie to her hip and loaded her plate, talking to the younger girls without once sending a desperate look in Rosemary's direction.

They ate in the front room, everyone visiting back and forth while exclaiming over the chicken-potpie casserole, the cheesy hash browns with ham, and of course the sweet rolls with pineapple and cream cheese filling and the turtle brownies oozing with caramel and crunchy pecans. While Rosemary had enjoyed Zanna's wedding feast, this informal lunch with her new friends, seated around Barbara Lambright's front room, tasted better than anything she'd eaten in years.

As she joined those who were carrying their dirty plates and silverware toward the kitchen, Rosemary felt a hand on her elbow. "Emma!" she said. "I'm glad to finally meet you and chat a bit, since it seems we'll be neighbors before the summer's out."

Emma stepped out of the stream of women with her, to stand back beside the sewing machine where it was quieter. She studied Rosemary's face for a moment. "So—you're Matt's new girlfriend, are you?"

Emma's tone and question sounded rather abrupt, after hearing all the other women welcome her and offer to hold frolics. "Might be a little soon for saying that," Rosemary hedged. "You know how girls Ruthie and Beth Ann's age like to carry on when there's the least hint of a romance—"

"Just thought I'd give fair warning about what you might be letting yourself in for." Emma stood slightly taller than Rosemary, and she was taking advantage of every inch as she gazed down her nose. "You see, with Matt the grass is always greener on the other side of the fence. He's got an eye for gals who live anywhere other than Cedar Creek, so once you move here with Titus—well, things might change once you're on *my* side of the fence, Rosemary."

As Emma stepped toward the kitchen again, Rosemary had the feeling she'd just been taken down a peg or two by a young woman who'd wanted to win Matt's affections and now felt rejected. Was it true, what she'd hinted about Matt? Or had that been Emma's disappointment talking? As Rosemary listened to the cheerful chatter all around her, she decided not to let the old adage about greener grass and fences dampen the rest of her day. If Emma had a problem with Matt, well, it was *her* problem.

While Eunice Graber and Aunt Lois redded up the kitchen, Barbara mixed the punch and arranged plates of cookies for Salome's shower. The rest of them cut border strips from a bright fuchsia twill Abby had brought over from the mercantile, while Rosemary pressed the finished blocks of the Friendship Star quilt top so Treva could stitch them into rows. By two o'clock, the rows had all been joined and the outer border was sewn on. An entire top for a queen-sized quilt had been completed in a single morning.

As Phoebe and Gail held the upper corners high to display their project, Rosemary's heart beat joyfully. "What a beautiful gift!" she exclaimed. When Beth Ann looked up from her rag rug, she sprang from her chair to see the quilt top from a better distance.

"Oh, Rosemary," the girl murmured, grabbing her hand, "that mix of bright colors is like nothing we've ever had at our house. Mamm and her sisters always used up the old clothes for quilts and rugs."

Abby came up beside them, a sly smile lighting her face as she lifted the rug in Beth Ann's hand. It was rectangular, already more than a foot wide and two feet long. "Jah, and look at how far you've come with your mamm's fabric strips, too. And you just learned how to crochet them this morning!"

As all the other women complimented Beth Ann on her rug, Abby leaned toward Rosemary. "If you'll let me know which colors she likes best, I'll pick out the border fabric and the brightest of our remnants at the mercantile," she murmured. "It'll make the move easier if her new room has a fresh quilt and—"

"Oh, Abby," Rosemary exclaimed, "everyone's already done so much by setting up another sewing frolic, offering to help us pack, and organizing a painting party." Rosemary couldn't swallow the lump in her throat. "How can I ever repay you for so much kindness and—"

"You can accept our gifts in the spirit they're given."

"But at least let me buy the fabric for Beth Ann's quilt," she pleaded. "You've been such a gut friend to the both of us."

Abby shrugged. "Sam just got in a big shipment of cotton prints, so I have to clear out some of our older stock to make room. And besides," she added as she slung her arm around Rosemary's shoulder, "you've already given us a gift of yourself by focusing on the positive points of serving God. You're an inspiration to us all, you know—the way you took on Titus's household and raising his daughter."

Rosemary blinked. "I did what somebody had to do for Joe's family."

"You opened your heart where a lot of daughters-in-law wouldn't have," Abby pointed out. "You could've stayed with your mamm and your sister. Or you could've caved in to your grief. But you chose to *serve*," she insisted. "And meanwhile, because Beth Ann didn't have to run her dat's household at the age of twelve, she has a chance to be a young girl yet. That's quite a gift you've given her, Rosemary."

Again her heart thudded in her chest. When had anyone ever told her she'd made an important difference in someone's life? "Denki, Abby," she whispered. "And many thanks for making Beth Ann your special project, too."

Abby winked. "Just maybe I have an idea about how she can spend her summer, once she gets settled in her new home."

And what might that mean? Rosemary looked again at the beautiful quilt top as Phoebe and her sister draped it carefully over one of the long tables. Wasn't it a fine thing, what they had accomplished with the work of their hands?

When Salome Bontrager arrived with her young son and daughter, she couldn't say enough in praise of the quilt. Her gratitude and bittersweet tears struck a chord with Rosemary. She, too, felt caught between going and coming, standing with a foot still in the life she knew while stepping into an unknown future whether she was ready or not.

She knew now that she was moving to Cedar Creek. Just as the triangles and squares formed the blocks of that Friendship Star quilt—and just as the rows fit together with a balance of dark and bright colors, framed by a border the color of the redbuds in Matt's pasture—Rosemary's heart and soul had pieced together her decision before her mind could resist again. Abby and the other women had shown her a new vision of home, and she now believed she could live here quite happily, no matter how Emma Graber had tried to warn her away from Matt.

Rosemary wasn't going to tell Matt she'd made up her mind, though. How long would it take him to figure it out?

As the buggy headed down the county blacktop toward Queen City, Matt glanced over to where Katie had fallen asleep in Rosemary's lap, and then behind him, where Beth Ann was stretched out on the backseat with her eyes closed. He scooted closer to the woman who was making his pulse pound with curiosity and hope.

"You must've had a gut time at the frolic," he murmured near her ear. "Beth Ann has a nice chunk of rug to show for her day, but you . . . well, your face has a glow to it, like you know something now that you didn't realize when you came this morning."

Rosemary's lashes fluttered and she glanced away, confirming his impression that she was keeping a secret. "Must have been the turtle brownies," she hedged. "They were huge, but I had to have two . . . all that gushy caramel and nuts over that moist, chewy chocolate, you know?"

"I don't suppose you brought me one," Matt teased. "Even if you women left any, Dat will gobble them down before I get back."

"Too bad for you, ain't so?" When she widened her eyes at him, Matt's heart turned handsprings.

"Give me a taste, Rosemary. Katie and Beth Ann won't know."

Her breath caught when she realized his meaning. She glanced back at Beth Ann, who was now breathing deeply, and then cradled her daughter more closely. Even in her stark black kapp and dress, Rosemary was still the prettiest young woman he'd ever seen, yet she was a conscientious mother first and foremost. And he liked that about her, a lot. Matt checked to see that no cars were coming, wrapping the reins securely in one hand even though Cecil would hold his gait steady. Then, when Rosemary's eyes found his again, he didn't wait to be invited twice.

Matt eased his face closer to hers, holding his breath as her lips parted. He closed his eyes . . . got so caught up in the sweet softness of her mouth that all thoughts of chocolate and caramel left him. Rosemary wasn't just letting him kiss her, like some girls he'd dated; she was kissing him back.

A screech of tires and the blare of a horn made them spring apart. With the revving of its engine and a loud *whoosh*, a low-slung black car sped around them, honking again and again. It was all Matt could do to rein in his spooked horse, and as Cecil raced down the highway, Katie began to wail.

"What was *that*? What happened?" Beth Ann cried out as she sat up behind them.

Amid this chaos, however, it was Rosemary's expression that stabbed at Matt's heart. "Of all the nerve, to be going so fast—to get so close he nearly ran into us." She was clutching Katie, desperate to quiet the toddler's cries against her shoulder. She looked around the slowing carriage, wide-eyed with fear, and then focused on him. "My word, I lost track of what time it must be, and—well, it's nearly dark. Do you have your lights on, Matt?"

How had dusk fallen and he hadn't noticed? The answer, of course, was Rosemary . . . the woman with the softest, warmest lips he'd ever kissed. Matt flipped the toggle switch beneath the windshield, his pulse pounding with fear and guilt as the headlights beamed on. While that car had been traveling well above the speed limit for this stretch of blacktop, he knew better than to lose track of the road—and the light—that way. It went without saying that they all might have been killed . . .

He eased Cecil over to the shoulder and stopped the buggy. His mouth was so dry he could hardly speak. "I'm sorry," he rasped.

Rosemary let out a shuddery breath. "Me, too. That was a close one."

A strained silence hovered between them for the rest of the ride. He knew better than to hope for another kiss when they arrived at the Yutzy farm. Beth Ann hurried past him to get into the house—probably to tell Titus how they'd nearly been hit—and Rosemary hugged her daughter against her shoulder. "Denki for the ride, Matt," she murmured as she ascended the wooden stairs to the porch. When the screen door banged behind her, it had the sound of finality.

Matt stepped back up into the buggy, still shaken. It was going to be a long ride home—and a long time before he got back into Rosemary's good graces.

Chapter 20

Matt sat in the phone shanty, listening to the ringing . . . ringing . . . of the Yutzys' phone. How could he apologize again and get Rosemary talking to him if no one picked up? It would be so helpful to hear her voice, to regain the confidence he'd felt in her kiss—

A loud knocking on the windowpane startled him out of his thoughts. "This isn't your private phone, Matt," a familiar voice reminded him. "If it wouldn't be too much trouble, I'd like to make a call."

Emma was glaring at him through the glass. While it was no surprise that she was still angry, it wore on him that both she and Rosemary were upset with him.

"I've watched you come in here four times in the last hour," Emma continued in her impatient tone. "What's the problem? Is Rosemary not taking your calls now? Could it be she listened to my advice?"

Matt came up out of the wooden chair so fast it banged against the shanty's back wall. "That's not fair, Emma! I apologized to you, so— What'd you tell her?"

"That's none of your never-mind, now, is it?"

As she held his gaze, it saddened him to see the glint of vengefulness in her eyes. How had he gotten two young women crosswise enough to conspire against him? Matt sensed this conversation would go nowhere positive, so he walked away. Judging from the familiar horses and buggies hitched alongside the mercantile, it looked like a good place to hear basic male conversation.

As he stepped inside, he inhaled the heady scent of bulk grass seed and the dry tang of onions set in bins near the door. At this time in the afternoon, the large rooms of the mercantile were much dimmer than the bright sunlight outside, so he allowed his eyes to adjust as he listened to the ongoing discussion.

"Who do you suppose folks'll be naming as their choices for a new preacher, come time for the falling of the lot on Sunday?" Rudy Ropp asked as he loaded two salt blocks into his shopping cart.

Pete Beachey, their deacon, stood an aisle away, looking at mousetraps. "Better be one of our younger fellas, like Carl Byler or maybe Leon Mast. Gets to be hard on an older man's nerves—and his pocketbook—when he reaches the point he's only got enough energy to support himself with his own business."

"When Preacher Paul and I would go fishin'," Merle Graber chimed in, "he'd tell me how he'd visit a member and get told it was none of his business if they were usin' their kid's cell phone or that they'd been attendin' church with the Mennonites. Nobody *wanted* his preachin' job, yet they were always tellin' him how he should do it." He let out a short laugh. "Sure hope I'm not picked to be the preacher. I've already got somebody tellin' me how to do every little thing."

Matt chuckled along with the rest of the men in the store. Even though Merle's memory wasn't as sharp as it used to be, his sense of humor—especially concerning Eunice—was still on target.

"Jah, and preachin's a thankless job, too," said Ezra Yutzy. "I've heard Abe Nissley tellin' how, more than once, he's been called away from his orchard to settle somebody's dispute on a gut, sunny day, only to lose some of his crop to hail damage when he couldn't get his apples picked in time. Kind of a shame to saddle a younger fella with that lifetime burden when they've got kids comin' along."

"But that's part of the vow we men take when we join the church," Matt's father pointed out from his high stool at the checkout counter. "I'd hate to think about keeping up with the mercantile while studying Scripture and preparing to preach, though. There's only so much a man can concentrate on at one time."

Matt headed down the aisle where they sold bags of roasted peanuts in the shell, hoping not to draw the men's attention as they talked about Cedar Creek's most crucial, controversial topic. His mother and grandmother had discussed this subject with Aunt Abby nearly every day this week, so it was good to hear the opinions of the menfolk. As he rounded the end of the snack shelves, however, Rudy caught sight of him.

"Well now, Sam, here's your boy," the older fellow announced. "Matt's plenty sensible enough to run the store when you'd need to be gone on a preachin' errand or studyin' up on the Bible."

Matt grabbed a bag of peanuts and hurried toward the front counter as though he had somewhere he needed to be. "Not so sure that'd be a gut idea," he replied, feeling all the men's gazes focused on him. "I'm lots better suited to being a shepherd than a shopkeeper. Right, Dat?"

His father looked pointedly at him as he accepted his money. "The man chosen will rely on his family to stand with him—to step in and help keep bread on the table. A preacher's whole family lives with a new set of priorities."

"Jah, well, I'll deal with that when the time comes," Matt murmured before he headed outside again. The afternoon had gotten off to a rocky start, and when he saw that Emma was no longer in the phone shanty, he hoped the sound of Rosemary's voice might improve his mood—except his dat had followed him outside.

"I get the feeling something's been bothering you all week, son. And maybe we don't need to share it with all the fellows in the store."

It was the sort of statement Matt knew better than to duck. Anytime his dat left the mercantile to talk with him, it was a sign Sam Lambright intended to conduct an entirely different type of business . . . and maybe it was time to turn loose of the concern that had burdened him since Saturday.

"While driving Rosemary and the girls back to Queen City last week, I, um, nearly got us all killed." The bag of peanuts crackled as he gripped it. "A car ran up real close behind us. Then the brakes squealed and he swerved around us, honking up a storm. Scared the daylights out of us," Matt continued in an urgent voice. "And when Rosemary pointed out that I hadn't turned on the buggy lights, I—I apologized, but she hasn't returned any of my calls since then."

His father's face tightened with concern, yet he remained calm. "We can't know what English drivers are thinking—or if they're just *not* thinking—when they come up behind our buggies too fast. And sometimes it's sheer orneriness when they make sport of spooking our horses. I've forgotten my lights a time or two," he added, stroking his dark beard. "And jah, it was usually when I was distracted by the young lady in the seat beside me."

Matt swallowed, waiting for a lecture about the precautions, the responsibilities everyone assumed while they were driving. There was no getting around how he needed a talking-to, yet when his dat's broad hand settled on his shoulder, Matt felt a solid strength rather than any signs of anger.

"Truth be told, a close call usually scares us into remembering the lights after that," he went on. "But it was God's doing—and probably that slow-moving vehicle reflector on the buggy—that kept you from being killed. And for that I'm thankful. It was a blessing, the day you were born, son, and it's too soon to lose you."

Matt went warm all over, basking in the love his father seldom put into words. Dat loved Phoebe and Gail and Ruthie, of course, yet he had always felt favored because he was the only son. "But I feel bad because Rosemary's not speaking to me or letting me—"

"She was scared, too. And what with Titus buying the Bontrager place, she has a lot on her mind right now." His father smiled wryly. "But we can never know what women are really worried about, jah? Your mamm has been upset all this week, thinking that if I'm chosen to preach she'll have to quit her midwifing. So it's a wise thing you've done, telling *me* about your highway incident instead of talking about it at the table, Matt. We're both better off for that!"

Matt enjoyed the sound of his father's low laughter as it blended with his own.

"We'll believe the best, come Sunday, when God chooses his servant for Cedar Creek, too," Dat went on. "Just as we'll believe He knows what *you* ought to do after that, and what path Rosemary should choose, as well. It's all a lot simpler if we let God be in charge."

Matt felt a glow when he met his father's gaze, as though his dat had pronounced a benediction, a blessing just for him. It was a holy moment, shining like a vibrant green leaf, when he better understood the strong, silent bond that had deepened over his lifetime . . . the sort of love he yearned to experience with Rosemary, and with Katie and his own children someday.

"Thanks, Dat," he murmured.

"We both feel better for talking this out. So now it's back to business."

Matt watched his father walk through the mercantile door, with a prayer that he himself would conduct God's business and his family's business in a mature, responsible way. He opened his sack and enjoyed a couple of fresh peanuts. Off to the west, the sky had darkened with rain clouds, so after one more try at talking to Rosemary he'd get back to checking the pasture fences.

One job at a time, one day at a time. It was the best way to get things done.

Rosemary divided the big batch of bread dough into four balls and then sprinkled the countertop with more flour. It was a humid, rainy afternoon, not ideal for working with yeast, but then it was one of those days when nothing else was going well, either. School had let out for the summer today, and Beth Ann's mood hung as low and dreary as the storm clouds.

"I—I hurried home by myself. I couldn't stay a single minute after we were dismissed," she said between sniffles. "Couldn't say good-bye to Teacher Rachel or to Fannie and Mary Etta Schlabach, or—well, what if I never make such gut friends in Cedar Creek, Rosemary? What if—"

Rosemary slipped her arm around Beth Ann's shaking shoulders. "Jah, it'll take some time, but Ruthie and the Coblentz twins already think you're pretty special, you know. And with the Ropp girls just around the bend, too, why, you'll have a new buddy bunch in no time. You'll see, Beth Ann."

The young girl drew a loud, shuddery breath and began to cry in earnest. "It's just so *hard*, Rosemary. Dat doesn't understand that it's more than leaving my gut friends. It's . . . well, I'll be leavin' Mamm behind, too."

Rosemary sighed along with her young sister-in-law, feeling the same pain on an adult level. All her life she'd lived either in the home where she'd grown up—even after she'd married Joe— or just down the road from her mother and sister. And how would she explain to Katie that they wouldn't be seeing Mammi and Aunt Malinda every day once they moved? She was glad her daughter was napping now instead of listening in on this tearful conversation. Like Beth Ann, Rosemary would miss taking wild-flowers to the little cemetery where they had laid Joe and Alma to rest.

When she saw Titus coming out the barn door, she stood taller. "Better dry your eyes now. Your dat's got something on his mind, and he's headed this way."

Beth Ann swiped at her wet face with her sleeve and began kneading a dough ball, her back to the door.

Rosemary picked up another lump of the bread dough, glad for the chance to work her arm muscles until they tired . . . losing herself in the age-old rhythm of flattening, then folding the dough with the heels of her hands until it felt pliant and springy. The screen door banged. With the sound of water running in the mudroom sink came the tang of Titus's muck-covered boots.

Rosemary felt him watching the two of them as he dried his hands in the doorway. "Just now making bread?" he asked. "Thought you'd be putting supper together."

Oh, but that remark rubbed Rosemary wrong, even though he'd said it in a pleasant enough voice. But then, hadn't a lot of ordinary things bothered her this week? "Had some pies that didn't cooperate today," she explained. "The filling got too thick, and then I forgot to set the oven timer so I had to make four more. Sorry."

Titus grunted. "Could be, if you'd return Matt's calls, you'd be in a better frame of mind. Just now picked up the phone in the barn, and it's him again, asking if you'll please come talk to him."

Rosemary closed her eyes. "You're wondering why supper's late, and I'm up to my elbows in flour and dough."

"I've got no time for playing messenger boy," he replied. "So when I come back from telling him your answer, you're going to explain what this is all about. And then we'll discuss the offer I got on the farm and your land today."

As the door closed, Rosemary's heart thudded. All week she'd avoided the subject of Matt's close call in the buggy, and Beth Ann had merely mentioned that a fast car had squealed around them and spooked the horse. Emma Graber's remark about Matt had been bothering her, too. There would be no avoiding the two of them once she became their neighbor, and she wanted no part of getting caught up in their quarrel, either.

"Uh-oh," Beth Ann murmured. "Sounds like there's no backing out now, if Dat's got a buyer for this place."

"Jah, life's moving forward and we'll have to move with it."

When Titus returned to the house, they were putting the loaves of bread in the pans to rise. He slipped out of his boots in the mudroom and then settled into his chair at the head of the table as though he might stay there until his meal was served—or until he got the answer he was looking for. "Matt tells me he forgot to turn on the buggy lights last Saturday while bringing you home, and a car came up on you too fast. Is *that* what this silent treatment is all about, Rosemary?"

Color and heat flooded her face. What else might Matt have admitted to Titus?

Her father-in-law chortled. "Why do I get the feeling something— or somebody—distracted the poor boy? Maybe you don't remember this, but Joe wrecked *two* courting buggies, paying attention to his girlfriends instead of watching the road. Cost me a pretty penny to keep wheels under my son before he married you, Rosemary."

Beside her, Beth Ann's expression brightened. "Jah, I remember that. You were none too happy with him, Dat."

"But boys'll be boys. Matt's trying real hard to grow out of that, and with the help of a gut woman, he will." Titus leaned his elbows on the table, expecting an answer.

Joe had been five years older than her, so most of his teenage recklessness had happened when Rosemary was too young to be concerned about it. She still didn't feel it was any of Titus's business what had gone on between her and Matt. Then again . . . if Matt had told her father-in-law exactly what they'd been doing, maybe Titus was testing her to see if she would admit to that kiss. "I have a lot of things to consider when we move to Cedar Creek," she said as she set the four bread pans in the oven. "And marriage is pretty low on my list."

"But you're going with us? For sure and for certain?"

Not in the mood to hand him an answer so easily, Rosemary reached into the cabinet for their dinner plates. "How much will this potential buyer pay for my land? You must be satisfied with what he's offered or you wouldn't be telling me about it."

Titus grunted at her change of subject. "Twenty-two hundred an acre. He likes the looks of the house and the barns, and wants to run cattle in the pastures. Figures to raise hay and oats on your parcel." His gaze sharpened as he rose from the table. "If you can't forgive Matt for a simple mistake, I wonder if you're setting your sights so high you'll never find another man. A bird in the hand's worth two in the bush, you know." Titus went into the front room, as though he didn't want to talk any more while he waited for his meal.

Tired of timeworn adages about greener grass and birds, Rosemary wiped the flour from the countertop. At the price Titus had quoted, her forty acres would bring eighty-eight thousand dollars . . . not a lot more than Joe had paid for it, but it would make a nice nest egg for her future.

When the floorboards creaked as Titus walked across the room above the kitchen, Beth Ann moved closer. "You know," she murmured, "I always thought a bird in the hand sounded really . . . messy."

Rosemary stifled a loud giggle as Beth Ann joined in. No doubt Titus would assume they were laughing at him, but she welcomed the relief from the afternoon's heavy mood. Maybe her father-in-law had made a good point about Matt's mistake being fairly common, and maybe the aroma of baking bread was lifting her spirits, but she felt better, and sensed she could share an important decision with Beth Ann. She opened the towel drawer and pulled a Lehman's catalog out from under the dishrags. "You know how you've been hoping to sew for Abby once we move to Cedar Creek?" she asked quietly.

Beth Ann nodded, curious about the catalog that was filled with all manner of nonelectric farm and household equipment.

"Well, I'm going to bake for Aunt Lois's café and find other places to sell my pies, too. Baking is my talent, like sewing is yours, and it's time to set myself up with a business that'll support Katie and me . . . something that's all my own, just as Abby has done." Rosemary smoothed down a page that displayed several models of gas cookstoves and ovens. "I'm going to invest some of the money I get for my land in gut, dependable appliances. No telling what condition the Bontrager kitchen's in—and it could be that Salome and Perry will take their stove and fridge with them."

"Oh, I like this one!" Beth Ann said as she pointed to a modern gas range. "It'll be a lot less trouble than this wood-burning stove of Mamm's. But mostly I'm happy you're coming with us, Rosemary. It makes the move seem a whole lot easier."

Beth Ann's words confirmed that Rosemary had made the right decision, for Joe's little sister as well as for herself. She hugged the girl, and for a moment they stood together with the aroma of warm bread surrounding them . . . a homey scent that set a lot of things right. "When I thought about staying here in Queen City, building a house and living there with just Katie and me, it didn't feel so gut," she confessed. "You're a ray of sunshine for me, Beth Ann. We help each other a lot, ain't so?"

"I was hoping you'd see it that way, Rosemary." Beth Ann looked purposefully into her eyes. "So, what about you and Matt?"

"I'll figure that out eventually. Now that I'll have my own money coming in, I won't be dependent on Titus or Matt either one," she mused aloud, "and that means I can make my own decisions. I like the way that feels."

Rosemary glanced at the clock, contented with the way this difficult day had worked out. "I got out stew meat for tonight. Shall we brown it in the skillet? Stir in some gravy makings and serve it over noodles?"

"Oh, *that'll* make Dat happy. He loves anything with gravy."

Rosemary smiled. Now that she had opened her heart to new possibilities—made *herself* happy—she was finding more satisfaction in making others happy too.

Chapter 21

As Abby sat in the biggest room of James's workshop among the other women for the preaching service on May 21, the air around her vibrated with the congregation's anticipation. It was the day God would choose their new preacher.

"'What doth it profit, my brethren, though a man say he hath faith, and have not works? Can faith save him?'" Pete Beachey read from the big Bible.

How appropriate that today's sermons would be inspired by the third chapter of James, about proving out one's faith by doing God's work. Here in the carriage shop, where special tools hung on the walls, they sat surrounded by evidence of James Graber's service, his calling. Abby remembered the work James had done on behalf of members in need, as when he'd replaced the vehicles the Ropp family lost in their fire last December and when he'd built a special carriage with a lift for Joel Detweiler's wheelchair. James would make a fine preacher, but only married men's names would be whispered to their deacon after worship this morning. Every man and woman present sat forward in earnest, awaiting the falling of the lot that would determine which family's life would be changed in a heartbeat.

As Vernon rose to preach the morning's main sermon, Abby noticed how the men looked among themselves, wondering who would be called to serve. Any fellow whose name got mentioned by at least three members would be summoned to the front for the choosing . . .

"As we are all well aware," Vernon began, "today marks a milestone in the life of our community." He gazed about the crowded workshop, first at the women and then at the men. "Preacher Abe and I can attest to the gravity of this process, this ordination by the Lord our God, which our departed brother Paul knew, as well. Paul Bontrager's life bore out the verses in the tenth chapter of Mark, which tell us that 'whosoever of you will be the chiefest, shall be servant of all. For even the Son of man came not to be ministered unto but to minister.'"

Bishop Gingerich clasped his hands before him, solemn yet joyous about the wondrous act they were about to witness. "We came not to this earth to be served, my brothers and sisters, but to serve. And while God has known from the beginning of all time which of you men will be chosen today, we will witness His presence in a profound way as He makes His will known to us. What a marvel it is, to participate in this ceremony today!"

Two rows in front of Abby, Barbara shifted on the pew—as did the wives of other men who might have to answer the call. While Vernon spoke of the privilege of becoming Cedar Creek's new preacher, everyone in the room realized that the new leader they chose would be required to put his spiritual duty before all personal commitments and earning his living. He would be called to correct them when they strayed from the righteous path. He would stand before them and preach God's word without any training or notes, regardless of how terrified he might be and how inadequate he might feel.

As Vernon continued his sermon, a little child chattered. Abby smiled back at Rosemary, who hushed Katie with a finger and a stern look. Titus had brought them into town yesterday, and they'd stayed at Lois and Ezra's so they could attend their new preacher's selection. Time had sped by these past weeks since Titus had first mentioned his desire to return. Not only had the best stitchers among them completed the Friendship Star quilt for Salome, but Zanna had also hosted a frolic where they had made a smaller, more colorful version of that pattern for Beth Ann's new room. Rosemary had mentioned that Beth Ann would celebrate her thirteenth birthday next week, so Abby was excited about presenting the quilt this afternoon after the common meal.

As they sang the final hymn, Abby felt the tension escalate. After the benediction, Vernon, Abe, and Pete stood silently before them to instill the solemnity of the moment and to prepare their hearts for the process of naming candidates they felt were worthy to carry out the Lord's work as their leader.

"Deacon Pete will await your nominations at the front counter," Vernon announced with a nod toward the shop's main room. "As we speak freely and with utmost sincerity, we are doing our part in God's great plan for our lives. It is a holy mission we fulfill here. A journey toward our spiritual future."

Abby waited, barely breathing, as the men filed into the front room first. Again and again Sam's name had come up at their frolics and in the mercantile—but other fellows had also been mentioned. The big room rang with silence broken only by the movement of folks going out and then walking sideways to resume their places in the tightly packed pews.

Abby rose with the rest of her row of women . . . Eva Detweiler, Hannah Hartzler, Marian Byler, and other friends near her age walked quickly into the other room. Each whispered a name to Pete and then returned, most of them white-knuckled. Ever since Paul's passing, each of them had considered the consequences to her family if her husband were chosen. It almost felt like a betrayal to mention a friend's man for this duty, yet God's will was to be carried out.

When Abby reached Deacon Pete, she leaned close. "My brother,

Sam," she whispered—not because she wanted to burden him and Barbara but because she believed Sam's wisdom had increased so greatly last year during their difficult days with Zanna. She returned to her pew with her eyes lowered, to await the next step in this nerve-racking procedure.

During the nominating process, James had helped Vernon set a table front and center, and they had gathered hymnals to use in the selection process. The whole room held its breath as Pete returned with the list of men who had been mentioned at least three times. Vernon studied it for a long moment.

"From the gospel of Matthew, which tells the parable of the talents," he said as he held up a slip of paper he'd written on, "'His lord said unto him, Well done, good and faithful servant; thou has been faithful over a few things, I will make thee ruler over many things: enter thou into the joy of thy Lord.' We have received the names of five fine men, whom you and the Lord have summoned to this holy moment."

As James and Matt placed five chairs behind the table, the bishop slipped the Bible verse into one of the hymnals, mixed the books around, and then laid them across the table. "Will you please come forward as I call your name?" he said in a voice that quivered with anticipation. "Moses Hartzler—"

Beside Abby, Hannah gasped and covered her mouth.

". . . Samuel Lambright," Vernon continued, and Barbara bowed her head.

"Amos Coblentz . . . Carl Byler . . . Ezekiel Detweiler."

Abby clasped her hands in her lap, gazing at the five who came forward, tight-lipped and apprehensive. Quite a mix of personalities and life experiences were represented: a chimney sweep, a storekeeper, a master carpenter, a farmer, and a mechanic, who ranged from her own age of twenty-seven to about fifty. Vernon stood solemnly, flanked by Preacher Abe and Deacon Pete, studying each man who stood before him. Indeed, the bishop seemed to be the only fellow in the place who radiated a quiet joy at this moment of utmost importance in all their lives.

"I never once doubted that our members would choose the best among us, but I shall ask the time-honored questions nonetheless," he said in a voice that carried to all corners of the big shop. "Are you men in harmony with the ordinances of the church? And in harmony with the articles of our faith?"

Down the row, each man nodded.

"Please kneel as we invoke our Lord's blessing on this holy selection process."

During the moments of silence, Abby was aware of how quickly her heart was beating. She heard only the shallow breathing of the women around her.

"And now, if you would each have a seat and choose a copy of the *Ausbund* from the center of the table," the bishop instructed, "we shall determine how the lot has fallen and whom the Lord has chosen. This ritual takes us back to the book of Acts, where Christ's apostles chose Matthias to replace Judas Iscariot. We are grateful that with today's lot we choose a man under more positive circumstances."

Abby and those around her craned their necks to watch as each man reached for a hymnal and then placed it on the table in front of him. What must be going through their minds? Certainly, this moment had rendered her brother and her friends a solemn bunch. Their faces looked tight and pale above their white shirts. Their foreheads glistened with sweat.

"Lord of all generations," Vernon intoned, "show us which one you have chosen from among these brethren." He reached over Carl Byler's shoulder and then opened the hymnal in front of him and fluttered its pages. The whole room exhaled when no slip of paper fell out. The same happened as he shook Zeke Detweiler's hymnal and then Mose Hartzler's.

Abby clasped her hands tighter. Only Amos and Sam remained.

The glance they exchanged was a weighty one. Both men ran thriving businesses and were raising children who would soon be of an age to join the church. Until those sheep were out of their rumspringa days and into the fold, all eyes would watch the new preacher's offspring very closely.

Across the room in the men's section, James caught Abby's eye. A few rows behind him, Matt pressed his lips into a tight line as he watched the bishop reach over his dat's shoulder for the hymnal in front of him. As Vernon ran his thumb over the edges of the pages, the piece of paper fluttered out like a white dove. The members sucked in their breath as one, while Adah Ropp slipped her arm around Barbara's shoulders.

"In this holiest of moments, God has reached down to us from the heavens," Vernon said softly, "and He has chosen a new shepherd for our flock. We, in turn, must pledge our support and assistance as Sam Lambright yields himself to God's will and gives himself up to a higher cause on our behalf. Let us all share a moment of prayer to praise our Lord for this marvel He has worked among us today."

Abby squeezed her eyes shut. Her heart was pounding so hard she could barely hear her own thoughts. *Lord, You're always with us and I ask that You guide Sam and the rest of us to live out Your will . . . to live as examples of Your truth and divine love. Help me not to falter as I step in wherever my brother and my family need me. Help me to speak Your peace when conflicts arise in the coming days, as our family adjusts to Sam's new calling.*

After Vernon spoke his benediction, Abby filed out with the other women to prepare the common meal. A crowd of men had gathered around her brother, and several women huddled around Barbara to assure her that they'd help with whatever she needed as Sam prepared himself to be a minister. As Abby stepped into the Grabers' kitchen, Emma grabbed her shoulders.

"Abby . . . Abby," her best friend murmured. "Such a gut thing for all of us in Cedar Creek means such a commitment and sacrifice on Sam's part—and for your whole family," she murmured. "How will Sam leave the store at the drop of a hat to visit a member who's stepped outside the lines? Will you still be able to run your sewing business?"

"Will Barbara continue to be a midwife?" Eunice chimed in, her face etched with concern. "Gals hereabouts depend on her, but once a fella becomes a minister, everybody in his family has to toe a straighter line."

Abby took their hands, smiling gratefully. "Jah, we've been called to face some new challenges," she replied in a tight voice. "Seems to me the best answer would be for *all* our members to toe that straighter line so Sam won't have to nudge them for confessions or tell them to put away the gadgets and habits forbidden by the *Ordnung.*"

"Jah, there's that," Emma replied as she pulled bowls of fruit-filled gelatin from the fridge. "Might not make things any easier, but everyone's pleased Sam was chosen. He's a gut man. Strong and dependable. Already a leader among us."

"Denki for that, Emma," Abby murmured. "Your prayers and best wishes will be greatly appreciated."

Chapter 22

The meal following Sam's ordination was quieter than most, yet as she ate Rosemary enjoyed listening to her new friends discuss the divine process they had just witnessed. Marian Byler, Eva Detweiler, and Hannah Hartzler had shared their relief in the Grabers' kitchen, while Nell Coblentz, Amos's wife, now sat at the table alongside Barbara Lambright. How must it feel to go to church as a merchant's wife and leave with a preacher for a husband? Within a few fateful minutes, life had changed dramatically for the entire Lambright family . . . including Matt. Rosemary shifted sleepy Katie on her lap, considering.

Would Sam's new calling affect the way Matt made his living now? Would he feel compelled to help his dat manage the Cedar Creek Mercantile rather than becoming Titus's partner? Titus had already settled up with Perry Bontrager, so it was too late to back out of the move.

"Rosemary?" Beth Ann came up behind her and gripped her shoulders. "Abby says she has a surprise for me! We're to go to the Lambrights' whenever we're ready—"

"And you're ready right now, ain't so?" It was good to see Beth

Ann looking so excited, considering how everyone else seemed subdued after the drawing of the lot. "Shall we give Abby a little longer? She might want to help Emma in the kitchen or—"

"Ruthie wants me to come right over," Beth Ann insisted. "She says her sisters and their friends are making plans to paint the Bontrager house next Saturday, and I think she feels left out—and worried about her dat being the new preacher."

Rosemary's emotions welled up at the thought of how many wonderful things their new neighbors were doing to welcome them. "No reason you girls can't do your visiting," she replied. "Abby will let you know about your surprise when she's ready, and meanwhile you can share Ruthie's concerns. She's made you feel a lot better about leaving your friends, ain't so?"

"Jah, she has." Beth Ann glanced up as Ruthie rose from the table, waving across the crowd. "So, do you know what Abby's got for me? Will you come to the house to see it?"

Rosemary smiled slyly. "Jah."

Beth Ann blinked, expecting more of a response. "And you're not going to tell me what it is?"

Rosemary spooned up a bite of butterscotch pie for her daughter. "Nope."

With a playful swat on Rosemary's shoulder, Beth Ann took off down the narrow aisle between the tables. Rosemary shifted to face Aunt Lois, who sat beside her. "It's gut to see her laughing. She had a rough time on her last day of school in Queen City."

"And how're *you* doing, concerning the move to Cedar Creek, Rosemary? A while back I had the idea you weren't real excited about coming." Joe's aunt leaned closer to smooth the loose wisps of Katie's hair. "We all would've understood, had you decided to stay near your mamm and Malinda."

Lois's face was creased with crow's-feet at her eyes and smile lines that framed her lips like parentheses. What a busy woman she was, putting in six mornings a week at her bakery while running

Ezra's household and tending the huge gardens around his pallet-making factory. And what a kind woman Joe's aunt was, too, to express concern about how she and Beth Ann were handling such a major change. "I can't explain it, exactly," Rosemary replied, "but while I was quilting at Barbara's the other day, I felt like I already fit in. And mostly I realized how long it's been since I had *fun*."

"Jah, we've got a fun bunch around here, for the most part."

"And when Titus told me he'd found a buyer for his farm—and my land, should I care to sell it—you know what?" Rosemary tingled with the anticipation of sharing her decision. "With some of the money I get from that sale, I plan to order a really gut cookstove from Lehman's, along with an extra oven for making pies! I'm going to start up my own business, helping you and whoever else will buy what I bake."

Aunt Lois grabbed her in a hug, making Katie coo between them. "Oh, Rosemary, that's such gut news! I can cut back on my hours and get off my feet more. And it's just as well you're already shoppin', too," she added, "on account of how the Bontragers loaded up their cookstove and the fridge and freezers and took them away with them. You'll have to buy appliances one way or the other, so it might as well be you choosing them instead of Titus."

Rosemary's eyes widened. "They've moved out already? I can't imagine how Salome got everything packed up—"

"We neighbor gals held a packin' frolic there last week. You're about to find out how everybody here pitches in on the hard work and has a gut time while they're at it." Lois hugged her again, laughing out loud. "Jah, Sam can order anything you want from Lehman's through the mercantile and Jonny Ropp's just the fella you want puttin' those appliances together for you, too. I can't tell you how wonderful-gut this makes me feel, Rosemary. Like a burden's been lifted—off my poor old feet, mostly."

Rosemary basked in the glow of Aunt Lois's words. It felt good to share her dream with someone who understood it. And didn't it brighten this solemn day with the promise of a new beginning for herself and a lighter load for Joe's aunt? "Let's hope Titus doesn't feel like I'm overstepping by setting up the kitchen the way I want it," she murmured.

"Puh! You leave Titus to Ezra and me. We'll be sure he appreciates the fact that you're still willing to keep house for him."

Rosemary allowed herself a moment to enjoy the way another piece or two of her future had fallen into place. She wrapped her arm more securely around Katie and scooted her chair back. "I think I'll see how Beth Ann's doing at waiting for her present from Abby."

"Turning thirteen, is she?" Aunt Lois shook her head. "Couldn't hardly believe how the time's been passin' when Barbara mentioned Beth Ann's birthday while we were sewin' up that quilt. It turned out especially pretty, too."

As Lois wiggled her fingers to get Katie to wave back, Rosemary passed sideways between the backs of peoples' chairs. She chuckled when Katie kept right on waving at several of the gals she recognized from her previous visits. As Rosemary stepped out of James's shop into the fresh air, she felt happy all over—so good, she simply stood for a moment with her eyes closed and her face raised to the sun. It seemed that so many opportunities were presenting themselves now that she'd decided to take her future in hand. She could even envision herself in new dresses of various colors . . .

Katie began to wiggle and laugh, a sure sign someone was approaching.

"It's gut to see you looking so pleased and peaceful, Rosemary," Matt said as his footsteps crunched in the gravel behind her. "Wish I felt that way myself right now."

"Puppies! Play with the puppies!"

Rosemary hugged her squirming toddler, saying a quick prayer that she would respond to Matt with words that moved them both forward, where God would have them go. She turned to greet him— and then released Katie as she leaped into his open arms. "You hit the nail on the head, far as how things are going for me," she said. "All of a sudden, Cedar Creek feels like my new home. I'll be baking for Aunt Lois and . . ."

The hopeful, joyful expression on Matt's face warned her to tread carefully. He looked delighted to be holding Katie, who clapped her hands on both sides of his face and then kissed his nose, a sight that tugged at Rosemary's heart. But she couldn't let the emotions of the moment determine her future. "Maybe I overreacted to that car giving us such a scare the other—"

"That was careless of me to forget about the lights," he insisted, holding Katie aside so he could focus on Rosemary. "And I'm sorry if calling you so many times made Titus grouchy with you. I—I was just hoping I hadn't lost my chance to see you again, Rosemary. To court you."

She felt lighter now that they'd both apologized. But she had more to say, and she couldn't allow Matt's dazzling smile to divert her. "I know a lot of changes are coming for your family now, Matt. Just as they are for mine," she said. "I hope you'll understand that I want to be myself for a while. Not a man's widow and not another fellow's wife."

"Ah. So that's to be the way of it, then?" Matt closed his eyes to think while Katie toyed with his shirt collar.

"Maybe that sounds odd to you," Rosemary continued. "But today, for the first time since Joe died, I feel . . . like *me* again. Open to new opportunities. Ready to see this move as an adventure rather than a problem to be overcome."

His lips twitched. "Maybe I should look at Dat's new job the same way," he remarked. "Could be that an adventurous woman will help us all see our new challenges in a fresh light."

Rosemary considered this as she headed toward the road and the tall white farmhouse on Lambright Lane. It pleased her that Matt hadn't dismissed her need for more time to adjust. "Do you suppose we could take a look inside the Bontrager house after I see if Beth

Ann's opened her birthday present? It would help me think about what to bring from Titus's house, or what I might try to talk him into selling off. He and his wife tended to stick stuff away—"

"And now's the perfect time to unload some earthly possessions, ain't so? Especially since they're not *your* possessions."

Rosemary laughed as Matt fell into step beside her. "That's a wonderful-gut way to put it. With all due respect to Alma—"

"She had her ways, and they're not your ways. Just like Titus isn't your husband." Matt swung Katie up over his head, shaking her to make her laugh out loud. "And while Titus has gotten used to you running his house, it won't be that way forever. Ain't so?"

There was no missing his meaning as he looked at her. "True enough. But meanwhile I'm going to set up my business in his kitchen," she reiterated as they strolled up the lane to Matt's home. "So if you convince Titus to go along with these ideas when you're talking to him, the move will be easier for all of us. Even though the kitchen's not his territory, he'll be more inclined to listen to you, as another man."

"And then you, as a woman, would be more inclined to listen to me."

Oh, but this fellow had a smooth tongue in his head! And yet, as they stepped onto the Lambrights' front porch, Rosemary realized that Matt's attention felt totally different from the way Joe had treated her. Her husband had loved her and provided well for her, but he'd kept his thoughts to himself, mostly. Joe hadn't been one to discuss her dreams and ideas, while Matt seemed to be taking them in stride—even if it meant putting his own hopes on hold.

As Matt held the door open, Rosemary paused so her words would be for him alone. "Thank you for understanding what I need," she murmured.

He set Katie on the kitchen floor, and as she toddled toward where Beth Ann, Ruthie, and Abby sat at the table, he placed his hands lightly on Rosemary's shoulders. "You, Rosemary, are exactly what *I* need," he whispered. He looked ready to kiss her, but then nodded toward the ladies at the table, silently promising her his affection when they could be alone.

Girlish laughter filled the kitchen. "Shall we go to another room?" Ruthie teased. "Easy to see what you've got on *your* mind, Matt!"

"Isn't that what courting buggies are for?" Beth Ann piped up, but then her face flushed. "I mean, we're having an early birthday party here, and you two are *welcome* to join us!"

Rosemary raised an eyebrow, as her mother had done when she and Malinda had smarted off. "Someone here is sounding very—*thirteen*," she teased as she approached a table littered with wrapping paper. She winked at Abby. "But then, some days the rest of us wouldn't mind being that age again. What have you got here, young lady?"

Beth Ann sprang from her chair and grabbed the corner of a twin-sized quilt while Ruthie took hold of the opposite side. "Isn't this the most wonderful-gut comforter you ever saw, Rosemary?" she gushed, gesturing at the crisp, fresh Friendship Star design. "And look at these colors! I can't wait to move into my new room—and Abby was just saying that, as gut as I can sew, she wants me to help with some of her Stitch in Time orders so she can spend more time managing the mercantile."

Abby nodded, her face alight. "Best idea I've had for a long time, too. Gail and Phoebe have already agreed to work at the store now instead of in Lois's bakery. They're experienced at shelf stocking and they've helped with the ordering, so the place will be in a lot of gut hands when Sam can't be there."

"And what do you know about that?" Rosemary felt a rush of goose bumps, a sure sign that everything was working out in a marvelous, mysterious way none of them could have planned. "I just told Aunt Lois I'm buying a new cookstove and a new oven so I can help with her baking. So everybody's jobs are covered—"

"Because it was meant to be!" Ruthie crowed. "I knew it from the moment I first met Beth Ann at Zanna's wedding. Life is a mighty happy place, you know it?"

Rosemary felt caught up in the gladness that filled this kitchen. She hoped the girls' happy attitude would carry over. Once the rest of the Lambrights returned from visiting over at the Grabers', the realities of Sam's new preaching responsibilities would sink in. She glanced at Matt and was momentarily stunned by the intensity of his smile.

"Couldn't have said that any better myself, Ruthie," he remarked. "Anybody want to join me for a look inside the new Yutzy homeplace?"

Chapter 23

Matt matched his stride to Katie's as she toddled between him and her mamm. Was it his imagination, or did the grass shine with a brighter green now? Did his ewes look fluffier, clustered out there with their lambs in the pasture? And wasn't it a fine sensation, crossing the road and feeling like a family? His pulse thrummed as he held the tiny hand of the little blonde in braids, who beamed up at him with such trust—such love—that for a moment he couldn't speak.

Beth Ann and Ruthie raced ahead toward the house the Bontragers had vacated. Matt knew that any words he might speak to Rosemary as they explored their new home wouldn't remain private in rooms that echoed with the emptiness of bare hardwood floors.

"Rosemary, look! The paint's here, along with the rollers and ladders," Beth Ann called out. She opened her arms. "Katie, come see your new house! Help me pick out my room."

Katie hurried toward her aunt and then the three girls disappeared inside. Matt held the door for Rosemary, watching her reactions so he could gauge the details that didn't suit her. While this was Titus's house, and he would have the final say on who would have which rooms, Matt intended to influence his new partner's thinking. Titus was much better at raising sheep than he was at housekeeping; he would choose options that seemed easiest for *him* rather than asking Rosemary for her opinions.

Rosemary gazed around the front room. "Jah, now that I'm standing in it, this front room's bigger than what we've had . . . Titus's couch and recliner would fit on this side, and we could put the table his dat made there by the picture window," she remarked in a far-away voice. As she looked at the paint Owen Coblentz had brought, rapid footsteps thundered above them. "Looks like we've got antique ivory, some white enamel, and a can or two of pale butter," she said. "Beth Ann will want that yellow for her room, no doubt. It would look nice in the kitchen, too. Who do we pay for this paint, by the way?"

"Rosemary."

She straightened to look directly at Matt. The sparkle in her green eyes told him she'd been stalling . . . fully aware that with the girls upstairs, they had a few moments alone.

"Matt." She clasped her hands in front of her. Even in her black dress and apron, Rosemary had a new radiance about her today.

He closed the space between them, his pulse thundering. Did he dare kiss her a third time? With his hands on either side of her face, Matt lowered his lips to hers. She accepted his kiss, tentatively at first, and then with a sweetness that made the concerns of the day melt away. He savored the pleasure of having Rosemary all to himself, focused on giving and receiving affection. While his parents obviously loved each other, he'd never witnessed more than the occasional squeeze of a shoulder or the way they sat close together on the porch swing . . . so he relied on instinct. As Matt kissed her again, he hoped Rosemary would find him as desirable as Joe—

No, better than Joe! She's with me now.

She eased away. "Got quiet upstairs," she whispered.

Matt nodded, clearing his throat. "Like I've told Titus, I'll help you folks bring the sheep and furniture over here whenever you're ready," he said in a loud, purposeful voice. "So what've you got in mind for your kitchen? What with getting a new stove plus an oven, we might need to ask Amos to make a few adjustments."

"Did the Bontragers have gas? Or did Salome cook with wood?" Rosemary asked as she preceded him into the kitchen.

Matt was no expert, but this room looked the worse for wear . . . dingy compared to his mamm's kitchen. "Well—there's a gas pipe where the fridge would've been and another one here for the cookstove. So if all you need's a hookup for an oven, it would be pretty easy for Jonny Ropp to run you a new line."

"Jah, Aunt Lois said he was the man for this job. I'll check my Lehman's catalog and call my order in to Sam tomorrow." Rosemary's eyes glimmered. "Do you know how nice it'll be to have all new appliances, Matt? And with a fresh coat of white enamel, these old cabinets will sparkle!"

His heart skipped in his chest. If Rosemary was happy, he was, too. Above them, his sister's giggles rang out and Beth Ann's joined in as their footsteps clattered in the hallway. While he'd grown up with three younger girls in the house, Phoebe and Gail were out of school and worked most days—and they were beyond the giggling stage now—so Ruthie led a pretty quiet life when she got home from school. It was good to hear her laughing. This house felt homier already, just having the girls spreading their sunshine upstairs.

And Rosemary—she makes it feel like a home, too. What man wouldn't want her in his kitchen . . . in his life? Matt had a quick vision of a long table where he sat at the head with Rosemary at his left while kids of various ages filled the chairs along each side. He could almost smell ham and redeye gravy served up with fresh biscuits . . .

But this wasn't his house. It belonged to Titus Yutzy.

Matt caught Rosemary watching him. Had she guessed at the pictures in his mind? Did he dare ask his dat if he could build a home down the blacktop a ways, on their property? Most young couples lived with the bride's parents until they could afford a house, but with Rosemary's mamm living in Queen City that would hardly be his case.

Since Rosemary had been married before, maybe she didn't want to live with his family until he could have a place built. He wasn't too keen on it himself. What with his grandmother staying in the dawdi haus and his parents and three sisters sleeping down the hall from his room, all of them sharing the one large bathroom, he and his new wife would have no privacy whatsoever.

"What're you thinking about, the way you're frowning, Matt?"

He stuffed his thumbs under his suspenders. Would Rosemary think he was jumping the gun if he asked her preferences in a house? Or, if he had Amos Coblentz draw up some floor plans, would she think he was a good provider, a man who planned ahead for his family? "Truth be told, I—"

"Rosemary!" Footsteps echoed in the stairwell, and Beth Ann burst into the kitchen with Ruthie close behind her. "Have you seen— Is Katie down here with you?"

Rosemary's eyebrows flew up. "No, I thought she was with you."

Beth Ann's stricken expression sent Matt's pulse into high gear. "Have you looked in all the upstairs rooms? Checked the closets?"

His sister's expression matched Beth Ann's as she took off to search the main level. "Katie?" Ruthie called out. "Katie, are you playing hide-and-seek?"

"We were just— I'm so sorry, Rosemary!" Beth Ann replied in a tight voice. "We got busy chatting about which room I'd like, and—"

"It's all right, Beth Ann. Let's spread out and look for her," Rosemary murmured. "She's probably poking around in all these new rooms. You know how she likes to have us chase after her now that she can go down the steps on her bottom."

Matt was already heading for the door. "Check the house and yard," he suggested, "while I look outside. Could be if she's seen folks still visiting up at the Grabers', she went to find her grandpa."

Rosemary nodded, keeping a purposeful calm about her. After all, the first time Matt had met her, she was looking for the pixie who had considered it a game to get away from her mamm. This time, though, they had no idea how long Katie had been gone. And once Matt stepped outside, he realized how many hiding places the empty outbuildings offered an inquisitive little kid.

Puppies! Play with the puppies! As Matt heard Katie's excited voice in his mind, he circled Titus's new house and then looked across the road toward his own pastures. The redbud blooms had almost all changed to green leaves. Katie was wearing a dress the color of a thistle, with a white pinafore, so she should be easy to spot.

Matt jogged across the blacktop ahead of Mervin Mast's carriage. "Seen Katie?" he called out.

Mervin and Bessie shook their heads. "We'll keep an eye out," Bessie replied. "Can't have her on this road now that everybody's driving home."

The thought of a horse spooking, maybe trampling the little girl who was unaware of the damage such large animals could do, sent Matt's heartbeat up a notch. How far could Katie possibly have gone in such a short time? Had she slipped down the stairs while he was kissing Rosemary? Surely those unsteady, dimpled legs couldn't have carried her much beyond the yard. Yet, as he recalled the toddler's agility when she'd darted away from Rosemary at Zanna's wedding, he realized he could take nothing for granted.

Matt reached the fence at the edge of the Lambright property and ran faster, toward the barns. Maybe Katie had headed this way, thinking to play with Abby, or—

Where are the dogs? Ordinarily Pearl and Panda rushed out to greet him, barking and wagging their tails. Once past the sheep barn, Matt clambered over the wooden gate and sprinted around the barnyard. "Panda?" he called out. Then he whistled between his two fingers. "Pearl! Come on up here, pups!" he hollered.

No sign of movement. He'd never thought about it before, but Matt was now aware of how far their pastures spread in every direction . . . how easy it would be for a little girl to wander along Cedar Creek and stumble on tree roots before falling into the water. Or if she went up to one of the ewes, thinking it was an oversized dog . . .

Matt gazed back toward the Bontrager place. Rosemary and the two girls were out in the yard, calling Katie's name, and even from here he could read the fear on their faces. Should he bridle a horse and go looking along the front fence line? Should he run to the Grabers' and form a search party while some able-bodied fellows were still there? Truly worried now, he let out another loud whistle.

A single *woof!* made his head swivel. Matt didn't know whether to laugh or cry, to run or stand stock-still. Tiny Katie was toddling through the lush spring grass with Panda on one side and Pearl on the other, blissfully unaware of the turmoil she'd caused. She was over where the lambs liked to play, not far from the feeders and watering troughs. However, a handful of ewes stood off to the side, where they could charge over at the first sign that Katie intended to handle their offspring.

"Thank you, Lord," he murmured. For a moment he watched his wonderful dogs escorting the little girl across the green pasture dotted with dandelions. "And a little child shall lead them" from the Book of Isaiah came to mind.

But Rosemary's little girl wasn't out of danger. Had it not been for his dogs instinctively flanking her, keeping the contrary ewes in their places, Katie might well be a lavender heap in the grass, mauled by those protective mother sheep. Matt stepped slowly toward the trio, signaling to the dogs to keep them from running toward him.

Their tongues lolled and their tails wagged as though they knew they were the heroes of the moment. When Katie saw him and cried out in delight, Panda and Pearl remained beside her as she walked faster, her little arms extended toward the sky in excitement.

"Matt!" she squealed. "Katie play with the puppies!"

Matt swallowed a big lump in his throat and strode toward her, his arms outstretched. What was this crazy sensation crackling through him, as though he'd been struck by the arc from a welder? For a fleeting moment, Katie was *his* child and he'd nearly lost her in a dozen potentially hazardous ways and places. But she was safe! Happy to see him and at ease with his dogs, even though Panda and Pearl stood taller than she did. He covered the last ten feet in a rush and grabbed her up.

"Katie, you gave your mamm and me quite a scare," he said sternly, yet he couldn't be angry with her. He held her sweet weight against him, nuzzling the flyaway tendrils that had escaped her pulled-back pigtails. "When we get you back to your mamm, I wouldn't be surprised if she swats your bottom—"

Katie clapped both sides of his face between her chubby hands. "I love you, Matt!"

So much for lecturing her about the dangers of running off and the punishment that might follow. Once again her words rendered Matt speechless, head over heels in love . . . awash in the wonder of having a child declare him worthy of her affection. Katie looked so much like Rosemary, with intensely green eyes and a turned-up nose, that he already knew she'd have fellows seeking her out sooner than he cared to think about.

"You say it, too, Matt!"

His breath stuck in his chest. Was it putting the cart before the horse to say those three little words to this pixie again before he'd said them to her mother? Was she manipulating this serious situation with her affection? Yet if he didn't respond . . .

Katie's eyes coaxed him.

"I love you, too, Katie," he whispered.

"Jah, I know it." She giggled before nuzzling his nose.

Matt wasn't aware of crossing the road. He surely must have floated, for his feet didn't seem to touch the ground as he made his way between the buggies pulling away from the Graber place. Folks he'd known all his life called out relieved greetings when they saw who was in his arms.

Rosemary ran toward him, followed by Beth Ann and Ruthie. "You little imp! I was worried half out of my—"

"Jah, I know it." Katie's matter-of-fact tone made Matt shudder with trying not to laugh while Rosemary disciplined her. "How much do you love me, Mama?" When Rosemary stopped beside him, reaching for her daughter, Katie threw her arms around his neck.

Matt's heart danced. This moment, this memory, would live on through his lifetime . . . this sweet scene in which Rosemary stood looking up at him with such relief and gratitude while her child clung to him as though she'd never let go. What kind of love was this that held him so close, so effortlessly as mother and daughter staked their claims on his heart?

"Oh, but you're a sly one, buttering us up so we won't punish you," Rosemary murmured. "But you're not to run off from Beth Ann—or any of us—ever again. Understand me, Katie? You could've gotten hurt or lost. We didn't know where to find you."

"Those big sheep could trample you," Matt joined in. "They get really mean when strangers come too close to their babies."

"But they *know* Katie now," the little girl murmured. "Like the puppies do. Like Grandpa's sheeps do."

I am the good shepherd . . . I know my sheep and am known of mine . . . and I lay down my life for the sheep.

The familiar Scripture came to Matt out of the blue and drove home a point in a way nothing else could. This lamb in his arms was a precious gift, and she had just become *his* lamb in an inexplicable, irrefutable way. So as Beth Ann and Ruthie gathered around them to complete the circle, what else could he do but treasure this moment of closeness they all shared? The Good Shepherd had watched over them from above—thanks in part to the four-legged shepherds Matt particularly cherished.

Life—and love—simply didn't get any better.

Chapter 24

Abby settled herself on one of the tall stools at the workbench in James's carriage shop, clearing a space for her writing tablet. Ordinarily she wrote her letters for the *Budget* before she went to bed, but she craved the sound of James's voice . . . a different inspiration for this piece. It wasn't easy to come up with something fresh and interesting to say each week as she reported the news of Cedar Creek.

She smiled at James, who was working with his shirtsleeves rolled to his elbows on this warm evening in late May. "You're sure you don't mind me keeping you company?" she asked. "I haven't seen nearly enough of you this week."

James looked up from the bright red open carriage he was constructing. "That's not going to change for a while, either," he remarked ruefully. "Just when I'd had ideas about disappearing with you on Saturday nights, I got all those extra orders. Then Perry left me shorthanded. Can't expect Leon or Noah to work much overtime—"

"Jah, when you're the boss, you keep the show running."

"—and when you're single, you're not giving up as much family time as your employees with kids, or so it seems to me. I feel bad about Emma having to spend the evening with the folks after tending them all day, but bless her, she's not one to complain." James picked up a shiny black wheel and slipped it onto the front axle of the carriage.

Abby slid down from her stool. She placed her hands on his shoulders from behind him and began to massage the stiff muscles. "They were well into a game of Settlers of Catan when I stopped by a few minutes ago," she said as she kneaded the tightness between his shoulder blades. "Your dat was all excited about the bricks and wool he was collecting as resources. Said it brought to mind the way Titus Yutzy would be pasturing his flock next door by the end of this week— almost like we're playing a real-life game of Settlers of Cedar Creek."

James laughed. He flexed his shoulders as she continued to rub his muscles. "It's gut he sees it that way. Gives him something to focus forward on instead of thinking about his best buddy Paul being gone."

Abby enjoyed the warmth that came through James's twill shirt as she pressed her thumbs in circular motions at the base of his skull. For several moments they stood that way, giving and receiving comfort by sharing each other's company. Not a romantic Saturday night, but it was an improvement over staying home while Phoebe, Gail, and Matt went out on dates, wasn't it? Certainly better than that evening she'd cried after James hadn't kissed her.

"And how are things at the store, Abby?" James asked as he turned to face her. "It's not like I've seen a lot of you, either, since the lot fell to Sam last week."

She drank in the timbre of his voice . . . the way his hair looked rumpled and needed cutting . . . the shine in his chocolate-brown eyes as he gazed at her. "Jah, there's that. Even with the girls helping, sometimes we're stretched pretty thin without Sam," she replied. "He's set aside a few hours on weekday mornings for studying his Scriptures and meeting with Vernon and Abe. I suppose there'll come a time when preaching will be second nature to him, but he still feels overwhelmed by what he doesn't yet know."

"Any fellow would," James agreed. "But truth be told, I was glad your brother was chosen—not just because he was my choice, but because Carl, Zeke, and Mose aren't as . . . seasoned."

"I picked him, too." Abby climbed back onto the stool. "He's the wisest man I know, now that Dat's passed. Not that I go around telling him that!"

James's laughter echoed in the upper spaces of the workshop. He gave her a quick peck on the cheek. "His sister Abigail would make a gut preacher, if she were a man. But I'm glad she's not."

And wasn't that a fine thing to say? As James returned his attention to the red carriage he was working on, Abby opened her notebook and picked up her pencil.

An incredible change is coming over Cedar Creek. We are rolling along life's highway like carriages, some of us leaving town—like Perry Bontrager, gone to live closer to Salome's parents. And we are welcoming Titus, Rosemary, Beth Ann, and Katie Yutzy to town with their wagonloads of furniture and sheep.

Carriages play an important part in Plain lives, and our local carriage maker, James Graber, has been blessed with many new orders for specialty rigs as a result of a magazine article featuring one of his open coaches. The modern world is embracing Amish craftsmanship, and we are pleased to share the work of our hands with those who value our dependable products. We gals have recently enjoyed two frolics, to present Salome Bontrager and then Beth Ann Yutzy with quilts, because when we share our time and hand-sewn projects, we express a love that outlasts words.

James looked up from tightening the bolts on the second wheel. "You've got a mighty intent expression on your face, Abby. Must take that sort of concentration to be a writer."

"Jah, you could say that," Abby replied in a faraway voice. "Although the custom work you do requires a skill I could never hope to have. But I suppose I put words on the page as well as the next scribe."

"Puh! No one writes pieces like you do, Abby. My folks—and everyone else in these parts—turn to your letter first thing each week when the *Budget* comes in the mail," he declared. "So where do you get your ideas for weaving Plain ways into our local news?"

Heat crept up her neck. She couldn't admit she'd been gawking at James while he worked . . . but even so, would everyone realize that scribe Abigail Lambright was head over heels for the man she was writing about? "Oh, the ideas come from all over," she hedged. "Instinct and thin air, mostly."

He rolled the third black wheel toward the opposite side of the carriage. "You don't give yourself enough credit, Abby. You could put all of your pieces together and come up with a real gut book—and folks would snap it off the shelves, too," he added. "Takes a special talent to do that, you know."

A book? While she had saved the drafts of her *Budget* pieces in her loose-leaf notebook, the thought of compiling them had never occurred to her . . . and when would she have the time to take on such a project? "Everybody has a special talent or two, James. They're part of the package God gives us when we're born. And from there, as we grow up and grow in our faith, it's up to us how we use those gifts," she said. "It would be wrong for me not to write—or not to sew and mind Sam's store—just as it would be a waste of your gifts to farm or to make pallets instead of creating extra-special carriages."

She watched him tighten the shiny black bolts on the final wheel. It was a pleasure to observe a master craftsman at work. The man and his tools accomplished so much, seamlessly and with no apparent effort. Abby had noticed this while Owen and Amos Coblentz had built her house, too—but they weren't nearly as fascinating as James Graber. "So . . . are you going to tell me about this rig, James? You've never built a bright red one—although your Mardi Gras coach was mighty colorful."

His face lit up. "Seems Santa needs a new carriage for the Christmas parade at Disneyland, clear out in California," he replied. "And while Santa's not part of our Plain celebration, the fellow ordering this rig told me how many homeless kids would be receiving food and warm clothes from his company, for Santa to deliver after the parade. That made it more worth my while."

"Well, what do you know about that?" Abby whispered as she considered this. "Who would've thought such a rig would come from Cedar Creek, Missouri?"

She loved the way his cheeks colored. James apparently had no idea how special the outside world considered his work. "It's my calling, getting folks where they need to go," he replied, "just like you sew wonderful-gut clothing, and write, and make everyone you meet feel special."

The heat rose to her face and she stared at her writing tablet. "Oh, James, you say the nicest things."

"I speak the truth, is all. And I'm happy you came over to spend this evening with me," he added. "I don't ordinarily like having somebody hang around while I work, but you? I realize now how much I crave your company, Abby. It brings me a lot of happiness. A lot of peace."

Who said she was the only one whose words could change the world? Abby's heart fluttered like a hummingbird's wings as she gripped her pencil. "I—I like spending time with you, too, James," she whispered.

The world went still as he laid his wrench on the carriage seat and came to stand in front of her. He took her hands in his, and she rose to face him. "Abby."

Was he going to say something life-changing, like *I love you* or *Will you marry me?* Abby held her breath, unable to shift her gaze from his. She'd known her answer to that question for years, but it still made her tingly to think that he might express his affections, his intentions, in this unexpected time and place. "Yes, James?"

He looked right through to her soul. "I . . . This isn't how I expected our lives to work out, but—" He paused, looking as nervous as Abby felt. "Well, our feelings for each other have raced along lately, and I'm happier than I've ever been. But I hope you'll understand that I can't commit myself for a while," he said hoarsely.

James sighed and looked away. "This isn't coming out the way I intended. Much as I want to court you, Abby—and maybe get hitched—it wouldn't be right for me to work such long hours here in the shop while you waited dinner, or waited up, or—"

"I've been waiting for most of my life, James. I wouldn't mind—" Abby clapped her hand over her mouth. What would she accomplish by interrupting this man when he was discussing their future together? "I—I'm sorry! I didn't mean—"

James laid a finger lightly across her mouth. "Took me long enough to notice how you feel about me, ain't so?" He stepped back, pressing his lips into a tense line, as though what he was about to say pained him. "But it's not fair of me to keep you waiting even longer while I get these orders out and hire a new fella in the shop, and— well, if you want to see somebody else, Abby, you should do that."

Abby's heart sank like a stone. Just when she'd been carried along by the power of his wonderful words, flying high on her lifelong hopes, she'd hit bottom. She blinked rapidly. She couldn't answer him, her throat felt so tight, so she stared down at her notebook page.

As she seated herself and reread what she'd written several minutes ago, Abby kept her eyes lowered and her mouth shut, desperately trying not to cry. James went back to the carriage he was working on, and soon the whine of a pneumatic drill filled the room. She wrote in a hurried scrawl:

Sometimes we ride along life's highway fine and dandy, with the clip-clop! clip-clop! *of the horse's hooves singing its age-old song, and other days we hit potholes or an axle breaks or life takes a turn we didn't expect. It's times like those when we ask our Lord to take the reins and we trust Him to get us where we need to go—even when we don't think it's the route we want to take. Here's wishing you a good ride in the right direction this week.*

—Abigail Lambright

She glanced up as she folded the page in half. James had gone to the front room, so it seemed a good time to slip out. While she had never been one to back away from serious discussions, it didn't feel right to keep sitting here with such a cloud of disappointment shrouding her. The dusk would disguise her tear-streaked face as she crossed the road and went home.

Abby let her tears fall unchecked as she made her way down Lambright Lane. What with the tourists from four buses that had kept them so busy at the mercantile today, it seemed a good time to let her hair down and read for a while before she turned in. Tomorrow wasn't a preaching Sunday, so she could recopy her *Budget* piece and prepare it for the mail before she went over to Sam's to share breakfast . . .

But making a batch of muffins would be better than sticking her nose in a book; it would use up those two really ripe bananas in the fruit bowl. And banana-nut muffins were Sam's favorite.

Abby opened her door, glad to have this muffin mission. Wasn't it better to bake someone happy than to stew in your own juice?

James watched out his shop window as Abby walked toward her house, her head bent low. He kicked himself. How had such a pleasant evening turned such a disastrous corner? She had given him a shoulder rub, had spent time with him while they both worked on their separate projects. He'd made such a light shine in her eyes when he'd told her he wanted to court her and impetuously kissed her cheek. And then he'd broken her heart.

You hurt the feelings of the most patient, loving woman on the face of this earth, and for what? So you could work on this devil-red carriage? Is there a message here?

"Jah, there's a message, all right," he muttered as he thought back over his part in their conversation. He'd gone on and on about how much work he had to do, how shorthanded he was. He couldn't have foreseen Perry's departure, but hadn't it been his own idea to accept orders for more custom carriages that required so much extra time? Stress, that's what this was. Working overtime alone, feeling so much pressure to produce, went against Old Ways. It smacked of outside-world commercialism, where orders called the tune and workmen danced faster and faster to keep up with the music.

And that was just *wrong*. The way he had treated his dearest friend tonight was inexcusable.

As James put away his tools, he fretted. Should he apologize to Abby now, or the next time he saw her? It would serve him right if she did what he'd suggested. Spending her time with another man probably sounded like a fine idea to her, now that he'd disappointed her so badly a second time.

Tense as his insides felt, though, he couldn't let this stretch into the night and keep him—and Abby—from sleeping. Wasn't it the prophet Isaiah who had said there would be no rest for the wicked—no peace for them because they were like a troubled sea casting up dirt and muck? His stomach and his conscience certainly felt that way, even if he hadn't hurt Abby intentionally.

James closed the shop door behind him and headed for the road. The *clip-clop! clip-clop!* of an approaching carriage made him wave even before he could distinguish Zeke and Eva Detweiler in the front seat, waving back at him. They were driving the carriage he had designed with a hydraulic lift so Joel's wheelchair would sit securely in the back, and as he saw the orange triangular sign on the back, it struck him: *"Slow-Moving Vehicle." That's exactly the speed you were meant to travel, too, James Graber.*

The Detweiler carriage was one of the finest customized rigs he'd ever designed. It gave a family with a partially paralyzed child a way for them to be with other folks. There was a message here, too: Had God given him his carriage-making talents so he could serve a theme-park Santa? Or was he to put his time and skill toward vehicles that helped families and thereby honored his commitment to Christ and His church?

James hurried up the long gravel driveway, past the big white home where Sam's family had turned on the lamps. It was twilight, and he hoped he wouldn't catch Abby getting ready for bed. As early as she rose each morning, the lamp in her bedroom window was often out by nine thirty. He knew this because he watched from across the road most evenings, wishing her good night from his upstairs room. James stepped onto her front porch and knocked, praying that he'd say the right thing.

Abby didn't answer.

James curled the brim of his straw hat in his damp hand, wondering if he'd already upset her enough—until the curtain fluttered at the window. The knob turned. Abby peered out the crack in the door. "Yes, James?" Her eyes looked puffy and her voice sounded hoarse.

He cleared his throat. "I came at a bad time but—well, I just couldn't leave things the way they were, Abby. I'm *sorry*. And I'm stupid, too."

She blinked. "I've taken off my kapp. And I've got muffins in the oven."

The thought of Abby's brown hair cascading down her back teased at him. He'd never seen her without either a prayer covering or a kerchief, and only a husband was to be with a woman when her hair was undone. "It's a lot to ask, Abby, but please can we talk for a bit? I'll wait out here, for however long it takes you to wind up your hair."

Abby sighed, sounding weary. "All right," she finally replied. "We can sit on the porch."

He took a seat, comforted by the creaking of the wooden swing's chains. It was probably best that Abby had insisted on following the Old Ways of modesty, for it gave him a chance to think about what he'd say. And frankly, it had been too long since he'd sat on a porch on an early-summer's night, taking in the velvet sky dotted with stars and the gentle warmth of the breeze, which carried the earthy fragrance that came ahead of rain.

When Abby stepped outside, her hair was tucked under a kapp and she held a small tray with muffins and two glasses of milk. James inhaled the heavenly scent of banana-nut muffins and was glad her swing was wide enough only for two. He groaned with the first bite of a muffin that filled his mouth with the flavors of banana and black walnuts and a basic old-fashioned goodness that was so like Abby Lambright.

"Denki for seeing me. It's more than I deserve."

"Puh," she protested. "We've both of us been under more pressure lately. I shouldn't have made that remark about waiting—"

"That doesn't excuse what I said, Abby. And on the way over here, I—I made a decision." He took another bite of the muffin to fortify his new commitment. "After I finish these three specialty carriages for English customers, there'll be no more work of that sort. I bit off more than I could chew. I had no call to burden you with my troubles."

Her hand found his in the darkness. "But you enjoy making those fancy rigs."

"It's not my best work. Not when it takes me away from the folks who matter most to me—my parents, my sister, and certainly *you*, Abby," he said, not daring to stop for a breath and lose his nerve. "Can you forgive me for saying you should see other fellas, when that made you feel so bad? Or . . . I *think* it did, anyway."

Abby's chuckle wafted around him, as soothing as the milk they sipped. "No real danger of that happening, you know. A maidel my age doesn't exactly have men banging her door down."

"Puh! Your *age*!" he protested as he turned in the swing to face her. "The way I see it, other fellas have never tried hard enough—never realized what a fine woman you are, Abby. Me included, for a long while. I hope I haven't blown my chances, considering how I've upset you twice now."

Abby's dark eyes glimmered as she took another bite of her muffin. Was she being coy? Or was she seriously considering whether she would see him again? James agonized as she raised her glass to her lips . . . Had he unwittingly said something else that had struck her wrong? It was so hard to figure out what went through a woman's mind. He'd found that out when he was courting Abby's younger sister, hadn't he?

Ah, but Abby is nothing like Zanna. Thank you, God!

James relaxed. He slipped his arm along the back edge of the swing as she took her time replying.

"You're an easy fella to forgive, James," she whispered. "I'd be foolish to send you packing just because you took on more work than you bargained for, ain't so? Your heart has always been in the right place, and that's what counts."

Oh, but he wanted to place his heart in her keeping, for now and for always, when Abby gazed at him this way. Did he dare tell her he loved her?

Better not to push his luck. He'd said enough for one evening.

James savored the final bite of his muffin, thankful for small pleasures that made life worth living. "Next time I get all cranky about being overworked, will you tell me straight out that I'm being a pain?"

Abby laughed and set the tray on the porch floor. "I will, if you'll do the same for me," she said as she scooted closer to him. "We're all in this together. With Sam working at his new calling, I'm already—"

"Let's not talk about Sam." James kissed her softly. Abby's forgiveness tasted sweeter than the banana muffins she had shared with him, so he kissed her again. He lingered over this moment, deepening the kiss as she sighed with him . . . and responded with a fervor he hadn't anticipated. Oh, but he'd waited too long to share Abby's affection.

As she rested her head on his shoulder, James thanked the Lord for making Abby such a wise, wonderful woman. He felt like a man who'd been wandering lost but had found his way home again.

Chapter 25

Monday morning, after Beth Ann had left for a day with the Schlabach girls and Titus had gone to tend his sheep, Rosemary started emptying the kitchen cabinets. Matt would soon arrive with a few women from Cedar Creek who had volunteered to help her pack, and she wanted to be ready for them. Mamm and Malinda clomped up the porch steps, carrying a roaster full of sausage-and-bean casserole for their noon meal. After they'd made over Katie's new dress, the color of sunflowers, they began the enormous task of emptying Titus's home of more than forty years.

"Oh my goodness." Her mother stared at the stacks of cookbooks, musty tablecloths, and plastic food containers. "You said Alma was a pack rat, but I had no idea."

"No sense in filling up your new cabinets with this old stuff," Malinda declared as she threw open the doors of more crammed cabinets. "Titus will be none the wiser if we take these items to the recycling center."

"The Mennonite gals over in Memphis are collecting for another overseas relief project," Mamm added, "and they need clothes and books and kitchen utensils. Nothing will go to waste."

The clatter of wheels announced the arrival of their helpers from Cedar Creek. Rosemary swung Katie to her hip and went outside to greet them. She didn't foresee any problems with the women getting along . . . but would her mother and sister approve of Matt Lambright? Here came a high-sided wagon, which Matt was driving, followed by an open carriage full of women who called out to her and waved excitedly.

"Many hands will make light work of this huge job, Rosemary," her mother remarked as she and Malinda came outside. "Don't you worry about—"

"Matt! Where's the puppies?" Katie called out when she saw him. She squirmed frantically, and when Rosemary set her on the ground, she scrambled toward him. "Matt, play with *me!*"

Rosemary's heart fluttered at the sight of the sturdy, broad-shouldered man in the straw hat who crouched and opened his arms. At the moment Katie threw herself into his embrace, Rosemary closed her eyes, hoping . . .

"Well, now," Mamm said softly. "That pretty much tells the tale. If you want to run out there the way your daughter did, you don't need my permission, you know."

Malinda laughed. "You didn't say he was nice *and* gut-looking, sister. Does he have a brother?"

As Rosemary turned to introduce the women, Barbara and Treva Lambright greeted her mamm and sister, as did Eunice and Emma Graber. They were all talking at once, picking up the pans of sticky buns and bars they'd brought.

"We've got empty boxes from the store," Treva said, pointing to a big supply of flattened cardboard crates. "And I brought along some strapping tape."

"Went over and took a look," Eunice declared as she adjusted her pointy-cornered glasses. "The young folks did a fine job of painting your rooms—"

"And the kitchen cabinets got three coats of white enamel," Emma added. "It'll be like moving into a new house."

"Your cookstove and oven from Lehman's got delivered on Saturday." Barbara climbed down from the driver's seat of the carriage. "Abby's already called Jonny Ropp to put them together for you. He'll deliver them by week's end, so you'll be baking those pies for Lois Yutzy in short order."

"Sounds like you're taking gut care of my girls." Mamm's voice was higher than usual, but she didn't waver as she accepted the pans of food they handed her. "I feel better already, seeing what all you're doing to help my daughter settle in."

"Lois has nothing but gut things to say about your Rosemary," Eunice said with a decisive nod. "We're glad to see her and Titus moving next door instead of not knowin' who might buy it."

Rosemary's cheeks tingled as Matt stepped toward her with Katie riding atop his shoulders. "Mamm and Malinda, this is Matt Lambright, Titus's new partner with the sheep—"

"Puh!" Malinda exclaimed. "Looks to me like the sheep are just a way for him to pass the time whenever Katie's not got him wrapped around her little finger."

"Jah, just one more female making me toe the line," Matt agreed as they all chuckled. "I'll get on over to the barn and help Titus load his hay and equipment. Seems safer than going into the house, where you gals might put me in a box and tape it shut."

Rosemary's helpers started toward the house with their moving supplies, chatting like they'd been friends for years. Katie fussed when Matt peeled her arms from around his neck, but when he whispered something in her ear, she nodded and kissed him loudly on the cheek. "See you at dinner," he reassured her as he handed her to Rosemary.

"Jah. You can sit by *me*!" Katie exclaimed.

Rosemary situated her toddler on her hip and grabbed a picnic hamper sitting beside the carriage. She walked quickly to catch up with the other women, who were making their way to the house with Mamm in the lead. "And what did Matt whisper in your ear?" Rosemary asked her daughter.

Katie giggled. "A secret."

"Ah, and what sort of secret was it?" A few steps away from the kitchen door, Rosemary caught up to Emma . . . hoping that since she'd come here with Matt and his mother, her opinion of him—and her mood—had improved.

"Matt says he loves me. And he loves you, too, Mama!"

Rosemary's face prickled with heat as she glanced at Emma. "You just never know what Katie will say next."

Emma shrugged, looking rueful. "It's easy to see she speaks the truth, though. I—I wish you all the best with Matt, Rosemary," she murmured. "Tried real hard to catch him for myself, but it wasn't meant to be. And I'm real sorry about the way I talked to you at the frolic. It scared me when I realized I was sounding as snippy as Mamm, so I've made my peace with Matt, too."

What could she say to make her future neighbor feel better? Rosemary wondered. It had taken some courage to come here under such circumstances . . . had cost Emma some pride to admit that her affection hadn't been returned.

"It's never easy to predict how our lives will work out, Emma," Rosemary replied. "It came as a complete surprise that Matt noticed me, when I wasn't ready to give up loving my husband, Joe. Katie's made things happen faster, and most folks can't help but go along with her."

"Jah, Katie has that way about her."

"I never dreamed I'd be moving away from Queen City," Rosemary went on as they stepped into the kitchen. She noticed that the other women were listening to her, too, so she included them in what she wanted to say. "But now that I've met my new neighbors—and such helpful, cheerful ladies you are, too—the move isn't so scary. It was gut of you all to come today."

"I left Sam studying the assignments Bishop Gingerich gave him, while Abby and the girls are running the mercantile," Barbara remarked.

"I can't imagine what it must be like, movin' your mother-in-law's belongings out and startin' fresh in a whole new town," Eunice chimed in. "Been livin' in the same house we built when Merle and I hitched up more than fifty years ago."

Treva placed her roaster in the oven. "I came along because it's a lot more fun to clear out somebody else's closets than to work on my own!"

"Jah, I know all about that," Mamm agreed. "Malinda and I have filled up a house where a family of nine used to live. I pity the poor soul who cleans it out after we're gone."

For the rest of the morning, they worked and chatted in a way that made Rosemary very grateful. How many weeks would it have taken her to complete such a daunting job? Even with Beth Ann's help, it would have been an overwhelming challenge to decide the fate of Alma Yutzy's belongings. But these ladies knew of benefit projects sponsored by other church groups or places to donate items.

Zanna Ropp had asked for fabric and old clothing for making her rag rugs, so Rosemary and Emma tackled the closets upstairs where Alma had kept her craft supplies. They tugged boxes and plastic bags of all sizes into the room that had been Joe's.

"Beth Ann doesn't want these lengths of fabric?" Emma asked as she emptied a box onto the bed. "Abby says she's a gut seamstress."

"Jah," Rosemary replied as they sorted through the musty twills and cottons. "But most of these fabrics have to be ironed, and she's not one for doing that when polyester blends can be hung on hangers straight from the washer."

"Gut point." Emma emptied another bag of fabric onto the bed. "Oh, now these look promising—dresses that were cut out but never sewn together, and they're a nice summer-weight crepe. Abby's made Mamm and me a slew of dresses from this fabric, and you can't find anything easier to care for."

As Rosemary held up the cut-out pieces, something about the shade of green whispered to her heart . . . and the purple made her soul sing. Wouldn't it be perfect timing, to wear these dresses when she moved to the new house? The one color reminded her of the cedar trees growing at the bottom of Matt's pasture, while the other—well, the iris along the side of the house were this same shade of purple. "Wouldn't take Beth Ann but a couple of hours to whip up these dresses, fast as she sews," she said. "Why donate such nice pieces when one of us can surely wear them?"

"That's what I was thinking." Emma held the back of the green dress against Rosemary's shoulder blades. "This is just the shade of your eyes, you know. And it's big enough that you can cut it to your size."

"Jah, Alma was heavier than I am . . . at least before the cancer caught her," Rosemary added sadly. It tugged at her heart to be handling Alma's unfinished dresses, yet wouldn't it be a tribute to Joe's mamm to wear them as she came out of mourning? She put a determined smile on her face and neatly folded all the purple pieces together, and all the green. Then she and Emma headed downstairs to see how the kitchen crew was doing.

The rich aroma of Mamm's sausage-and-bean casserole made Rosemary realize how hungry she was. Malinda and Barbara were carting loaded boxes to their rigs while Mamm and Treva were setting cookies and sticky buns on plates.

"Would you look at this?" her mother said as she opened the lower cabinets. "We did right well this morning."

"My stars, Mamm! They're clean as a whistle—and I've never seen this set of dishes," Rosemary remarked as she looked at the table, which was set for their noon meal. "What a pretty pattern of pink roses."

"Found them tucked away behind a bunch of old cottage cheese cartons." She smiled ruefully. "This gives me the bug to clear out my own cabinets. No telling what treasures I might find."

"Same here," Matt's grandmother replied. "We figured to work in the cellar after dinner. The men won't have patience enough to pack those crocks and canning jars right, let alone wash them so's they're ready to use again."

Rosemary's heart throbbed with gratitude. "I can't thank you enough," she murmured. "What with keeping track of Katie and—well, I just haven't found the time to redd up those cellar shelves."

Both women smiled as though they shared a secret. "Consider it our housewarming gift to you, Rosemary," Treva remarked. "Happy to help."

"Jah," her mother added. "You'll have plenty to do, getting that new place settled in. If you think of us when you see all those shiny-clean jars and these rose dishes on your shelves in Cedar Creek, that's thanks enough."

Rosemary broke a slice of Barbara's fresh bread into soft chunks and put them on Katie's high chair tray. As Titus and Matt washed up in the mudroom, she dished up the sausage-and-bean casserole. Wasn't it nice to have such a bunch of people around this table, where they would eat only a few more meals?

Titus sat down and ran a gnarled finger around the rim of his dinner plate. "Can't recall the last time I saw these dishes. Alma's sisters gave us this set for a wedding present," he murmured. "A little frilly, to my way of thinking. And once the kids came along, she put them away and got that set of Melmac."

As his eyes misted over, everyone got quiet. They bowed and prayed.

Treva passed the casserole to Titus. "We thought these dishes were too pretty to hide away, but if you'd rather we packed them—"

"No, that's not what I mean." Titus looked again at the rose pattern on his plate and then focused on Rosemary. "Alma was real happy you married into our family, so if you like these dishes we'll use them. The Melmac's pretty well shot after thirty years, if I say so myself."

Rosemary chuckled. "Denki, Titus. That's a wonderful-gut way to remember her every time we eat."

As the bread basket went around, Matt shot her a secretive smile from across the table. "Dat says your new cookstove and oven arrived from Lehman's," he remarked in a purposeful voice.

"Jah, I was amazed at how fast they got there." Rosemary bit into a chunk of sausage simmered in Mamm's colorful mixture of seasoned beans. How long might it be before she tasted this favorite casserole again? When Katie squealed and pounded her high chair tray, Rosemary put more of the casserole on her plate and then pressed her tiny fork into her hand. "Use this," she instructed gently. "You'll need to eat like a big girl at the new house."

Titus cleared his throat. "I'm mighty grateful that you're moving to Cedar Creek, willing to cook and clean for me, Rosemary. And glad you'll be baking for Lois, too. So I'll be the one paying Sam for your new appliances. Least I can do."

Rosemary nearly dropped her fork. "But I can use the money from selling my property. You were gut enough to find me a buyer—"

"Nope. My mind's made up." Her father-in-law's expression went crooked when he realized every woman at the table was gazing at him. "Hasn't been easy for you, looking after Beth Ann and me. Least I can do," he insisted again. Then he focused on his food, as though this show of gratitude hadn't come easily to him.

Rosemary stole a glance at Matt. Had he given Titus this idea? And wasn't that a thoughtful way to make her happier in the new house? Indeed, she felt surrounded by warmth and friendship as she considered how many folks within sight of the new place would be there when she needed a helping hand.

By the time Beth Ann got home from visiting the Schlabach girls, the canning jars in the cellar were packed and Matt had a load of hay bales ready to haul to Titus's new farm. The young girl gaped when Rosemary opened the kitchen cabinets and recounted how much packing and recycling they'd accomplished during their frolic. As the Grabers and the Lambrights loaded up to go home, Beth Ann thanked them all. "And tell Ruthie I said hullo!"

"I'll do that," Matt's mamm replied. After their final good-byes, the women headed for the carriage.

Rosemary waved one last time at Matt and at the carriage that followed him. Then she looked at Beth Ann, hoping the idea she'd been cogitating on would appeal to her. "You'll want to see what Emma and I found while we were clearing out those cabinets upstairs—the ones where your mamm kept her fabric and whatnot."

Beth Ann wrinkled her nose. "I've pawed through them a time or two. Those cottons would make for a lot of work if I sewed dresses from them."

"But now that you're making rugs—" Beth Ann's wide-eyed reaction made Rosemary laugh as she led the way upstairs.

"Well, jah! I wasn't needing strips to crochet those other times I went through Mamm's boxes."

"We saved you a nice stack of colorful fabric and gave the older clothing to Zanna for her rug making. And then there's a favor I'd like to ask." Rosemary stepped into Beth Ann's room and gave the girl a moment to exclaim over the colorful florals, calicos, and ginghams for her rug . . . waited for her to find the dresses that were already cut out.

"I can recall when Mamm started these, way last year before she got so sick." As she held them up, Beth Ann seemed a little sad—until she looked slyly at Rosemary. "Why am I thinking you'd like to wear these instead of your black dresses? Maybe someday real soon—like, once you move across the road from Matt?"

Rosemary blushed. It seemed everyone had ideas about how she and Matt should be together, sooner rather than later. "You'll be busy packing up your room, but—"

"It'll be a snap to make these, Rosemary. If you'll redd up the supper dishes," she suggested slyly, "I could have them all sewn up for you by tomorrow." Dish duty wasn't Beth Ann's favorite chore.

"I can do that, jah! You're so much better at sewing than I am."

Beth Ann got a faraway look on her face. "It's like Abby told me," she mused as she restacked the fabric. "I knew my best talent early on, so it's up to me to do some gut with it. If I can help with her Stitch in Time orders while she runs the mercantile for Sam, I'll be doing worthwhile work for Abby and her customers, too. It seems a fine way to start out our new life, ain't so?"

Rosemary felt a rush of goose bumps. "That's a wonderful-gut way to look at it," she murmured as she hugged Beth Ann. "Your mamm would be so pleased—and so am I."

Chapter 26

Matt polished off his French toast and sausage on Tuesday morning and excused himself from the table. "Titus is bringing a load of sheep first thing, so I'd better get to my chores," he said. Everyone in his family was watching him with knowing expressions, so he added, "He's paying an English fellow with a truck and a big stock trailer to drive the sheep over today and then move the furniture tomorrow. Meanwhile, Rosemary's still packing in Queen City."

Ruthie snickered as though she saw through his attempt to keep Rosemary out of the picture for the day. She stabbed another slice of golden-brown French toast. "To hear Beth Ann tell it, they'll be all out of that house in a day or so. I can't wait!"

Matt liked the sound of this. It meant the move was going more smoothly than Titus or Rosemary had anticipated. "We'll be starting Titus's flock in the alfalfa field that cuts in behind the Graber place, as that's the best grass to get them through the summer."

"It'll take a couple years to convert those fields to gut grazing land," his dat remarked as he sopped up the syrup on his plate with his last bite of French toast.

"Jah. Titus is keeping Carl Byler on as his farmer, to overseed a lot of that place with timothy and canary grass—including our pastures, so his sheep can graze here some of the time while his new pastures get established." Matt rose and scooted his chair under the table. "It'll take some planning and rethinking, considering how that farm has been worked before, but Titus and I are convinced it'll benefit the both of us."

His grandmother filled the sink with dishwater and then pointed out the window. "If that big red stock trailer coming down the road has sheep in it, your day's off to an early start, Matt. It's wonderful-gut, the way things are working out for you."

"Mostly, Grandma thinks it's wonderful-gut that Titus is moving into the Bontrager place," Ruthie teased. "Preacher Paul wasn't her cup of tea, but—"

"Ruthie, you'd best watch your smart remarks," Dat warned her with a stern look. "It's one thing to be excited about Beth Ann coming, but there's no call to let your tongue wag out of turn. Folks'll be paying attention to such details, now that you're a preacher's daughter."

Matt headed outside, glad to leave the kitchen. While their father had always been mindful of talk that went astray, lately he'd been lecturing Gail and Phoebe along these same lines; they should be wearing their kapps farther forward to cover more of their hair and should be hemming their skirts longer, too. Now that they spent their days in the mercantile, where the locals could monitor their behavior and where they would come in contact with more English, Dat was making them all toe a higher line. Mamm was already wearing black capes and aprons in public, as a preacher's wife, and Dat was telling her to limit her midwifery to emergency situations. He expected her to ease herself out of it altogether by the time he started preaching sermons later in the summer.

In short, a lot of Lambrights were silently gnashing at the bit, like retired racehorses feeling the reins tighten while they were being trained to pull Amish carriages.

Matt called to his dogs, who loped up from the barn to trot

alongside him. He felt fortunate that English ways had never been a temptation to him. Broadfall trousers, suspenders, and home-cut hair were no stigma to a fellow who spent most of his time with sheep. However, just to be sure none of his kids jumped the fence, Dat had insisted it was time for him and Phoebe and Gail to commit to the Old Order Amish church. But then, a certain someone more compelling than his dat was incentive for him to take his vows so he'd be ready to marry.

As the shiny red pickup truck and stock trailer pulled into the lane down the road and stopped, that certain someone stepped out of the back door of the cab and looked right at him.

Rosemary!

Matt broke into a jog, his heart thumping. While Titus and his English driver came out of the truck's front doors, the dogs raced ahead to check out the sheep that were blathering in the trailer. But Matt was focused on Rosemary's dress, which was the same deep green as her eyes. He entered the lane looking like a man lost in love, no doubt, but he didn't much care what Titus and the other fellow thought.

Rosemary turned to lift her daughter out of the truck's cab, and Katie threw her arms out toward him. "Puppies!" she crowed as she kicked to get down. "Katie play with the puppies all day!"

"It's gut to see you, Rosemary," he said in a breathless voice. "Didn't think you were coming along today."

Rosemary's gaze didn't waver as she set her wiggly daughter on the ground. "I'm nearly done with the packing, thanks to you folks coming out yesterday. I wanted to see about my new cookstove and oven at the mercantile, and figure out what'll go in which cabinets before we move the furniture tomorrow."

Those were her *words*, anyway. She was thinking of her new business, but her shining eyes told Matt she had also come to see him—and when had anything ever made him so happy? Rosemary's brown hair shimmered in the sunlight, tucked beneath a fresh white pleated kapp, and the green dress made her eyes look ever so large and pretty as she gazed at him.

"And Matt here's gonna be my new partner," Titus was saying as he and his driver approached. "Matt Lambright, this is Dylan Mc-Grew from over west of Queen City—and I've gotta tell you the trip was a whole lot shorter by truck than it is by buggy!" he added with a laugh. "We'll unload these sheep out in that back pasture and then fetch the rest of them so's they're all here together, getting used to their new place before nightfall."

"Jah, that'll work," Matt said as he shook Dylan's hand. "We've got the new troughs filled and the mineral blocks out, and Mose and Carl have helped me reinforce the fences. Panda and Pearl will get those sheep unloaded for you and tell them exactly where they're to go."

"Nothing like border collies to keep livestock—and their people—moving where they're supposed to," Dylan agreed. "Better than having a hired man, for a lot of things."

"That's the way I've always seen it, too," Matt replied. "And they don't ask for time off or pay raises, either, ain't so?"

He winked at Katie, who was stroking both dogs' heads as they sat patiently accepting her attention. Then he focused on her mother again. "I'll ride back to that pasture with these fellows and the dogs, but we'll not be gone long. If you need any help in the house, let me know when I get back—and then I'll tell Mamm to set more places for dinner," he added happily. "She's already figuring on Titus and Dylan, so you two girls will be a nice surprise."

Rosemary's eyes widened. "I brought along a basket of sandwiches and a pie for us, but—"

"Pie?" Matt's grin widened. "We'll add your lunch to Mamm's menu, then. The more the merrier, ain't so?"

Her cheeks bloomed as she playfully lifted Katie to her hip. Had there ever been a prettier woman? A more devoted mother? Surely

God had created Rosemary just for him! Something inside him glowed, just being near her today.

Charity suffereth long and is kind . . . charity envieth not; charity vaunteth not itself, is not puffed up . . .

The familiar Scripture passage came to him, most recently from Zanna's wedding. Aunt Abby had suggested to him when he was younger, struggling to understand the Bible, that he could substitute the word "love" for "charity"—so the passage described Rosemary perfectly. Didn't it? Love was patient and kind, just as she was.

"See you in a few," he murmured as he followed Titus and Dylan toward the truck.

"I'll be here, Matt."

Along toward noon, Abby's head began to throb. Only Tuesday it was, and already she felt she was running behind for the week. All morning she'd tried to focus on filling out the order form for bulk spices, cereals, and baking staples from their supplier in Lancaster County, but every time she had a moment, Gail would have a question or a customer came in wanting her to sew. Vernon Gingerich had ordered four new summer dresses for his aunts this morning and curtains to go with the rag rugs Zanna had just completed for their room. Amos Coblentz had bought a new set of dishes for Nell's birthday next week, so Mary and Martha wanted two long tablecloths made from a sturdy, no-wrinkle cotton-polyester blend as a present to their mother.

And Barbara had insisted that because Sam would soon sit up front with the bishop, Preacher Abe, and Deacon Pete, it was time to replace his black church trousers, vests, and *Mutze* coat. And now that he was a preacher, he needed more than one suit, and new dress shirts to go with them.

When would she have time to sew all of these items? Phoebe and Gail were learning the finer points of managing the store, but they had realized right off that running the Cedar Creek Mercantile was a bigger responsibility than baking at Mother Yutzy's Oven.

Abby looked up from her paperwork. Gail was patiently describing the different cheeses in the refrigerated section to Merle Graber, who had come to fetch some for Emma's dinner casserole, while Phoebe was valiantly counting out the bolts Mervin Mast needed at his wooden pallet factory. Mervin, like a lot of fellows, preferred to deal with Sam when it came to supplies for his business—but wasn't everyone in Cedar Creek having to be more patient while her brother did the homework that would enable him to serve them in a higher capacity?

Abby began to mentally add up the amount of payment to send with the order, but about halfway down the long column of figures she felt someone gazing at her. She swallowed a sigh, wishing she'd used the adding machine. Yet when she saw Merle's gentle expression, her exasperation vanished. He laid three different kinds of cheese on the counter.

"You know, when I came over here I was missin' my buddy Paul," he murmured as he fished for his money. "And Eunice won't let me go to the fishin' hole by myself, you see. But what with Gail talkin' so nice to me about these cheeses, and you and Phoebe bein' so kind and perty, why, I might just take up shoppin' as my new hobby!"

Abby was so touched, she didn't know whether to laugh or to cry. Emma had probably told him exactly what kind of cheese she wanted when she'd sent him out half an hour ago, yet Merle was unconcerned about such details. He had focused on the silver lining rather than the cloud—paying her a compliment instead of bemoaning the loss of his longtime friend. "Denki for saying that about us, Merle. You come over and shop anytime you like. I'm sure it's a big help to Emma."

"That poor girl needs to get out even more than I do—but not for shoppin'," he added sadly. Then he brightened again. "But at least my

James is socializin' again, and I'm mighty happy it's you he's seein',
Abby. When he came home whistlin' and grinnin' the other night,
why, I felt like a young fella again myself."

The heat rose in her cheeks as she totaled Merle's order. Would
James have his dat's endearing smile and benevolent nature as he got
older? Abby looked forward to finding out. "Give Emma and Eunice
my best," she said as she handed Merle his change. She winked at
him as she put his purchase in a small sack. "Your dinner's going to
taste awfully gut with this cheese in it. You picked all my favorite
kinds."

He winked back and patted her hand. "Jah, Abby, you and I have
gut taste, ain't so?"

The bell above the door jingled as Merle left, a lighthearted
sound that matched her mood now. Abby resumed adding up the
amount for the order she'd been working on all morning. She wrote
the check, signed the order form, and finally slipped all the paperwork into an envelope. "I'll be back by one o'clock so you girls can
take your lunch break," she called over to her nieces. "Sam will surely
be ready to come in by then."

Phoebe and Gail waved as she headed toward the door. And
when Abby placed the order into the mailbox by the road, her smile
found her again. Titus Yutzy and his driver were striding toward her,
along the shoulder of the blacktop, while behind them Matt strolled
beside Rosemary as Katie toddled between them, her hands holding
theirs. Matt carried a picnic basket, as though they were a family ready
to sit on a quilt beneath the trees and enjoy their lunch together.

And isn't that a picture, Lord? The worries and pressures of the
morning faded away. No doubt there would be a wedding in their
future, but it wasn't her place to push for that.

Then Abby's eyes widened. "Rosemary! What a wonderful-gut
surprise, to see you wearing *green*!" she called out. She hurried toward
them, drinking in the sight and the meaning of the young widow's
new clothes.

"Abby, hullo!" Rosemary shrugged modestly, keeping a grip on her toddler's hand as a car went past them. "Emma and I found the pieces of this dress cut out amongst Alma's fabric, and last night after dinner Beth Ann put it together in no time. She's taught her best friends how to make rag rugs, so they're having their own frolic today."

Abby quickly assessed the dress. It appeared to be as well made as the clothing she sewed in her shop, perfectly proportioned to Rosemary's body even though it had been originally intended for a taller, larger-boned woman, from what she recalled about Alma Yutzy. "I figured right, when I suggested to Beth Ann that she might sew for me," Abby said. "And my stars, do I have as much work as that girl would care to take on."

As they opened the kitchen door, the aroma of pot roast baked with potatoes and carrots greeted them, as did Barbara and Treva. "Gut to see you girls again so soon," Abby's mother said as she placed silverware around the places at the extended table.

"And gut to see you in such a fresh color, too," Barbara chimed in. "You fellows get washed up, and we'll be ready to sit down in a few. Meanwhile, I'll just have to tickle this Katie girl, won't I?"

As the toddler giggled in anticipation, it occurred to Abby that Barbara was looking forward to having a grandchild to play with. What a fine sight, to see her chasing Katie around the kitchen table as Mamm stepped out of their path—and then lo and behold, her mother started around the table in the other direction to ambush the child with a hug. Laughter filled the kitchen as the three of them came together, with Katie the filling in a sandwich made of grandmotherly love.

Abby noticed then that Sam had come in from the downstairs bedroom, which they had set up as his study. As he paused in the door to watch the merriment, his face lit up.

Oh, but he needed this moment, Abby thought. And she hoped they'd have many more like it as they helped Sam toward his new calling.

As Titus introduced Dylan to everyone and the men took their places at the table, Abby placed Rosemary's sandwiches on a platter and set her pie alongside an angel food cake. They bowed for a moment of silent grace, and then Sam passed the platter of pot roast to Titus.

As Abby looked around the table, it seemed Rosemary, Titus, and little Katie were already adding a welcome new dimension to their family. She wished that Phoebe and Gail could have been here to share this gathering. Rosemary glowed as she cut up roast and vegetables for her daughter's smaller plate. No doubt they would soon need a second high chair for meals when Zanna, Jonny, and little Harley joined them. This growth in their family meant a fresh start in ways they hadn't been thinking of lately as they'd focused on the responsibilities Sam's new position had added to their lives.

As Rosemary received the basket of fresh, warm bread, she inhaled its aroma with her eyes closed. "What a treat. While I can make pie crust in my sleep, a gut, chewy-soft loaf of bread doesn't come so easy for me."

"Treva's the one we beg to bake the bread and rolls," Barbara said with a smile for her mother-in-law. "It's another reason we're pleased she's living in the dawdi haus, close to the kitchen."

"It's a treat to be here amongst all of you Lambrights, too," Rosemary continued in her low, compelling voice. "Makes for more interesting conversation than Titus, Beth Ann, and I have at our table."

"Jah, you betcha!" Katie piped up.

As everyone laughed, Dylan McGrew grew pink in the cheeks. "You know, I said that a time or two on the way over here, and it seems someone has picked up on it."

"She doesn't miss much," Titus agreed. "And I can tell you she keeps us all on our toes, too, now that she's walking so gut. Won't be long before she'll outrun us."

"Jah, Zanna's Harley already reminds us of how busy we were when Matt was a tyke," Sam said as he sopped up gravy with his bread. "Keeps you young and alert, having the little ones around."

"And you know," Rosemary said in a thoughtful tone, "I'm thinking *you* will keep us young, too, Sam, with your preaching. One of the reasons I'm glad we're coming to Cedar Creek is the way you considered all sides of the situation when Zanna was having a baby before she was married. I was impressed as I listened to the stories about that when I came to her wedding."

The kitchen got quiet as Rosemary gazed directly at Sam, smiling with sincere respect. Abby had seldom seen her brother appear utterly speechless, yet he had stopped eating to gape at their guest.

"Our preachers in Queen City would have shipped her off without considering anything but the Old Ways," Rosemary insisted. "Your response—the way your whole family took up Zanna's cause—makes me think you'll breathe fresh ideas into the church here and you'll keep some of the young people from jumping the fence, too. It's a real talent, a true gift from God, to stand firm in the Old Amish beliefs while allowing love to lead us into the future."

"You said a mouthful there," Abby murmured. And wasn't it a fine thing to see Sam blush as he soaked up Rosemary's compliment?

"Couldn't have said it at a better time, either," Mamm chimed in gratefully. "Sometimes we get so weighted down carrying our crosses, it takes an outsider to see us for who we are. I'm mighty glad you're not an outsider anymore, Rosemary."

"Jah, so am I," Abby added as she rose to fetch a knife. There was no doubt in her mind that Rosemary's rhubarb pie would be as much of a treat as the company of the delightful young woman who had baked it.

Chapter 27

Early the next morning, Rosemary drove to Mamm's by the sun's first light. What with moving the furniture and spending the night in their new place, Titus's house would be swarming with neighbors and emotions would be running high. Beth Ann was keeping Katie for her while she made this final trip to her mother's house to say her farewell.

Lord, help me be strong, she prayed as she pulled in. The buggy wasn't halfway up the lane before her mother and Malinda stepped out on the porch to greet her.

"And would you look at that perty purple dress?" her sister called out.

"Jah, that's a sight for sore eyes," her mamm agreed. "It tells me you're ready to move on, Rosemary, so there's to be no tears or saying good-bye this morning. Hear me? Do you think we'll not come to Cedar Creek to see your new place—and Katie, of course?"

"We'd be helping you move, you know," Malinda added, "except you've told us a dozen times to stay put."

Rosemary clambered down, grateful for their positive attitudes. "Titus has Dylan and a few other fellows driving trucks for him, so I'll let them do the heavy lifting—and meanwhile I'm saving your backs, too. Beth Ann and I are taking Katie with the first load and staying over there so we can point out where all the furniture's to go."

"As long as you stay out of Titus's way—and let him think he's in charge—everybody'll be happy," her mother agreed.

When Rosemary reached the porch, there was a moment of awkward silence as the three of them looked at one another. "Well," she murmured, "I'll go upstairs for a moment, and then I'm off. No tears," she agreed, echoing her mother. "No reason to act like it's the last time we'll see one another."

Rosemary entered the house where she'd spent most of her life and took a slow, sentimental journey. She'd been born in the downstairs bedroom . . . had eaten her meals and learned to cook in this kitchen . . . had listened to countless Bible readings in the front room . . . had shared the north-corner bedroom first with Malinda and then with Joe—and had given birth to Katie there, too. As she entered the room, the morning light glowed on the butter-colored walls and she drew in a deep breath.

"Joe?" she whispered.

She waited, gazing out the window toward the land that was no longer hers . . . And that felt all right, didn't it? No regrets about selling it, no what-ifs about the house she wouldn't build there. Her pulse thrummed in spite of the finality she felt while standing in this room. *You were taken from me too soon, Joe, but your love made me strong enough that I can stand on my own now.* She ran her hand over the quilt Mamm had made for her wedding gift, content to leave it here with other mementos of her marriage and childhood.

Lo, I am with you always, even unto the end of the world.

Rosemary let out the breath she'd been holding. It seemed to her Joe had murmured these words from the gospel in her ear as a blessing—a benediction. No matter where life took her, she would never be alone.

When a little sob escaped her, she blinked away her tears. Hadn't she just received the highest promise that everything would work out if she believed it would? Rosemary smoothed the purple dress with a sense that the best was yet to be. It was as Abby had told her weeks ago. If she opened her heart, all things were possible because she loved the Lord.

And I love Matt, too!

Finally, after everyone around her had told her how she should feel about him, the words rang true. Rosemary turned and went downstairs. "Don't be strangers," she said as she passed through the kitchen where her mamm and Malinda were washing the peas they'd picked earlier. "I'll let you know when we're ready for a visit."

"Jah, and we'll be there, too," her sister replied.

"Have a gut moving day!" her mother chimed in.

As Rosemary climbed back into the buggy, her mother and sister were putting on a cheerful front—too cheerful—yet it had gotten them all through a potentially difficult visit that could have left her feeling blue all day.

Hadn't they given her the best gift of all? The gift of their acceptance and best wishes as she moved on?

Rosemary drove off with hope riding high in her heart.

A few hours later, Rosemary pointed toward the longest wall in the freshly painted front room as Matt and Mose Hartzler carried the couch inside. "Right there will be fine," she said. The room was stacked high with boxes and the chairs weren't placed just right, but all the main furnishings were accounted for. "That's the last of this truckload, ain't so?"

"Jah, we'll take a breather and help Dylan when he gets here with the stock trailer." After he and Mose scooted the long sofa into place, Matt grinned at Katie, who was climbing on each piece of furniture to check it out. "Did I see a plate of fried pies in the kitchen before we piled so much stuff in there?"

"Jah. Abby brought them over before she opened the store, bless her. Your family's been so gut to us, Matt."

"Fried pies?" Katie piped up with a hopeful expression.

"Jah, you can share one with me, punkin." Rosemary slipped between the stacked boxes into the kitchen, which was an obstacle course of opened crates and tables covered with unpacked dishes. "We'll set you in your high chair—"

"Big chair!" her daughter exclaimed. "I's a big girl now, in the new house."

Rosemary offered the tray of fried pies to Mose and Matt. "We've been talking all week about how, at the new house, big girls pick up their toys and eat with a fork and spoon. So far, she's doing pretty gut at it."

Matt took a bite of a pineapple-lemon pie, and then he placed a small box on a chair and lifted Katie onto it as though accommodating her was second nature to him. "We'll find the booster chair and bring it over," he said as she smacked her hands happily on the tabletop. "It's held a gut many little Lambrights up to the table, so it'll work just fine for you, too, Katie."

Rosemary felt another flutter inside. What with all the details of getting out of one house and into another, it hadn't occurred to her that her daughter might be ready to advance to the table, yet Matt had seen that immediately.

"Jah, won't be long before you'll be scurryin' around with my little ones and the Detweiler girls after church," Mose remarked as he chose a cherry pie. Then he glanced toward the road. "I hear that big red truck pullin' in out front."

"Titus said he was loading the bedroom sets this go-round," Matt remarked, "so you might want to point us toward which rooms each piece goes in, Rosemary."

"Beth Ann's upstairs hanging her curtains, so I'll let her help you with that." She led the two men between the boxes in the front room, where Dylan and Titus were coming in with a headboard.

"This walnut set's going to the rooms in the back," her father-in-law was saying as he walked backward in that direction. "Decided I was done with going up and down the stairs to eat and get myself to bed. Preacher Paul had the right idea about that."

"Fine by me," Dylan agreed. "This set's by far the heaviest."

Rosemary blinked. This was the first she'd heard that the stairs were becoming a problem, as Titus still got around quite well.

"We'll be right behind you with the dresser," Matt said as he and Mose headed out the front door.

Was that a secretive smile she'd seen on Matt's face? Or was she keeping track of so many men moving so many pieces of furniture, asking her so many questions about where to put it all, that she was imagining that part? Rosemary climbed the steps and headed toward the farthest bedroom down the hall. "How's it going, Beth Ann?"

"I'm as far as I can go until my bed gets here."

Rosemary smiled. Beth Ann was so excited about her new room, ready to use the colorful new Friendship Star quilt she'd gotten for her birthday as well as the rag rug she'd finished. As she stepped into the room, Rosemary couldn't help but throw her arms out and spin in a circle. "What a fine room! Look at those curtains—and your dresses are in place already," she exclaimed. "How about if you point the fellows toward where all the bedroom pieces go up here? It seems your dat is taking his set to the dawdi haus."

Beth Ann's eyes widened. "When did he decide that? I mean, he's not *that* old!"

Rosemary wandered into the hall. "So . . . if he's not taking that big room at the other end of the hall—"

"You should have it! Katie's crib would fit in the alcove by the window, so you won't be nearly so crowded," Beth Ann pointed out. "And when she's ready for a regular bed, she can have that smaller room next door."

And when did my baby get so big that we're talking about a regular bed?

Rosemary ambled into the larger bedroom, as the men would soon need her to point the way for more large, packed boxes. The room looked too big for the furniture she'd been using in Titus's house, but it made sense for her to be next to where Katie would eventually sleep, didn't it? She hadn't wanted to ask Mamm for her furniture from home, for that would have left an empty room there.

Downstairs, Mose and Matt were hoisting the box springs toward the dawdi haus while Titus and Dylan followed with the mattress. The men had arranged the contents of the livestock trailer in a logical order, and they'd put flattened cardboard boxes on its floor to keep any animal odors from getting on the furniture. Rosemary glanced around for the boxes of bedding, figuring to make up the beds as soon as they were assembled.

Matt returned to the front room. "Did I see a cooler of lemonade?"

"Another generous gift, from the Grabers," Rosemary replied as she led him to the kitchen.

Matt frowned and then jogged to the window. "Oh, but this has to *stop*!" he declared as he hurried toward the back door. "Katie's just slipped between the boards of the pasture gate. I'll take care of it."

Alarm rose within her, and Rosemary hurried outside in Matt's wake. A loud bleating caught her attention. Sure enough, Katie was toddling toward a lamb that had gotten its head caught between a trough and the pipe of the pump used to fill it. As it cried out pathetically, its mother approached at a wary gait. In the distance, Rosemary spotted the border collies, but they were too far away to prevent Katie from approaching the crying lamb and causing a crisis at the water trough.

What had possessed her daughter to dash off yet again? At Titus's, Katie hadn't shown any inclination to get past a fence, yet she'd clambered down from the elevated chair, moved the box she'd been sitting on so she could reach the doorknob, and then let herself outside. Yes, this *did* have to stop.

Rosemary watched as Matt nimbly scaled the gate and within seconds he'd grabbed Katie. He pivoted, unlatching the wide, heavy gate with one hand as he held her daughter in the crook of his other arm. He was a man on a mission, his expression taut, yet he showed no sign of losing his temper as he closed the gate and then set Katie firmly on the ground. As Matt crouched in front of her little girl, Rosemary stayed out of Katie's sight. The way Matt handled this moment might determine a lot of things, as far as how Katie reacted—and how *she* felt about it, too.

"Katie, this is not a game," he stated sternly, "and those sheep are not like puppies. And you are *not* to run off by yourself ever again. Understand me? Big girls stay where their mamm puts them—because once you're a big girl, you can be punished for not behaving. When I was your age, my mamm whacked my bottom with her wooden spoon and stood me with my nose in the corner."

Katie's eyes got wide and her face fell. She looked away from Matt's intense gaze, but she knew better than to try to escape. She hadn't been talked to this way by a man . . . Joe had died before she was steady on her feet, and she was intimidated enough by Titus's gruffness not to follow him around outside.

Rosemary smiled in spite of the situation's seriousness. She could well imagine Matt standing with his nose in the corner as Barbara scolded him, just as she had received similar discipline from her own mother. Plain parents believed in nipping misbehavior in the bud and impressing their children early on when it came to the dangers of living around livestock and machinery.

"I'm going to help that little lamb now," Matt continued, pointing to the bleating animal, "and you're going to sit right here on this stump and wait for me without moving. Ain't so?"

Katie glanced at the stump beside the gravel driveway, which was just the right height to make a seat for her. She sat down without protesting and then clasped her hands in her lap.

"Gut girl. I'll be back in a few, and then we'll go back to the house." Matt still spoke in a no-nonsense tone of voice, but he had relaxed some. "Your mamm'll be real glad you listened to me and that you won't ever, ever run off from her again. Ain't so, Katie?"

The little girl's face remained somber as she considered what Matt had said. She nodded.

"Tell me that part, Katie, about what you won't do ever again."

Katie focused intently on Matt, whose eyes were on the same level as hers. "I . . . won't run off no more. I a big girl now."

"Jah, you are. I'll be right back."

As Matt returned to the pasture, Rosemary remained on the back side of the nearest tree, watching her daughter. As she had promised, Katie sat absolutely still on the stump, watching Matt approach the lamb and the ewe who waited close by the water trough. In a low voice, he spoke to the fluffy, fleecy mother while his two dogs sat alertly on either side of her, trained not to interfere unless she charged.

"We're gonna get this busy baby of yours out of this hang-up," he said in a low singsong voice. "You're Titus's ewe and you don't know me yet, Mama, but you will. I can see how your little one's head is stuck where it was never intended to be . . ."

Rosemary listened closely. If the ewe perceived Matt as a danger to her lamb, she would attack him. Indeed, the fluffy sheep stood stiffly, not at all confident about what he intended to do to her baby. As he reached into the narrow space between the trough and the water pipe, the lamb squirmed and freed itself. Matt took hold of it, chuckling.

"Jah, see there," he said, "you got to climbing around when your mamm wasn't watching—probably ran off, just like our Katie over there," he added as he massaged the little lamb's neck and checked its windpipe. "And you see what sort of trouble it got you into, ain't so? Little ones were meant to stay with their mamms while they learn how to be big girls."

Rosemary covered her mouth so Katie wouldn't hear her chuckling. Matt had not only gotten the lamb out of its predicament, he had turned the situation into a fable for her little girl to follow. And follow him Katie did, watching between the gate slats from her seat, not missing a single word as Matt soothed the little lamb.

And what a picture, when he took the lamb in his arms and held it to his chest to let it become accustomed to his voice, his scent. The little ball of fleece pressed its head against the strong, gentle hand that still caressed it. Then it turned to gaze at Matt full in the face with a look of such utter love and trust that tears sprang to Rosemary's eyes.

Matt was the picture of the Good Shepherd, right here in Titus's pasture. After a few moments he gently set the lamb on the ground, and it bounded over to its mother as though nothing scary had happened to it.

Rosemary sighed. It took a special sort of man to be a shepherd, just as it took a special sort of man to be a dat. And it seemed, as Matt closed the pasture gate and then opened his arms, that he was indeed a most special man. He took to her daughter better than a lot of natural fathers related to their children. Plain men were known more for their discipline than for their affection, yet Matt Lambright had just demonstrated the perfect combination of both. Katie sprang from her stump and rushed toward him, aglow in the forgiveness she sensed in Matt's smile.

"You did real gut, Katie," he assured her as he swung her up to his shoulder. "Your mamm will be glad to see you're safe and— Ach, there she is now, come to look for you, no doubt."

Katie swiveled. "Mamm!" she cried. "Matt fixed the lamb! He fixed me, too, so I'm a big girl now, ain't so?"

As Rosemary closed the distance between them, she considered her words carefully. "So what does it mean that you're a big girl, Katie?" she asked pointedly. "You look the same to me as when I left you at the table eating your fried pie. And when I looked again, you were gone. Do you know how scared I got when we couldn't find you?"

Katie's finger went to her mouth, but then she perked up again.

"I won't go again, Mamm. Me and Matt decided," she declared with a nod.

Me and Matt decided. Rosemary couldn't miss all the situations that phrase might apply to. As they walked toward the house, she let the emotions of the moment carry her—relief, because Katie was safe . . . hope, for she realized her little girl was indeed maturing to meet the challenges of this move to Cedar Creek . . . contentment, because walking alongside Matt as he held Katie to his shoulder felt so right. She could even chuckle at the folks who had come outside to find them. Titus, Dylan, and Mose had stopped carrying furniture while Beth Ann had come downstairs. Every one of them looked so pleased right now.

"Got the lost lamb back in the fold, I see," Titus remarked. Then he focused on his granddaughter. "And what do you say to Matt? He kept you from getting hurt pretty bad, ain't so?"

Katie beamed and threw her arms around Matt's neck. "I love you, Matt!"

"And I love you, too, Katie. Awful much," he replied without missing a beat.

Yes, Rosemary thought, this moment was about gratitude and growing up, but it was mostly about love. It was something special indeed that Matt Lambright broke the mold of most Amish men when it came to saying how he felt.

And didn't Matt's response say more than mere words? Maybe this incident, and his response to it, could be a springboard for the big leap of faith everyone had been encouraging her to take.

Rosemary gazed up at him, noting the color that crept into his cheeks. "Maybe we can talk sometime soon, jah?"

Matt's face glowed as he handed Katie back to her. "Jah, we can, Rosemary. Anytime you're ready."

As Matt helped the other fellows heft the rest of the bedroom furniture up the stairs, the dressers and wooden chests felt weightless.

He floated along, carried on a stream of ecstatic thoughts. Rosemary wasn't the only one who was ready to talk, however. As Titus helped Matt put her bed together, a grin flickered on his lips.

"Figured I might was well save us all a lot of trouble," her father-in-law began as he fitted the metal frame into the simple wooden headboard. "Knew it was only a matter of time before you and Rosemary tied the knot, so here's my offer. You kids can live in the main part of this house, like it was your own place—if you want to," he added.

Matt rocked back on his heels, grabbing the edge of the headboard to steady himself. "That's mighty generous, Titus. But maybe you want to settle in first and then think about—"

"It worked for Paul, staying in the dawdi haus, and it'll be fine for me, too," his partner insisted. "Keeps me fed and dressed, gives Beth Ann a gut home with a woman to help her grow up—and it saves you the trouble of squeezing into a room at your dat's place as newlyweds, ain't so?"

Matt's cheeks went hot. "There's that, jah. But it all depends on Rosemary, what she wants."

Titus's eyebrow rose. "You'll want to be careful about giving her so much say-so, son. Once a woman gets a taste of having her way, there's no end to it. Just ask my brother, Ezra, or Abe Nissley," he said. "Adah Ropp's another one who takes it upon herself to rule the roost, and that's not the way nature intended. God created the man first for a gut reason."

Matt had heard this sort of logic all his life, and he sensed it was a fine time to keep his opinions to himself. Far as he was concerned, everything did depend on Rosemary—and for all of Titus's insistence on the Old Ways with the man running the house, he probably wouldn't have kept up with his sheep, much less entered into this business partnership, had Rosemary not gotten him through the winter.

"We'll work that part out," Matt replied as they positioned the box springs on the frame. "But I appreciate the offer, Titus. Having us live here makes a lot of sense for you and me as partners, too. And it saves me the expense of getting a house built."

"But anytime you wanna do that, it's fine by me," Titus insisted.

As they positioned the mattress, Matt's thoughts were spinning. While it would be very convenient for all of them to live here, maybe Rosemary was fed up with looking after Titus . . . She had made plans to build a house with Joe, after all. And she would be starting up her baking business, so maybe he and Titus were putting the cart before the horse, assuming she'd marry him anytime soon. Could be, when Rosemary wanted to talk, she would thank him for keeping Katie out of harm's way rather than encourage his attention.

There was only one way to find out.

Somehow Matt made it through dinner, with everyone chatting at the table as though they had nothing pressing to do, nothing twitching in their minds. Soon they would be packing up another trailer load, but he sensed an important moment might be lost if he returned to Queen City with Titus and Dylan.

"I'm going back over to make up the beds, in case Katie's ready for her nap," Beth Ann said as they rose from the table. "Can you help me unpack your clothes and toys, Katie?"

"Jah, I's a big girl," the toddler declared as she scrambled to the floor. "Unpack. No nap."

As everyone laughed, Matt silently thanked Beth Ann for opening this conversational door. "I'll get this morning's boxes rearranged so we'll have places to put all the stuff that's still to come over," he said.

"Jah, and we'd best get moving, too," Titus replied with a knowing smile. "Dylan and I can handle this load, and that'll still get him home before dark."

As Matt took his straw hat from its peg behind the door, it occurred to him that someday he would be hanging his hat in a different spot.

Are you sure about that? She hasn't said yes yet.

His dat and Abby headed down Lambright Lane to the mercantile, chatting with Beth Ann and Katie. Rosemary and the other women began to redd up the kitchen, so amid the clatter of their dishes and chitchat, Matt slipped out the back door. From the swing in the yard, he often gazed out over the pastures, keeping watch. Whenever he needed to gather his thoughts, this was the peaceful place he chose.

Last time he'd sat here with Rosemary, she'd run off because he kissed her.

He settled into the slatted seat and began to rock, letting the familiar creak of the wood and the chains soothe him. The rolling pastures glowed a lush green, and the clusters of grazing ewes and lambs helped his tired body relax. Carrying furniture up the stairs was harder work than tending sheep, but it gave him a sense of hope. For even if Rosemary didn't give him an answer today, she would be living across the road. He would have the chance to truly court her then—and maybe that would be the better plan. She had a hundred things on her mind right now, and if he waited for a quieter moment, maybe when they were alone in the buggy . . .

"Hope you don't mind if I join you," Rosemary murmured as she slipped into the swing beside him. "Seems your mamm and sisters don't want my help with the dishes, so they shooed me out. I suppose I could go back to the house and empty those boxes in the kitchen—"

"Rosemary." Matt took her hand, pleading with his eyes.

She twined her fingers between his. "Jah, Matt?"

Oh, but there was no getting around it, was there? Mamm and the girls were probably peeking out the kitchen window behind them. But if he walked Rosemary over to the other place, they might get interrupted by Katie or Beth Ann—and those piles of boxes would compel Rosemary to unpack. She was never idle—always a willing worker, a woman who served the Lord and everyone around her with gladness.

The freshness of her pretty face, and the way she looked ten years younger wearing purple instead of black, encouraged him. Changing out of her widow's clothing was a big signal, and if he didn't follow up on it, he might go a long while before he found another opportune moment.

Matt cleared his throat. Maybe he was making this way too complicated. "Will you marry me?" he asked in a strained whisper.

Rosemary clapped her hands together. "Oh yes. Yes!" Then she drew in a long breath and sat back. "But, Matt, I want to be courted a gut long while," she began, as though she'd been thinking about it more than she'd let on.

His heart throbbed hard. "I—I can understand that, jah."

"And meanwhile, I'll be baking pies for Aunt Lois and setting up my business." When her hand found his again, her grip was as firm as her voice. "It's only fair to both of us to know how that part of my life will work out before we jump into being married. You might change your mind about having a wife who spends a part of her days working at something for herself. And we need to court long enough that you know I'm not perfect. I'm sure to have habits that will aggravate you—and you'll do things that irritate me, too."

Matt felt light-headed. He had hoped her answer would be an immediate yes . . . and yet she spoke wisely. "Truth be told, while I'm best at tending sheep, I might have to help Dat more while he's learning to be a preacher," he murmured. "But I won't change my mind, Rosemary. I want you for my wife."

"Jah, Matt. I want that, too."

Applause and squeals came from the kitchen. *Jah, the window was open, dummy. It's June, after all.*

But he had to make the situation perfectly clear so Rosemary would have no regrets. She had opened her heart to him, and he wanted nothing to stand in the way of her complete love and acceptance. Matt kissed her with great restraint, so he would have concentration enough to continue. "What would you say to us living at Titus's place?" he asked her in a low voice. "He's offered it to us—"

"So that's why he wanted the dawdi haus!"

"—but I can see why you might rather have a home of your own, like you were planning with . . . Joe."

Rosemary's face resembled one of the roses about to burst into bloom in the flower bed beside them. Her deep green eyes made him think of the cedars along the creek, ageless and peaceful. "What I had with Joe is a wonderful-gut memory now," she whispered. "What I can have with you, Matt, is a whole new life. A whole new world."

He liked the sound of that. A lot.

"And if you can stand to live with a grumpy old fellow, a teenage girl, and my runaway toddler—"

"Ah, but Katie's a big girl now," he corrected her.

"—and you can tolerate me riding herd on all of them—"

Matt shrugged. "I have two border collies. Herding is an everyday thing."

"—then I—" Rosemary stopped short. Her eyebrow rose into a distinctively independent angle. "Puh!" she declared. "You and I will decide what we want and where we'll live, in our own gut time. Everyone else can fall into step and find their places, ain't so?"

As more applause and female laughter came through the kitchen window, Matt's heart thumped like a drum. "Jah, you've got that right, Rosemary. You see life pretty much the same way I do . . . and I can't wait to see our life now that we'll be together."

Chapter 28

It finally struck Rosemary then: she was getting married! And on her own terms, too. She was wildly, deliriously happy. She had loved her Joe truly and deeply, but this time around she was much more aware of the commitment she had agreed to. She knew for sure and for certain that along with Matt providing a good home, he would bring *joy* into her life. The women in his family rushed out into the yard to congratulate them, full of ideas about their future in the home across the road.

After a few moments, Rosemary grabbed Matt's hand. "Now that everyone here has heard our gut news, we should stop by the mercantile. Wouldn't want your dat and Abby to feel we've left them out."

"Jah, there's that," he agreed. "And then we'd best get ourselves across the road to make room for the next trailer load. I don't want Titus hefting any more furniture or boxes than he has to. He's more tired than he realizes."

As the two of them strolled down Lambright Lane, Rosemary realized she had many important things to learn about Matt, but they had time for working together and playing together . . . and praying together. That was an important habit for any couple to cultivate. When they reached the back of the mercantile, she smiled up at him. "I think we're going to make a couple of folks here mighty happy with our news."

"Dat's ready to hear something cheerful. I've got to say, when you told him he'd make a fine preacher for Cedar Creek, he really took it to heart," Matt said. "That was a thoughtful way to handle the challenge that's come to our family."

Rosemary entered the mercantile's storeroom and inhaled the savory scents of the bulk spices there. The bins of rolled oats, noodles, and other foods the Lambrights bagged in this room were neatly arranged along the walls and the worktable was spotless. As they passed into the main room of the store, she glanced up toward the loft level and then waved.

"Abby!" she called out to the woman who sat sewing next to the railing. "When you told me at Zanna's wedding that I'd be glad I stayed for dinner? And that I could open my heart to a whole new world? Well, you were right! Matt and I have agreed to start courting."

Abby shot up from her chair, clapping her hands. "Oh, but that's wonderful-gut!" she said as she hurried toward the wooden staircase.

"Is that so?" James Graber stepped from a side aisle holding a bag of sweet potato chips. "I could've predicted it from the moment Matt laid eyes on you, Rosemary," he teased as he pumped their hands.

Sam, who had been restocking a display of flower seed packets, straightened to his full height. "Well, now. That's the best news I've heard in a long while. A reason to celebrate. Bringing Rosemary into our family has already blessed us beyond measure, ain't so?" He clapped his son on the back and placed a hand on Rosemary's shoulder, as well.

Once again Rosemary felt welcome and loved . . . and as she caught sight of a bookshelf along the back wall she got an idea. "I have a couple of requests," she said. "It seems like a gut time to acquire one of those fine Bibles you sell, Sam."

Matt's eyes widened. "Pick the one you'd like, and it'll be my gift to you, Rosemary."

"And now we have a gut excuse for another sewing frolic or two," Abby declared as she came around to hug Rosemary. "So be thinking about what all you'd like for quilts and curtains."

Sam opened his arm to allow Abby into their huddle. As James took his place beside her, Rosemary noticed then that a few English customers were in the aisles, probably listening in on their conversation. But why should it bother her to let the whole world know how happy she was?

"And what else is on your mind, young lady?" Matt's father teased. "I've heard only one of your requests."

"I'd like you to be the preacher who helps Bishop Gingerich marry us, Sam."

Was it her imagination, or did his face go pale? "It'll be a long while before I'm ready to preach sermons on a Sunday, much less—"

"I didn't say you had to be ready anytime *soon*." Rosemary gazed at him and then at Matt, enjoying the resemblance between father and son. "We won't be setting a date for a while. Courtship is the best chance to have fun getting to know each other before the serious business of being husband and wife sets in."

"I think it's a wonderful-gut idea, Sam," Abby chimed in. "And with Phoebe and Owen engaged, why, you can have *two* couples to practice on before you marry anybody outside the family."

"Practice makes perfect," James agreed. "I was thinking at Zanna's wedding that there might be several Cedar Creek couples getting hitched in the coming months."

Was that a secretive smile on James Graber's face as he glanced at Abby? Rosemary kept the question to herself, but it was a wonderful feeling to be so surrounded by love in bloom, among members of the Lambright family who had made her, Katie, Beth Ann, and Titus so very welcome.

Sam relaxed as Rosemary's idea settled into him. "Do you suppose folks would notice if I used the same sermon for both ceremonies?"

As their laughter filled the large, open store Rosemary reveled in the sound of it. It was a welcome sensation to feel her soul soaring again, on the wings of a love as fresh and vibrant as this June day. And as she gazed around this circle of loving hearts, she knew her life with Matt Lambright would shine with a light that came straight from heaven.

For more heartwarming Amish romance,
look for Book Three in the Home at Cedar Creek series,
available in trade paperback and
e-book in November 2013.

In the meantime,
have you read Book One in the series?
An excerpt follows of

Abby Finds Her Calling

It's available from New American Library
wherever paperbacks and e-books are sold.

James Graber inhaled the crisp October air and grinned up at the rising sun. It was his wedding day! All his life he'd lived in anticipation of something grand, something beyond the immense satisfaction of his carriage-making trade, and finally, in about an hour, he would achieve that dream when Suzanna Lambright became his wife.

As he gazed across the road, at the lane where horse-drawn carriages were entering in a steady stream, the Lambright place took on a new glow in his eyes. There was the Cedar Creek Mercantile, where Zanna's elder brother, Sam, sold groceries and dry goods and where her sister, Abby, ran her sewing business. Beside it, Treva Lambright, Zanna's mamm, had a glass greenhouse where she raised and sold a variety of vegetables and flowers. Down the long drive stood the tall white farmhouse where Treva lived with Sam's family—his wife, Barbara, and their four children, Matt, Phoebe, Ruth, and Gail. And farther up the lane was the little home Abby had built for herself this past spring. These places, surrounded by sheep sheds, the barn, and acres of rolling green pasture, felt more special to James today, even though he saw them every time he stepped off his own front porch.

And who could believe all these wedding guests? Nearly four hundred family and friends—some from as far away as Pennsylvania, Ohio, and Indiana—were arriving to celebrate with the Grabers and the Lambrights, families who had moved here to Missouri generations ago. The *clip-clop! clip-clop!* of the horses' hooves made his heart sing to their ageless rhythm.

ZAN-na! ZAN-na! James heard in that beat. Silly, the things he thought of when he envisioned her pretty face as she gazed at him in that playful way she had. *Lord, please help me make her happy every single day of our lives!*

James was glad to be marrying on a perfect autumn day, after the harvest was in but before the traditional marriage month, because it meant these folks from back East had a chance to celebrate with them. Here in Missouri, Old Order Amish married anytime during the year, not just in November, when the many weddings meant that folks had to pick and choose which ones they attended. And what a backdrop the countryside provided: the sweet gum and maple trees blazed in their red and orange glory, with a hint of frost to make them sparkle in the sunrise.

James's younger sister, Emma, joined him in front of the house, smoothing her new purple dress. "That's a mighty fine smile you're wearing, brother. I hope to see it gracing your ugly face every day from here on out," she said, her brown eyes sparkling.

James cocked an eyebrow. "And what would you have to make fun of if I were a handsome man, Emma?" he countered with a laugh. "Zanna thinks I'm downright perfect, you know."

"Gut thing, too. Old as you're getting, none of the other girls would have you."

"We'll see what you say about that when *you're* within spitting distance of thirty," James shot back. Then, with a welling up of love for this young woman who kept their household running as well as anyone could now that their parents were aging, he slipped his arm around her. "Denki for keeping Mamm's head from spinning off these last couple weeks, getting ready for this wedding," he murmured. "A lot of the weight falls on your shoulders, taking care of her and Dat."

"They're our parents, James. They've been taking care of *us* all our lives."

"Of course they have, Emmie, but . . ." James sighed, focusing on the window of Zanna's upstairs room in the white farmhouse across the road. He couldn't see inside, of course, but he liked to imagine her there . . . putting on her new blue dress and white apron about now, with Treva and Abby helping her get ready. "Not my place to ask Mamm and Dat to move into the dawdi haus, but I can't help wondering . . . Do you think it'll go all right, when Zanna comes to live with us?" he asked quietly. "Mamm's tongue wags pretty constant and cuts pretty sharp, and we all know how Dat's hearing gets worse, and his brain a little fuzzier, when he doesn't want to listen to all her carrying-on. And neither of them is able to handle anywhere near as much as they used to."

"Zanna's known them all her life, same as everybody hereabouts. It's not like she's walking in blind," Emma replied, resting her head on his shoulder. It was a rare moment of physical affection from this girl who was usually busy at the stove or the sink or the washer, or looking after their parents, while he built custom carriages in his shop beside the house. "Truth be told, brother, Zanna's all grins and giggles when she talks about you. Her eyes light up, and she's been a different girl since you asked for her hand. I'm real happy for the both of you."

James smiled. His sister hadn't been as generous with her praise for other young women he'd courted over the years. Maybe he was making up things to worry about—wondering how Zanna would adjust to the Graber household—which wasn't normally his way. All in all, his times with Zanna had been among the happiest he'd known. He looked forward to a long life with her and many children to bless them.

Even Sam, James's good friend and Zanna's older brother, had remarked what a fine couple they made—and had thanked James for asking to court Zanna rather than keeping his intentions secret, as was the custom. James had felt that the passing last spring of Leroy Lambright, Sam and Zanna's dat and the head of the Lambright household, was an important reason to get Sam's blessing early on, out of respect for Leroy and the family's feelings. Sam had said right out that he thought James would be the steadying influence his youngest sister needed now that their father was gone.

Imagine that—Sam Lambright, a stickler for the proper order of things, thought he, James Graber, could fashion Suzanna into a fine wife and mother. James suspected that might take some doing. Zanna wasn't one who took to being molded into anyone else's ideal. But what a happy challenge it presented. And what a fine-looking woman she'd grown to be. Truth be told, James secretly admired her tendency to think and speak for herself rather than to automatically submit to the men in her life.

"Over the next several weekends you'll spend visiting kin and collecting your wedding presents, we'll all have time to adjust to Zanna's being in the family," his sister continued. "It's the same kind of change every family goes through after a wedding."

"Change has never been Dat's favorite thing. And he hasn't been the same since his stroke."

"And Mamm's gotten crankier, keeping after him. There's that," Emma agreed with a sigh. "But Lord love them, they're getting by as best they can. I'll work on them while you and Zanna make your family calls these coming weeks. They may as well get used to the fact that their last two kids have lives of their own."

And what would they do when Emma married? James wondered. Would she move away like their two elder sisters, Iva and Sharon, had? James breathed in deeply and then exhaled, consciously relaxing the tightness this thought caused in his belly. Inevitably, the day would come when his sweet, capable sister would cleave to her own husband and start a home . . . which would leave him, as the only son, and Zanna, as his wife, to care for his parents. As well they should.

But this was no time for such concerns. His bride was waiting for him. James lightly kissed Emma's temple and then released her. "I'd best go over to help Sam with the last-minute details. See you in a few. Or would you rather I took Dat over to—"

"Get out of here! What with Daniel and Amos, our big, burly brothers-in-law, staying with us last night, I've got lots of help with Dat this morning. And Sharon and Iva are in there helping him dress." Emma shook her white apron at him to send him on his way. "If you dare to poke your face into that Lambright kitchen full of women, you might see how Mamm's doing. Tell her I'll be there directly."

James hurried down his family's gravel lane, pleased to see the pie pumpkins that remained in Emma's garden. He stopped beside his shop to wave at Zeke and Eva Detweiler in one buggy, and the two buggies full of Detweiler children that followed them—including the carriage he'd designed to accommodate young Joel's wheelchair. Then he crossed the road and strode alongside the mercantile, which was closed on this Thursday so the Lambrights could celebrate this special day.

It struck James how many of the tipped-up buggies behind the Lambright barn had come from Graber Custom Carriages—how every family in Cedar Creek depended upon his vehicles and repair work. It was a blessing, indeed, to live among the friends he served and to be entrusted with getting their families where they needed to go. And today it seemed every man, woman, and child for miles around was showing up to wish him and Zanna well. Fellows in their black hats and suits stood chatting in clusters outside the house while their wives gathered in the kitchen to finish preparing the wedding feast.

He gazed again at Zanna's upstairs bedroom window. As he recalled tossing pebbles against it those first Saturday nights he'd courted her, James grinned like a kid. She'd looked so pretty in the moonlight, smiling down at him before she'd let him into the kitchen. She'd seemed tickled that a successful, established fellow she knew so well wanted to win her heart.

Had Zanna come downstairs for the wedding yet? Did she feel as frisky and excited as a new foal, the way he did? In his black vest, trousers, and high-topped shoes, with a radiant white shirt, James was filled with an excitement he'd never known. He greeted Matt's border collies, Panda and Pearl, with exuberant pats on their black and white heads. "Dressed for the wedding, I see," he teased.

In less than an hour, Zanna would be seated with him and their four newehockers. It might be difficult to sit through most of the long wedding service, and Bishop Gingerich's lengthy sermon, before they were at last called to stand before this gathering of family and friends.

James paused when a familiar figure stepped out the Lambrights' front door. Ordinarily folks came and went through the kitchen entry, but something about Abby Lambright's expression announced that she was on no ordinary mission. She glanced across the yard, where their many male guests stood visiting, and then she headed straight for him.

"Gut morning, Abby!" he called out, hoping to dispel her gloomy frown as she pulled her shawl tighter around her shoulders. Abby was a maidel, a few years older than he, and in his entire life he'd never known her to raise her voice or lose her temper.

"James," she replied with a stiff nod. Her eyes looked puffy, but her gaze didn't waver as she stopped a few feet in front of him. "There's something we've got to tell you, James. And since Sam's talking with the bishop, he's asked me to let you know that . . . Well, there's no easy way to say it."

Frowning, he stepped closer. "Did somebody fall sick? Or get hurt carrying all those tables and pews and—"

"I wish it were as simple as that," Abby interrupted. She bit her lip and took a deep breath. "James, Zanna is nowhere to be found. As far as we can tell, she didn't sleep in her bed last night . . . and we have no idea where she might have gone."